A SIEGE OF BITTERNS

A BIRDER MURDER MYSTERY

STEVE BURROWS

A Point Blank Book

First published in Great Britain and the Commonwealth by Point Blank, an imprint of Oneworld Publications, 2016

First published in English by Dundurn Press Limited, Canada. This edition published by Oneworld Publications in arrangement with Dundurn Press Limited

A CIP record for this title is available from the British Library

ISBN 978-1-78074-843-6
ISBN 978-1-78074-844-3 (ebook)

Printed and bound in Great Britain by Clays Ltd, St Ives plc

Visit our website for a reading guide
and exclusive content on THE BIRDER MURDER SERIES
www.oneworld-publications.com

Oneworld Publications
10 Bloomsbury Street
London WC1B 3SR
England

A SIEGE OF BITTERNS

ABOUT THE AUTHOR

Steve Burrows has pursued his birdwatching hobby on five continents. He is a former editor of the *Hong Kong Bird Watching Society* magazine and a contributing field editor for *Asian Geographic*. Steve now lives in Oshawa, Ontario.

For Mom and Dad
Yours is the best story of all

Acknowledgements

This is a work of fiction. The actions of the characters should not be interpreted in any way as a reflection upon the birders of Norfolk. At Cley, Titchwell, and elsewhere, I have always found the birders to be helpful, knowledgeable, and, above all, law-abiding. Similarly, in the real world the RSPB always keeps the rights and wishes of the landowner in mind when handling rare bird reports. As for scientists, what can I say? Tony Holland is entitled to his opinion.

Many people have contributed to this work. Fellow birders have generously shared their knowledge and skills, Simon Wotton of the RSPB provided information on the status of Bitterns in the U.K., and Sylvia McConnell, Allister Thompson, and Allison Hirst have offered valuable insights, opinions, and advice on the text. I thank them all.

Finally, my beautiful wife, Resa, had unwavering faith that one day this would happen; so sweetheart, I would like to acknowledge in print, just this once, that you were … you know, not wrong.

1

At its widest point, the marsh stretched almost a quarter of a mile across the north Norfolk coastline. Here, the river that had flowed like a silver ribbon through the rolling farmlands to the west finally came to rest, spilling its contents across the flat terrain, smoothing out the uneven contours, seeping silently into every corner. From this point on, tiny rivulets, no wider than a man's stride, would trace their way between the dunes and shale banks to complete the river's final journey out to sea.

At the margins of land and water, the marsh belonged to neither, and it carried the disquieting wildness of all forsaken things. Onshore winds rattled the dry reeds like hollow bones. The peaty tang of decaying vegetation and wet earth hung in the air. An hour earlier, the watery surface of the wetland had shimmered like polished copper; a fluid mirror for the last rays of the setting sun. But now, the gathering gloom had transformed the marsh into a dark, featureless emptiness.

To the west of the marsh, a row of ancient willows rose out of the flat landscape, marking the inland limits of the wetland's spread. Beyond the trees, the land climbed gently to a small, flat-topped rise, where a single house perched on the crest. Lights burned in the downstairs window, a small whisper of defiance against the darkness; a beacon to declare a human toehold on the edge of this raw, unnatural nature.

On a narrow path threading between the willows, two silhouettes moved in loose harmony. The recent tidal surges had left the water levels lapping over the edges of the pathway, so that it was no longer wide enough for the pair to walk side by side. Instead, the man picked his way along carefully in front, one hand clutching the binoculars dangling from his neck, to prevent them from bouncing against his chest. The dog roamed along easily behind him, stopping occasionally to paw at the debris on the path left behind by the now receding waters. The man scooped up a branch from the path and flung it out over the water, sending the dog crashing after it in a silvery spray. He looked at his watch and quickened his pace along the path, as if the coming darkness might hold danger. Or opportunity. The water-soaked dog scrambled ashore and fell in behind him, its hard-won prize dangling from its mouth.

As the path turned away from the marsh, it began to widen out. The dog surged ahead of the man now. Guided by long habit, it pressed on alone, sure of the route as it began to wend its way deeper amongst the willows. By the time the man arrived at the first bend, the dog had disappeared from view. The man checked his watch again and looked behind him, ahead, all around. Satisfied, or otherwise, he pressed on along the path.

Perhaps he had caught sight of it before he rounded the bend, sensed even, somehow, that it was there. Had there been a feeling of foreboding, of uneasiness, as he approached? All he knew for certain was that his first reaction was not surprise. Alarm, certainly, at the grotesque sight that greeted him. And horror, naturally. But by then, the dog had begun barking, rearing up on its hind legs to confront this unnatural apparition.

He knew immediately what it was, and that, too, lessened the shock. He did not need the groaning of the willow branch to confirm its burden. Even against the dark spiderweb of branches above him, the man could make out the form. Even before the freshening wind from the coast began to slowly twirl the shape and ease it out to describe its perfect, dreadful arc above the path, he knew.

He sat down on a log and took out his mobile phone. And waited for it to ring.

2

Tony Holland cursed again as his Audi A5 hit another pothole and bounced violently. He was certain he was going to snap an axle if he had to go much farther down this rutted laneway. No wonder Danny Maik had been so quick to accept when Tony had offered to pick up the new DCI. He should have known; Maik smiling that sly smile of his and thanking Tony for helping out like that. Holland owed him one. I mean, a joke was a joke, but putting his new Audi through this ... that was right out of order.

Holland looked out at the monochrome countryside surrounding him. He didn't need daylight to remind him what this part of the world looked like. Not for the first time, he wondered what would possess anyone to choose to live out here. Okay, if things were really tight and this was all you could afford, maybe. But on a DCI's salary? His new boss could have bought one of those brand new condos down near the waterfront — wave pool, exercise room, the lot. Instead, he had chosen this, living out his very own remake of *Little House on the Prairie*, or whatever, out among the mud and the fields and the rutted, pot-holed driveways.

The car lurched suddenly to the right. A water-filled crater wide enough to swallow his front tire all but wrenched the steering wheel from Holland's hands, sending the headlight beams up into the treetops. That was it. Any more of this and he was parking up. The new DCI could bloody well walk down. But the pothole proved to be the laneway's last hurrah, and Holland lurched gratefully to a halt in front of the DCI's house.

The cottage was a two-storey gabled affair: a solid, stone-walled structure with corners dressed in brick. Holland had seen a thousand like it throughout the county. Never once had it occurred to him that he might like to live in one. Like most properties of this age, this place looked like it needed a bit of a touch-up here and there, though it would be cosy enough on the inside, no doubt. Just what was it, this fascination the townies had with renovating these aging places, when you could get something new and maintenance-free for the same money?

A young woman was leaning in the open doorway as Holland pulled up, cradling a coffee mug to her chest. She was wearing a pair of faded jeans and a loose-fitting cableknit sweater. Holland suspected that the sweater might belong to the new DCI. Not the jeans, though; they were clearly all hers. He checked his smile in the mirror and ran his fingers through his hair before getting out of the car.

"It's so wonderful to be able to see the stars. In the city, it never seems to get dark enough," said the young woman by way of a greeting. She laughed, "Don't mind me. I suppose we are all the same when we first come out here, aren't we? I'm Lindy." She offered a hand and flicked her head toward the open door. "He'll be out in a minute. I'd offer you some coffee, but I suspect he will want to be off right away."

Well, she certainly wasn't Canadian, judging by that accent. They must have met over here. Holland introduced himself, giving it a little bit extra. If Lindy was going to be drawing any lines between the local yokels and tony ex-urbanites, he was keen to end up on the right side. And not just for his boss's sake, either. She was definitely worth some attention, this one. And some might say paying attention to deserving females was Tony Holland's specialty. So if it was stars she wanted to talk about, well, then, Lindy would learn how the stars out here were always best after a heavy rain, and how, sometimes, they seemed so close you felt like you could just reach out and touch them with your fingertips, and ... Holland heard a man's voice calling from somewhere inside the house and Lindy rolled herself off the door jamb and went inside. Holland leaned on his car and lit a cigarette. His celestial poetry would just have to wait for another time.

Domenic Jejeune was hunting for his mobile phone amidst piles of newspaper on the dining room table. Lindy picked up the phone from a sideboard and handed it to him.

"I thought you said he would be an antique, the one picking you up. 'Standard issue ex-army plod,' I believe was the term. I was expecting some grizzled old sapper with a broken nose and a cauliflower ear. This one looks younger than you."

"Perhaps he uses Botox," said Jejeune, shrugging himself into his jacket. "Have you seen my notebook anywhere?"

"Quite dishy, in fact," continued Lindy, producing a small black book from among the piles of paper on the table and handing it to Jejeune, "in a predatory, ladykiller kind of way, of course. Not that I'd get much of a look in, I suspect. The way he nursed that car along the driveway, I'd say any young lady is going to be coming a distant second in Constable Holland's affections. Are you okay?"

She paused and examined Jejeune's face carefully. It was the same look she had seen so many times recently. Uncertainty? Reluctance? It wouldn't be surprising. It had been a trying few weeks; the move, the new position, all the attention. A few doubts would be perfectly understandable. But Lindy knew it wasn't just that.

"It's going to be fine. Really, Dom. You've earned this. Everybody knows that."

Domenic looked at her. "Why don't you go back to bed?" he said gently. "You must be exhausted."

"I'm up now. I may as well do some more unpacking." She kissed his ear. "Good luck. And remember, be nice to Constable Holland. It's not his fault you've been called out at this ungodly hour."

"I'll keep it in mind," said Jejeune.

He gave her a peck on the cheek and walked out to the waiting car. Nodding an acknowledgement to Holland, Jejeune folded back the front passenger seat and got into the back. If Holland had any thoughts about this, he kept them to himself.

"Sergeant Maik sends his regrets, sir," said Holland, straining to make eye contact with his new boss via the rear-view mirror as he pulled away from the house. "It takes him a bit longer to get going these days, especially with him just coming back to active duty and all. Not to imply anything, sir. Sergeant Maik is a fine police officer. It's just that …"

"How is he at keeping his eyes on the road when he drives?" asked Jejeune. "I can't imagine what sort of damage an uneven driveway like this could do to an A5's suspension system."

And having successfully punctured Holland's conversation balloon for the remainder of the trip, Detective Chief Inspector Domenic Jejeune settled back into his seat and stared out the window at a soothing composition entitled *Saltmarsh Countryside by Night.*

3

Jejeune stood at the edge of a rise, staring down into the arc-lit theatre of activity below. White-suited officers moved about purposefully, pursuing their singular tasks, seemingly oblivious to one another, or even the shrouded body lying at the foot of the giant willow tree. A border of yellow police tape enclosed the area, and even from here, Jejeune could hear it snapping in the wind. He drew up his collar. The wind had picked up, carrying in the damp air off the sea. Proper daylight was still some way off, and he knew these officers would be cold and tired by the time they wrapped up their activities.

Jejeune knew his presence had been noted the moment he had arrived, even before he had issued the order to bring the body down. Word had already spread that the chief superintendent had delayed calling in SOCO. There would be nothing much in the way of forensic evidence at such a windswept, uncontained scene of crime anyway, but she clearly intended this to be Jejeune's investigation. He knew that if it was this obvious to him, it had already occurred to the other officers on the scene, the ones who were now waiting expectantly for him to finally descend into the arena himself. He took a deep breath and exhaled slowly. A local celebrity, a TV personality at that. And with a world-famous wife. It was hardly the sort of introduction he would have wanted. But putting it off wasn't going to make things any easier. He took his hands from his pockets and rubbed them together. Time to act.

For a big man, Danny Maik moved across the soft ground with surprising nimbleness. He picked his way along the edge of the marsh and stopped on the far side of the willow tree. From this point on, he would approach the body with his eyes only.

Tony Holland was leaning against the tree smoking a cigarette.

"So you got the old short straw, eh? With Captain Canada," he said. "What a welcome to come back to."

Maik shrugged. "And here I'd led such a charmed life up till now, having officers like you for company. Besides, I've never had any problems with Canadians. The ones I've met have always seemed all right."

"I hear they've already found the stepladder," said Holland, when Maik failed to rise to the bait. "In the shed next to the house. A bit clever, that."

Maik nodded his agreement. It was. Present the evidence to the police on a plate like this, and you discouraged them from poking around trying to find it on their own, when they might turn up who knows what else. Maik knew that murder generally induced a state of panic. A killer thinking clearly enough to replace evidence like this would also have the presence of mind to remove any incriminating clues. Forensics would check out the mud-caked stepladder as a matter of course, but there would be nothing there to help them.

Maik's eyes remained fixed on the plastic-covered form on the far side of the tree. "Did he say why he wanted the body down so soon?"

Holland shrugged. "Didn't want him swinging round in the breeze when the press arrived, I suppose. Grain sack over the head, wrists and ankles in chains. Might hog the spotlight, a thing like that."

"And did he tell them they should set it there, or did they come to that brilliant decision all by themselves?"

"He just said to bring it down. He didn't say where to leave it."

Holland stubbed out the remains of his cigarette and eased himself up from the tree trunk. He seemed to spot a situation requiring his attention and began walking toward the centre of the clearing. If Danny Maik was going to start making a fuss about something, a bit of distance was never a bad idea.

Maik retraced his steps along the edge of the marsh and rounded up a small posse of uniformed constables. From a distance, Jejeune watched the easy authority with which Maik addressed the young police officers. Steady, measured tones; clear, precise instructions; and just the right amount of eye contact. Born to command, some people.

"Again," Maik told them. "Approaching from the head and feet only, two men each end, and lifting straight up. Then moving off to the right. Remember, he's going to be a lot heavier than you expect, and the mud isn't going to help any, either. So go slowly. And let's show him a bit of respect, shall we."

"I think he's past caring, Sarge," said one of the young constables.

"Then we'd better make sure that we're not, hadn't we," said Maik evenly. "Because when a man's death stops affecting you, Constable, it's time to find another line of work."

The group moved off silently, tracked by Maik's unwavering gaze. He didn't turn as Jejeune approached, speaking over his shoulder instead. "He didn't mean anything by it, sir.

They're not quite sure how to handle it, that's all. I doubt any of them have been this close to violent death before."

But you have, thought Jejeune. *You know about violent death, and indignity, and lifting bodies out of the mud.*

"Another footprint?" asked Jejeune. Two sets had been found on the path leading down from the house, but they had disappeared in the morass of mud beneath the willow tree.

Maik was still watching the group as they approached the shrouded form beneath the tree. "Can't be sure until they lift the body away, but there's definitely something there, just by the left hip."

At the first lift, one of the men lost his footing, causing the entire group to lurch to one side.

"Steady," shouted Maik, leaning forward like an anxious football father on the touchline. He turned to Jejeune. "Of course, whether it'll still be there or not after this bloody lot have finished performing is another matter. Er, Chief Inspector."

An awkward silence settled between the two men, amplified by the activity and commotion going on all around them. Jejeune extended his hand. "I'd hoped to get acquainted under better circumstances."

Maik inclined his head. "Yes, sir."

Jejeune was not sorry the sergeant had missed his introduction to the ranks the day before. The breathless entrance into the cafeteria; the detective chief superintendent with Jejeune in tow; the startled look of the ambushed diners, before most of them had even done justice to the day's first cup of tea. Jejeune had been not so much presented as thrust upon them. The media were already onto the story of Jejeune's appointment, the DCS had explained as they were hurrying toward the cafeteria. God knows how they got these leads. Still, she had managed to get them a couple of minutes before the story was released to the online editions.

Jejeune had returned DCS Shepherd's terse smile.

It was important, the DCS continued, that the station hear it directly from her first. Better to set things straight right from the start. After all, who knew what spin those idiots in the press were likely to put on this.

"I'm assigning you Sergeant Maik," she had told Jejeune as they walked. "He's good, but he's just back from medical leave, so you'll have to keep an eye on him."

And suddenly they were at the cafeteria and, without further ado, it gave her great pleasure to announce the appointment of Detective Chief Inspector Domenic Jejeune, an officer whose extraordinary rise through the ranks was already well-documented, and was yet all the more remarkable given his … his lack of … grey hair. A weak smile, met by a few forced returns from the crowd.

And there it was. In a single sentence, the two themes Domenic Jejeune would rather have avoided at all costs: his fame and his youth.

"No point pussyfooting around, Domenic. It's not as if they won't have noticed, is it? Better get things out into the open, so they can come to terms with it and get on about their business. Glad to have you on board, of course, delighted, but the less disruptive your appointment turns out to be, the better all round. Agreed?"

Agreed. But exactly how was it going to be better all round for him to have to prove himself once more against suspicions about his age and his reputation, instead of just getting on with his job? So even as Jejeune stepped forward to articulate, in that slightly accented, self-effacing style that the media loved, just how proud and privileged he felt to be a part of the North Norfolk Constabulary, which was itself renowned for its forward thinking and innovative approaches, he was aware that the job that lay ahead of him had suddenly become that much harder.

He had noted their responses. Nothing overt, no rolling of the eyes, no smirks; but then, there hardly would have been with the formidable presence of the DCS by his side. But a slight stiffening of shoulders, the faintest turning away of a head; it was there if you knew what to look for. And Jejeune did. But could they see through his veneer, too? Could they tell, as he delivered his speech in a tone as smooth as melting chocolate, what was really in his heart? Could they sense his doubts and fears? His reluctance?

Jejeune stole a glance now at Maik, still watching the recovery party. *No, you weren't there,* he thought, *but there would have been no shortage of people lining up to tell you about it.* Like this one approaching now. Holland.

"Terrible, eh, sir? And him a television personality, too. Did you know him at all?"

Jejeune didn't answer.

"I've had a word with the man who found the body. Not much help." Holland consulted his notebook. "Dr. Michael Porter. A local vet. He's a bit cool, though, all the same. Just called us straight off and sat down and waited. Made no effort to get the body down, do CPR, nothing like that."

"No," said Jejeune thoughtfully, "he wouldn't have."

Holland looked at Maik.

"He's a vet," said Maik. "He'd recognize a lost cause when he saw one."

"Still, you'd think he might try, if only for form's sake. He was out here doing a bit of birdwatching when he found the body. Avid birder, apparently. He made a special trip tonight looking for something called a Bittern. Word is you do a bit of birding yourself, sir. Have you heard of that one?"

"Avid. That's what he said? Not a professional then."

Holland couldn't suppress a smirk. "I don't think he's won any medals at it," he said, cocking a sly grin toward Maik. "But he seems keen enough. He said he'd only been here about ten minutes. Parked his car on the far side, and walked around here with his dog."

"We've got his details, so what do you reckon, sir? Send him home?"

"No," said Jejeune, "not just yet."

Jejeune stared at the man sitting on a fold-up chair in the tent. Michael Porter looked unconcerned, distracted almost. A man used to pronouncing death; sure, confident, controlled. A man aware that he is at the centre of a great commotion and doing everything he can to portray himself as the soul of calm. He might still be fighting the shock of finding the body, but inwardly, Dr. Porter would surely be relishing this role.

Jejeune approached the man and took a seat opposite him. Holland made the introductions.

"So, what were you doing out here, Dr. Porter?" asked Jejeune amicably.

"Birdwatching, I was hoping to get a Bittern. There's some excellent habitat for them here, and one was reported in the area recently. I have actually covered all this with the constable, Chief Inspector."

"I meant what were you actually doing, under the guise of birdwatching?"

"I beg your pardon. What are you suggesting?"

"I'm suggesting that you are not telling us the truth about why you were here, Dr. Porter." Jejeune indicated the mud-splattered dog lying contentedly beneath the vet's chair. "No birder serious enough to make a special trip out here in the hopes of seeing a Bittern is going to allow his dog to go splashing around in the marsh and trundle unleashed up and down the pathways."

Jejeune paused, but Dr. Porter had nothing to say.

"I have no reason to doubt that you are a birder." Jejeune nodded toward the man's binoculars, a pair of high-end Opticrons. "But that's not why you came here tonight."

Porter's anger was palpable. "This is ridiculous. No wonder people are reluctant to get involved these days. You try to help out, and this is the way you are treated."

Jejeune kept his stare fixed on the man, but Maik's and Holland's eyes were locked unwaveringly on the chief inspector. When he spoke slowly like this, his accent was all but undetectable.

Jejeune sighed. "Dr. Porter," he said, "the Bittern habitat you spoke of is over on the far side of the marsh, close to where you parked your car. There is virtually no cover at all on this side for a secretive bird like the Bittern. It's far too open. And besides, anyone looking for a crepuscular species would have been in position long before you got here. So why were you here, Dr. Porter, if not to look for a Bittern? Would you please show the sergeant your mobile phone?"

"I most certainly will not."

Jejeune leaned forward and spoke quietly and evenly, like a man explaining the rules of a game to a child. His tone was as calm and reasonable as before. "Dr. Porter, I need a clear picture of what happened here tonight, and at the moment, you are casting shadows. How deeply I have to dig into your personal affairs to get my clear picture is up to you."

Jejeune paused again, waiting to see if it would be enough.

There was no physical indication that Dr. Porter had capitulated, no drooping of the shoulders, no slumping forward. He remained sitting upright, staring into the middle distance as resolutely as before. Only his voice changed. It was quieter now, less assertive.

"I was meeting a man, he … I buy drugs from him.

It's not what you think. Medical supplies, for my practice. Acetylpromazine, Tranexamic Acid, that sort of thing. They're incredibly expensive and, well, he gives me a good price. I … that is to say, they may not be stolen. I don't ask. I don't even know his name. He calls me, ID blocked, before we meet, just to confirm there are no problems. I waited for his call tonight and as soon as he rang off, I called the police about this awful business, I swear it."

"What did you tell him?"

"Nothing. Just not to come. That there had been a murder and the police would be arriving shortly. That's all. He said he was calling to cancel anyway. He said he would get in touch with me later. Then he hung up."

"He didn't ask about the body?"

The vet shook his head. He rubbed his face with his hands, letting his fingers run up into his hairline. Beneath the chair, the dog stirred into life and raised its head.

"Please wait here."

Jejeune led Holland and Maik out of the tent and turned to face them. "Constable Holland, take Dr. Porter home and collect all the drugs he has bought from this man. Let's see if we can trace the supplier through their batch numbers."

"You think there might be a connection?"

"A man tells you a body has turned up at a place you are supposed to meet, and you don't ask any questions. At all?"

Maik reached for his own phone. "I'll try to run a trace on that incoming call, shall I?"

Jejeune pulled a face. "Anybody that cautious will be using a pay-as-you-go disposable, but I suppose it wouldn't hurt to be sure. I'll check what else we have here and then you and I can go on up to the house."

Jejeune marched off toward the crowd of officers still working the crime scene. The two men watched him go.

Holland let out a long, theatrical breath. "And just what the hell does *crepuscular* mean?"

"It means," said Maik, his eyes tracking the senior officer into the crowd, "that Chief Inspector Jejeune has just announced his arrival. I believe what you have just seen, young Holland, is the unusual sight of somebody auditioning for a role after they've already been given the part. Now get this bloke home and pick up those drugs."

4

Dawn was still some way off when Jejeune and Maik climbed the small rise to the house. They entered from the garden and found themselves in the kitchen. A uniformed constable approached Maik and murmured quietly to him. If Jejeune was concerned that the officer had gone to the sergeant, rather than himself, he didn't let it show. He paused to look back at the doorway, through which the killer had almost certainly led his victim on his final journey.

"The wife is with her doctor, apparently," said Maik. "Her personal assistant was wondering if our interview could wait. She can stay to give us her own statement, if necessary, but she would prefer to be upstairs, too. They have both been away for a couple of days. Just got back late last evening. Saw nothing, heard nothing. Oh, and the record company is asking to be kept informed of developments. Just as a courtesy."

Jejeune looked at the tall young woman hovering at the foot of the staircase. She was right out of the PA mould, impeccably dressed, pretty enough, but careful to keep it in check; presentable and professional, but not enough to take the shine off her boss. She had the right amount of detachment, too. She would use the word *regrettably* a lot when she told people they wouldn't be seeing Ms. Brae today. And there would be the smile, the one that told them there was no room for argument. She knew enough not to smile at the two men now, but she conveyed her thanks with a slight nod as Jejeune waved her upstairs.

The detectives went down a wide hallway into a large sitting room. Even to Maik's untutored eye, there seemed a lack of balance in the furniture. Small, homely items, a well-worn chair, a battered side table, fought for space among the high-class furnishings, as if someone had tried to accommodate them long after the room had been expensively and professionally set up.

A robust fire burned in a fireplace on the wall opposite the door. A brittle air of calm hung in the room, poised, as if the slightest disturbance might shatter it. In a wing-backed chair near the fire, a man's profile was visible. He was gazing into the flames, his face pale, unclouded by expression. A uniformed constable standing near the doorway nodded his head subtly in the direction of the man. Jejeune motioned for Maik to take the lead. Perhaps it was some sort of test, like in the army. *See what the chap's made of, what?* Maik was unconcerned. He would just do his job, and leave others to worry about the performance reviews. He approached the man and drew up a chair to sit beside him.

"Malcolm Brae? I'm Sergeant Maik. Please accept my condolences. However, we do need to ask you a few questions, sir."

The man nodded without speaking.

With a skill born of long practice, Maik walked him through the rudimentaries. Brae had come straight over as soon as the call came from the police. He had been at his own house, in his workshop, actually, finishing up a special order. Maik moved on to the secondary level inquiries, covering his points carefully, but not endowing any of them with particular significance. When had Malcolm Brae last seen his father? Was it normal for his father to be home alone in the evening? Anything special about this night of the week? Each question was met with a sullen, monosyllabic response, as if Malcolm Brae was determined to provide as little information as possible.

Maik continued, unfazed. Had his father been involved in any disputes lately? Had there been any unfamiliar visitors or strangers hanging around the house, any hint at all that he might be in danger? "There's no record of any police reports, you see, but with an ... incident of this nature —"

"It doesn't appear to be a random attack. Is that what you're saying? Yes, thank you, Sergeant, I had got that far on my own, actually." Malcolm Brae turned to examine the flames again.

"We can wait until later to do this if you like," said Maik, in the same even tone as before, "but the quicker we fill in the gaps, the more likely it is we'll be able to catch up with whoever did this."

With an effort, Brae drew his eyes from the fire and looked at Maik. "Gaps, Sergeant? Since the success of *The Marsh Man*, my father's life has been pretty much a matter of public record, especially since his marriage to that woman. I can't imagine there are too many *gaps* that have escaped the public's attention."

Jejeune had begun a slow walk around the room, carefully examining the various artifacts as if he might know a thing or two about this quality of art. But Maik was pretty sure that he wasn't letting it distract him from Brae's answers. He turned his own attention back to Brae.

"Your father courted controversy at times in his TV show; the proposal for the North Norfolk National Park, for example."

"Oh, yes, that. The dailies loved that one. Complete nonsense, of course. My father wasn't above making an outrageous statement or two, if he thought it might attract publicity."

"Even the wrong kind?"

Malcolm Brae leaned forward confidentially. "There is no wrong kind of publicity, Sergeant. Just ask my stepmother.

Besides, it caused nothing more than a bit of bluster in a couple of editorials." He spread his long white hands. "Nothing that I ever heard about, anyway."

"But others might have?"

"My father's wife was his confidant on personal matters. The rest of us generally just got warmed-over press releases. As for other secrets," continued Malcolm Brae, "I'm sure my father would have entrusted those to his beloved marsh."

"He spent a lot of time there?"

Malcolm Brae let out a short, angry bark. In another context, it might have been a laugh. "I think it's fair to say that marsh saw more of him than any of us ever did. Everything else, the TV programs, the books, the wider environmental activism, they all grew out of his obsession with that place. Still, at least he really did care about his subject. I suppose that in itself made him unique among television presenters these days."

Jejeune's tour of the room had brought him to an ornately paneled door on the far side. "Your father's study?" he asked Malcolm Brae. He opened the door and entered without waiting for an answer.

It was a surprisingly small room, with built-in bookcases around two walls and a faded oriental carpet on the floor beneath a dark cherrywood desk. A battered filing cabinet sat in a corner of the room. Jejeune could see nothing other than the mirrored reflection of the room through the darkened windows behind the desk, but he guessed that in daylight the view looked out over the marsh. And the willow trees.

The desk, like the rest of the room, was tidy, but not immaculately so; a sheaf of papers loosely stacked in Brae's in-tray, a slender black pen perched uncertainly in a holder, a silver letter opener roughly aligned with the top of a blotter. It was the desk of a man who liked order.

Jejeune opened the drawers and found the same general order and organization. He looked at the desktop again, carefully. The pen had been returned to the holder upside down. Easily done, the two ends were virtually identical. The simple mistake of a busy man, preoccupied with getting on with his day-to-day affairs. Perhaps.

He picked up the sheaf of papers from the in-tray. It was a collection of birdwatchers' lists, records from local sites dating back for the previous five years or so. Most were computer printouts, but several were typed or even handwritten. All different hands, as far as Jejeune could tell.

Brae's day planner lay to the left of the blotter, opened at the page for the previous day. Jejeune lifted it and riffled back the pages from the previous few days. Amid the smattering of bird sightings and other observations about the marsh were several meticulously recorded appointments. Cameron Brae's day was unlikely to involve missed engagements or forgotten assignments.

At first, Jejeune thought he must have misread the entry, perhaps merged two words in the blur of flickering pages. He thumbed back urgently through the pages. There it was, from three days ago. He drew a deep breath. The pages of the day planner were divided into three columns, for morning, afternoon, and evening. Various entries were scattered over the page, a local hotel listed under "Breakfast," initials at 6:30 in the evening. But in the centre column there was only one entry. It was underlined twice and circled in red: *am.bittern.*

Jejeune looked back at the birdwatchers' lists. It would take a long time to search through them all, longer than Jejeune had at the moment, but he would be willing to bet there were no other sightings of an American Bittern among them, underlined and circled in red, or otherwise. Eurasian Bitterns, such as Dr. Porter had claimed to have been searching for, certainly, but not American Bitterns. Lying in the tray beneath the bird lists was an Ordnance Survey 1:25,000 map showing the marsh and surrounding areas in great detail. At a point on the northern boundary of the marsh, someone had marked a crude red *X*. To Jejeune's eyes, the ink looked the same as that used for Brae's circled diary entry. He took the upside-down pen out of the holder and scribbled on the blotter. Red.

Jejeune turned to leave the room, but stopped suddenly and went back to the bird lists. He leafed through the top three again, carefully clipping each together when he had finished and replacing it in the pile. Coupled with the pen, it left him in no doubt. So you hang your victim out on public display, brazenly replace the ladder in the shed outside, but then try to hide the fact that you had ever been in this study. What sense did that make? But then, what sense did murder ever make?

Jejeune stepped back through the open doorway, motioning to the constable.

"Have everything from the desk bagged and bought to the station. Don't let anyone else near that room until it's been fingerprinted. You'd better check that the station has my prints on file. If not, have a set sent over from central records." He should have worn gloves, he knew, but no one had offered him any at the scene, and he hadn't been expecting to be handling any evidence up here in the house.

In his absence, an uneasy truce had been reached. Both Maik and Brae were silent now, the only sounds coming from the fireplace, where the flames were spitting out impurities in the wood with angry crackles.

Maik approached Jejeune.

"The victim had been home alone for the past couple of days. With his wife away, he saw no need for the staff to be here, so he dismissed them. He and the son apparently had a row about something a couple of days ago, too, but I get the feeling that's not unusual."

Jejeune nodded. He addressed the man in the chair. "Did your father entertain people in his study?"

Malcolm Brae turned to look at Jejeune. The detective was standing just far enough behind the chair to force Brae to twist his body in order to face him. Jejeune made no move to make the man's pose any more comfortable.

"No, it was his private sanctuary. If he wanted to talk to anyone, he did it out here."

Malcolm Brae seemed to catch on something, perhaps his use of the past tense. It was a moment before he was able to recover himself.

"The nature of your father's work," said Jejeune softly, "I imagine he consulted scholarly papers, species lists, things like that, quite often."

It was clear to Maik that the interview was now no longer his, but he didn't put away his notebook. Instead, he seemed to decide it was an ideal place to rest his gaze.

"I rarely saw my father without a book or journal of some sort. Face buried behind one at the breakfast table, absorbed in one in front of the fireplace at night. People forget, beyond all that television celebrity nonsense, he was first and foremost an academic."

"You didn't approve of his television work?" asked Jejeune.

"We didn't see eye to eye on many things. My father had a very singular view of the world, Chief Inspector, and if you didn't agree with him, there was very little room for compromise. Few arguments measured up to his standards. Few people either."

Brae's temples were shining with sweat now, and right on cue, he began to shiver. Maik motioned the constable over and told him in a discreet murmur to go upstairs and tell the doctor that Mr. Brae was beginning to go into shock.

Jejeune needed Malcolm Brae to stay with them for a few moments more, and he hurried into his last question. "I wonder, do you happen to know what your father's county life list was?"

"Somewhere around 385, 390? I'm afraid I can't ..."

But Malcolm Brae was gone. He returned to his sullen examination of the fireplace. He was trembling now, beads of sweat forming on his brow, his hair damp at the temples and collar. As soon as the doctor arrived, Jejeune signalled to Maik and the two of them left the room in silence.

They paused on the front steps. Despite the lights and activity in the marsh behind the house, only stillness lay across the dark fields in front of them.

"Brae didn't seem to take to your questions overly, Sergeant. Why do you think that was?"

Maik turned his collar up against the night. For a moment, there was silence between the two men.

"I don't imagine it's easy, being the child of a television personality," he said finally. "You spend your life in their shadow. Then, when they've gone, the first thing you find yourself doing is answering more questions about them. Of course, I'm no psychologist, but it could be something like that."

Jejeune nodded almost imperceptibly. "Aggression's a handy thing, though, if you want to deflect unwelcome questions. There's some psychology in that, too, isn't there, Sergeant?"

Of course, it could just be that the poor bugger has just had his world cave in on him, on account of his old man being found swinging from a tree in his back garden. Who knew how anybody would respond to such a situation. Maik had seen grown men laugh out loud at the sight of a dead colleague, only to see the same men crushed by grief a few hours later. Normal responses take a holiday when Death comes calling. But he didn't say any of this. Jejeune's handling of the inquiry had left him feeling vaguely uneasy, but he was unable to put his finger on why. Right now he just wanted to go home and get some sleep. He did have one further thought, though.

"His county life list? Are you talking about birds, sir?"

"His lifetime list of species seen in the county."

"What did he say? Three hundred and eighty-five? Sounds like a lot."

"Or 390. It is. An extraordinarily high number."

"Whatever it was, it won't be getting any higher," said Maik matter-of-factly. He got into his car and drove off, leaving the inspector staring up at the star-filled sky.

Jejeune took in a deep breath of the sweet night air. Dysfunctional families, a policeman's insecurities, rare bird sightings. Where, beyond the shadowy recesses of a few human hearts, did any of them register in the grand scheme of things? But murder, that mattered. Murder introduced a terrifying dissonance that knocked the whole world out of its equilibrium. Murder set everybody's alarm bells jangling. And now, once again, it was to him, Domenic Jejeune, that the daunting task of silencing them had fallen.

5

The incident room at the Saltmarsh division of the North Norfolk Constabulary was filled to capacity for the morning briefing. Detectives and uniformed officers, many of them still bleary-eyed from their overnight exertions, had scattered themselves around the desks, but there were also a number of other bodies, community support workers and clerical staff, who found a reason to be in or around the station at this particular time. Some stood in small clusters near the windows, others leaned against corridor walls and door jambs.

The new DCI has some pulling power, thought Maik, *I'll give him that.* If Maik could have put a name to the mood, he would have gone for curiosity rather than anticipation. He was already aware of one or two rumblings from those who had seen Jejeune in action at the crime scene. Now they were wondering if that performance was a one-off. Maik doubted that anybody had gone so far as to make up their mind about him just yet, but anybody who came to Saltmarsh with this kind of fanfare wasn't going to get the benefit of the doubt for long. Reputations didn't count for much in this part of the world. They were going to want to see some proof that the DCS's star recruit was worth the blaze of publicity that had accompanied his appointment.

Perhaps in a moment they would get to see the magic that was the real Domenic Jejeune.

Certainly, Jejeune's entrance raised a few eyebrows. He was the last to arrive, but he made no move to take control of the briefing. Maik took up a position in front of the whiteboard, and as the sergeant gradually brought the meeting to order, Jejeune hopped up onto a desk at the back of the room and began leafing through a battered book. Perhaps it was a Canadian thing, thought Maik, this lack of formality. But no, Jejeune had been in England long enough. He knew how these briefings went. So this casual attitude was just his own particular approach, then.

The inspector looked up momentarily from his book and gave a slight nod toward Maik, to indicate he should begin.

"Right, let's get on with it. The victim has been formally identified as Cameron Brae, television presenter of the show *The Marsh Man*, author, environmental activist, part-time lecturer at the university, but most importantly of all to you lot …" Maik spread his hands out invitingly.

"Mr. Mandy Roquette," chorused two or three of the assembled choir near the front.

"The Party Animal herself. Enough to see anyone off, that would be," offered Tony Holland, to a laugh or two.

"In her prime, maybe. Well past her sell-by date now, though," added a robust blond constable perched on the edge of a chair, who obviously felt more than comfortable about her own shelf-life. There was more derisive laughter, until Maik shut it down.

"Cause of death: hanging. Still to be confirmed by the M.E., but it should be straightforward enough. No other evident wounds. Crime scene a wash. No useable physical evidence, bar one impression of the foot of a stepladder, presumably the same one found in the victim's shed, forensics to confirm. No witnesses. No apparent motive. No suspects." He looked around the room. "That about it? Right, so where do we start? With the backstory, Sergeant Maik, that's where. Now, thanks to television, I doubt that there is anybody here who is *not* familiar with Dr. Brae's work, especially in and around these parts."

Maik paused and looked significantly in Jejeune's direction, but the inspector's attention seemed taken by something in the book.

Maik moved on. "And thanks to our friends in the media, we know a fair bit about our victim, for once. Talk to anybody and the message is the same: With Cameron Brae, what you saw on TV was what you got; a person who cared deeply about the environment and dedicated his life to sharing his knowledge and his passion with others. As far as anyone can tell, 'Leave it for the next generation' wasn't just a TV mantra, it was the philosophy that governed his life. So it looks like our biggest problem in the short-term will be coming up with a list of suspects. All indications are that Cameron Brae was a well-respected and admired man, much loved by one and all."

Jejeune looked up from his book, "Are we sure about that, Sergeant?"

"No one we have talked to has had a bad word to say about him."

"Then perhaps we should look at some of the good words. Let's do that, can we? Let's have a list of all the adjectives we have heard about Cameron Brae. Everyone. Sergeant Maik can write them down as you call them out."

Maik, who looked like he would sooner consult a psychic than pursue this line of inquiry, said nothing. Gradually, the words came, first a trickle, and then suddenly a flood, as the group caught on, and saw their contributions validated in washable black marker. Maik scribbled rapidly to keep up with the input, some of the entries barely legible when he had finished.

Jejeune looked up again when the participation had run its course, picking out a few of the words: *Passionate, Zealous, Fervent, Dedicated, Committed, Devoted, Determined, Eager, Keen.*

"What does it say to you, that list?" he asked.

"Somebody who loved his work and was very good at it," offered Holland. "But we knew that already."

"Wouldn't fancy working for him, though," said the blond constable. "Sounds like a pain in the … er, neck." She was obviously going to leave it to one of the others to find out how comfortable the new DCI was with his officers using the vernacular, as it were.

Jejeune smiled. "Some might have an even lower opinion, Constable …" He hesitated.

"Lauren Salter," supplied Maik quietly.

"But your point is well taken," continued Jejeune smoothly. "Crusaders, the overly committed, the evangelists, are not always the easiest of people to get along with, in my experience. Professional admiration is one thing," said Jejeune, "but it doesn't mean people liked the man personally. And make no mistake, this was a very personal crime."

"There's no human stuff," said Maik. He surprised even himself by saying it aloud, but now he had, he felt compelled to continue. "All anyone wants to comment on with Brae is his work. There's nothing about *him* up there. You know, what a laugh he was, how good he was to his family. That's usually the first thing people talk about when somebody has died."

He stopped suddenly. Everyone in the room realized Maik was drawing on a well of experience that no man his age should have accumulated.

Constable Salter, who had just finished mouthing the words *lower opinion* to Holland, picked up on Jejeune's earlier point. "So the field's wide open, then, really. We could be looking at colleagues, co-workers, just about anybody."

Maik looked at the board thoughtfully. "In the absence of any other obvious suspects, the best route we've got at the moment seems to be the family. Regardless of whether you think his wife can sing or not, and those of us who know what real music is have our own thoughts on that. . . ." Maik held up a hand against the furor. "Regardless, as I say, we know she has got a few quid of her own, making money an unlikely motive, even if she was, *is*, the beneficiary of Brae's will. But a thirty-odd-year age difference between the spouses, now that has been known to produce a motive or two, so it might be nice to know if the grieving widow had any boyfriends. Lauren?"

"On it," said Salter in response to Maik's gaze.

"And the son . . ." began Maik.

Jejeune looked up from his book again and shook his head slowly. "Yes, I'm not sure I can put family in the frame for this."

"With respect, sir," said Maik, in a careful tone that the others in the room recognized as the first signs of danger, "fair enough that he may not have been as well-liked as we first thought, but we have no forced entry and the house conveniently empty. And family is the first place we would normally start in a case like this, even without those two."

"And normally it would be the right place to start. But in this case, I think we need to consider the nature of the crime. A hanging is a message. Traitors are hung, those who have sinned against society, or the common good. I can't recall ever having heard of hanging as a means of murder in a family dispute. Poison, the slow route, weapons for the impulse murders, even strangulation or suffocation. But hanging? And think about the sack over the head. No, this killing was a humiliation, a public punishment. It doesn't feel like a family member to me, not at all."

Holland blew out his cheeks and leaned toward Constable Salter. "Tell me he has actually run a murder inquiry before," he whispered.

"I think we're into the realm of male intuition here," she whispered in reply.

It wasn't in Maik's nature to publicly question a superior, but he too would have liked some indication that Jejeune had the faintest idea what he was doing. "So everybody else is in the frame, just not the family?" Maik struggled to keep his respectful tone in check.

"Oh, I'm sure the family will provide all sorts of interesting leads. No, we have a look at them, most definitely. I'm just saying it won't turn out to be one of them who committed the murder, that's all."

An awkward silence settled over the attendees. Jejeune seemed to realize that, having sucked all of the oxygen out of the room, the responsibility for kick-starting the proceedings had fallen to him.

"Right, so, what else do we have?" he asked brightly.

"Cameron Brae's last telephone call was to Peter Largemount," said Salter, sifting through her notes. She looked up at Jejeune. "He's a local businessman, sir, owns a large wind farm near Brae's property. Oh, and there's an email from Brae to a Professor Alwyn at the university requesting some data. He didn't use email very much, so this one kind of stood out. No evidence of any reply from the professor."

Jejeune nodded. "Very good. We should definitely have a closer look at anything Brae was working on in the days leading up to his death."

"Archie Christian should be one of our first stops, too," added Holland.

Jejeune raised a questioning eyebrow.

"Local villain, sir. Hard core. He's originally from down your patch. London, I mean, not Canada...." A few smiles from the assembly accompanied Holland's own. "He claims to be a reformed character these days, a legitimate businessman. Usual story, relocated city dweller, tired of the hustle and bustle, came up here for a bit of peace and quiet and the idyllic country life."

Holland didn't dare catch Maik's eye, but both men knew the others in the room wouldn't have missed this little dig at Jejeune.

"The thing is, he was a player in the organized crime scene, back in the day. He earned himself a bit of a reputation with the serious crimes squad. Two stints inside, but nothing ever stuck. He's certainly got the 'skill set,' as you might say, for this sort of thing, and he's on record as having a number of run-ins with Cameron Brae over the years."

"Really? What about?"

Holland looked around him at the others, as if perhaps this was information a new DCI should already know. "Well, sir, Brae blocked a number of development projects here, and at least a couple involved Archie Christian. I thought that might be, like, you know, a motive?"

Before anyone could tell if Holland had pushed things too far, the door opened and all eyes shifted toward it.

If Jejeune was surprised by the arrival of the chief superintendent, his body language gave no hint. Among the general shuffle that accompanied her entrance, Jejeune stayed perfectly still, his loose, informal pose unchanged. Only by looking directly into Jejeune's face would you have been able to detect any flicker of emotion betrayed there. And Danny Maik was the only person in the room facing in that direction.

DCS Shepherd swept her eyes over the white board as she entered. "I see they've started making a list of your qualities already, Domenic. I just dropped by to see how things were progressing. Arrested anyone yet?"

"Sergeant Maik has just been leading us through the preliminaries," Jejeune said, in a voice that suggested he felt that comedy was best left to the professionals.

"Yes, well, an early result would go down very nicely. Very nicely indeed."

She turned to the room in general. "This one will be different from any murder case you have worked before. The media spotlight will be on us, and everything you do or say will be noted and pored over and held up to scrutiny. That's okay, welcome even, as long as we get it right, but just as our successes will be noted, so will any cock-ups. And everything, good or bad, will be magnified out of all proportion. Just remember that. Fortunately, I have already recruited someone who knows all about the pressure of the media spotlight in a high-profile murder case, so we can all look to Inspector Jejeune as an example of how to handle ourselves. But for anybody who's thinking that all this attention might be their road to stardom, just remember this: You and this story will be old news as soon the next big football transfer goes through. But your superiors won't be as fickle, and if anybody's been giving the media any behind the scenes tours, slipping them the odd tidbit of unauthorized information, just to get on their right side, I'll make it my business to find out who it was."

The DCS's face softened; the precursor to the nurturing side she was about to show. Maik wondered if this ability to display a greater emotional range had anything to do with the increasing numbers of female officers he was seeing among the senior ranks these days. Certainly, he could never have switched personas this quickly. Not that he had another one to go to, anyway.

"Because Cameron Brae was such a well-known TV personality, the pressure to solve this case will be intense," continued Shepherd, "but I am certain I have assembled one of the finest squads in the country here. If you do your jobs efficiently, professionally, competently, just like you do them every day of the week, I'm convinced we'll get a result. Now, I'm sure the chief inspector doesn't want to let you go without some well-chosen insights. Domenic?"

Jejeune raised an eyebrow.

"Words to the wise? A few pearls of wisdom to help them on their way."

The assembled crowd gazed at Jejeune expectantly, a few sharing his palpable sense of unease as he walked toward the front of the room and took his place before them. When he spoke it was as if he was giving voice to inner thoughts, drawing them up from within, as if they needed expression out here, in the light of day, to become fully formed ideas. It was not at all the performance of a man they had all seen so at ease in front of the television cameras.

"A sixty-two-year-old man was taken out of his house, led to the end of his garden, and hanged. His last thoughts would have been of the family he would never see again, the things he had left unsaid, the work left undone. He would have died afraid and alone."

Jejeune paused for a long moment. Just as the silence was about to become uncomfortable, he spoke again, his voice steadier now, measured and deliberate.

"We can't change any of that. We can't hope to undo any of the damage that's been done by this crime. All we can do is find the person who did it and bring that person to justice. If we are being honest with ourselves, it is a ridiculously inadequate response to a horrific crime like this, and in the big picture, our success or failure won't really change anything. Not for the family, or for those who admired the man and his work. They will have some closure, some sense of justice, whatever that means, but their loss will still be there, their despair, whether we find the killer or not. So we are doing this for ourselves, really. And we do it because it's the only thing we can do. It's the only response we have."

A stunned silence settled over the room. Holland leaned back in his chair and whispered out of the side of his mouth to Salter again. "Blimey, I thought I was at Agincourt for a minute there."

A muscle twitched in DCS Shepherd's jawline. She obviously didn't feel Jejeune had channelled the ghost of Henry V either, and judging from the eerie stillness in the room, the assembled crowd was as bemused by the speech as she was. Still, they placed their loyalties in some surprising people, this lot. They thought the world of Sergeant Maik, who seemed to Shepherd to have all the personality of a granite wall. All it would take was one flash of brilliance from Jejeune, one insight, one bit of inspiration, and they would see what all the fuss was about. *Then watch that whiteboard fill with accolades.* But she was forced to admit, judging by the dumbfounded looks on their faces, that moment might be some way off yet.

6

The house felt different. Daylight had opened up the rooms, revealing the high cathedral ceilings and flooding the hallways with light. But the oppressive sadness that had shrouded the rooms had also gone. With the new day, the house seemed to be quietly regaining its equilibrium. It was as if the inhabitants had tacitly recognized that it was this, the pattern of chores and duties, the day-to-day business of carrying on, that would gradually guide them back toward normality.

Maik waited in the hallway while Nancy the PA went off to see if her boss was up to receiving visitors. Despite himself, he was still bristling at his exchange with Jejeune before he had left to come here. Not so much the request itself, odd as it was, but more the way he had put it. Seeing the sergeant in the front lobby, Jejeune had only one thing to say as he hurried by with his battered hardback in his hand: "See if Brae made a habit of discussing his weight with people. And if you could be subtle about it."

Subtle? Maik was so flustered by Jejeune's remark that he had been uncharacteristically curt in his reply, so much so that even the desk sergeant had looked up. "And what will you be doing, while I'm busy being subtle?"

"Me?" Jejeune brandished the book in the air. "I'm off to see a man about a bird."

And with that, he was gone. The desk sergeant had raised an eyebrow in Maik's direction, but it didn't look as if Maik was in any mood to entertain witticisms about birdwatchers as he barged out the door.

Nancy returned and led Maik down the hallway to the sitting room. He found Mandy Brae in the same chair her stepson had occupied the night before. She smiled a meaningless smile at the sergeant and motioned him into the room, thanking Nancy politely, which was apparently how people like this dismissed their PAs.

"Would you like some breakfast, Sergeant? There are some things in the kitchen. Nancy made them for me, but …"

Maik declined, pausing awkwardly at the end as he considered how he should address her. *Ma'am* seemed ridiculously antiquated for a woman who was still, despite what some blond police constables would have you believe, barely into her thirties. And yet *Mrs. Brae* also seemed inappropriate for a woman who had walked the red carpets of the world under a stage name of Mandy Roquette. But *Ms. Roquette*? Maik wondered why it suddenly meant so much to him to get it right. She had just lost her husband. What further assaults from the world did he imagine he was trying to protect her from?

The old soldier in Maik was always more comfortable on his feet, but with his subject sitting hunched in the chair beneath him, it made for an intimidating setting for an interview. He opted for distance, and strolled away to rest an elbow on the mantle. Music was playing softly in the background, languid saxophone phrases laid over a satin-smooth rhythm section. It seemed oddly out of place. In Maik's experience, the bereaved usually chose to bear their burden in silence; afraid perhaps that a familiar song might distract them from the business of mourning. But Maik could sense that music was a safe haven for her, perhaps the only thing that could help her through this time.

"We are obviously aware of your husband's environmental activism, his opposition to certain projects, for example. Would you know if he was involved in anything like that at the moment?"

She shrugged. "My husband was always on the lookout for anything that might hurt the environment. That didn't always make him popular with the local developers and business owners, not that he gave a toss about that, of course. But as far as I know, there was nothing recently."

She brushed a strand of dark hair away from her face. Without the pancake show business makeup, her skin was unnaturally pale, but it was immaculately smooth, and even in her grief, her delicate, China-doll features exuded a fragile beauty.

"How about his work at the university? Can you tell me anything about your husband's current area of research?"

"Pretty much the same as always. I think. It varied quite a bit. Birds, marshes, that kind of thing. We didn't really discuss it much, to be honest."

Maik wrote without comment. The music floated in the background of the silence that had settled between them. "Junior Walker," he said. "Haven't heard him in a while."

"A Motown man, Sergeant?"

Maik nodded. "The early stuff especially. Smokey Robinson, Marvin Gaye. Nothing to touch it, in my opinion."

She smiled wistfully. "Mine too. I grew up with it. My dad had an amazing collection; still does. I sang along to all of them when I was a kid. The Supremes, Martha Reeves, Mary Wells. Remember her? Those duets with Marvin Gaye?"

Maik shook his head slowly. "Voice like an angel, that girl. 'What's the Matter with You Baby,' 'Once Upon A Time.'"

"'Once Upon A Time.' God, I'd forgotten all about that one." She began rocking slowly from side to side, hugging her sweater tightly around herself, murmuring the words to the song, barely audible. She tilted her head and looked up at Maik. "Certainly puts 'Party Animal' in perspective, doesn't it?"

"Your music brought a lot of pleasure to a lot of people," said Maik simply.

She sighed. "Where does it come from, Sergeant, all the bad stuff in life?"

Maik looked at her for a long moment as a wave of sadness swept over her. Pragmatism. The life raft that would save them both. "Would you know if your husband had started working on anything new recently, or if he was planning to?"

She looked vaguely puzzled as Maik drew her back into the present. "He had so many things on the go, articles, ideas for the TV show. It was always hard to know exactly what he was working on at any given time. I mean, we talked about his work now and then, of course we did, but he spent a lot of evenings out. He said he was working at the university. When he came home, well, we had better things to do than compare careers."

Maik made another note in his book. In the background, Junior Walker had given way to Stevie Wonder. For once in his life, he wasn't going to let sorrow hurt him.

"Jamerson at his best," she said, catching Maik listening. "That's who I was going to be, when I grew up. The female James Jamerson."

Maik was confused for a moment. By the time The Roquettes had struck it big, they had onstage backing musicians, so the girls were free to concentrate on jumping around the stage in those elaborate dance routines. But now he remembered that, in the early days, they had played the instruments themselves. So she was the bass player? Maik allowed himself an inward smile. It was nice to have goals, but looking to be the next James Jamerson, king of the Motown session players, was aiming a touch high, to put it mildly. They listened in silence for a few moments.

"While it's more likely that this was in some way related to your husband's professional life, it could have been personal." Maik made a stab at looking uncomfortable at the line of questioning.

"Did you ever see my husband interviewing somebody, Sergeant? What would somebody call you, by the way, if they didn't want to keep calling you 'Sergeant'?"

He told her.

"One of his guests said it was like being drowned in treacle. He just used to question them and question them, and question them some more. But it was just his thing. And he was always polite. He was never sarky or vit … what's that word?"

"Vituperative," said Maik, surprising himself. Perhaps not, he thought, but he was sure such an approach could be irritating, for all that. He had seen Brae's show once or twice on TV when he had been flipping through the channels. Once, he remembered, he had watched him dismantle a guest's arguments strand by strand until there was nothing left but clichés that sounded as hollow and forced as they undoubtedly were. Brae had brought about the meltdown with such gentle probing, such polite questioning, that a viewer could have genuinely believed that he was innocent of any ulterior motive. But in light of what Mandy Brae was saying, Maik recognized the performance now for what it had been, as meticulous and systematic a destruction of a person's point of view as you could wish to see. Impressive, certainly, but hardly the way to make a raft of new friends.

"I know what you're thinking, that he must have been a pain to live with. But Cameron saved his performances for the public. When we were together, he could be really great.

Clever, funny, charming. He was a complex man, for sure, and no doubt some people found his ways a bit off-putting. But privately he was different. He was just really, really nice."

A discrete tapping on the door preceded Nancy's unbidden entrance. "Beverly Brennan has just telephoned with her condolences. Quite the parade today, I must say. Still, I suppose it wouldn't do to have the papers find out the local dignitaries hadn't even been in touch with the resident celebrity in her moment of distress."

Maik looked toward the PA, but it was Mandy Brae who offered the explanation. "Your DCS came by early this morning, and one or two other of the town worthies. Nancy feels I haven't been exactly warmly received by the community since I moved here. Personally, I couldn't care less, but that kind of thing seems to matter to Nancy, doesn't it, love?"

"Did you mention the watch?" asked Nancy.

Maik raised an eyebrow.

"My husband's Rolex. I bought it as a gift. I don't think he ever really liked it, but he wore it to please me. It's missing. We think the ... person must have taken it."

Maik made a note in his book while he collected his thoughts. This was no robbery, but perhaps the killer just couldn't resist a piece of high-end jewellery on offer. He noted down the details as Mandy Brae dictated them.

"I wonder, Sergeant, could we put off anything else until later?" asked Nancy. "Ms. Brae's publicist is coming in soon, and she needs to get prepared." Nancy turned to Mandy. "And perhaps a few minutes rest, too." She was back in her role as Mandy's protector. So where did that leave him?

Mandy flashed Maik a faint look of resignation. "We never even got to chat about whether Dennis Edwards outdid David Ruffin on 'I'm Losing You.' Still, perhaps next time. You will come back to keep me updated, won't you, Danny?"

It's the distance, he decided, that invisible gap that stars keep between you and them. That's what sets them apart, the space they have reserved for themselves, as if it could offer some kind of protection from the real world. Mandy Brae exuded vulnerability, a frailty that made Maik want to guard her against … what exactly? But it didn't matter. Whether she had put them on a first name basis or not, he knew he would never be allowed to get that close.

"Er, just one more thought. Sometimes, in these cases, if someone has been receiving threats, they won't say anything to their family, for fear of worrying them. But there are other signs. Had anyone commented on your husband looking ill recently? Losing weight, perhaps? Not eating?"

"I don't think so." She turned toward Nancy and then back toward Maik. "As far as I know he was about the same weight as always. I'm sorry, I don't know. Perhaps I should have paid more attention."

A wave of sadness seemed to sweep over her again, as if Maik's question had been a reproof. Subtlety be buggered. He wasn't going to make a young widow cry because she thought she had been a negligent wife. That was all Jejeune was going to get, whether he liked it or not. He stood up abruptly and closed his notebook.

"If we need anything else, we'll be in touch."

"Goodbye, Danny. Perhaps you should bring your Motown collection next time. We could sit down and have a good old reminisce about happier times, eh?"

"There's an idea," he said.

But it won't bring them back, he thought. *I know. I've tried.*

7

Jejeune wheeled his Range Rover into the parking lot of the Titchwell Marsh reserve and pulled up near the railing. A birder in olive-green jacket and trousers was standing beside a car with its boot open, dismantling a spotting scope. He cast a critical look at Jejeune's binoculars as the detective approached him.

"You'll be needing a scope if you've come for the Red-necked Phalarope."

"I'm looking for Quentin Senior." Jejeune inclined his head toward the reserve. "Is he out there?"

"Not sure. It's a big area," said the man. There was a shimmer of movement in the bushes above the man's car. Jejeune looked up reflexively.

"Bullfinches," said the man without bothering to look up.

"Isn't that Senior's car?" Jejeune began to reach for his warrant card.

"No need for that. I know who you are. You could try the Island Hide overlooking the freshwater marsh. He might be there."

"Is that where the Phalarope is?"

"At the back," said the man, slamming the boot shut and getting into his car hurriedly. He had pulled out of the car park by the time Jejeune reached the entrance to the reserve.

The gravel along the pathway crunched beneath Jejeune's shoes; the only noise in an otherwise quiet marsh. A gentle breeze stirred the tall grasses on each side of the path, but Jejeune detected little bird life. It was mid-morning, and the early period of feeding activity had subsided, but he remained alert. In this part of the country, a rarity could appear at any time.

About a hundred yards along the main path, Jejeune turned off and followed a trail along a grassy berm. In the distance, he could see other similar pathways, separating the water into lagoons of various sizes. Water levels and vegetation varied from cell to cell.

The trail ended at a low wooden hide. The door opened outward and was offset from the line of the horizontal wooden slats that served as viewing windows. Anyone opening the door to enter or leave the hide could do so without offering a backlight through the viewing windows that might startle the birds on the marsh beyond. At the far end of the hide, a man was sitting on a low bench, staring intently through a pair of battered binoculars. A telescope stood ready at his side. He was probably a little beyond sixty, heavily built, with a luxurious white beard and full head of pure white hair, worn long and shaggily to his collar. His florid features spoke of a life spent outdoors, meeting Norfolk's salt air and keening onshore breezes head on. He looked up and smiled at Jejeune as he entered. Jejeune smiled, too. As a spot for a quiet interview, he could hardly have chosen a better place.

"Phalarope's just gone, I'm afraid. Flew off to the west." The man must have noted the disappointment in Jejeune's face. "There is a pair of Spoonbills on the mudflat to the left, though. Feel free to use the scope, if you like."

Jejeune stooped to peer through the telescope. He noted the elegant profiles of two white birds tucked into a far corner of the marsh as they shifted the water with their side-to-side action. After a few moments of silent appreciation, he took a seat next to the man. He introduced himself and produced his warrant card. The man half-turned and offered a meaty hand.

"Quentin Senior. Good to know ya. Word on the jungle drums is that you're a birder. Well you've certainly picked the right part of the world to get posted to. We've got it all here. Coastlines, inland marshes, grasslands. Little wonder many people consider it the premier birding area in the U.K. But you're not here today for the sales pitch, are you? You'll be wanting to talk about Cameron's murder." He drew up his binoculars again and began to scan the marsh. "Well, I don't know how I can help you, but feel free to fire away."

"I've been reading quite a bit on the society's web page about this race to four hundred species," said Jejeune. "Actually, I suppose even before I came out here, I had already heard a lot about it. You would have to think that most dedicated birders have. One of the greatest prizes left in British birding, I would imagine."

Senior nodded enthusiastically, his flowing locks bouncing in harmony. "Indeed, yes. All seems rather silly to outsiders, no doubt, but as a birder yourself, you'd understand the significance. Imagine it. Four hundred species listed in a single English county. Nearly seventy percent of all recorded British birds in about two percent of its land area. Be a fitting culmination of any local's birding career, I should imagine. Certainly would be of mine."

"As I understand it, Cameron Brae was leading the race."

"Still is. Three hundred and ninety-four species at last count, I believe. The rest of the pack shortly behind."

"With you leading them. But with Mr. Brae now out of the running, and two or three new species showing up every year, at some point you will inevitably pass him."

Senior brought down his binoculars and turned his alarmingly blue eyes on Jejeune. "As you say, Inspector, I'm at the head of the chasing pack at the moment. Currently at 392, in case you're wondering. But as you well know, nothing is certain in birding. There are a number of others in contention. Duncan out in Salthouse is well up there, got to 390 just recently, as a matter of fact. Slender-billed Gull down at Blakeney. After that, Thompson and Harris, both in Cley. I don't know their numbers off the top of my head, but they would both certainly be in the running. And I could give you a list of at least half a dozen others who have 370-plus sightings. Anyone of them arguably has as good a chance as me of being first across the line."

Jejeune was annoyed with himself. "I didn't mean to imply …"

"No harm done," said Senior, with a terse smile. "Just doing your job."

"Cameron Brae had a number of birding records on his desk the day he died. Would you happen to know why?"

Senior nodded. "Indeed, mine would be among them. He called around about a week ago and asked everyone if we would mind submitting our old records to him. But I have no idea what he wanted them for. I just assumed it was something to do with his research. Or his show."

Senior had resumed his scan of the cell in front of them, and Jejeune raised his own binoculars. The Spoonbills had been joined by an Avocet. Jejeune watched it as it used its delicate upturned bill to probe the mud for food. It was astonishing to him that he should be able to see these two species, each so rare elsewhere in the country, on the same mudflat at the same time. But that was north Norfolk birding for you.

"I imagine it takes a great deal of effort to stay at the leading edge of a race like this. If you relaxed even for a few days you might find yourself losing ground."

Senior nodded. "Especially when one is so close to the goal. The odd miss here or there wouldn't have mattered so much at 360 or 370, but now, every sighting is vital. And of course, the more you add to your list, the fewer there are left to find, which makes it even more difficult."

"So you would certainly be aware if anything interesting had been sighted recently. Something awaiting verification, even?"

Senior lowered his binoculars and looked at Jejeune carefully. "We have a fairly sophisticated network out here, rare bird alerts, hotlines, phone apps, and such. As you can imagine, I keep a close eye on them. Of course, something could always have slipped past, but I doubt it. Beyond Duncan's Slender-billed Gull, there's been nothing out of the ordinary of late, as far as I know. Can I ask what bird you're interested in?"

Jejeune seemed to pause, as if aware that he was about to set out on a path with an uncertain destination. "An American Bittern."

Senior raised his eyebrows. "*Botarus lentiginosus.* And Cameron claims to have seen one? Don't look so surprised, Chief Inspector. I hardly think you would come down here just to chat about rare sightings with an open homicide on your desk. May I ask where? And when, exactly?" The news had evidently regained any ground Jejeune had lost with his clumsy earlier gambit.

"Possibly the inlet at the north end of Great Marsh. The sighting was recorded in his diary on the Monday morning, three days before he died, but there were no other details. I'm right in thinking it would be an extraordinary find?"

"Absolutely," agreed Senior, nodding. "A mega-rarity. Certainly never been one in Norfolk, at least not in living memory. Last one confirmed in Britain about ten years ago, I think. Well, well, well, an American Bittern for Norfolk. At last. And right on our doorstep, too. But you say you have no other details?" Senior shook his head. "No notes. That is most unlike Cameron."

He snapped the binoculars up to his eyes, and then lowered them again just as quickly. A common bird, or none at all. With the naked eye, Jejeune could see nothing moving in the marsh. Senior opened a well-worn daypack on the bench beside him and dug out a pack of battered sandwiches wrapped in cellophane. He offered one to Jejeune, which the detective was only too happy to refuse.

"An American Bittern," said Jejeune as the two men resumed their scan of the marsh. "Wouldn't it be difficult to be sure, under normal viewing conditions?"

Senior looked at Jejeune again. "Could he have mistaken it for *stellaris*, you mean, a Eurasian Bittern?" Senior stroked his beard and considered the proposition. "There would be a few reliable field marks to distinguish *lentiginosus* from *stellaris*. In flight, there would be the contrasting dark wings and pale coverts, the bird not as deeply winged as *stellaris*. Cameron could have identified the American Bittern by its call, of course. Markedly different to *stellaris*. I don't suppose we know if he heard it? Really this is maddeningly frustrating, Inspector."

Jejeune shook his head. "But assuming it was a visual ID, there would have been little chance of Brae misidentifying the bird?"

"Not if he got a decent look. Of course, given the secretive nature of bitterns, the best any of us can usually hope for is a brief glimpse through the reeds or a quick fly-over. Ever seen one yourself?"

"Eurasians? A couple," conceded Jejeune. "Glimpses. I've never had what you might call great looks."

"Not sure many have," said Senior. "Especially with only about sixty-odd breeding pairs in the whole country. That said, Cameron would have seen more than most. There are a couple of places up and down this coast where they are reliable enough. Cley's one. They breed there. He would have seen one or two over at Thornham, too. Let's say he would have seen enough Eurasians to know the difference."

"So you think it's unlikely he would have been mistaken about this."

Senior stopped chewing long enough to let Jejeune know he was considering the possibility carefully. "The Shetlands," he said, through a mouthful of bread and cheese.

Jejeune looked momentarily puzzled.

"I once travelled up to the Shetlands for a bird, based solely on an identification from Cameron. Long-billed Dowitcher. Saw it, too. He was a first-rate birder, Chief Inspector. If Cameron Brae says he saw an American Bittern, then I can assure you that's what he saw. If he wasn't certain, he would have listed it as *unidentified, probable, possible,* whatever, but if he called it, it was because he had seen enough to be sure."

A flash of movement from the left had both men raising their binoculars reflexively. A Hobby swooped in over the water, sending a fling of Dunlin spinning up into evasive flight. The bird of prey banked sharply to its left and made a deft pass at one of the waders, but its strike was unsuccessful. Having lost the element of surprise, the Hobby abandoned its lightning raid and flew out over the surrounding fields.

"Good bird," said Senior.

It was. Jejeune had been hoping to add a species or two to his year list today, but he had not expected a Hobby to be among them. But then, the unpredictability was one of the aspects of birding he found most intriguing.

"I was just thinking," he said, "those records …"

Senior smiled indulgently, showing a row of large yellowing ivory. "As I said, I have no idea why Cameron wanted them, but if you're thinking he was checking them for past American

Bittern sightings, I'm afraid you're barking up the wrong tree. Cameron had been birding in this area for over half a century, man and boy. He wouldn't have needed the records to confirm that there had never been a previous sighting in these parts."

Jejeune stood up to leave. "Mr. Senior, I am going to ask you if you could avoid spreading the word about this sighting. It might be important to the investigation. Frankly, I'm not sure quite how at the moment, but since Mr. Brae chose not to report it himself, for now I'd like to keep it quiet."

An expression flittered over Senior's florid features, but it was gone before Jejeune could register what it might have signalled.

"Of course. But that said, you must realize, Inspector, that in this part of the world, secrets do have a way of rather seeping through the cracks. If Cameron did mention this to anyone else, I would be very surprised if this stays suppressed for very long." He hesitated for a moment. "I suppose you wouldn't object to me having a quiet wander over there on my own, though. So long as I was careful to give your chaps a wide berth?"

"The site is well away from the investigation area. But if you do find an American Bittern, I'd appreciate it if you could make me the first call on your list."

Senior nodded his agreement, though whether Jejeune's interest was purely professional, or otherwise, just at that moment, he wouldn't have liked to say.

8

"Well, it's not the most plausible theory you've ever come up with," said Lindy. "Actually, let's put it how the locals might. It's daft, Dom. Utterly bloody ridiculous."

They were in the kitchen, a long, narrow room with a floor of red flagstones and a wide picture window above the sink offering an uninterrupted view out to sea. Lindy was preparing mussel crumble, listening to Dom's out-loud thinking and tossing terse comments over her shoulder as she worked. Since they'd moved from the city, she had developed an interest in preparing local recipes from raw ingredients. The results thus far had been mixed at best.

"All I'm saying is, I've known weaker motives. Well, probably as weak, anyway."

"But murdering someone over a bird list? I mean, it's so preposterous. Even a fanatical birder like you must admit that, for God's sake. Just to be the first to see four hundred birds. Who cares? Well, you would, obviously, but I mean among normal people."

Birders versus the real world was a discussion they had held before, at various levels of seriousness, and Jejeune had little hope that this one would turn out any different, especially given Lindy's current mood. She had come home in a foul temper, and although she had calmed down after ten minutes on the porch swing with a glass of Chablis, she was still in a combative mood.

"It's four hundred in Norfolk. Listing four hundred species in one English county would be an astonishing achievement, by any measure of birding. It's the sort of thing that would get your name mentioned in the birding circles not just locally, but internationally. Besides, I said it was a possibility. At this stage, most things are."

"But even if Brae saw this bird, and no one else did, nobody could be sure he would still become the first to see four hundred. Another rare bird could pop up tomorrow. If Brae missed that one, and his rivals saw it, they would be right back in the race." She put her knife down with a clatter and turned to face him. "I can't believe I'm even discussing this."

Jejeune shook his head slowly. "These days the top birders know where their rivals are at all times, every day, every hour even. If anyone is on a good bird, the others will know about it almost immediately. Given the information network out there, the chances of listing more than one rarity without your rivals getting on it is very small. It means a lead of three birds for Brae would be as good as insurmountable. I know the whole thing sounds a bit far-fetched —"

"A bit? It's madness. Truly. Honestly, Dom. Take it from a non-birder, from somebody out here in the real world. People just don't kill each other over things like this."

Jejeune understood Lindy's disbelief, and probably the idea was ridiculous. In truth, in the face of other, more plausible motives, he may not have given this idea more than a passing thought himself. But that was the problem. It was all very well Lindy implying that there were other, more rational reasons for hanging a man from a willow bough at the bottom of his garden, but if there were, Jejeune had yet to come up with them.

He stood up and gazed out the window. An unbroken field of blue stretched out to the horizon, the sea as smooth as a satin sheet. Though clifftop dwelling could result in some blustery days, and promised some punishing winter conditions ahead, sunny days like this were all the compensation either of them needed for choosing such a remote location to call home.

"By the way, your sergeant dropped by today. He's a pretty formidable character, isn't he? Eyes as cold as a November rain. I don't know why the army would have bothered giving him a gun. One look would have been enough. I've seen less intimidating stares from people wearing sunglasses."

"What did he want?"

"He asked me to let you know Brae's weight hadn't come up in conversation recently. Subtly or otherwise."

Jejeune shrugged. It had been an idea, no more. "I called you at the office today. Ellie said you were in an emergency meeting."

Lindy looked up from the crumble and brushed a stray strand of hair back from her brow with a wrist. "No secrets from you coppers, is there? It wasn't really a meeting, more a frank exchange of views."

Jejeune had been on the end of some of these frank exchanges of views. He suspected that Lindy had enough self-control to limit her outbursts in her professional life, but it was quite clear she had carried the residue of her anger home with her, and it hadn't all disappeared yet.

"Eric wants to capitalize job descriptions — he claims it is expected by the public and we need to be careful we are not perceived as being disrespectful."

"What sort of job descriptions?"

"The queen, the pope, the president of the United States." Lindy emphasized each title with finger quotes in the air. "I told him I wanted to work for a news magazine, not a comic. He can't arbitrarily change the rules of grammar just because people's feelings might be hurt. You don't capitalize occupations, not even important ones. You might as well start capitalizing noun phrases, such as Illiterate Halfwit Editor." Again the rabbit-ear fingers twitched.

"You didn't really say that, did you?" Jejeune had no doubt that she had, but he was hoping to coax a smile out of her anyway. But Lindy's ire was roused again, and she wasn't ready to let her indignation subside just yet.

"The rules are there for a reason. You capitalize titles, not jobs. Queen Elizabeth is the queen of the nation. It prevents confusion. What's next, for God's sake? Avoiding capitals in proper nouns in case somebody gets offended? So all of a sudden, a Giant Panda becomes just a really, really big one."

"And a Little Gull just a small one." he offered in support. Domenic could see her point, but it surely wasn't enough to cause a tirade like this. Not for the first time recently he had the feeling that there was something more fundamental troubling Lindy. Over the past couple of weeks he had caught an off-guard expression now and again that was unfamiliar to him, and a million miles away from the mischievous pirate-smile that had so beguiled him two years before. But Lindy would come around to telling him in her own way, and in her own time.

He could see that she was waiting for a further contribution from him, but he was at a loss as to what to offer. "I could send over a couple of boys from the grammar squad, if you like."

But Lindy wasn't ready for humour just yet.

"It's all right for you, Dom. People aren't constantly trying to challenge your professional integrity. They can't do enough for you. Their biggest concern is how to keep their Golden Boy happy."

Lindy softened. Despite her agitation she realized this was dangerous territory. She had put a lot of time and effort into the construction project that was Domenic Jejeune's self-belief, and she was well aware that its foundations were built on sand.

"Look, nobody is saying you don't deserve your success. You're brilliant at your job, and what you did ... well, people want to recognize that, reward it, it's understandable. But things are not like that for the rest of us. Our standards, our principles, our ability to do our jobs properly, every day people are trying to chip away at these things. That's just the way it is. All I'm saying is, you're lucky you don't have to put up with it, that's all."

Lucky? He didn't feel lucky. In truth, he envied Lindy, doing a job she genuinely cared about. Could he have ever gotten so passionate about his own work? His curse, if he cared to think about it that way, was that people considered him to have talents, a gift, even, for a job that he neither liked nor particularly wanted to do. But when those talents were in the area of policing, well, he could fully understand how everybody from his parents back in Canada to his superiors would be urging him to follow his talents as far as they would take him. He had heard all the arguments, and he had long since stopped offering counters to them. Now he just did his work, as quietly and efficiently as possible, and said nothing. But lucky? No, he didn't feel lucky.

Still, if he couldn't get to the bottom of Lindy's current unhappiness, at least he knew he had a cure for it; short-term anyway.

"It's probably about time we invited some of your friends up to see what life in the wilderness is like. Do you think they'll have had their shots?"

"They're *our* friends, actually," said Lindy, but it was obvious that Domenic had scored a direct hit. Her face lit up and her movements became suddenly more animated. "Do you think so? When? How about next weekend? We could do a small dinner party. Nothing extravagant, but if they came down in the afternoon we could take them down to the beach first. No birding, though, please Dom."

"No birding," he assured her.

9

"I'm sure I don't need to stress the importance of making some early progress," said DCS Shepherd. "The media will be all over us on this one. Obviously, you can be our point man, but easy does it. I want them eating out of our hand. And you'll clear everything through me first. Right?"

They were standing in the corridor outside the incident room. Showing up at the previous briefing session hadn't gone quite the way the DCS had planned, so this time she had intercepted Jejeune just as he was about to go in for the morning update.

"Cameron Brae was the closest thing the greens had to a hero out here," she continued, leaning in close to make sure her message was getting across. "Even if he hadn't been married to Mandy Roquette, the public would still be baying for justice."

Jejeune's general rule was to say nothing unless he had something useful to add, but the habit had a way of turning dialogue into monologue that some people found disconcerting, especially if they were trying to make a point. Shepherd felt compelled to add more.

"This is to have the highest priority, Domenic. Whatever you need, manpower, resources, anything at all. I don't want it being said that this case suffered for want of a few paperclips."

As far as Jejeune could tell, neither paperclips nor anything else the DCS could provide would bring the case any nearer to a conclusion just yet. But he promised he would let her know if he thought of anything.

"By the way, there's a function at the Saltmarsh Hunt Club Thursday evening. Black tie. Our MP, Beverly Brennan, will be there, and it will be a good chance for you to rub shoulders with some of the other local dignitaries, too. Usual fare, I should imagine. Honestly, I've been to so many of these things, these days I basically look at them as a chance to wear a nice frock for a change. You're girlfriend's welcome, too, of course."

Jejeune watched the DCS disappear along the corridor toward her office. Plenty of hours down the gym, judging by the muscle tone in her legs. She had a body type that would tend to widen out as she got older, but it hadn't happened yet, and she was clearly working hard to delay the process as long as possible.

After the carnival-like atmosphere of Jejeune's first day, attendance for this morning's briefing session had shrunk back to only those with a legitimate reason for being there. Jejeune went directly toward the back of the room as before. He perched on a desk, his feet resting on the chair in front of him like a benign gargoyle. He began flipping idly through his battered hardback while he waited for Maik to bring the session to order.

A young police constable entered the room carrying a manila file. Maik stretched out a hand like a one-armed scarecrow, his other arm folded across his chest. The constable hesitated. According to protocol, the file should have gone to Jejeune, as senior officer, but the constable had always found Maik a particularly intimidating presence, and what with the chief inspector looking so preoccupied and all.... He set the envelope in Maik's calloused paw and left without a backward glance. Maik opened the file and took a quick look at the single sheet of flimsy blue paper inside. It was the investigation file copy of the M.E.'s report.

He set the form to one side and addressed the room. "Right, death by hanging, more or less instantaneous. So no surprises there, then. Family all alibi out." A glance flickered in Jejeune's direction. "So who are we looking at?"

Jejeune laid the book aside as Maik began, but the sergeant could already see that if *Rare and Vagrant Birds of Norfolk* no longer held the chief inspector's complete attention, neither did the proceedings here. Jejeune cast long, languid glances out the window, returning his gaze to the room only to focus on some indeterminate spot in the middle distance. But it was already evident that Jejeune's apparent lack of interest didn't mean that he wasn't paying attention. Sooner or later, when he came across something he liked, or more likely the opposite, the assembled troops would no doubt be hearing from Domenic Jejeune.

Constable Salter consulted her notes. "Records show the call to Largemount wasn't answered. Nothing back yet from the professor about the email." She turned to Jejeune. "Sir, I've been thinking. If you were out of work, and you missed out on a potentially well-paying job through Cameron Brae's activism ..."

Jejeune raised his eyebrows. "It's worth a closer look. Let's get a list of anybody who was promised a job at a project Brae subsequently had shut down."

"Gold star for Lauren," whispered Tony Holland. "Would you like me to follow up on Archie Christian, sir?" he asked. "In my opinion, he's definitely worth a look."

Jejeune shook his head. "I've seen Mr. Christian's file. As you say, he attracted a fair amount of attention in his younger days, but a bit of overzealous debt collecting doesn't necessarily mean he is a killer. Besides, this crime seems all wrong for a professional enforcer. Apart from the chains around the wrists and ankles, there wasn't a mark on Cameron Brae's body. I've never actually met Mr. Christian, but I'm betting he would have taken a more direct approach, especially if it was revenge he was after."

Holland got there just before Maik. "More direct? Brae is about as dead as you can get, sir."

Jejeune nodded. "True, but killing somebody by hanging is not as clear-cut as you might think. If the drop is too short, the neck doesn't break and the victim strangles to death. To kill a victim cleanly, you need to break the neck between the second and third cervical vertebrae, and to do that, you need to calculate the drop height pretty carefully, using the person's weight."

"I don't get it," said Salter. "Why would the killer care one way or the other? You've already said this was a punishment; a humiliation. I would have thought the more Brae suffered, the better the murderer would have liked it."

"Except it can take up to forty-five minutes to strangle to death in a noose. No killer would want to wait around that long to make sure his victim was dead. And besides, someone went through those lists in Brae's study."

It was Maik's turn to look puzzled. "I thought those lists were still in his in-tray. How do we know anybody touched them?"

"They were out of order. It's not a mistake an academic like Brae would have made. Then there's the return of the stepladder. No, this killer spent a lot of time pottering about at the scene, and that breaks all the rules for a professional like Christian."

"Absent any other clear motive, perhaps we should look at the wife's career," said Maik, breaking the silence that had followed Jejeune's pronouncement.

"Somebody killing her old man as a way of getting to her, you mean?" asked Holland, warming to the idea. "Why not? Plenty of crazies out there."

"We should think about some sort of protective detail," said Maik. "Just until we're sure she's not in any danger."

"I wonder, was there a pre-nuptial agreement?" said Jejeune.

Salter shook her head. "A lot of people thought it would be a good idea. Brae even brought it up himself, apparently, but she refused. She was very firm about it, so everybody just let it drop."

Jejeune nodded. "Thank you."

And that was it. No discussion of Danny Maik's cavalier promises to provide round-the-clock security for Mandy Brae, or crazed fans, or unreturned emails. Just the pre-nup that wasn't.

Salter sighed. If Jejeune had any idea where he was going next with this case, she was fairly sure he was the only one who did.

10

Just why Jejeune had sent him to conduct the interview with the professor alone, Maik wasn't quite sure. But as a soldier, and a son of a soldier, Danny Maik had spent a good deal of his adult life following orders, many of them a lot more cryptic than this, so he accepted his duty without question. Loyalty to one's superiors had been drilled into him from an early age by his father. It was about the only thing the serial adulterer had provided for him in his childhood, apart from a series of images of his mother sitting at their kitchen table, sobbing quietly. But the lessons of youth, however learned, stay with us, and Maik would always strive to obey those higher up the chain of command. And if that involved interviewing one of the world's leading experts on the biochemistry of salt marshes, whether Maik had the first clue about the subject or not, then so be it. At least Jejeune hadn't asked him to be subtle this time.

For Maik, universities were the physical embodiment of all the opportunities that had eluded him: the learning, the connections, the privileges. He was not resentful, but he recognized how different his life might have turned out if a university education had been one of the options available to a boy of seventeen living with his abandoned mother. As it was, a chance to escape the stifling miseries of his home life, and a regular paycheque to send home to ease his conscience proved too alluring, so he had enlisted in the army at the earliest opportunity.

Maik walked down the corridor between the soaring galleries rising on both sides, his footsteps echoing off the polished wood walls. He realized this was a world now beyond him, and found his old sense of tribalism rising; us and them, the mindset that had taken him through so many conflicts. Even here, in the tranquil halls of North Norfolk University? Blimey, son, time to get some help.

Maik found the laboratory and entered after knocking. Professor Miles Alwyn was a slightly-built man, and his wardrobe seemed chosen especially to emphasize the fact. An oversized white cotton shirt billowed about his slender torso, dangling off his shoulders and gaping woefully around the neck. Baggy corduroys were gathered at the professor's narrow waist by a thick black belt. Maik had no previous mental image of what a salt marsh biochemist might look like, but with his black-rimmed glasses and wispy brown hair, the man before him put the sergeant more in mind of a minor civil servant in a long-forgotten colonial outpost than a world-renowned academic. Alwyn's reedy voice did little to dispel the impression.

"Yes, yes, come in, Sergeant," he said, making no secret of his annoyance at being disturbed. "I understand the need to investigate this dreadful business, really I do, but I fail to see the urgency. I mean, poor Cameron is already dead, after all, I don't see why this couldn't have waited until the end of the day."

A less seasoned police officer might have pointed out that, in a murder investigation, decisions about the urgency of inquiries are best left to the professionals. But the sergeant could already sense that trivializing the professor's work, especially *this* professor's work, was probably not the most productive path he could take.

"We found an email to you from Cameron Brae, dated four days before he died," he said perfunctorily.

"Yes, he wanted a copy of a survey we had done on Peter Largemount's land about five years ago. I've no idea why."

"You didn't ask?"

"I receive requests for data all the time, from people all over the world, many distinguished academics themselves. Each has his own reasons, I assume. All I can say is that Cameron had certainly never shown any interest in the survey results before."

"Did you arrange to have the report sent to him?"

"I sent it myself."

"Rather than asking one of the admin people to do it?"

Alwyn waved a dismissive hand. "It was a ten-minute job, for goodness' sake. In the time it would have taken me to find somebody and explain the nature of the request to them, it was done."

"So the report was to hand then. You didn't have to go hunting around for it." Maik made a production of noting something down in his notebook. "Can you tell me a bit more about your relationship with Mr. Brae? I understand he was a colleague of yours here at one time."

Alwyn straightened, "Ah, I see you've been reading Cameron's press releases." He gave his head an emphatic nod. "Yes, he did assist me in some areas of my research, but *colleague* hardly describes Cameron's contribution to the work here, regardless of what he would have his adoring public believe. My studies concern the impacts of weather systems on saltwater marshes. There appears to be fundamental differences between the ways saltwater and freshwater marshes are affected by storms and flooding. It is partly to do with the root systems of the vegetation; how deep they run, how well anchored they are."

"I see," said Maik. Or at least I might, he thought, given time.

"Cameron's work, while interesting in its own way, I suppose, was really nothing more than a derivative of my research. He was looking at the impact of these weather systems on the populations of certain marsh species. Birds, mostly, of course."

Alwyn was hovering in a way that suggested he believed he had contributed all he could, or wanted to, and was now waiting to be dismissed, so he could get on with more important things.

"I understand you worked together quite closely, in the early days."

"Mostly on surveys for the government, of the sort we did on Peter Largemount's land. Phase one and phase two environmental studies, prior to a land sale or a change of use. I did the biochemistry and the microbiology. Cameron did all the macro stuff, the fuzzies and the furries. And the feathers, of course."

"Change of use? That would be agricultural to commercial?"

Alwyn looked at Maik over his glasses. "It's hardly likely to be the opposite these days, is it, Sergeant?"

Maik found himself wondering just how little pressure it would take to snap that scrawny chicken-bone neck of the professor's. Not that he was actually intending to do it, more as just an abstract academic exercise, the way they liked to do things out here in university land.

"Your collaboration stopped quite suddenly, by all accounts, but there was never a public explanation for your split."

"That's because it was a private matter. While some of us felt it was more important to remain in the trenches doing the real work, the hard science, others felt the call of stardom. There may be some redeeming features to standing before a camera and reporting on other people's findings. Call it what you will, but it isn't science. 'Professional differences,' I believe the newspapers would term it these days."

"And yet, even after he left, he still maintained an office in the department. And part-time status as a lecturer."

"Sadly, university administrators are every bit as sycophantic toward celebrities as the rest of you. They let him maintain a presence here, no doubt in the hope that some of the stardust would fall upon them. I'm not sure that it ever did. But I suppose it was useful at fundraisers."

"It must have been awkward, given the nature of your break-up, crossing paths all the time."

"Hardly. I told you, Cameron's idea of expanding the frontiers of science was standing in front of a camera and reading it off a script, or posing for photographs with that ridiculous wife of his. The tedium of data analysis was hardly his realm anymore. Plus, of course, I generally do most of my lab work at night. I enjoy the solitude."

"Do you know his wife at all, the current Mrs. Brae?"

"The Party Animal? Don't look so surprised, Sergeant. Most of these students grew up on The Roquettes' music. Even a few of the younger faculty, I imagine. I can't say I ever cared for it myself."

Nor did Maik, truth be told, but he got the sense he and the professor were in the minority. The Roquettes' *oeuvre* was hardly the sort of contribution to the history of music that was going to endure, but it had captured the imagination of an entire generation for a brief moment in time.

"I have never met her, but she did call me once, just after she moved to Saltmarsh. She wanted to know if I could explain the nature of Cameron's work to her."

"And?"

Alwyn shrugged. "I could have covered his contributions to the field, such as they were, in about ten seconds. His research was not what one would call far-reaching. I sent her a brief synopsis, really rather basic." He shook his head regretfully. "Sadly, even that proved beyond her. She called with some alarmingly naive questions. I told her it was obvious that this would simply be a waste of time for both of us. I thought that would be that. But she called back. Wanted me to tutor her, one on one. Offered to pay me any sum I chose. She was quite insistent. I suppose people like that are used to getting what they want. But she clearly had no capacity for such a level of study, and I told her as much. I never heard from her again."

Maik must have pulled a face as he wrote in his notebook.

"This is a university, Sergeant. More, we are a science faculty. Our entire raison d'être is the truth. I was not about to take her through a secondary school science curriculum on the pretense that one day she might be able to converse as an equal with her husband on saltmarsh ecology, not even if she was a paying passenger."

Alwyn watched as Maik made his notes in his laboriously slow handwriting. "You know, Sergeant, it strikes me that our work is very much the same in some respects. Endless days of sorting through irrelevances in search of that one immutable truth."

Maik had spent far too long in the army to worry about people insulting his intelligence, but he sensed that his new chief inspector wouldn't have put up with this nonsense. From what he had seen, Jejeune treated his own obvious intellect with the same casual insouciance he brought to everything else. Nevertheless, Maik suspected that he wouldn't stand for anybody taking liberties with it, especially condescending twonks like this, trying to change the subject by forging imaginary bonds with a fellow truth seeker. But as far as Maik knew, no crime had ever been solved by encouraging people to keep quiet, so he was quite happy to let Alwyn drivel on all he wanted.

"I expect you'll keep me informed of developments, Sergeant. Cameron was, as you point out, a former acquaintance of mine. I should like to know the matter has been resolved successfully. I take it you already have some ideas about who might have done this terrible thing."

But Maik's bland smile wasn't saying either way as he put away his notebook and bade the professor good day.

Maik sat in his car, staring at the imposing brick facade of the university, Alwyn's bastion of truth. His thoughts turned to a young mother, killed in a head-on collision coming home from working late one night. He recalled the utter desolation of her family; her husband's inconsolable sadness, her little boy's despair and confusion. The intermingled outpouring of love and grief from everyone who had known her. The perfect wife, so young, so beautiful, so much to live for. Only she wasn't coming home from work, was she? She was coming from her boyfriend's flat. And now that the boyfriend had moved on, the only one left with her secret was Danny Maik. How many other secrets did he hold in his heart, how many other deceptions and falsehoods had he kept away from the innocent over the years?

And now, as he thought of Mandy's Brae's words — *He said he was working at the university* — Maik knew this was yet another betrayal to be stored away. Because even if Mandy Brae was still trying to convince herself that her husband was working late, Danny Maik now knew differently. Wherever he was on those nights, Brae certainly wasn't at the university.

11

By the time Maik straightened up from retrieving his jacket from the back of the Range Rover, Domenic Jejeune was already staring up into the stand of tall beech trees that fringed the sweeping forecourt in front of Peter Largemount's house.

"Remarkable family, the corvids," said Jejeune, still staring up as Maik joined him.

Maik had actually started to consider whether he knew anyone called Corvid before he realized that Jejeune was talking about birds. He looked up to see a large gathering of Rooks fidgeting through the branches high above. Jejeune was watching the birds intently, observing their interactions as they jumped from branch to branch, cawing harshly and fluttering their wings.

"Villains of the bird world, of course. You've only got to look at the collective nouns. A murder of Crows, an unkindness of Ravens."

"Coined by farmers, I should imagine," offered Maik. "Especially in these parts."

"And yet there's a complex social system going on up there. The corvids are an extremely intelligent family. Did you know that Crows are considered to have the best-developed brains of all birds?"

"High praise, indeed," said Maik.

Jejeune offered a wry smile. It was like his own journey to cricket, he thought. You had to let people come to it of their own accord, and only then you could start explaining the nuances, the beauty, the hidden joys. Jejeune was delighted to share his birding knowledge and skills with anyone who was interested. But trying to convince the average non-birder, like, say, a battle-hardened police sergeant, was probably a waste of both people's time.

"Let's go and see if Mr. Largemount has any better appreciation for his tenants," said Jejeune, leading the way across the forecourt to the house.

Peter Largemount's house was a large three-storey structure topped by a balustrade that circled the roof like a stone tiara. Its pale stone facade was dressed up with red-brick trim and large Italianate windows, articulating the floors into neat rows. It was the house of a family that had known great wealth in the past, not all of it drawn from the rich dark soils of the surrounding lands. Despite the scars earned through two centuries of perching on the edge of a Norfolk sea cliff, the house appeared to be structurally sound, and there was evidence of much new repair work to the windows and the roof.

The fields surrounding the house were forested with tall grey pylons, at the top of which large-bladed turbines spun with a relentless determination. In the centre of the pylon crop stood a bare expanse of land, in which Maik could just see the faint reflection of water. Lesser Marsh had no doubt seen a lot of changes in the surrounding vegetation over the centuries, but Maik doubted the marsh had ever witnessed, or ever would again, anything as strange and unnatural as the forest of wind turbines that now surrounded it on all sides.

Peter Largemount stood in the imposing doorway of his home, waiting for the two policemen to approach. He wore an open-necked shirt beneath a sweater with a bold diamond pattern on it. Largemount gave his approaching visitors a wide-open smile, displaying a full set of large white teeth. He looked like the kind of man you might find leaning against the bar at a golf club, thought Maik, telling you all about himself and his latest exploits, in business or otherwise. A bit of a prat, perhaps, but you still found yourself secretly wondering what it would be like to have his kind of money and lifestyle.

"Officers, welcome. Come in, please."

The men stepped into the large entrance hall. Pastel patterning from a stained glass window on the second-storey landing trickled down the marble staircase and flooded the hallway. Polished wood and veined marble encased them on all sides. It was the kind of ostentatious display of wealth that would not sit well with the locals, and Jejeune could see why Maik had told him Largemount was not well regarded in these parts, despite a family pedigree going back centuries.

The men moved through the house to a large book-lined room at the back that seemed to be doing double duty as a business office. Along the back wall, the large windows were open to the sea air, and the sounds of the waves crashing on the stony beach below pulsed up toward them. A set of smaller mullioned windows along the north wall looked out over fields of windmills.

The officers declined refreshments, and Maik started the proceedings while Jejeune went off for a tour of the bookshelves.

"Can you tell us the last time you spoke to Cameron Brae?"

"No idea. Months ago, I should think. Probably at some function or t'other."

Largemount spoke with the briskness of someone who had other things to do, other places to be. But for now, he was at least giving the officers the benefit of his full attention. Especially the younger one, wandering around the room trailing his fingernail across the spines of a row of books.

"First editions, mostly, Inspector. Excellent hedge against inflation. Though I must confess, I don't read as many of them as I would like. Time, you know, the enemy of the busy man."

He smiled to show how bravely he was enduring the unbearable pressure of making a fortune.

"Your telephone number was the last one Mr. Brae called," said Maik.

"First I've heard of it, but that's no surprise." Largemount aimed his explanation toward Jejeune, on the far side of the room. "I'm not often home in the evenings. This line's been acting up a bit lately, as a matter of fact. Wiped out the memory recently, call display, messages, the lot. Seems to be working all right now, though."

"So no record of any incoming calls then."

"No, Sergeant. But you do have my word. I received no call from Cameron Brae." It was meant to be a smile, but Maik got some sense of the last sight a swimmer might see when a Great White Shark approached.

"An operation like this," Jejeune indicated the windmills beyond the window, "I would have thought it was just the sort of thing to attract the attention of Cameron Brae. Did he ever voice any concerns?"

Largemount shook his head. "Not as far as I'm aware. There are many roads to a sustainable planet, Inspector, not all of them compatible. Clean energy is a complex business. There is a delicate balance between energy production and nature conservation. I believe Cameron Brae appreciated this. We are all working toward the same goal, after all. Or rather, we were, poor chap."

Largemount joined Jejeune at the window and gestured toward the windmills. "I understand the locals didn't care for 'em much at first, but I'm sure they've come around. Clean, quiet, solidly constructed, what's not to like? I wouldn't say they're prettier than a stand of trees, but they're a damn sight more productive. Each tower can generate over two thousand kilowatt hours per year. Besides, I feel we've done what we could to be good neighbours. Chose the light grey paint, least conspicuous under most lighting conditions. Matte finish to reduce reflected glare. That sort of thing."

Maik doubted that sensitivity to local aesthetics was high on Peter Largemount's list of priorities. More likely, the light grey matte paint was the one on sale that week. Peter Largemount did not strike him as a man to take the opinion of a few local greenies to heart either, despite the fact that, as Maik understood it, power estimates for wind farms were dodgy at best. For one thing, they were based on constant wind speeds, which, as anybody who lived here would appreciate, was something you couldn't actually count on in north Norfolk. He said as much now.

"Don't you believe all that twaddle, Sergeant. Wind power is the future in these parts, and in a big way, too. In fact, within a few months we plan on expanding our operations here."

Jejeune had been staring out the large windows down at the bay below and had begun to turn away when he paused. *Froze* would have been Maik's word.

"Do you have any binoculars — a telescope would be even better, actually." The chief inspector spoke with the suppressed urgency of a man who is afraid that his excitement might break a spell.

Largemount produced a pair of EL Swarovisions from a shelf and handed them to Jejeune. "Something interesting?"

"I can't … I think that could be an Ivory Gull down there, feeding on that seal carcass."

Jejeune took a long look through the binoculars, leaving the other two men to raise their eyebrows at each other in silence. The dazzling clarity of the Swarovskis stunned Jejeune for a second. But it made the identification unequivocal.

"It is. This is astonishing. I can't believe I'm actually looking at an Ivory Gull." He continued, commentating the features to himself as he tracked the bird through the binoculars. "Plumage, size, behaviour. It's all spot on for an Ivory. This is an incredible find!"

The others looked at each other, aware that Jejeune's zeal had taken the moment beyond flippancy, but unsure now what might constitute a meaningful contribution.

"So, it's an unusual bird, then, is it, sir?" said Maik at last.

"Incredibly. This is a top, top sighting," announced Jejeune triumphantly, "possibly a first for this area. Unbelievable. Here, take a look."

Maik took the bins because he had no real option to refuse. He could see the bird clearly enough. Pure white, with coal black eye. And a hint of something at the tip of its slender black beak. Yellow? Orange? The bird was quite small, Maik would have said, compared to some of the gulls around here. It was sitting on the bloated belly of a dead seal, reaching into the carcass to tug out strands of what, Maik didn't particularly care to know. A pretty enough bird, with its snow-white plumage brilliant in the bright sunshine, but whether it was worth getting this excited about? Certainly not to him.

He handed the binoculars back to Jejeune, who snatched a quick one-handed look again as he flipped out his mobile phone and began scrolling through the numbers. "I need to report this to the rare bird hotline immediately. I take it you'll be okay with me revealing the location, Mr. Largemount."

Largemount's face darkened. "I'd rather you didn't, Inspector."

Jejeune stopped dialing.

"As you know, this area is a mecca for birdwatchers, and consequently they have a significant voice in this community. Someone finds a rarity, and the next thing you know, the government will be shutting down my operation here and designating the property as a reserve or some damn thing."

Jejeune was still stealing one-handed glances at the bird through the binoculars.

"Expropriations of land are extremely rare, Mr. Largemount, and certainly not for a migratory bird like this. I don't know the local birding community all that well, of course, but I have to tell you, if the news gets out that there is an Ivory Gull on your property, and you are refusing access, I imagine it will create an incredible amount of resentment."

"Nevertheless, I would still prefer to protect my privacy. I believe that is my right." He smiled to rob the words of offence, but it was clear there was no room for negotiation. "Now, Inspector, if there is nothing else, I'm afraid I have a rather busy schedule today. You may, of course, stay and observe the bird yourself for as long as you like."

Jejeune folded away his phone. "As you wish, Mr. Largemount. But I am required to report the sighting of a rarity like this to the county bird recorder, who will undoubtedly refer it to the British Birds Rarities Committee. I will request that they suppress the details of the location."

Jejeune took another long look at the bird, until it flitted farther into the cove, where he no longer had the angle to see it. He silently handed the binoculars back to Largemount.

Maik took his time returning to the Range Rover, taking a moment to stroll around on the forecourt, enjoying the sunshine. He looked down again on the grey crop of turbines in the fields below him, their reinforced polyester blades spinning hypnotically. The turbines stretched out to the edge of Largemount's property in every direction. Right in the centre was the marsh, its outline traced by the pylons so definitively it looked almost as if someone had carved it out with a pastry cutter. On the far side of the property, Maik could see the two widened parking areas along the road, where birders could pull in to view the wetland without trespassing. There were no cars parked there today.

When Maik got back in the vehicle, Jejeune was speaking animatedly into his mobile phone. He didn't need his years of detective experience to guess who Jejeune was talking to.

"Yes, yes, absolutely convinced. Full adult plumage, no spots at all ... the Collins guide. I realize that, but nevertheless, I am quite sure.... No, I haven't got a camera with me.... That's right, the beach below Peter Largemount's property. There is a little cove with a beached seal carcass. It was feeding on that ..."

Maik waited patiently until Jejeune hung up.

"Got the local birders riled up?"

"It would, if he would permit the bird line to post it. But from what I've just heard, it sounds like the locals wouldn't exactly be shocked to learn that Largemount was refusing access to his property. He has something of a reputation with them already."

"You can't understand some people, can you?" said Maik. "I mean, I'm no birder, but what could it have hurt, especially if this bird is as rare as you say it is, to let a few people come onto his land for a quick look."

"It would be more than a few. Well into the hundreds, I should think, for a bird like this."

Maik's head snapped round.

"Conservatively. When a White-crowned Sparrow turned up at Cley in the winter of 2008, over four thousand people came to see it. Now it was sedentary, so people from Finland, for example, could be fairly sure it would stay around for a while, making their journey a bit less of a gamble. An Ivory Gull is classified as an 'accidental' species out here, and considered extremely transient. If we are lucky this one may stay around for a couple of days, but I would be surprised at anything beyond that. Still, I would have thought it was well worth a trip from anywhere in the U.K., on the off-chance."

Anywhere in the U.K.? thought Maik. *Finland?* He wouldn't travel to Finland to see a Motown reunion concert. Well, he would, but that was different. Surely. Wasn't it? Maik, who had encountered more than his share of eccentric behaviour in his time, could now add another arrow to that particular quiver.

He was about to point out that they were driving in the wrong direction when he realized they were heading down to the coast. Jejeune was going to see if he could get out to the promontory to see around the point. Where the bird was.

"Any thoughts?" asked Maik, as the Range Rover lurched over a deep rut in the track, slewing them both violently to one side.

"About what? Oh, Largemount? He's lying. Why, I'm not sure, but if he didn't speak to Brae on the night of his death, he was at least aware of his call. You said Brae had called him. You never mentioned that it was in the evening. And anyway, the natural assumption would have been that someone calling at night would have called Largemount's private number. But he latched straight on to the business line, the number Brae actually called."

It was a subject that, in Maik's opinion, probably warranted further discussion. But when they bumped up onto the grassy promontory and parked near the edge, Jejeune grabbed his binoculars and scrambled out of the car almost before Maik realized what was happening. He followed his inspector up a steep path nearby, where he was straining around to look back in toward the beach where it ran below Largemount's property.

Jejeune's view of the cove was blocked by high boulders. From here it was impossible to see if the Ivory Gull was still there or not. Maik was by now beginning to get the idea that scrambling over the boulders and down toward the beach was definitely not out of the question for Jejeune. And if he went, Maik would be forced to go with him.

"You won't be able to get out far enough to see back into the cove," said Maik. "The headland juts out too far."

With a sigh and a last, longing glance toward the hidden beach, Jejeune turned and scrambled back down the path toward his vehicle. As his boss was looking over his shoulder to reverse, Maik allowed himself the briefest of smiles. For all he knew, that business about the headland might even be true.

12

Jejeune had hardly stepped through the door of the Saltmarsh Hunt Club before the formidable presence of Largemount materialized by his side.

"Taking some terrific abuse from your mob." said Largemount by way of an introduction. "Birders," he said testily, in response to Jejeune's puzzled look. Largemount was holding what appeared to be a hefty gin and tonic in his hand, sloshing it around as he made his point.

"You told me you would only report it to the county recorder. I'm getting phone calls, texts from all over the place. Good God, is that the way Englishmen speak to each other these days? Even had a couple confront me right on my own driveway as I was heading here this evening. All over this rumour about some bloody seagull."

Jejeune hardly knew where to start. The word *rumour*, perhaps, or even *seagull*. His discretion got the better of him at the last moment.

"As a member of the RSPB, I had a duty to report a sighting of a rare species, especially one with a globally 'near-threatened' status. I did request that the location be withheld, but I did tell you at the time that it was an especially significant sighting. Somebody somewhere obviously felt the same. Is the bird still there, by the way?"

"How the hell should I know?" asked Largemount tersely. "I want you to find the idiot who leaked the location. And when you do, you may inform them I intend to initiate legal proceedings against them."

Despite his bombast, Jejeune sensed that Largemount wasn't entirely uncomfortable in his role of stage villain. He was, in truth, the kind of personality who would revel in it. Still, he seemed determined to play the aggrieved victim to the hilt.

"I can't see any sense in bothering Colleen with all this," he continued, "since you're already involved, in a manner of speaking. So I can take it you'll deal with it, can I?"

It was the first time Jejeune had heard anyone refer to the DCS by her first name. Message received and understood.

"Frankly, Mr. Largemount, it could have been anyone at a local level, or on the Rarities Committee. If it came from the RSPB, there are fourteen hundred staff and over a million members who could have leaked this. Trying to track down the source would be a waste of time. Still, you are within your rights to restrict access to your land, and you shouldn't be getting harassed for it. If you still have any of the correspondence, I'll have my sergeant check into it."

"Another bird fanatic, is he?"

"I think you can rely on Sergeant Maik to be impartial, at the very least."

Perhaps it was Jejeune's unwillingness to be cowed that urged Largemount to ram the point home still further.

"I'm giving you fair warning. I shall take whatever measures I need to for the protection of my privacy and my property. Let me catch just one of these buggers on my land again … Excuse my language, my dear. Peter Largemount, pleasure to meet you."

It was Largemount's first acknowledgement of Lindy's presence at Jejeune's side, and Domenic felt the tensing of her hand on his arm. He hoped she wasn't going to do anything contrary. Like curtsying, for example. It was definitely within her repertoire, if she felt she was being patronized. But tonight, she decided a sweet smile would do. Largemount was a man whose own best attempts at a winning smile still came out like a scowl. He offered one to the couple now and melted off into the mass of evening gowns and black tuxedoes.

"How fortunate that you were duty-bound to report that Ivory Gull to the RSPB like that," said Lindy archly. "Just think, no one might have ever known you'd seen it, otherwise. Now they have the sighting on record, and your name beside it, too."

She looked pleased with herself, as she always did on the rare occasions she caught Jejeune in a moment of human frailty. He half expected her to start skipping along beside him at any moment.

"Has it been seen again?" she asked.

Jejeune shook his head. "Not as far as I know. But it has a rotting seal carcass to feed on, so the foul weather offshore might keep it here for a short while, providing it can avoid the avian botulism that is running through the gulls just now."

"Why, Domenic Jejeune," said Lindy in a faux-Southern accent, "I do declare, all this sweet-talkin', it's enough to turn a young girl's head."

DCS Shepherd approached them wearing a gown that was surprisingly flattering. "Domenic. And you must be Belinda. So glad you could make it." She extended a hand. "DCS Shepherd. Normally, that is. Tonight I'm just Colleen. Would you mind if I borrowed Domenic for a moment? There's an absolute catalogue of people waiting to meet him."

Lindy was magnanimous enough to imply that Colleen could have him for as long as she needed him, and she wandered off to find the bar on her own.

Shepherd took Jejeune's elbow and guided him over toward a distinguished-looking couple who were locked in earnest conversation. She presented her new DCI by name, but left the couple to furnish their own introductions. Jejeune, who had never had much trouble with names and faces, stored them away for future reference.

"Canadian, isn't it?" said Malford, Dean, ex-something in banking. "Well-liked in these parts. Acquitted themselves admirably during the war." He held up a mottled hand. "Oh, I know, ancient history now. But the past is still important to some of us out here. People in these parts have long memories."

If it was a message, Jejeune didn't have time to dwell on its import because the conversation had moved on to another topic: his own success.

"Popular chap these days, I must say," said Malford. "To be expected, I suppose, given the Home Office connection, as it were. Still, the praise is well-merited, no doubt about that."

Sensing Jejeune's discomfort, Malford's wife, Emily, swooped in. "How are things in Canada?"

"I don't really know," said Jejeune simply. "I only really get back for Christmases and the odd holiday. It's hard to pick up much of substance at family gatherings."

"I would have thought the dinner table was the perfect place to take the temperature of a country," said Malford. "Certainly is at our house."

"You'll have to forgive my husband," said Emily. "He's become quite evangelical since he worked on Beverly Brennan's campaign. Politics is all he talks about. And since she swept to power, he's been quite impossible, I'm afraid."

"Quite right, too. Breath of fresh air, that woman. Talks a lot of sense. I mean, I'm as much in favour of a bit of green space as the next man, but we can't stifle the local economy because of it."

"It's a funny thing, though, Inspector. I never quite remember him having the same fervor for politics when it was a bunch of crusty old men running for office."

Malford smiled the smile of an older man still thought capable of mischief. "As if the charms of a pretty woman would sway men like us, eh, Inspector," he said with a wink. "Perish the thought. Besides, you've already got quite a catch already. Journalist, isn't she? National something? Not with that paper anymore, though, the one she covered your case for?"

Jejeune was impressed. It wasn't the sort of detail that would have fallen under casual conversation about the new couple. It was one more thing to keep in mind about these parts.

"She has moved on to another publication. They do more in-depth investigative journalism, you know, the story-behind-the-story."

The couple's muted response told Jejeune all he needed to know about how Saltmarsh's upper crust felt about journalists digging into backgrounds for the story behind the story. In these post–phone hacking days, journalists still had some way to go to win back the public's trust.

"So how did you come to be over here, anyway?" inquired Emily Malford with a kindly smile. "Canada seems like such a lovely place."

Jejeune smiled blandly, but in his mind he could still see the friendly face of the police commissioner, feel his avuncular arm around his young shoulders. "*You've such a bright future in policing, Domenic. This business with your brother, sad as it is, it will hold you back. It shouldn't do, but it will. Go abroad, that's my advice, put some distance between you and all this. I shall look forward to watching your career soar.*"

"New horizons," said Jejeune. "You know how it is, greener grass."

"I do hope you can make a go of it here in Saltmarsh. It's the isolation, you see. Men rather seem to enjoy the solitude. But for the women, well, being so far from one's circle of friends can be hard. At first, anyway. Please do invite your … young lady to join us at one of our coffee mornings," she added.

Jejeune thought he might just do that, if only to watch Lindy's reaction. He followed Mrs. Malford's eyes across the room to a nearby group, where Lindy seemed to be making quite an impression with her mostly older, mostly male audience. It was understandable, he thought. But it was not just the white dress, showing off her lithe body and tanned, shapely legs to fabulous effect. Lindy was the youngest woman in the room by at least twenty years and her youthfulness and vibrancy seemed to dance off her like the light from a diamond.

"I must say," offered Dean Malford, "we would have never expected to have so many celebrities living out here. First old Brae gets himself on the telly, and then that singer woman moves out here, and now there's you. Back in the old days, about the best we could hope for was a member of the royal staff popping into the local sweet shop if HM was up at Sandringham."

The conversation swayed on around Jejeune, who listened for cues and responded accordingly without ever completely abandoning his survey of the room. Shepherd returned and he was guided around, hand on elbow, to meet various elements of Saltmarsh's elite and receive their considered wisdom on local culture, society, and police work. He was beginning to worry that the smile muscles in his cheeks would soon fail him.

Across the room, he saw the local MP, Beverly Brennan, laying her hand on Largemount's pleated barrel chest as they shared a laugh about something. It was a curiously unguarded gesture from a career politician like Brennan. But then, Peter Largemount was the kind of man who evoked strong emotions in people. He had certainly evoked them in Domenic earlier in the evening. Brennan seemed to sense him watching her and she made her way toward him. Jejeune detached himself from his conversation with an apologetic smile and wandered over to meet her.

Beverly Brennan offered her hand. She was a striking woman, with glittering blue-grey eyes and finely sculpted features. She wore her ashy blond hair drawn up loosely behind her neck, but let down, it would be shoulder length. It would complete what was already an impressive package. After the requisite pleasantries, she got down to business.

"Colleen and I discussed your potential appointment a number of times. We wondered what sort of impact it might have on the area, given the amount of media attention you seem to attract. But I know DCS Shepherd thinks very highly of you, and she fought very hard to bring you on board."

Beverly Brennan took Jejeune's silence as a rebuke. "Of course, we welcome anyone who has a genuine contribution to make to our community. It's just that with most celebrities, I find they can be more of a drain on resources than anything else. Police officers, of course, I would exempt from that statement."

She turned on her energy conservation smile, maximum wattage from minimal input. The policy statement over, she could now turn to other matters. "I understand you are a birder. You'll not get the best reports of me from certain quarters, I imagine. They seem to think my support for job creation and the economy in this area signals that I have turned my back on environmental concerns. But I understand the environmental issues rather better than some of my opponents might like to admit. Conservation and prosperity don't have to be an either/or proposition as far as I'm concerned. There are always areas for compromise. I'm just not convinced that the environmentalists in this area try hard enough to find them."

Jejeune nodded. He wondered if Largemount had decided to bring in reinforcements, since he had not shown himself to be sufficiently contrite over the Ivory Gull. It was certainly a pointed and forthright warning, but then Beverly Brennan didn't strike him as the type who would agree to be anybody's attack dog, so perhaps it was just that she delivered all her views like this. Jejeune seemed to remember that she had been something of an environmental activist in her earlier days. Always on the soft side of radical, but robust enough to get mentioned once or twice in the news reports. If Brennan was as self-assured and forthright in those days, it was little wonder she had attracted her own share of the limelight she now disparaged.

If the MP was waiting for a meaningful response from Jejeune, she was disappointed. He offered some platitudes about the value of compromise in all areas and turned the subject to what the economic future of Saltmarsh looked like from her perspective. It was a subject she warmed to, and it gave him the opportunity to listen politely and continue his appraisal of the room. Even though he was only half listening, Jejeune was struck by the number of references to Brennan's earlier positions on environmental protection. *Is she looking for absolution*? he wondered. *From me*? He had only been here five minutes. Why should his opinion have any special significance?

Brennan finally excused herself and Jejeune went over to where Lindy was holding court, motioning for her to detach herself from her covey of admirers and join him in a corner.

"Having fun?" he asked.

"Terrific, yes, it's like being trapped in a sixties time warp. Most of these men seem astonished that I actually have a career all of my own. I suppose they think I should be spending my days at home in the kitchen."

"They've obviously not tasted your cooking."

"What about you, Chief Inspector Jejeune? Where do you think I should be spending my time?"

"Right here by my side," said Jejeune, who felt it was never too early to start digging out from under a remark like that.

"You spent a long time talking to that MP. I didn't know you had political aspirations, darling. Or was it just that cute colonial accent that got her meter running?"

"I doubt we have much in common. She's heavily behind development in these parts. Her idea of compromise seems to involve having the local environmentalists meekly accept whatever mitigation measures are proposed by the developers."

"Oh dear, and you such a greenie, too. Let that be a lesson to you, young Domenic. People's politics are not always as attractive as they are. And she is quite a looker, isn't she? Speaking of which, who's your dolled-up boss got her eye on?"

"No one, as far as I know. This is supposed to be just a PR thing for her, I think."

Lindy sighed. "Oh Domenic, you are so thick when it comes to women sometimes. Look at her. Do you really think a woman would go to that much trouble just to shake hands with a few society high-lifes? It must have taken her over an hour to do her makeup alone. She really wants to impress somebody. Not you, is it? You need to be careful, Inspector Jejeune. From what I hear, they're all at it, this lot. They're like a bunch of ferrets. It's a proper little hotbed of hot beds we seem to have landed ourselves in."

"Business," said Jejeune. "It's a business of ferrets."

He was hardly surprised by Lindy's revelations. It had always seemed to him that adults fell broadly into one of two categories: those who slept with their own partner, and those who slept with someone else's. *"Bedrooms and boardrooms,"* Lindy had once told him, *"the nerve centres of our society. But bedrooms most of all."*

"How are you doing, anyway?" she asked.

When she had had a drink or two, Lindy had a way of leaning dangerously close. She was doing it now, stroking the silk lapel of Jejeune's jacket with the palm of her hand in a way that made it very difficult for him to concentrate on what she was saying.

"Well," he said with a smile frozen on his face for the benefit of passersby. "I've spent most of the night listening to people who want me to use my influence with the government for one thing or another. Most of them seem to think I've got the PM on speed dial."

"The Home Secretary did acknowledge a personal debt of gratitude to you, darling. On national TV. That sort of thing hardly goes unnoticed." Lindy surveyed the room. "You know, if these sorts of events are going to be part of the package from now on, I suppose we'd better get used to it. By the way, I had a nice chat with a lady who writes the local gossip column. She wants to do a piece about our hobbies, but I thought birdwatching and organic cookery seemed a trifle dull for a couple of transplanted urbanites. She's obviously going to be looking for something a bit spicier. I thought leather porn and crack cocaine. Sound all right to you?"

"Fine."

This was more like the old Lindy, with her dangerous, buccaneering wildness. It was something Jejeune had seen a lot of in the early days of their relationship, but it had been noticeably absent these last few months. He hoped its resurfacing tonight was a sign of things to come.

13

Domenic Jejeune drove without haste beneath a sky the colour of sorrow. Between the high hedgerows to his left, he could see tantalizing glimpses of the rolling north Norfolk landscape, with its clear, unbroken views to the horizon 'promising forever' as Lindy put it. To his right, swollen rain-clouds hung low over the sea. The freshening breeze coming in through the Range Rover's open windows suggested that the storm wouldn't be long in coming.

Normally, coastal drives like this were one of the great pleasures of living out here. Casually scanning the fields and hedgerows for a potential addition to his county list, his mind could remain blissfully unoccupied. But today, a number of gnarly questions turned the sights and sounds on this dark summer's day into little more than background noise. Jejeune didn't hold out much hope that his destination would do much to quell the disquiet, either.

Jejeune pulled off the road and began a long, bumpy drive along a rutted cart track. Maik's Mini was parked beneath a large oak tree at the far end, and Jejeune marvelled, as ever, at just how the sergeant managed to fold his formidable frame into the tiny car. Maik was leaning back on the front fender, his face turned toward the sky. Jejeune couldn't hear whether there was an old Motown track coming from the CD player, but he wouldn't have bet against it. As Jejeune got out of his car, the first heavy, coin-sized raindrops began to splatter on his windshield. He nodded briefly to Maik and the two men hurried up a well-travelled pathway between the trees just as the downpour began.

Malcolm Brae's cottage sat in a clearing, surrounded by the remains of an ancient apple orchard. In the sunshine the air would be alive with birdsong, but with their uncanny radar for weather systems, the birds had already taken cover. Only the sound of a high-speed drill was audible over the drumming of the rain. It was coming from a large barn beside the cottage. The detectives entered the barn without knocking and stood inside the doorway for a moment, shaking off the water from their jackets and shoes. The rain was hammering down on the metal roof with ferocious intensity now, threatening to drown out even the sound of the drill.

Malcolm Brae was leaning over a makeshift workbench. He looked up when the two men entered, but continued working until he had finished his task before turning off the drill and taking off his safety goggles.

"Chief Inspector. Questions, or answers?" Malcolm Brae was forced to shout above the noise of the rain. Somewhere in the distance, a thunderclap boomed.

"The former, I'm afraid." Jejeune had to move closer to make himself heard. "But we are beginning to narrow the field of suspects down quite considerably."

This was news to Maik, but he said nothing. As Malcolm Brae shifted his position to look at them, Maik could see what he had been working on. Instinctively, he placed a warning arm across Jejeune's chest. Although it was broken down into its component parts, Maik had seen enough guns close up to recognize one in its raw form.

"It's perfectly harmless, Sergeant," shouted Malcolm Brae. "I always remove the firing mechanisms while I'm working on them. I was just cleaning up the scrollwork on the face plate."

"I don't see a locking steel cabinet anywhere, sir," bellowed Maik in return. Another deafening thunderclap sounded overhead. Somewhere outside, the landscape was being lit up by a flash of lightning.

Brae smiled indulgently. "I think you'll find that requirement only applies to working firearms, Sergeant. As they are, disabled old Churchills like this are little more than glorified wall hangings. Which, of course, is exactly what the townies want. And before you ask, I do have all the requisite permits." He picked up a grimy cloth and began wiping his hands. "Did you want to see me about anything in particular?"

Now that his eyes had adjusted to the light, Jejeune could see a number of old firearms in various states of disrepair, lying on surfaces or propped up against the walls. All had either the trigger mechanism or the firing pin removed. The intensity of the rain had increased, and Jejeune looked up, as if to satisfy himself that the roof wasn't going to collapse under the deafening hammering.

"I wonder, can you tell me a bit more about your last contact with your father? You said you had argued."

A flicker of sadness touched Brae's eyes. "I tried to call him, on the night he died, but he didn't answer his phone." He paused, perhaps to let a loud passage of rain subside, perhaps for some other reason. "I wasn't surprised. My father could be a very stubborn man. He wasn't one to do the kiss and make up thing very easily."

"Can I ask what the row was about?" asked Jejeune, leaning closer to avoid shouting over the storm.

"About? About nothing. About everything. About my being his son, and he being my father. I don't think either of us was ever very comfortable with the arrangement."

Outside, two flashes of lightning were followed by two rapid thunderclaps.

"Was there ever any conflict between your father and Peter Largemount over the wind farm?"

Maik fought hard to conceal his bewilderment. As far as he knew, Largemount had a solid alibi and there was no evidence linking him with anything. He was certainly full of surprises, this DCI. But in Maik's book, that wasn't necessarily a good thing.

Brae shook his head. "Though he never publicly criticized the project, I know my father had some misgivings; he felt the potential impacts of the turbines on bats hadn't been studied enough, for one thing. As for Largemount himself, my father couldn't stand the man. Hardly surprising, really, chalk and cheese. I must confess, I did always find it rather curious that the two never butted heads over that wind farm."

"Mr. Largemount has some powerful allies. Perhaps your father recognized it was a battle he couldn't win."

Brae looked at Jejeune quizzically. "You didn't know my father, did you, Inspector? He relished those kinds of battles. In his earlier days, grinning Peter Largemount was exactly the kind of target he would have sought out."

Jejeune began to stroll around the barn. Maik had been sure it was coming. There were just too many interesting objects lying around for the inspector to have foregone his customary pottering. Jejeune lifted an old gun from its resting place and looked along its length.

"A Powell, Inspector," called Brae, "an 1895 Boxlock, with a Deeley pull down latch, in case you're interested. Look at the exquisite detailing on the plate. You really can see how collectors consider them works of art."

Jejeune leaned the shotgun back against the wall. He was ready to find beauty in many things, but in some it was harder than others. "Disabled or not, this is not the most secure environment for firearms, Mr. Brae."

"I told you, I remove all the dangerous bits before I start working on them. Those you *will* find locked up in my safe in the cottage. I would like to build a workshop in there rather than work out here, but we can't all afford to undertake English Heritage–style renovations, Chief Inspector."

Someone else who had heard about Jejeune's plans for his cottage, thought Maik. Or his girlfriend's plans, more likely. Even if Jejeune could claim it was the police force's idea to transfer him here, he was still, in the eyes of the locals, just another one of those townies who had swanned up from the Big Smoke to snap up a prime piece of the Norfolk coastline, and, if not exactly act the part of the country squire, at least be close enough to the cliché to be tarnished by association.

The intense, machine-gun drumming of the rain had eased off to a residual pattering on the roof. In the distance, the thunder was now just a faint rumble as the storm rolled its way across the countryside.

"I understand your father left a lot of unfinished projects," said Maik. "Any idea what will happen to them now?"

"Mother may make some efforts with the charitable work, I imagine, but as far as the academic research …" Malcolm Brae shrugged. "Perhaps the university … I don't know."

"You wouldn't have any interest in pursuing your father's work yourself? I understand you studied something similar at university."

Brae smiled sadly. "A generous way of putting it, Sergeant. My father was understandably delighted when I chose Conservation Biology as my discipline. Sadly, I'm afraid it was discipline that let me down in the end. My own. Another career opportunity lost to the demons of alcohol. Not exactly a unique tale of woe in our current society, I realize, but true nevertheless."

"That must have been a …"

"Disappointment, Sergeant? Yes, my father was never able to disguise his true feelings very well — not that he tried too hard in the first place. I never touch the stuff now. But that's horses and stable doors, unfortunately, as far as any academic career for me is concerned."

"And your … the current Mrs. Brae. She seems very keen that your father's memory be preserved. I would imagine she would be interested in seeing his goals pursued."

"I doubt she knows much about father's goals. Or anything else, for that matter. She certainly doesn't have a clue about his environmental work. She couldn't offer you a fact about my father's studies if you offered her a new recording contract. A disapproving look, Sergeant? You have interviewed her. Am I wrong?"

"Some of the ideas are quite complex, as I understand it."

"Really? Take care of the environment, and we might just have a healthy place to live in the future? Well beyond the realm of a Roquettes song, I realize, but hardly quantum physics. Does it not strike you as a somewhat strange relationship in the first place? People from her world only marry for three reasons: money, looks, or status. Despite my father's success, money was clearly not a factor, certainly not the kind of money she's used to. And without wishing to speak ill of … as it were, my father was no prize physical specimen. No, what she wanted from her marriage to my father was some veneer of intellectual status. Intelligence by association, however tenuous that association might be. Being with my father and his circle provided her the *gravitas* missing from her ridiculous previous existence. Really, I ask you, can there be anything more pathetic than a fading airhead starlet looking to be taken seriously?"

"Hardly a crime, though, is it, wanting to improve your

mind?" said Maik reasonably. "After all, not everyone gets a crack at a university education."

"But merely wishing to be thought clever, without putting in any of the requisite effort, there's a word for that, isn't there, Sergeant? Don't be misled. My stepmother's desire to make over her image has little to do with any genuine desire for greater knowledge."

How well had it gone down with the rest of the Saltmarsh *cognoscenti*, this quest of Mandy Roquette's to be admitted into their little circle? It occurred to the listening Jejeune that she probably had more money than the rest of the Saltmarsh elite put together, and yet she had been conspicuously absent from the list of invitees to the Hunt Club function.

"Your stepmother told the sergeant your father *said* he was working at the university," said Jejeune casually. "Do you happen to know where she thought he was really going?"

Malcolm looked puzzled.

"Most people would just have said 'he was working at the university.' But he's a very literal man, the sergeant," said Jejeune, "not much given to linguistic license. If he states that Mrs. Brae used the word *said*, I have no doubt that is exactly how she put it. *Said* as in *claimed* you see. It doesn't necessarily mean that she believed him. In fact, it suggests the opposite."

"Insecurity is a disease that can become an epidemic very rapidly, Inspector. I would suspect that after you have attended enough dinners where the conversation swirls around above your head all evening, it would be easy to start imagining all sorts of things. But I would say if my father was having an affair, it can only have been because he was not satisfied with his life inside of his marriage."

He paused and looked at the two men. The rain on the metal roof was barely audible now. But the sound still seemed to fill the barn.

"You will let me know when that field of suspects gets narrowed down to one, won't you?"

Brae hefted the stock of the Churchill rifle back onto his workbench and reached for a jar of polish. A rich, sweet scent of oily resin filled the air. The detectives left him to his work.

Jejeune sat in the Range Rover, looking out at the sky, an unbroken shroud of grey weeping gentle tears. "No metaphors, no similes, nothing," Lindy had said after Maik had called in to the cottage to report on Brae's weight. "It's his army training, I suppose. All that precision and drilling."

Jejeune had not noticed it until she had pointed it out, but he supposed he had been unconsciously registering the sergeant's speech patterns since. He sighed. Perhaps he had no business commenting in public on how his sergeant expressed himself. Still, it was too late now. The engine coughed into life, and Jejeune eased the Range Rover out toward the grey horizon.

Maik sat in his own car for a long time, staring out through the veil of soft rain at the stunted, unkempt apple trees, with their fallen garlands of fruit beneath them. Just his imagination, running away with him. He snapped off the CD player. Sometimes even silken harmonies of The Temptations couldn't soothe away the problems. *So I speak plainly? Well how about this for plain speaking, then? If Jejeune thinks he can find a motive for murder in Mandy Brae's suspicions about her husband's infidelity, he is wrong.* Whatever else she might have been, Mandy Brae was a loyal, loving wife. Maik was sure of it.

14

Archie Christian's house was set well back from the road, but the long single-storey facade still set an imposing barrier between a visitor and the rest of the property. The house sat on a small rise, looking out over a vast expanse of flat, tilled soil. The wide porticoed entrance and lavish three-winged layout spoke to the affluence of the original owner, a landowner with a healthy share of the local onion trade.

The wings ran off the house at ninety degrees from the main block, forming a three-sided courtyard behind the house. Along the back, forming the fourth side, was a long ramshackle greenhouse. A set of large padlocked gates connected each end of the greenhouse to the side wings of the house. When they were shut, as they were now, it formed a fully enclosed courtyard. For a man with Christian's past, the setup could hardly have been better, well away from the prying eyes of the public and secure against unwanted visitors. Well, almost.

A judas gate on one side gave under Maik's attentions. "Appears to be open, sir. Can't see why we can't just go in, as long as we announce ourselves properly."

"Are we sure he's here?" asked Jejeune.

The sergeant shrugged. He had not called ahead. Archie Christian was not the sort of man to whom you gave advance notice of a police visit. Not if you wanted him to be at home when you got there.

Jejeune looked skeptical, but followed Maik through the gate without comment. He noticed fresh tire tracks in the mud that didn't match either the battered Transit van or the tan late-model Aston Martin, both of which were parked on the far side of the courtyard.

A short, stocky man with a grey bouffant hairstyle and chiseled features came out of the greenhouse as the two detectives approached. He wore a silk shirt of alternating blue and purple stripes and grey trousers with a crease that could have cut through flesh. A thick coil of rolled gold chain glittered around his neck. Black patent leather shoes of a style Jejeune hadn't seen for a generation completed the outfit. Judging by his appearance, whatever he was up to these days, Archie Christian wasn't spending a lot of time in the onion fields.

Christian walked toward them briskly, pushing his hands deep into the pockets of his trousers. He had the exaggerated swagger and easy self-confidence of someone who was comfortable coming at you head on and standing right in your personal space. It was a useful trait to have, thought Jejeune, if you intended to do them bodily harm for non-payment of debts.

"Blimey, Danny Maik. I thought they had sent you to the glue factory. Dodgy ticker, wasn't it? Don't look so surprised, old son. Lots of loose lips in the North Norfolk Constabulary, if you know who to ask." He tapped the side of his nose with a forefinger and turned toward Jejeune. "And you must be the new bloke. The TV star." Christian waved his hands in front of him like a bad impersonation of a vaudeville star. "So what is this then, promotion? Or purgatory? I mean, one of the kids still died, didn't they? And if I remember rightly, there was a whisper that if things had been handled differently.... Still I suppose we'll never know, eh? At least you managed to save the important one, the Home Secretary's daughter, that's the main thing."

Maik made a move toward Christian, but Jejeune lifted his hand. It was a slight, almost imperceptible gesture, but it was enough to quell the storm brewing inside Danny Maik.

"We're making inquiries into the death of Cameron Brae," said Jejeune evenly, "and your name came up."

"Now there's a surprise." Christian cast a glance at Maik. "Every time anybody gets so much as a parking ticket out here, my name comes up. Do you know why that is, Inspector Hollywood? Because your coppers down at the station are too bloody lazy to do their job. Instead of going out and looking for the real villains, they'd rather just sit on their fat arses in front of a computer screen and pull up the names of people in the area with a bit of history. Never mind that these people have been decent, law-abiding citizens for years. Well, I was here that night, all on my own. All night. We done?"

"As a result," continued Jejeune as if Christian hadn't spoken, "we have a few questions to ask you."

"I don't know anything," said Christian.

"Be a short interview, then, won't it?" said Maik, matching Christian's surly tone exactly. He indicated the greenhouse. "Mind if we have a look around inside, Archie? The DCI has never seen your little setup before."

Christian shrugged and led the men into the greenhouse. Most of the space to the left was dedicated to rows of tables with trays of plants arranged along them, and hanging down in luxuriant fronds from baskets suspended from beams above. But the entire right hand section of the structure had been converted into a sunroom. A large wicker sofa and two matching chairs surrounded a low bamboo coffee table, the furniture set to look out through the oversized windows at the vast flat quilt of fields beyond. Christian's laptop sat on the table, the monitor having already retreated to his screensaver. Behind each chair was a wicker bookcase filled with the sort of bric-a-brac one might associate with the worst of seaside souvenir shop, and modern fiction, to Jejeune's mind at least, of a similar pedigree. Separating the space from the rest of the greenhouse was a polished teak bar, trimmed with brass rails and flanked by two large bamboo screens. An impressive array of liquor stood against the mirrored back of the bar. Through a small gap between the screens, Jejeune could see a large bed. It looked like the glass in that part of the room had been painted over, creating a dark space not visible from anywhere but here.

All around the room, evidence of Christian's outlandish taste screeched at them. Nothing could have been more out of place in the tranquil pastels of the Norfolk countryside, and Christian seemed intent on making sure it was so. If you won't have me in your inner circle, he seemed to be saying, then you can just bloody well put up with me being on the outside making a spectacle of myself.

Christian stared insolently at the two policemen, challenging them to begin. By now, Maik was beginning to get the idea of the pattern the interview was going to take. He would take the lead, while Jejeune pottered around examining the furniture until he felt like making a contribution. Maik found this constant fiddling irritating, and for the interviewee, it must have been as distracting as hell. But then again, perhaps that was the point. One thing certainly seemed to be becoming clear. Domenic Jejeune rarely did anything without a reason.

On the draining board near the bar were two glasses, still wet.

"Been entertaining, Archie?" asked Maik.

"A punter. Not that it's any of your business."

"I'll tell you what is my business: the run-ins you've had with the victim. There was a fair few of them, wasn't there,

Archie? Public set-tos, claims and counter-claims, harassment, threatening behaviour. It was all there on the computer screen when I sat there checking it out this morning."

"We had our differences of opinion. I wanted to get a backhoe in to pull up some hedgerows. I needed permission, because it was a public right of way. But Brae opposed it. 'In contravention of existing by-laws,'" quoted Christian in what was meant to be the lofty tones of a solicitor. "By-laws, my arse. It was just showboating. Local greenie takes on the big, bad businessman. So yeah, we had a history, me and him."

"Not like you to worry about planning permission. In the old days you would have just ripped up those hedges without a second thought."

"Yeah, well, this was different, wannit? I was looking at setting up a GM project on my land. Plenty of investors were interested so the lawyers wanted everything done above board. Only somehow, Brae got wind of my plans. Mobilized the local bumpkins, and that was that."

Christian pulled out his BlackBerry and checked it. If it had vibrated, neither Maik nor Jejeune had heard it. Satisfied, or not, Christian turned and tossed the device onto the table beside his computer.

"So what happened?"

"Made such a fuss, the investors lost interest. GM's a dodgy prospect anyway; last thing they wanted was a big song and dance attracting negative publicity. Brae knew exactly how to play it. So they pulled out and went somewhere else, somewhere with a bit more progressive ideas. Suffolk, I think."

"And the threats?"

"He started a whispering campaign with the investors. About me, my background. Not enough he was killing off a highly profitable enterprise. I told him to lay off, that's all."

"Not quite all, though, was it Archie?" said Maik. "You said you'd do him. And you said it in front of witnesses. Not very clever that."

"Yeah, well, that wasn't really me talking, was it? It was the old Greene King. I'd had a bit of luck on the gee-gees at Folksham and I was out celebrating. I saw him in the car park as I was coming out of the pub. We exchanged a few pleasantries and went our separate ways. And that's all there was to it."

"Except now the man you threatened is dead," said Maik, "and you don't seem to have an alibi for the night in question."

"No, I don't have an alibi. And let me tell you what you don't have. You don't have any reason to zero in on me. Don't you be fooled by that softly, softly crap Brae showed on TV. He was a calculating bastard, out to stop anybody who wanted to make a decent living if it involved using any of his bloody 'green spaces.' There will be plenty of people glad to see the back of him, take my word."

"Just what is your business these days, Mr. Christian?" asked Jejeune, apparently taking an interest in proceedings for the first time.

"I'm a consultant."

"At Folksham Race Course?"

Christian shrugged. "Among other places. What's that got to do with anything?"

"And what do people consult you about, exactly?"

"They want me to whisper to their horses. Get them to run faster. You pair done? I've got a lot of work to catch up on."

Jejeune noticed the momentary flicker in Maik's features. He had good ears, the sergeant.

"You can see, Mr. Christian, Archie, how a history of conflict with the victim could put you in the frame for this."

Christian's sneer at Jejeune held real malevolence. "Oh yeah. Bleedin' obvious, innit? We have a bit of a ding dong. He hurts my feelings, so I do him in. Then I think to myself, the best thing you can do here, old son, is to hang his body from a fakkin great tree. Nobody will ever suspect you. I mean, it's not as if the two of you have been having a public dispute, and he's slagged you off every chance he got." Christian fixed Jejeune with a cold-eyed stare. "Is that what passes for brains in the police force these days? You're as bad as these Earth Front nutters who keep giving me all these threats and nasty phone calls."

"Threats?"

"They think, like you, that I've got nothing better to do than string up old men from trees. That's how it was, though, taking him on. Never mind you was in the right legally, morally, whatever. As far as the public round here was concerned, opposing Cameron Brae was like kicking Bambi to death."

"Are you asking for police protection, Archie?" Maik asked with feigned concern.

"From a few kids with acne all over their faces? Do me a favour. Besides, what kind of protection am I going to get from a useless invalid with a bad heart and a pretty boy who talks funny?"

Maik closed the distance between them. His face had darkened with the effort of keeping control. "Mind your manners, Archie. Your act might impress some over-the-top greenies, but I've seen genuine hard men in my time. You don't even come close."

Christian smiled pleasantly. He had spent his formative years facing down situations like this in pubs and snooker halls throughout the east end of London. You didn't flinch, not if you wanted to come back tomorrow.

"You want to watch it, a man in your condition, getting all agitated like that. Understandable, though, I suppose. Must make you feel a bit impotent, this dodgy heart business. Perhaps you should think about early retirement. But then what kind of a life would that be, eh? Nitro pills, and nights in front of the telly with your slippers and a glass of warm milk? Not much of a prospect for an Action Man like you, is it, Danny boy?" A thought seemed to strike him. "Here, listen, when the old ticker does finally give out, can you ask somebody from the station to let me know? I'd like to say a few words at the funeral."

Maik moved closer to Christian, and leaned closer still. "They'll be putting you in the ground long before me, Archie. You like a flutter, bet on that."

Neither man batted an eye, even though their stares were locked less than a handspan apart.

"Don't try throwing your weight around here, Danny boy. You want to intimidate people, you should have stuck to waterboarding Arabs in the desert. Exporting democracy for fun and profit, eh? Well, we don't stand for that kind of thing round here, am I right, Chief Inspector? It's all about rights in this part of the world, and I've got 'em. So don't come back here unless you've got a warrant. And you won't get one 'cause you got nothing. No motive, no opportunity, no witnesses. So piss off."

Outside, Jejeune paused to look around the courtyard before getting into the car. He waited until they were well along the driveway before he spoke.

"I don't like my officers threatening members of the public, Sergeant. Not even a little bit. Besides, anybody who didn't commit the crime can potentially offer us assistance in solving it."

"Assistance?" Maik couldn't suppress a derisive laugh. "I don't think Archie Christian does 'assistance.' What makes you think he didn't do it, anyway? He's certainly got the means, and without an alibi, we have to assume opportunity. And despite what he says, public ridicule and harassment would be motive aplenty for Archie, even without the lost income from the GM business. If you're worried about the weight thing, Christian's got the head for numbers. Lightning fast on odds calculations at the track."

Jejeune shrugged a little. "The calculations are not so much the issue. You still need a branch of the right height. That willow tree had at least eight boughs strong enough to take a noose, but only one of them was the right height to kill Brae cleanly."

"Odds of seven-to-one wouldn't faze Archie," said Maik. "But I take your point. It's all a bit fussy for an old-school villain like him. I don't know if he would have the patience for something like this. That said, I wouldn't put anything past him. He's a lot of things, is Archie Christian, but stupid isn't one of them."

"Still, it wasn't an entirely wasted trip, was it?"

"His job, you mean? You want me to follow up with the vet?" Maik obviously relished the idea, but Jejeune shook his head.

"Let's leave that for a while. I still think Mr. Christian knows more than he is saying about this case. We might need his assistance yet. And now we know how to get it."

Jejeune saw a smile touch the corners of Maik's lips. He had handled himself well back there, the sergeant, picked up on the cues very nicely. They had combined smoothly and ended up with a productive interview. Teamwork, some might have called it. Except for that, you needed team players. *And that's not us, is it, Sergeant? Not quite ready for the group hug yet, are we?*

15

"So, Sergeant Attenborough, got your RSPB membership form in yet?"

Holland entered Maik's workspace holding a sandwich in one hand and a mug of tea in the other. The cubicle was a small, bright space separated from the rest of the office by a pair of dividers that came out perpendicularly from the back wall. Holland set his tea down on the window ledge and reached over to pick up a file that was fighting for space on a desk piled high with books, papers, forms, and coffee mugs.

"Birders?" he said through a mouth full of chicken salad. "Gah, these anoraks and their lists. They're worse than train-spotters. Probably got their own secret handshake, too, like that Star Trek bunch. Nanoo, Nanoo."

On the other side of the dividers, the room hummed with undefined activity, but Maik had spent most of this day and the previous one on the phone with members of the local birding community. And his mood hadn't been lightened any by a flying visit from the DCS, on her way through the squad room to who knew where.

"It's a difficult one in these parts, isn't it, Sergeant?" she'd said. "I suspect it's going to be necessary to remind our birding friends what is a right and what is a privilege. The local community is very supportive when they close off the beach at Blakeney Point, to protect the nesting sites of those ... *birds*. You might want to remind them of that."

"Sandwich Terns, ma'am. I have mentioned it," said Maik, who liked to be told how to do his job about as much as anyone else.

"Good, good." If Shepherd had any thoughts on Jejeune's use of key personnel this way, in the middle of a high-priority murder investigation, she was keeping them to herself. She leaned in close and Maik caught a scent of something sweet and expensive. She was certainly taking good care of herself these days, the DCS.

"And you're doing okay, yourself, Sergeant? Physically, I mean. Not feeling the strain or anything."

"The files aren't all that heavy," said Maik flatly.

"Yes, well, please tread lightly, however you proceed. Keep in mind that birders are a very important part of our community, and there are some highly placed citizens among them. Let's not turn this into one of your usual us-and-them routines. We all need to be on the same side going forward."

As opposed to going backward, Maik supposed. He had contempt for modern idioms at the best of times, but reserved special scorn for idiotic redundancies like this. But she did have a point. Far from being contrite about their harassment of Peter Largemount, the birders that Maik had spoken to thus far were, to a person, outraged that they were not being allowed on the land to search for the Ivory Gull. Some had inquired about the laws on public thoroughfares, others what sort of sentence they might be looking at for trespassing. Still others were interested in a landowner's rights concerning forcible denial of entry, and their own rights with regards to defending themselves, should it come to that. In Maik's experience, birders normally respected the rights and property of local landowners with equanimity, but since seeing an Ivory Gull was an opportunity that was unlikely to occur again in anyone's lifetime, the prevailing sentiment seemed to be that it would be far better to ask for forgiveness afterward than for permission beforehand.

He shouldn't have been surprised, really. This was the most concentrated area of dedicated birders in the country, possibly in the world. A disproportionately high number of birding experts lived around here, drawn by the variety of species, and the expertise and insights of others of their ilk. Maik had encountered local birders often enough over the years, and had witnessed first-hand their relentless intensity. He knew that even if he didn't share their passion, it would be a mistake to underestimate their commitment to their hobby. But even he was surprised by the depth of feeling he was encountering today. If he was not yet ready to embrace the four-hundred list as a valid motive for Brae's murder, by now Maik was at least some way closer to understanding how Jejeune could consider it.

He picked up the various emails, messages, and letters Largemount had provided and considered them once again. For the most part it was transparent outrage and bluster, nasty but not vitriolic. But two of the threats worried him. They were colder, more calculated, a lot more careful in what they promised and how they were worded. And they weren't signed. Those he set aside for further consideration.

Holland riffled through the list of local birders, a veritable who's who of Saltmarsh society. "I just don't get it. I mean, I like birds, I suppose. I like to see them flying around, hear them singing and all that, but species and sub-species and migration patterns and distribution maps. Why bother with all that crap?"

Maik shrugged. "I don't know, the same as any hobby, I suppose. The more you know, the more you want to know."

But there were other reasons for immersing yourself in a hobby. Maik had known a lot of policemen who had sought outside interests as a way of dealing with the stresses of the job. Sports, vintage cars. And of course, the bottle. Some just needed an outlet, any outlet.

Holland flipped the file back onto the desk. "And all this extra work you're having to do is because of a bird he found? A seagull? On the beach? Blimey, no wonder he's up for detective of the year. You must be well pleased to have gotten roped into this."

"It's caused a fuss, I know that much. I spent as much time discussing that bird yesterday as anything else. Did I see it myself? Did it have such and such markings? Did he get photographs? I even got a call from the Netherlands about it."

"From what I hear, the locals don't think it was a, whatever it is, Ivory Gull. They think he's just trying to make a name for himself. Done the opposite, though, made a right rickets of his reputation with the local birders, apparently. None of them has reported seeing it, have they?"

"The Rare Birds Committee said the only bird in this area pending verification at the moment is an Egyptian Vulture. There's a Baikal Teal, too, but that is an old chestnut that surfaces every couple of years or so, apparently. Usually an escape."

Holland's mouth fell open in mid-chew. "Steady on, Sarge, you'll be out there in your anorak and camouflage trousers before long, you keep this up. Not cool, not cool at all."

"If I wanted to be cool, I'd open the window," said Maik testily.

"Still, I suppose it's a nice break from bashing your head against a brick wall on this case. Any idea where he's going with it?"

Maik shook his head. Having counted out the family, and gotten nothing especially useful from either Largemount or

Christian, he had no idea what lines of inquiry Jejeune would be pursuing now. Maik was still uneasy about the cavalier way they had eliminated so many potential suspects just on Jejeune's say so. But the inspector had such a way of putting his point across, so positive and matter-of-fact, you almost felt compelled to go along with him. Of course it was possible that Jejeune was just streets ahead of everybody else on this, but for the life of him, Maik couldn't see where they were heading next.

Seeing Maik preoccupied with his own thoughts, Holland started to leave. Suddenly he turned around. "Here, Sarge, you're starting to fancy yourself as a bit of a birder, have a go at this one."

Maik looked up to see Holland holding his chicken sandwich, open-faced in front of him.

"So what do you reckon, Leghorn or Rhode Island Red?"

16

DCS Shepherd tapped on the door to Jejeune's office. "Report of firearms discharge on Peter Largemount's property. Domenic, with me, please."

By the time Jejeune had grabbed his jacket, the DCS was halfway down the corridor. There was no time to question if Sergeant Maik should accompany them. There was little point, either, since it was clear the DCS would be handling this one. The sergeant would just have to continue with his phone calls.

Shepherd revved her car out of the parking space and plunged into the Saltmarsh high street traffic with barely a glance. The DCS's features were cinched up tight, though whether this was purely concentration, or something else, Jejeune couldn't have said. They sped out through the light mid-morning traffic and in moments they were into the countryside.

Sunlight filtered through the branches of the hedgerows that lined the road, dappling the tarmac in extravagant patterns of light and shadow. In the fields along the roadside, large pools of standing water lay on the black earth like patches of silver, remnants of the tidal storm surges of the previous week. The salt marshes and lagoons along the shoreline had flooded rapidly and breached their boundaries, spilling their contents across the flat inland terrain. Thankfully, the storms had subsided quickly, and there had been no repeat of the massive property damage of the 2006 inundations. Still, it had served as a reminder that even living in an idyllic place like this had its perils.

"This will turn out to be nothing, I'm sure," Shepherd said finally. "In fact, I think I already know what it's about." But if she was trying to convince herself, she wasn't doing it well enough to ease her foot off the accelerator. "So tell me more about this birdwatching theory of yours. Something about a four-hundred list?"

Jejeune wasn't really sure where he had imagined this conversation would take place. He only knew he wouldn't have chosen it to be here, in the DCS's car with her eyes focused intently on the road in front of her as the north Norfolk countryside flashed by. He had no idea who the DCS's source would have been, but he was fairly sure his theory wouldn't have been presented in a positive light. It wasn't even a theory at the moment, just a loose set of ideas, not ready to see the light of day. He would have preferred not to discuss it at all, just yet, but he realized that option wasn't available to him anymore.

"The race to record four hundred species in Norfolk is a matter of intense competition amongst the local birders. In birding circles it would be one of the crowning achievements, and it would ensure prestige well beyond the local societies, nationally, certainly, perhaps even into the world birding community. Cameron Brae was leading that race and two days before he died, he made a record of an extremely rare sighting, an American Bittern. But he never reported his sighting to the records committee, or to anybody else, as far as I can tell. It doesn't make sense."

Shepherd effected a creditable racing change as she accelerated into a sharp left-hand bend. A flock of Wood Pigeons exploded off the road in front of them in a flurry of wings and feathers. Jejeune let his fingertips touch the dashboard.

"Well, perhaps he just realized he had made a mistake. I'm sure it happens all the time. I'm no birder, but I know I couldn't be sure of something if it was just the briefest of flashes as it went by."

Jejeune thought about the entry, the circling, and the double underlining. "I don't think so. I believe he was absolutely sure about what he had seen. There's also the lists. Bird orders consist of certain families, and they're arranged that way in birdwatcher's lists. It wouldn't make sense to do it any other way. But in the lists on Brae's desk, one of the families was misplaced, put in the wrong order. It's not a mistake a birder of Brae's quality would have made."

Shepherd flicked a glance at him, as though she was waiting for something more. Realizing it wasn't coming, she summarized for herself. "So we don't know why he didn't report this bird in the first place, but you think somebody killed him in case he had second thoughts and tried to put it on his list afterward? And you think, what, this person checked these other lists after killing him? Why would they do that?"

In truth, Jejeune had no idea what the disordered lists meant. "All I know is that Brae's behaviour is completely inconsistent with someone who has invested so much effort in a bid to list four hundred species."

He hesitated. He knew that, as a motive for murder, it was paper thin. He could have given her the other things, the particular family of birds involved, the significance of a three-bird lead so close to the final goal. But he knew these details wouldn't be enough to convince someone who was so manifestly not a birder. They were barely enough to convince him.

"I see." Shepherd's response was a good deal more subdued than it might otherwise have been, had she not been simultaneously negotiating a left-hand bend at speed and imagining a scenario where she stood in front of the Deputy Assistant Commissioner trying to explain this theory to him.

They sped through a tiny village, its stone-walled cottages so close to the road that if anyone had opened a window outward, Jejeune was sure it would have ripped off the mirror on the passenger side of the car. But with the appearance of Largemount's property on the horizon the DCS seemed to ease off some of the urgency in her driving. She pulled into the forecourt and pointed at a figure about a hundred metres beyond the house. "I'll talk to Peter. You handle Ivan."

Jejeune began walking down the dirt track while the DCS crunched over the gravel toward the house. As he approached, Jejeune recognized the man from the Titchwell car park.

"Somebody needs to do something about him," said Ivan by way of a greeting. "He's a maniac. He fired at me. Twice."

Jejeune could see that the man was still shaking slightly. He could hear it in his voice, too. "I was down in the marsh, walking across the shale bank. I saw a flash of white come in to land. I thought it might be the Ivory."

Jejeune looked over Ivan's shoulder. He hadn't realized Largemount's property was so close to Great Marsh. Or to Cameron Brae's house.

"As soon as I crossed over the creek, there was a shotgun blast in my direction," he continued, "and then he appeared. It was almost as if he had been hovering there, waiting for somebody to trespass. He became very belligerent and demanded I leave immediately. I told him, if he wanted me off his property, he would have to call the police." There was more outrage than fear in Ivan's words now. "That's when he raised his shotgun again and pointed it directly at me. Then he lifted it slightly and fired directly over my head. Both barrels."

Jejeune didn't need to make notes, but he did so for form's sake. He asked about Ivan's sightings for the day down in the marsh, but there was nothing that made it worth suggesting a side trip to the DCS on their way back. The sound of an approaching car caused them both to turn quickly. Shepherd was driving down the dirt track toward them. She pulled up and got out, looking flushed.

"We won't be taking this any further, Ivan. Mr. Largemount has no wish to press charges."

"*He* doesn't?" Ivan was indignant.

The freshening breeze on the rise coloured the DCS's cheeks. "The land is private and it is posted. In addition to which he tells me he spoke to you yesterday about trespassing."

"And I'm telling you the man fired at me. It was a criminally irresponsible act."

"He was shooting at pigeons," said Shepherd. "I happen to know Peter Largemount is an excellent marksman. I am certain you were never in any danger. Look, this is a simple trade-off. You will not pursue the matter any further and he won't press charges for trespassing."

The DCS's tone made it clear that she wouldn't be entertaining any other contributions to the discussion.

"Damned thug," said Ivan half to himself as he began picking his way carefully down the slope back toward the marsh. "Little wonder he's the most despised individual in the county."

Jejeune was silent as he watched him go. He remained that way until he and the DCS were in the car together, when he finally spoke. "Perhaps I should still have a word with Mr. Largemount."

DCS Shepherd was looking over her shoulder, reversing up the dirt track. "It's sorted. Besides, I hear you two have been jousting recently. Nothing to do with the investigation, I take it? He's not a person of interest?"

Jejeune shook his head. "There's a phone call from Brae that he doesn't want to talk about, but he has an alibi for the evening Brae was murdered."

"So, nothing then." She nodded as she turned the car around and started to drive back along the road. "I must confess I'm not sure where you're going with this bird list idea, Domenic. I'll back you, of course, but I'm going to need something substantive, and soon. I've been hearing from a lot of top line academics about this case," she said. "Politicans, too. They're starting to talk about Brae in exalted terms. If we suddenly end up with a martyr on our hands, it's going to make it a lot more difficult for us to hold on to this case. I need to show the higher-ups we know how to do Big Crime out here in the backwoods, to convince them that we are going to be able to deal with this at division level. Find me something, Domenic, will you? Some solid, tangible piece of evidence that I can point to and say, we are on our way to solving this case."

"I wonder," said Jejeune guardedly, "would Beverly Brennan have been one of those politicians you have been hearing from?"

Shepherd risked a sidelong glance at Jejeune before returning her attention to the twisting road. "Beverly Brennan is a good friend of the department, Domenic. A very good friend. And I happen to know she is a close personal friend of the Deputy Assistant Commissioner, too. You will want to be treading very lightly here."

"It's just that I can't seem to find out much about her. Her public life is obviously a matter of record, but her private life seems to be very much a mystery."

Shepherd was still letting the road claim her attention. "Out here you will find that private lives are exactly that. And why on earth are you looking into Beverly Brennan's private life in the first place? There are actual suspects in this case that I understand you have already dismissed. Might I suggest you have another look at them, rather than making enemies you really don't want to make."

"When I met her recently, she went out of her way to defend her green credentials to me. I wonder why she would do that."

"Perhaps she was simply trying to give you a bit of background. She knows you're not from around here. And in all honesty, it wouldn't hurt you to know a bit more about the local landscape. Yes, it's true she was an environmental activist and now she isn't. People change, Domenic, especially ambitious people. It's how they get ahead. It's a lesson you may want to take on board."

Jejeune nodded. People did change, he knew. Some got caught in the ever-changing tide known as life and ended up being carried in directions they never intended to take. But something still bothered him about the way everybody involved in this case seemed to be directing attention away from everybody else. To coin a phrase of Lindy's, he didn't know exactly what it was he didn't like, he just knew he didn't like it.

"Follow your bird lists for now, Domenic. But remember, I'll want to see some results, sooner rather than later."

Shepherd wasn't alone in that. Jejeune wouldn't have minded a few results, either. But just at the moment, he couldn't see where they might be coming from.

17

A cool wind blew in from the coast, lifting the peaty scent of the marshes and carrying it inland to the slight rise where Domenic Jejeune stood watching the activities in the reserve below him. Camouflage-clad birders with impressive-looking scopes slung over their shoulders were making their way purposefully toward one of the central hides. Whatever had come across the wires, Jejeune had missed it, but it was obvious from the number and haste of the birders that a significant sighting had been reported.

Jejeune returned to the car, where Maik was flipping through a music magazine. "Anything interesting?" he asked without looking up.

"Indeed, Sergeant. A lot of birders headed in the same direction in a hurry. That usually only means one thing."

"Anorak sale?"

If Jejeune was amused, he forgot to tell his face. Anorak, he thought, the cult, not the coat. *Nerds* he would have called them when he was growing up in Canada. A few years ago, he had no idea what an anorak even was, let alone how to interpret it as an insult. Not for the first time, Jejeune marvelled at how much of the British culture he had absorbed without even realizing it.

"Time we took a wander over to Bishop's Hide, I think."

Quentin Senior was standing behind his car, fitting a battered old telescope onto a tripod, as Jejeune wheeled the Range Rover into the reserve's tightly packed car park.

"Good morning, Inspector. Possible Semi-palmated Sandpiper. You'll know all about those, coming from Canada. It's already out on the wires, so I hope it's valid, though I have my doubts. Somebody trying to compensate for the missed Ivory Gull, I shouldn't wonder. It often happens, a report of one rarity touches off an epidemic of other sightings. Still, one has to be sure. Wouldn't do to miss out on a lifetime bird due to a bit of complacency, would it?"

He extended a hand toward Maik. "Don't believe we've met, certainly not here at Cley. Quentin Senior, self-appointed custodian of this place. At least I should be. I spend more time here than I do at home. That's how I can be fairly certain you've not been here before."

Maik offered his hand, but little by way of explanation. If it wasn't already clear that he wasn't a birder, it would soon be.

Senior hefted the scope onto his shoulder and began walking along the wooden path into the reserve.

"Local man, Sergeant?" asked Senior over his shoulder as they walked through the waist-high grass. "We can take a lot of pride in Cley, you know. It is the oldest bird reserve in the U.K. In 1926, a doctor named Sydney Long had the foresight to purchase this area to preserve it from hunting. It is often said that this is where birding properly began in Britain. It's an impressive bit of our local heritage, whether you're an actual birder or not."

By the time they arrived at the hide, there were already a lot of people crowded inside, huddled closely along the benches and standing in rows behind. An array of scopes and zoom lenses on tripods filled the remaining space.

Even in the darkened interior of the hide, Jejeune could feel eyes upon him. Senior's appearance had occasioned a wave of murmured welcomes, but Jejeune's own nodded efforts at a greeting went unreturned, as people returned to their binoculars with studious intensity.

Senior had settled into a spot made for him on the bench by two other birders, while Jejeune and Maik were left to stand behind the row of tripods.

"The inspector here should be able to give us the nod, or otherwise," Senior announced to the hide. "Must've seen plenty of Semi-palms back where he hails from. So where is it, exactly?"

Multiple contributions guided Senior to a mudflat toward the back of the cell, where a gathering of perhaps two hundred small grey birds sat hunched against the onshore wind. Maik wondered just how anyone could have identified one bird among so many similar shapes in such a sheltered location. But with so many expert eyes scouring these marshes on a daily basis, not many birds were going to escape scrutiny.

"Semi-palm?" asked Maik, more because it looked like being a long stay than out of any real interest.

"Semi-palmated, as in webbed," explained Jejeune. "The Semi-palmated Sandpiper has partial webbing between its toes, but its feet are not fully webbed like, say, a duck. There's never been a confirmed sighting in Norfolk in recent history, or so I believe."

Jejeune was suddenly aware that Maik was not the only one paying attention to his explanation. He was confident of his facts up to this point, but he felt it wouldn't hurt to quit while he was ahead.

Along the length of the hide the birders discussed in muted tones issues of size, coloration, and bill length. Tired of listening to comments that made no sense to him, Maik bent to peer through a telescope set up at one of the viewing windows. As Senior had said, Jejeune had seen many Semi-palmated Sandpipers in Canada; hundreds, if not thousands, so he was happy to hold back and let the sergeant take a turn first. As much as he understood the excitement and anticipation of the other birders over seeing one in Norfolk for the first time, he couldn't quite find the same enthusiasm. He remembered in particular viewing a hundred-strong flock once, at Hillman Marsh, north of Point Pelee, and watching as his brother painstakingly trained his scope on every one in turn until he found a Western Sandpiper among them. He still remembered thinking he would never be the birder his brother was. He didn't have that kind of confidence, that almost mystical certainty, that there was a rarity in there, in amongst all those Semi-palms, just waiting to be found.

After a few moments, Maik peeled back from the scope and straightened up.

"Well, I don't know what it is, but it isn't a Semi-palmated Sandpiper."

Senior shot Jejeune a surprised look and then turned a quizzical gaze on the sergeant.

"I was watching it just now as it lifted its foot up," said Maik. "There's no webbing between the toes on that bird."

"Yes, there is a bit more to bird identification than that, thank you," said one of the birders stiffly, looking at Senior for support.

"Is there, Daniel? We tend to get caught up with the possibilities sometimes, but I think in the end, what our eyes tell us should be the final say on the matter. If there is no palmation, then that would be enough to eliminate it for me. Anyway, as it turned I think I might just have gotten the faintest hint of braces, badly abraded, of course, but see what you think."

He backed away from his scope to allow the man a look. Senior turned to direct his explanation to Maik, who was beginning to regret having shown such an interest in the first place.

"Most of the Little Stints we see down here are juveniles. They have fairly distinct pale stripes on their backs. From a distance it looks like the little fellas are wearing braces. Our friend out there," he nodded toward the marsh, "doesn't appear to have any, which is why we thought it might be our long-awaited Semi-palm."

Maik tried his best to look engaged, but he was nevertheless relieved when the other man backed away from the scope. "Could be right, Quentin, faint, but the braces could be there, in this light."

There were subdued mutterings as the birders reconsidered their points of view, and before long the hide had reached a consensus that the bird was, after all, a Little Stint, albeit one with abraded feathers. Jejeune's reluctance to get involved in the initial excitement seemed justified now, but he sensed that, unfairly or not, his own relationship with the local birding community had hardly been enhanced by the way Maik's prosaic approach to birding had brought them all down to earth.

There was a rustle of activity as the men packed up their equipment and began to vacate the hide.

"Looks like it's only one lifer for you this week, then," said the last of the departing birders to Jejeune before the door banged shut behind him. Only Maik, Senior, and Jejeune remained in the semi-darkness of the hide.

Senior nodded toward the door. "I hope you'll forgive them, Inspector," he said with an apologetic smile. "A bit of the old green-eyes, I'm afraid. Part of them wants to believe the Ivory Gull in spite of themselves, and they can't bear the thought that they might have missed out on it simply because

Peter Largemount refused them access to his land. That and they're all a bit nervous, quite frankly. Understandably, of course."

"Nervous?"

"About their records. What they might have revealed."

"I'm sorry?"

"Within a week of asking for everybody's records, Cameron was dead. You can see how some of the chaps think there might be a connection between the two. Absolute tosh as far as I'm concerned, but folklore and superstition have long played a role in these parts, and there's still a surprising affinity for that sort of thing if you scratch below the surface. It doesn't take much for people around here to start adding up two and two and coming up with voodoo." He winked at the detective.

"And you still have no idea what he would have been looking for in those records."

Senior looked at him frankly. Even in the subdued light of the hide, the intensity of his blue eyes was quite startling. "As I've already told you, no. I was hoping he might tell me the next time we spoke."

"Do you think he would have?"

"I should have thought so. We were fierce competitors in the four-hundred race, certainly, but there was none of that acrimonious nonsense you may have heard about in other birding competitions." He shook his head thoughtfully. "No, I'm sure he would have been willing to share his thoughts with me, had he been given the chance."

"Could Brae's concern have been something about the four-hundred list, perhaps? The veracity of some of the records?" Maik tried to make it sound casual, but the implication was clear.

"If it was to do with false entries, I would have been especially interested in his findings, for obvious reasons. But I suppose we shall never know. And yet, you know, there was something troubling him. I called him to ask when we might be able to get the records back. He sounded a bit odd, frankly. Didn't say a lot, but it was definitely there, if you knew him well enough. *Uneasy*. Yes, that would be the word."

Jejeune was silent. Maik waited to see where the inspector wanted to go with this. It seemed like the first thing they had come across in a long time that was worth pursuing. But whatever Jejeune made of this news, it apparently wasn't enough to warrant a comment. Maik stepped into the breach instead.

"It seems strange, Mr. Senior, that somebody with your obvious love of the subject would resign from the county Rare Birds Committee. Can I ask why that was?"

"Optics, Sergeant, I believe they call it these days. Wouldn't do, me up near the top of the list and still deciding whose sightings would count and whose wouldn't. Wouldn't do at all. I offered, they accepted, end of story. There were plenty of good birders to take my place, and in Carrie Pritchard I really do believe they got one of the best."

"I was speaking to Ms. Pritchard just the other day, as a matter of fact," said Maik. "She tells me the committee would almost certainly have accepted a record from Cameron Brae solely on his say so. That means he may have been able to count that American Bittern, after all."

"Really?" Senior considered the possibility. "Normally it would be out of the question, of course, but given Cameron's reputation, and his status in the birding community, I suppose if he had actively insisted on it, there would be enough votes on the committee to push it through. Celebrity is as seductive there as anywhere, Sergeant."

"And if you still had a vote?"

"Me? Ah well, I'm from the old school, Sergeant. A man's word is good enough for me. Depending on the man, of course."

"In that case," said Jejeune thoughtfully, "there could be another reason he didn't report it right away."

"Trying to suppress it, you mean? Wait until he was sure the bird was gone, and then insist on counting it?" Senior shook his head vehemently. "Not Cameron's style at all, Inspector. The last thing he would have wanted was an asterisk by his list, literal or otherwise. To insist on counting a bird that no one else had been given the chance to see, had actually been cheated out of seeing? Well, turn the old victory champagne to vinegar in the mouth, wouldn't it, one would have thought."

Senior nodded at Maik, who was standing at the door with his hand on the latch. "Your sergeant looks as if he has had about all the birding excitement he can stand for one day. I wonder, do you think you will be able to release the records soon? I know the members will be keen to have them back. They represent years of work, and even if most of the lists have already been backed up on computers by now, I'm sure the blood, sweat, and tear-stained originals would still hold great sentimental value for them." A thought seemed to strike him. "You know, if you sent those lists over, I could have a quick look through them myself before I handed them back. I know the people and the places, and the birds, of course. If anything out of the ordinary jumped out, I might be able to spot it."

"That would be very helpful," said Jejeune with not very much thought at all. "I'll have them sent over."

Maik was quiet on their way back to the car. His silence suited Jejeune, who was casually scanning the mudflats and scrapes for odd shapes or flickers of movement. Had he inquired what was on Maik's mind, the sergeant wasn't sure how he would have answered. If, just if, Jejeune was onto something with this four-hundred list theory, how much sense did it make to hand over the most important piece of evidence to one of the people who stood to gain the most from the crime?

Jejeune appeared to have eliminated Senior as a suspect purely on the basis of him being a fellow birder, an approach that seemed to Maik to be about as logical as the *good chap* theory that had failed so spectacularly for MI6 over the years. Why didn't this DCI just let the evidence take its course, instead of simply writing off suspects on gut instinct? First the family, then Christian, and now apparently Senior.

And yet, Jejeune had jumped at Senior's offer so quickly, you couldn't help wondering if it was what he had had in mind all along. So either Jejeune was becoming distracted by all this talk of rarities and sightings, or there was a lot more going on in his mind than a simple sergeant like Danny Maik could work out. Whichever it was, Danny was grateful for the opportunity to keep his thoughts to himself. For now, at least.

18

If it had been a novelty at first, this constant flitting around, it was starting to wear a bit thin now. It could always be the caffeine, Maik supposed; those Canadians certainly loved their coffee, but he doubted the DCI's perpetual motion could be put down solely to a few alkaloid jitters. Yet here he was again now, perched first on a desk on one side of the incident room, and now the other. Not much knocked Danny Maik off his stride, but he could see how Jejeune's constant fidgeting could irk some of the others, if only because they couldn't be sure where he was, or who he was watching, at any given time. The result, Maik had to admit, was a good deal more attention being paid in these briefings than he had seen for a long time.

They had gathered expecting to hear the contents of a new report from the M.E., which promised an update on the time of death. But that had been shouldered offstage by the news that Maik had just delivered to them like a bolt from the heavens. The watch had been returned.

"I don't get it," said Holland. "I mean, that's a flash piece of hardware to be sending back without being asked."

No one else got it either. Murderers sometimes took trophies, but they did not, in the department's collective experience, return them a couple of days later, carefully wrapped in tissue, via the victim's mailbox.

Jejeune felt sets of eyes turning his way by increments, but he had no more idea than anyone else of the significance of this development. It was too important a piece of the puzzle to be ignored, and yet it seemed so out of keeping with the rest of the attack, Jejeune had no idea where it could fit in. He had noticed that neither Brae nor Mandy wore a wedding band, so was the watch the next best thing to taunt the widow with? Was Maik onto something with his theory of a deranged stalker targeting Mandy Brae? Jejeune had little doubt that she was safe for now. Maik had already set up a security detail for her. But Mandy Brae couldn't live like that forever. Sooner or later she would tire of the protection and venture out on her own. And when that happened, she could be in a lot of danger. The only way of preventing that was to catch this killer quickly. And perhaps, with the appearance in the doorway of the young constable with another file, they were about to get just a little closer. The constable handed the file over to Maik without a second glance at Jejeune.

"Right," Maik announced to the room at large, "based on the M.E.'s closer examination, we now have a more precise time of death. Still more or less instantaneous, but now fixed within an hour either side of eight p.m. Help anybody? Or otherwise?"

"Archie Christian is still in the frame," said Holland. "And his run-ins with Brae were a bit more than just a candid exchange of ideas, too. Even before the incident outside the pub, there was a report of a confrontation at Brae's house. Christian went over there after the GM contract was cancelled. Apparently, he lost a shedload of money and he made no secret of who he thought was responsible."

"So that's motive and opportunity," mused Maik, doing his best to ignore Jejeune, who was now handing him back the report, having come forward to take a quick glance at it. "Archie Christian is starting to slip into the picture very nicely."

Maik could see that Holland liked the way this was going. If Jejeune continued to ignore standard police procedures and dismiss suspects in order to push his bird list agenda, there would almost certainly be a day of reckoning coming. As far as Holland was concerned, Archie Christian's guilt or innocence probably didn't matter much one way or the other. But the good, solid police work took you in a more or less direct line to Christian, and the constable would be happy to be on record as the one who had pointed that out when the DCS was casting around asking where it had all gone wrong.

Salter flipped back through the notes on her yellow foolscap pad. She shifted uncomfortably. "Erm, Peter Largemount didn't get to his speaking engagement until just after 7:30. According to those who have caught his act before, he usually likes to arrive early for these things and have a couple of steadiers at the bar. When he wasn't there at his usual time, the MC phoned Largemount's house and cell but got no answer. Largemount eventually came flying in just before he was due to speak. Well flustered, by all accounts, although he put on a good show once he got started."

Maik nodded to himself. Murder in Saltmarsh and cocktails in Norwich half an hour later? Possible, if you knew what you were doing. Maik had seen the way Largemount threw his big Bentley around, and it was apparent he had no great affection for speed limits. If you were lucky enough, or good enough, Saltmarsh to Norwich in thirty minutes could be done. Of course, if you were going to go to all the trouble of manufacturing yourself an alibi, it seemed beyond careless to leave a hole in it this big.

"And, er, you had asked me if there had been any recent changes in Peter Largemount's financials."

Maik was looking down at the M.E.'s report as she spoke, but he knew who Salter was addressing. Maik hadn't asked her anything about Largemount, and it obviously wouldn't have been Holland. No, it was the DCI who liked Largemount. He had had his eye on him from the beginning. This was ridiculous. You couldn't have a murder squad all pulling in different directions like this. Him looking at Senior, Holland going for Christian, and the DCI after Largemount. What about Salter, did she have a favourite? Or was she just content to sift through the reports and offer up the details.

"I don't know if it's relevant," continued Salter, "but Largemount is trying to raise some cash, so he is looking at a new share issue. Since the wind farm productivity is not up to full capacity yet, according to Finance, the only way he could really justify the new issue is if he was to increase his operations. He's proposing a thirty percent expansion."

"How is he going to manage that?" asked Holland. "The only land he's got left is Lesser Marsh."

Enter Brae's request for that earlier biodiversity survey, thought Maik. He flashed a glance at Jejeune, but the DCI was already there. Still, Maik was pleased with himself. Sometimes, it took the old fella a moment or two to catch up, but he usually got there in the end.

"The thing is," continued Salter, "even though Lesser Marsh is on private land, any proposal to drain it would need significant political backing. Thanks to people like Cameron Brae, there's a lot more awareness out there now about the ecological value of wetlands. Only it looks like Largemount's already got some high-level support in place. When the IPO of the company was first floated, a feasibility study for draining Lesser Marsh was included, and the expansion plan received tacit support from ..."

"Beverly Brennan," said Jejeune, just loud enough for the others to hear. He tapped his index finger against his lips. "So

Brae doesn't oppose the wind farm in the first place, though nobody seems to know quite why," he said. "But perhaps this time he decides enough is enough. This is where he makes his stand."

"The Marsh Man facing the possibility of a wetland practically on his own doorstep being drained for development. That would certainly be enough to get Brae up in arms. And we know how adept he was at mobilizing opposition groups and rallying public support to bring an issue to national attention," said Salter. "With Brae's weight behind the protests, suddenly it's not a rubber-stamp approval anymore, even if it is on private land."

Maik considered the idea. As a motive for murder it was weak. Still, it probably had as much going for it as a race to see four hundred birds.

The door opened and DCS Shepherd leaned in, one hand on the doorknob and the other supporting herself on the door jamb. It was a dynamic pose, very American cop show, although one day, thought Maik, if she wasn't careful, she was going to pop right out of one of those silk blouses, and that would add a different kind of drama to her entrance entirely.

Shepherd was wearing the expression of someone who had recently spent a lot of time assuring people about things she was now finding might not be possible, after all. She looked over her spectacles at Jejeune, still perched on his desk at the side of the room, as if she felt he might be a long way from the action. She turned her attention to the incident board. No new additions. But then, no one had been eliminated yet, either.

"I thought Peter Largemount was in the clear. That dinner thing in Norwich."

"The M.E.'s report has revised the possible time of death, Ma'am. It puts him back in the picture."

Maik was never less than courteous to any superior officer, but he remained wary of this one. She spent half her time telling everybody how much she trusted them to get on with things, and the other half checking up on them.

She crooked a finger toward Jejeune and waited patiently while he joined her in the corridor. "Every time I think we have taken a step forward with this case, we seem to end up two steps further behind," she said, by way of an opening gambit. "Now I don't know why Peter Largemount has suddenly sprung back into the picture, and I don't much care. I understood you were pursuing this business about bird lists. Do you have any more on that?"

Jejeune looked at the DCS for a long moment, and when he spoke it was as if he was choosing his words with extra caution. The exaggerated care slowed the delivery to a trickle.

"I know for certain that Brae was looking at records of marsh birds in the area, waders specifically," he conceded carefully, "and it now seems that Largemount has made inquiries about the feasibility of draining Lesser Marsh to expand his operations. A connection between the two seems possible, at least."

It was Shepherd's turn to be silent for a moment. "This bird angle, whatever it is, is it a viable line of inquiry? Because if it's not, we need to establish that before we waste any more time on it. I want you to pursue it, Domenic, and decide one way or the other. If I have to go before the DAC and defend the idea of local citizens killing one another over a list of birds, I want to know we're not going to end up looking like idiots when it's all said and done. Firm it up for me, will you, Domenic, before we go off chasing any more shadows."

Jejeune wouldn't have minded doing just that, but it was going to be a lot harder than it sounded, putting any meat on those bones. And in the mean time, pursuing any other lines of inquiry, such as the links between Brae's interest in waders and Peter Largemount's development plans, would have to be put on the back burner. Or was that what Shepherd intended?

She turned a solicitous look on Jejeune. "And you're sure everything is okay? Personally, I mean? You just seem a little, well … subdued. This case not got you down, or anything?"

No, it wasn't the case. It was the job, the stifling, pointless, endlessness of poring over statements, sifting through evidence, when you knew the answers were never going to come from there. The work that had to be done, because it had to be done, for no other reason than because it met the expectations of those in command.

But how to put that into words, to someone who had shown so much faith in you, gambled a career, some might say, to bring you on board, and still reassure them that you would work to the absolute limits of your ability to solve the case. So Jejeune said nothing beyond assuring Shepherd that everything was okay.

Shepherd nodded absently. "Just a thought, of course, but you could try looking a bit more engaged. Just until they've gotten more used to your style, you know."

Jejeune promised he would. Try, that is.

19

At first glance, the home seemed to be unoccupied. There was no car in the driveway, and no signs of movement behind the wispy lace curtains. But Jejeune heard noises coming from the back of the house, so he made his way around to the garden and peered over the fence. A slightly built woman in her sixties was bending over a flowerbed, plucking weeds by hand and dropping them into a small plastic bucket. She straightened when Jejeune cleared his throat, her hand automatically moving to support her back.

"Chief Inspector Jejeune. How nice. I expected you would be coming by sooner or later. Come in, please. I was just about to stop anyway." She smiled and patted her hip. "These old bones don't take kindly to my gardening calisthenics these days, I'm afraid. Why don't you have a look around while I go and put the kettle on."

Jejeune wandered around the garden, taking it all in. The small, neat lawn was surrounded on all sides by planted borders; the shrubbery carefully arranged by height so that it seemed to slope up and out like the stands of a small stadium. The plants and foliage, an array of fruit trees, berry bushes, and smaller ornamental shrubs, had been chosen with care. It would have been difficult, thought Jejeune, to provide garden birds with a greater choice of habitat and food sources in such a small area.

Katherine Brae emerged from the house carrying a tea tray. She set it on a small wicker table and eased herself into one of the chairs. She patted the seat beside her and Jejeune joined her.

"I hope you're enjoying it out here," she said as she poured. She looked up at Jejeune. "If it makes you feel any better, you never really had a choice, you know, not once Colleen had set her sights on bringing you here. I was her teacher at junior school. She always tended to get what she wanted, even then. How is she? Any closer to revealing this mysterious new love in her life?"

Jejeune inclined his head to one side.

"No, and even if she were, you would keep it to yourself. Quite right, too. One hears things in a community this size, it's inevitable. But one does one's own position no good at all by repeating them."

Jejeune commented on the beauty around them. Until he came out to Norfolk, he had thought English country gardens like this were a thing of the past.

"Yes, I think Cameron probably found it more difficult to leave his garden than he did to leave me," she said with a soft smile, to show there were no hard feelings. "I'm not sure he was ever truly happy in that big new house. He liked being so close to the marsh, of course. He always hoped to live near it, but I think he would have preferred a smaller place. Not that he got much say, I imagine. I understand his new wife is a woman who is used to having things her way."

"Your son seems to have an uncomfortable relationship with her. That's hardly unusual, of course, but I get the sense there may be more to it."

"He thinks she is unworthy of his father's attention, and who can blame him, especially since he didn't get all that much of it himself. My husband was a man who found being a parent very difficult. But despite that, perhaps even because of it, Malcolm still wished for his father's approval. Which son doesn't? I always felt that was why he was always trying so hard with his environmental activism."

"He told us all that ended with his university days."

"His formal academic pursuits, certainly, but as for his involvement with grassroots organizations, as far as I am aware, he is as committed as ever. I don't think you leave a group like Earth Front that easily. He used to say it's like the mafia. Once you're in, you're in for life. I do worry about some of the activities they have been associated with, but Malcolm assures me they only ever indulge in forms of protest that are legitimate within a democratic society."

"Vandalism and arson are not legitimate forms of protest in any society. Earth Front has a pretty strong track record of violence and criminal activity."

"There are extremists in all organizations, Inspector, as I'm sure you know. As passionate as Malcolm is at times, I doubt he would ever become involved in anything illegal."

Jejeune looked around the garden. In the almost idyllic calm of a late summer's morning, it was hard to imagine how much turmoil and anguish this house must have seen when Cameron Brae had announced that he was leaving his wife for a newer model.

"If I asked you to talk about your husband, where would you start?"

The question was so direct and unexpected that Katherine Brae's hand shook a little as she put her teacup down.

"He was not always an easy man to live with," she said cautiously. "You had to be prepared to defend your position at all times. How could you enjoy chain store coffee and at the same time support sustainability, for example? He couldn't always appreciate the subtle shades of grey, those compromises that make us human. He was relentless in his pursuit of clarity. He really, genuinely wanted to understand your point of view, and the reasoning behind it, and he wanted to be sure you did, too."

She sighed, as if unwilling to go on, but she had not yet finished purging herself of the well of emotions she had kept to herself until now. "It was wearying, at times. If someone made an inconsistent statement on TV, for example, I'm afraid there was no one else around to hear Cameron's rebuttal except me."

"Still, there must have been some satisfaction in seeing the finished article, the crystal-clear intellect we all saw on TV, and thinking you had helped to hone it."

Katherine Brae smiled softly. "An anvil contributes greatly to the making of a horseshoe, Chief Inspector, but I doubt it gets a great deal of satisfaction from the final product. It's funny, though. I always felt there was an element of vengeance to his television interviews, as if he was trying to make somebody pay for something. What, I have no idea." She paused. "I just don't think it really brought him any real happiness. I'm not sure anything did, apart from that marsh. He really did love it, you know. Worshipped it in an almost spiritual way. He would leave before breakfast to watch the sunrise there. And at this time of year, the glimpse of a Spotted Redshank on its way down to its wintering grounds, or even a passing Ring Ouzel, it all was wonderful to him. He would come home for breakfast and sit there, where you are, with the kind of look that a wife could only dream of being able to bring to her husband's face. Well, this wife anyway."

Jejeune seemed to find something interesting about his tea cup. He turned it carefully in his hands, as if trying to memorize the delicate floral pattern around the rim. "Did he ever try his questioning techniques on Professor Alwyn?"

"I would doubt it. Professor Alwyn is one of those men who think professional achievement absents one from the need for any social skills. I'm sure he would have been quite forthright in rebutting any challenge to his beliefs. Besides, providing you were able to defend your position to Cameron's satisfaction, he was perfectly willing to let you hold it. Of course, that is still very hard criteria to meet. Not many people could hold opposing points of view to Cameron and yet maintain his respect. I suspect Professor Alwyn was one, though. Certainly at one time."

"Do you know why they stopped working together?"

"Cameron never really spoke about it. All I can tell you is that he was never quite the same man after they parted ways. He was still as committed to his work, of course, but there was more urgency, as if he needed to achieve something tangible in a hurry. Haste had never been an issue before. Cameron had always been so methodical, so patient. Of course, it was just after they parted company that he got his TV show. And then, a short time later ..."

She offered a small apologetic smile, though for whom the apology was intended, Jejeune didn't know. "There is not much more to say about it. In truth, I suppose our marriage had ended a long time before she appeared. It was just that neither of us had noticed. They just found each other, working on the show, and then at a few charity events. Once she bought that house by the marsh, I suppose their liaison was inevitable. Cameron was astute enough to realize the value of her celebrity status in promoting his causes. And for his part, I really do believe he saw her as his personal reclamation project, a little lost wilderness all of her own. Cameron could be remarkably naive in some ways."

A charm of Goldfinches swooped in and settled on a stand of thistles, pecking at the down. It was a scene Jejeune had seen a thousand times on calendar pages, one of the most picturesque in nature. It still gave him a frisson of delight and he paused for a moment before speaking.

"Beautiful, aren't they?" she said with the quiet indulgence of a person who has seen someone's attention stolen away on many such occasions. "Of all the birds that visit this garden, I believe the Goldfinches are my favourite. They seem so innocent, somehow, so ..." she searched the air for a word, "harmless, I suppose."

"Did your husband ever have an affair while you were married?"

There was, in Jejeune's experience, no easy way to ask the question, and he suspected that Katherine Brae would be insulted by any attempt to wrap it in euphemisms.

"The wife; the last to know but the first to suspect? No, Inspector, Cameron was never deceptive, even about her. He was perfectly candid about his intentions, right from the beginning. It wasn't in his nature to be dishonest. It would have gone against so many of his principles. I used to tell him he was the only truly honest person I had ever known. Wouldn't hear a word of it, of course. '*No, Katherine, I don't deserve that sort of respect.*' That was Cameron, you see, always harder on himself than anyone else." She paused, to give Jejeune's question one final consideration, and then shook her head. "No, I am sure of it. He was never unfaithful during our marriage."

She looked around at the garden. The Goldfinches had gone, leaving the thistles bouncing gently on their stems. "We worked on this garden together, tending it, changing it, even bullying it into shape when necessary. Even if we were pottering around in separate corners, I always felt we were linked in some way, working toward a common goal. But you know, I don't think either of us really wanted to finish it. It was the process, you see, the working on it together, that we enjoyed."

She sighed. "I think that is what I find hardest to understand. How can you simply abandon something into which you have put so much time and effort? Cameron was a complex man, but he was never a callous one. Not before her." She brightened. "Anyway, I suspect you have better things to do than listen to me chattering about my garden. And since you're not going to tell me who Colleen is seeing these days, I'm sure you will need to be on your way."

Jejeune stood up to leave. "Thank you for the tea. I enjoyed it, and your garden."

"I'm not sure my ramblings have been any use to you, though, Inspector."

"On the contrary, you've been most helpful," he said. And Jejeune meant it, too.

20

It has been like this forever, thought Domenic Jejeune. For a thousand years and more, men and women have been greeted by the same sights and sounds as they worked these coastal margins. The same play of sunlight on the waters, the same quiet rush of winds through the reeds. The ebb and flow of tides had changed the shape of the land over the centuries, but the essential rhythms of nature, the seasons, the weather patterns, those had remained constant for as long as humans had inhabited this land.

From his elevated wooden platform, Jejeune surveyed the coastline in a slow pass, squinting against the light spangles that bounced off the gently rippling water. Not a single element of modern life intruded. No buildings, no wires, no pylons. Just birds, by the hundred, resting on the tidal mudflats, or wheeling lazily in the sky above. And the sound, the beautiful sweet silence, broken only by the crush of the waves and the occasional plaintive call of a seabird. It brought a feeling as close to peace as Jejeune ever found these days.

Lindy shifted impatiently. "I do try, honestly Dom, but I just don't get it. We could go for a nice walk along the beach together, get all the fresh air you like and see just as many birds. But just standing here, watching, I mean, it's like fishing, without the excitement."

But there was excitement. Could she not feel it, the pent up energy surging through the stillness? It was, Jejeune knew, the strain of the hunter, the waiting, the stalking. Not now to strike with a bow, or a gun, but just watching, waiting for a flicker, a shimmer of movement in the tranquility of the landscape. But he was aware now that the spell had been broken and would not be recovered. He turned to Lindy and lent her his arm. They descended the wooden steps and began walking back toward the main intersection of trails.

They were almost upon it before Jejeune noticed a movement at the water's edge. Quentin Senior, his drab jacket gathered around him and a battered grey cap covering his white hair, melded into the reedbeds so completely it was a moment before Lindy could pick out what Jejeune was looking at.

"Anything special?" asked the detective.

Senior turned slowly and stared up at the two figures above him on the track. "Ah, Chief Inspector, and friend, I see. Another one who, if I may say so, bears the expression of a long-suffering non-birder. Really, Inspector, does none of your acquaintances share your passion for our pastime?"

He smiled warmly to rob his words of offence and made his way up the steep slope. He extended one of his meaty paws to Lindy. "Forgive me, my dear, but I see that look a lot around here. Quentin Senior, at your service. Welcome to Holkham. A couple of months early for the Pink-footed Geese, but there's plenty else to see. Whatdda they call ya, anyway?"

Lindy had been prepared for the worst, but instead found herself immediately drawn to this hulking, avuncular man. Besides, anybody who greeted her in such an unabashedly manly way could surely be forgiven a "my dear" or two.

After the introductions, Senior turned toward Jejeune. "I never did find your American Bittern at Great Marsh, Inspector, and perhaps more tellingly, there's been no mention of one at all on the wires. As far as I can tell, not even the most notorious rumourmongers have gotten wind of it. As I said before, in these parts, that can only mean that Cameron never mentioned it to anybody."

Jejeune looked thoughtful, but said nothing. Senior looked as if he might want to say something else, too, but for some reason was having trouble getting around to it.

Lindy felt the need to break the silence, which was threatening to become uncomfortable. "There's something moving in the grass down there," she said, pointing. Both men snapped an instinctive glance with their binoculars, but Senior didn't need to dwell on the sighting.

"Sedge Warbler. He's been there most of the morning. God knows what he's doing. Just keeps going up and down the reed stems. Just for the fun of it, I suppose."

"Do birds do that?" asked Lindy. "I thought there always had to be a reason for everything in nature."

"Is fun not reason enough?" Senior was shaking his great white head in mock chastisement. "Don't you believe all that nonsense about the mighty mechanical machine that is nature. Birds know how to enjoy themselves just as much as you or me. I remember seeing an article about Ravens some time back. There they were, sliding down snowy hills on their backs, jumping into snowbanks and the like. The only possible explanation could have been the sheer joy of it. Crows, too, I suspect, have a well-developed sense of mischief, and no doubt there's plenty of fun in that rookery near Peter Largemount's house, if you cared to watch 'em for long enough." Senior checked himself in mid-flight. "Forgive me, my dear, get me on the subject of birds and I could go on for hours. But I must get on, half a day here already and not much to show for it, I'm afraid."

"You've been here all morning? Here and I thought it was only senior police officers who could pinch half a day in the middle of the week to go birding."

Senior smiled indulgently. "Ah, but despite appearances to the contrary, my dear, you are looking upon a gainfully employed person."

"You're working?" asked Lindy. She saw a shadow flicker across Domenic's features, and realized a half second too late where this conversation was going.

"Indeed I am. I'm gathering a bit of data for the ministry so they can put it into a report and store it on a dusty shelf somewhere." Senior leaned forward conspiratorially and nodded toward Jejeune. "They all get that look, I'm afraid," he said with a wink, his tone halfway between humour and genuine apology. "And this is normally where the significant others would like me to shake 'em out of it, tell them what it's really like, the drudgery of sitting here for hour after hour studying birds. Wet Wednesdays in the wind and the rain, and all that." He straightened up. "Can't do it, I'm afraid. Birding for a living is every bit as wonderful as it sounds. To see a parcel of Oystercatchers sweep in first thing in the morning, wheedling and prodding away for their breakfast, or catch a glimpse of that shimmering green as a spring of Teal flashes by, I tell you, it's enough to restore a man's soul."

Lindy looked at Jejeune, whose expression had come to rest somewhere between sadness and rapture.

"I think you had him at Oystercatchers," she said. "But surely, you're only talking about short-term contract positions. And, I mean, not to be blunt or anything, but ministry studies are notoriously underfunded. I can't imagine someone being able to do this as a full-time job." At least somebody should be fighting Domenic's inclination to chuck his police career away so he could become a paid birder. Besides, there was no point in having a reputation as a feisty journalist if you weren't going to trot it out occasionally.

Senior smiled delightedly.

"Well, it doesn't pay as well as a chief inspector, certainly, but with the birding tours, the odd lecture, a pittance from the university grants committee.... Thankfully, my humble abode was paid off about four generations ago. A crust and a curd is enough to keep body and soul together. As long as Woodforde's don't keep raising the price of the Wherry, I should have enough to see me into my dotage. That's the beautiful thing about birding, my dear, it's so remarkably inexpensive. The greatest show on earth, sun up to sun down, all for the cost of a pair of binoculars."

He tapped his own battered Zeiss Jenoptems, and gave Lindy another of his wonderful yellow smiles. From the far side of the marsh a couple waved, and Senior waved back. "Canadians, over here on a birding holiday. They were telling me about a spot called Thickson's Woods, a little east of Toronto. Ever hear of it?"

Jejeune thought he had, though he had never been there.

"The chap claimed Ian Fleming would most likely have birded there. It's right next to Camp X, apparently, on the shores of Lake Ontario, where he did all that hush-hush training in the war. Well, we all know Fleming was a birder. Took the name James Bond from the author of a bird guide, of course, but I would say that claim was a bit circumstantial, eh, Inspector? Still, one never knows. I love to hear stories like that. Just goes to show, even the smallest of birding spots have their own bit of history."

"Few as storied as this coast, though, as I understand it," said Lindy. There was something lovely about this man's passion for birding, and Lindy, almost despite herself, couldn't resist the urge to prolong his enthusiasm.

"Indeed," said Senior brightly. "D'ye know, there are written bird records for this area going back over a thousand years." He held up a hand, as if anticipating a protest. "All right, I'll grant you, most of those early accounts were more to do with what was going to end up on the dinner table. I say *biodiversity list*, you say *menu*, but still, it's an impressive claim."

As much as he would have liked to allow Senior to continue with Lindy's birding seminar, Jejeune had a number of pressing matters to cover. "About those records?"

"Nothing yet, I'm afraid, Inspector. Other than the deliberate mistake, that is. Spot it? For the moment I'd thought perhaps you'd done it yourself. Wondered if they did things a little differently in Canada."

It was likely that Senior was joking, but Lindy knew that, for some reason, his opinion of Domenic's birding skills was very important to Dom. She could see he was fighting the urge to protest his innocence.

Senior turned to Lindy. "One of the families was in the wrong order," he said. He fished out his battered bird guide and riffled through the pages to make his point. "Each order of birds has certain families within it. Among the Ciconiiformes, for example, we have *Ardeidae,* our friends the bitterns, and also *Ciconiidae*, the storks. But, sandpipers, the *Scolopacidae* are part of Charadriiformes, so what on earth were they doing in amongst the Gruiformes order, the rails, moorhens, and suchlike?"

"Is it significant, do you think?" asked Lindy.

"Well, it's not for me to tell the inspector his business, of course. All I will say is that Cameron would never have made a mistake like that. Of course, I'm sure your young man is far too clever to have missed any of this himself."

Lindy knew Jejeune wasn't all that comfortable discussing just how clever he was, and she wasn't surprised that he let Senior's comment pass.

The joy melted from Senior's eyes. Whatever it was he had wanted to say earlier, he was going to get around to it now.

"Bad news on the Ivory Gull sighting, I'm afraid, Inspector. I'm hearing the committee won't be able to validate it. Without photographic evidence, and in the absence of a corroborating report … I'm sure you understand."

Senior had couched the news as delicately as possible, but the message was clear. Domenic Jejeune did not have sufficient prestige among the local birding community to have a report accepted at face value. Out here a reputation like that could take decades to earn.

"No reflection on your skills, I assure you," continued Senior. "It's just that, well, to be frank, one or two of the members are concerned about the number of rarities being reported lately. The committee is keen to ensure we don't harm our reputation. This month alone there has been Duncan's Slender-billed Gull, which at least appears genuine. But then, right on the back of it we had this business with the Semi-palmated Sandpiper that wasn't. Somehow it got out onto the wires as a confirmed sighting and now the committee is in the uncomfortable process of having to rescind it. The Ivory Gull, as you know, has already made its way out into the wider world, and I'm afraid validating another unsubstantiated first record in the same week as the Semi-palm debacle, well … you can see …"

"Of course," said Jejeune. "It's not important."

But Lindy could tell that it was. And while the two men stood in silence, she reflected on fascinating complexities of the man who shared her life. Here was someone who had been singled out for praise by the Home Secretary, who had been fêted by the national media for his role in solving a high-profile murder case. And yet to the untrained eye it had all simply washed over him, leaving not the faintest residue. But this, this smallest of slights from a tiny birdwatching committee on the edge of nowhere, had cut him to the quick. She felt a protective urge well within her, but she had no idea what to offer as support.

The men traded birding small talk, but the conversation was transparently forced on both sides, and it was clear that each wanted to go his separate way, to escape, if possible, the lingering tang of discomfort that Senior's news had brought.

"Well, I must be off," said Senior finally. "Something will be out there waiting for me. You never know what, but you always know it's going to be wonderful." And with a wave of his giant hand, he was gone.

"It doesn't matter, Dom," said Lindy, watching Senior's retreating form as far as the bend in the path. "You know what you saw. Maybe it will show up again. Or maybe you'll find this other bird, the one that Brae saw. The American Bittern. That would teach them, wouldn't it?"

Jejeune stopped to look over the mudflats and pulled the bins up sharply to his eyes, but Lindy sensed it was more to avoid eye contact than to view some phantom movement out over the water. The wind was beginning to pick up and she gathered her light jacket around her. "I'm going back to the car. Stay a while, if you like. I have a book to read. I'll be fine."

Jejeune watched her leave and then turned again to look out over the flat landscape. He watched as two incoming Mallards rowed hard against the gathering breezes, and his thoughts drifted once again to the earliest peoples to have called this area home. For all their contact with nature, they would still have been prey to human emotions: sadness, melancholy, disappointment. But what of other, darker human forces: treachery, jealousy, anger. Did those throb in the hearts of these people? Did they shape their actions, and reactions? He knew that there was anthropological evidence to suggest that there were murders back then. But over what? Partners, territory, possessions? Motives as old as human existence. But where were they in Cameron Brae's story? Like everything else, missing.

His thoughts turned to Quentin Senior. Jejeune had purposely avoided mentioning the mistake when he gave him the lists. Like Brae, Senior was far too good a birder to make an error like that under normal circumstances, but panic, especially murder-induced panic, could play havoc with a man's composure. But would Senior now so brashly draw it to Jejeune's attention, if he had been the one who incorrectly replaced the wader family list? It wasn't absolute proof that Senior was innocent, but was a brave gambit if not. *Here we go again*, thought Jejeune, *the willingness to interpret grey areas in a suspect's favour*. That was the problem with the truth. You only got to believe one version. The last time he had abandoned his objectivity and invested himself in a suspect's innocence, the results had made him vow to remain detached forever more. Would he ever learn? With a sigh, Jejeune turned away from the coastline and began a slow walk toward the car.

21

"You can keep up this surveillance all night, but I'm pretty sure this lot all have alibis for the time of the murder."

Lindy thrust a glass of wine into Jejeune's hand and kissed his cheek. It was true, he was watching them. It was something he did, instinctively, whenever he was in a crowd. Find a spot, a wall, a corner, a nineteenth-century oak beam, and watch. Watch the interplay of people, their unguarded expressions, their gestures, their body language. But if Domenic Jejeune could readily acknowledge that he was, by trade, a watcher, he could not have explained what it was that he was looking for. Perhaps it was just another way of trying to understand human nature. But Lindy was right. Tonight was not the time. Tonight was for soft banter and light-hearted humour, and immersing himself in the waves of genial good feeling that were swirling around his living room. But even here, in his own home, he couldn't let his guard down entirely. And if not here, he wondered with a slight sadness, when could he ever?

The small dinner party, he noticed, had somehow morphed into a gathering for twenty people or more. Apparently, a trip out into the wilds of north Norfolk did not hold the terrors that Domenic had hoped it might. In truth, he had deliberately avoided contact with most of these people for some time. But it was not, as had been assumed, because Domenic had outgrown the 'little people,' as they now referred to themselves. He simply found himself all too frequently put in the position of having to somehow explain his success. Nobody much mentioned his failure anymore. It was almost as if it was seen as bad form to bring it up. So people just tiptoed around it, wondering instead where all his marvellous insights came from, how he made those wonderful, vital links in his cases. But Domenic didn't tiptoe around his past failure. For him, it was a constant companion.

However, he had become aware, they both had, of an undercurrent of resentment as his refusals and regrets became a predictable pattern. Tonight, he hoped, would go some way to restoring Lindy, at least, to the group's good graces.

Jejeune watched her gliding effortlessly between the little knots of people crowded into their front room. She was among her friends here. *Their friends*, he reminded himself. Only not really. This group had been together since college, for the most part, long before Domenic had entered the scene. Looking around the room, other latecomers were easy enough to spot, standing on the fringes, smiling valiantly, trying too hard to break into the conversation. If he was honest, he had always struggled to find common ground with Lindy's circle of friends. It was tacitly understood that his work was off limits as a topic of conversation, and while that didn't stop them trying, Jejeune did little to encourage any questions that went down that route. And while he enjoyed the occasional *bon mot* himself, he didn't really share their desire to elevate witty ripostes into an art form. So that left birding. Out of politeness, one or two of the circle usually inquired about his latest forays, but like all hobbies, there was only so far you could progress into the subject without running up against the specifics. Cue the awkward silences, and the anxious glances around the room for other conversations to join. Domenic realized that without the allure of his job, he would have long ago faced excommunication from this group anyway. It was, he knew, the potential thrill of forbidden secrets that drew them to him. He understood. It was hard wired into all of us. It was the same with Lindy's work, their fascination with the inside story, all the hidden dirt on her latest investigations.

There was a sudden explosion of laughter as Lindy scored a direct hit. She had dismissed a proponent of a monorail system as having a one-track mind. A burst of spontaneous applause had even erupted from one or two of the group, and she was now basking in the glow. Dom wasn't even sure it was an original line. He thought the two of them had seen it somewhere — an email, perhaps. But what did it matter? He eased himself off the oak beam and moved into the room to join the throng. Observations on hold, time for some fieldwork.

Even if Jejeune was now adept at gently shifting conversations away from his work, there were other topics outside his comfort zone, and one was on the horizon now: the wine. Knowledgeable comments were beginning to build, and Domenic could sense that someone was soon going to be seeking his input. What was this one that Lindy had chosen? Some kind of reptile?

"Lizard Point," supplied a man in a leather jacket leaning into the circle.

Jejeune breathed a sigh of relief, Thank you, Martin. But his gratitude was short-lived. Because Martin's invoice wasn't long in coming.

"Listen, Dom. I was chatting to Lindy the other day, and she mentioned that the time might be better just now to ask you about that brief stint on the show."

The 'show' was the current affairs program Martin produced for one of the independent networks. They had discussed

Domenic's appearance before, but he had always been able to find reasons to avoid it. Martin stared at him frankly through his gold rimmed spectacles. Wiry black hair, greying at the temples, framed a lean face with sharp features. For a slightly built man, the producer had a remarkably confident presence, standing square to Jejeune with his wine glass held to attention at his chest.

"A colleague of mine has some fascinating theories on criminal behavior. I think it would make very good TV," said Jejeune. "I could put you in touch."

"Yes, only part of this segment's appeal would be that it featured you, specifically, you see. *Domenic Jejeune: Flavour of the Month*, and all that. It would be *your* insights, *your* approach that the public would want to hear."

Jejeune glanced around the room like a man looking for a hidden passageway. He saw Lindy again, stunning in her plain blue dress, with just a simple gold necklace and earrings to set it off. The jewellery was a gift from him, but he didn't recognize the dress. He wondered if she had bought it just for tonight. When had she found the time to go shopping? He realized that there were great gaps in Lindy's day, her life, about which he knew nothing. She sensed him watching and rippled her fingers in a wave. He smiled back.

Martin had given her some helpful leads early on in her career, and it would mean a lot to Lindy to repay the debt. Jejeune sighed inwardly. What did it matter, really? The segment would not change anything, for better or worse.

Martin was too experienced to miss the signs. He had closed many deals like this one, and had begun his thanks even before Jejeune had voiced his agreement. There was just a hint of triumph in Martin's smile as he wheeled away to savour his coup.

Domenic drifted slowly over to where Lindy was holding court. She was telling the assembled crowd about her latest feature for the magazine. He stayed at the edge of the circle, just outside it.

"Honestly, I sometimes think people would be more interested in a story about *no* corruption." Lindy dragged her hand across an imaginary banner headline. "*Honest Financier Found: Taxidermist Called Immediately*. What do you think? Oh God, I love this song."

He watched her, so full of life and so connected to her emotions, swaying gently, with her wine glass cradled to her chest, eyes half closed, dreamily immersing herself in the lyrics of a Leonard Cohen song. What could a young, vibrant, angst-free creature find in music whose sole purpose, it seemed to Jejeune, was to take away your will to live? Human tastes, he thought; a mystery far beyond the abilities of a simple policeman.

She opened her eyes and saw him watching her. She came over, popping a samphire spring roll in his mouth as she arrived. Lindy had taken on the food preparations for the party with zeal, and some of the dishes, such as the tempura oyster, had been a big hit. The mussel crumble had gone down well, too, even if one of the group had already christened it "mustn't grumble." But others, like the cockle fritters and this samphire concoction, had been less successful. Still, he doubted that the success, or otherwise, of her culinary efforts would matter to Lindy tonight. She was enjoying herself, and she was determined to see that everyone else was, too. And that included him.

"So, anyone mention your job yet?"

"One or two."

"It's a compliment, Dom. Your work is interesting, and people know you are good at it. I know it's uncomfortable for you, but they mean well. By the way, Simon and Nancy are staying over. I thought we could take them up to Heacham in the morning. We can have breakfast on the way."

Jejeune didn't disagree, though in his opinion, the undeniable beauty of the Norfolk Lavender Farm paled in comparison to the sight of the sea lavender that turned the marshes into a spectacular carpet of purple at this time of year. But he supposed he understood why Lindy would want to steer their overnight guests more toward tourist sites than birding ones.

She looked sad and paused for a moment, as if unsure if she should continue. "You've been thinking about that man, haven't you? Senior. I saw the look on your face. You think you just want to pack it all in and do the same thing. But that's not you, Dom. You solve crimes. It's what you are good at. It's what you were meant to do."

"It doesn't matter. Really."

"But that's just it. It does. I can tell. It matters more than your bloody job. And all you can do is pretend that it doesn't because everyone has built this little box around you called 'Detective Genius,' and now you are trapped inside. But I see how you come alive when you are birding, how much more enthusiastic you are, how much more excited. I never see that when you are going out to work."

"I'm usually investigating violent death. It's hard to get too enthusiastic."

"You know what I mean."

"I'm fine, honestly."

"Are you? Really?" The lightness disappeared from her. "I don't want to lose you because you're unhappy. It happens, you know. You're sad at work, and then suddenly your home life doesn't look so good either anymore, and so you start to look elsewhere for your happiness."

Jejeune started to protest, but a Lindy under full steam was not one to halt to take on arguments. Especially not a Lindy with a little too much wine in the fuel tank already.

"You need your job, Dom. You need somewhere to focus

your abilities, to use that, go on then, I'll say it, that *gift* you have; that gift nobody can buy or learn, that separates the great from the merely very good, from the rest of us. You have it, Dom. I've seen it. You hear things others don't; you see them in a different way. Why do you think the DCS is even considering this bird list idea of yours? Because it's you. Anybody else would have been laughed out of the force. And knowing you, it's probably going to turn out to be right. I'm not saying being a detective has to be all there is for you. A lot of people in this room no doubt have interests that they love far more than their jobs. But to have the kind of talents you have, and to let them all go to waste, just to watch birds … it's wrong, Dom. Just wrong."

Lindy backed off. She had said her piece and they both knew Domenic wasn't going to offer any resistance. Not tonight.

"I heard Martin saying you have agreed to be interviewed for his program. Thank you. I know how much you dislike doing them." She paused, tears starting to her eyes. The drink, thought Jejeune. And perhaps something more. "You're a good man, Dom. A really good man. It's just your rotten luck that you're a good detective, too."

Someone across the room called her and she was gone. It had been an odd way to put it. But good journalists sometimes had a way of capturing complex truths in a single phrase. And Lindy was a very good journalist indeed.

22

The orange glow was visible as soon as Jejeune's Range Rover crested the rise on the outskirts of the village. It was impossible to tell from here the size or intensity of the blaze, or how far off it was, but the savage starkness of the flames against the surrounding blackness alarmed Jejeune. He put his foot down, plunging on through the dark country lanes, heading toward the false sunrise on the horizon.

As he slowed down to make the turn into the driveway, Tony Holland approached and tapped on the window. "Pity you had to come out in the middle of the night, sir. No bodies that we know of, but as it's a person of interest, Sergeant Maik thought you'd want to know about this." He waved his gloved hand toward the other end of the driveway, as if to emphasise the distance between himself and the messy end of the action. "If you had gotten here a bit sooner, you would have run into the DCS and Beverly Brennan. Both gone now. Not sure why they were here. Still, if it's important, I imagine they'll fill you in, eh, sir?"

He withdrew without waiting to see how Jejeune received his report and watched the tail lights bounce along the unpaved driveway toward the house.

From the forecourt, Archie Christian's house showed no signs of damage, but all the noise, and the light, was coming from around back. Jejeune parked and walked around to the side. The judas gate swung crookedly, the lock having been crudely crowbarred. Jejeune stepped through into the rear courtyard, where he was greeted by scenes of controlled chaos. Shattered glass lay everywhere, and water-soaked furniture and possessions were piled in untidy heaps around the yard. Water dripped from the scorched metal skeleton of the greenhouse, and Jejeune could see pools where the runoff from the fire hoses had started to gather in the depressions in the ground. The far gates stood open, and a single fire engine was parked halfway inside. A number of cars were parked at odd angles around the courtyard, well away from the scene of destruction in front of the greenhouse.

The fire itself had been brought under control, but patches of grass and debris still smouldered and flared into occasional flames. In the flickering light, Jejeune thought he could make out words on the side of one of the buildings, but before he could read them properly, the guttering flames had died down again.

He saw Maik and Christian standing together near one of the halogen floodlights the fire department had set up. The conversation looked amiable enough from this distance, but Jejeune knew that both men were capable of making their point without waving their arms about. Christian was standing with his hands in his pockets, feet spread apart like a used car salesman. He was wearing a button down shirt with a tie loosely knotted just below the neck. He had on a pair of immaculate Italian silk trousers and highly polished patent leather shoes. Whatever he had been doing when the fire broke out, Archie Christian had been fully dressed at the time.

"I'm telling you, I can deal with this," Christian was saying evenly as Jejeune approached the two men. "It's just a couple of nutters at Earth Front, got it into their heads that I had something to do with Brae's death, that's all."

"You saw them?" asked Maik. "These Earth Front members?"

Christian shook his head. "Didn't see anything. First I heard was the glass breaking. By the time I got out here, they were gone. And then the fire kicked off and I had to get that dealt with. But it was Earth Front, all right. I told you, they've been sending me nasty notes. Besides, this is right up their alley, isn't it? Bit of damage, a few naughty words on the wall, then run away and hide."

"More than a bit of damage, though, Archie," said Maik. "There's nothing left of your sunroom. If you had been inside we might have had more to investigate than just criminal damage and arson."

"Investigate? You're having a laugh. You lot couldn't find a dog's tail if I showed you where the arse end was. Besides, whoever did this will be alibied all the way up to their you-know-wheres." He shook his head slowly. "Help from the plod. Nah, I don't think so." He wandered off to examine some charred debris the firefighters had just brought out into the courtyard.

"The senior fire officer says definitely arson," Maik said, turning to Jejeune. "They found a can in the driveway, an accelerant, probably petrol."

They heard a shout and spun around to see a man sprinting away from the front of the greenhouse. There was a screeching of tortured metal as a large part of the structure's frame broke away and crashed to the ground with a shattering of glass. A fire officer came around and moved everyone back toward the centre of courtyard. It was some moments before order was restored.

A young constable came over to Maik and passed him something. He had a big grin on his face. "Found it on the table in there, sir," he said, nodding toward the charred structure. "Blimey, I only just got out before the front fell in."

"The next time you're in a burned-out building and you hear it creaking, young Hennessey, you get out right away. Never mind the heroics."

He watched the young man slip away, no doubt with less praise ringing in his ears than he had anticipated. Maik turned the BlackBerry over in his hands, examining it as if it were a seashell. He rolled his thumb over the trackball and punched a couple of buttons.

"Here, leave that alone. Personal property that is." Christian strode over hurriedly and snatched the device from Maik's hand and stuffed it into his trousers pocket. "You ought to be careful. The last bloke who messed with my stuff has still got his hand in a cast."

"Oh, I doubt that would happen to me," said Maik pleasantly.

Christian was sobered by Maik's tone. "Yeah, right, sorry. I've spent ages customizing the settings on there, that's all. I don't want a clumsy git like you restoring all the defaults again." He sighed. "Look, it's been a long night, right? The fire's just about sorted. I'll have a look at the damage in the morning. Nothing else we can do tonight, is there? Besides, I could use some kip."

Christian walked off to survey what was left of his furniture. Jejeune, who had watched the conversation between the two men in silence, came up beside Maik again. His hands were tucked in his pockets. But his eyes were still on active duty.

"Who is that man, and what has he done with Archie Christian?" asked Jejeune.

"My thoughts exactly. You saw the place he had put together for himself in that greenhouse. He had put his heart and soul into it. The Archie Christian I know should have been talking about performing surgical procedures on somebody over this. Instead he sounds like an advert for the Samaritans. He might be planning to go after these people himself, I suppose, but I've never known Archie to soft pedal anything before. Something doesn't feel right here."

"Your restraint, admirable as it was, by the way, suggests that the BlackBerry was helpful?"

"Call log's been wiped out, obviously, but not his address book. Now, just having somebody's number in your BlackBerry might not be enough to get a warrant, but where Archie Christian is concerned, it's all the proof I need."

Jejeune looked thoughtful. "We still haven't been able to confirm the source of the vet's stolen drugs, I take it."

"We've asked at all the racecourse infirmaries and veterinary centres as far out as Great Yarmouth and Newmarket. Folksham was among the first we checked. They said there was no record of anything missing, but if Christian is involved, that wouldn't be a surprise. When it comes to helping himself to other people's property, Archie is no mug. This will be more than just a case of somebody pinching some packages off the shelf. The shipping manifests will have been altered long before the drugs got to the infirmary in the first place. I'll get on to the vets in the Folksham area to find out which labs supply their drugs. There'll be a paper trail somewhere. It will lead right back to Archie, sooner or later."

The two men watched Christian for a moment as he picked through the debris, careful as ever not to dirty his clothes. Maik shook his head again.

"Archie Christian, the Voice of Reason. Not on your life. You know he didn't even call this in himself? A couple driving by saw the flames from the road and got on their mobile right away. But if they could see it from the road, Christian must have been aware of the fire by then." He snapped out of his reverie. "The DCS was looking for you, by the way. I imagine she'll want a word in the morning. She's taking this Earth Front connection at face value. She's worried that they might ramp it up even further, now that they have gone this far."

"And you?"

"It could be them. I hate to agree with Archie, but it does have their mark, based on their activities elsewhere in the country. The trouble is, with Archie you can never be sure what else he's been into. This could be nothing to do with the Brae case at all."

Jejeune nodded thoughtfully. Earth Front had started off as just a bunch of overly zealous environmentalists, committed to aggressive anti-social acts to raise awareness for their cause. But there was enough of an over-the-top radical element to make the organization an attractive target for the professional anarchists, and in the past couple of years, things had become a lot more serious. If they were starting to get a foothold in this area, Jejeune could see why the DCS might be concerned.

"The connection between Christian and Brae is clear, though, just the same," said Jejeune, "and if Earth Front really believes Christian was involved in the murder, targeting him makes sense. Until something comes along to suggest otherwise, I suppose we need to look into where the evidence is leading us. Have Constable Salter take a poke around Earth Front's background in the morning. By the way, Holland said Beverly Brennan was here tonight. Any idea why?"

"Eco-terrorism is bad for business. Whether we like it or not, Christian has got some clout with the local business community. As far as they're concerned, he's a legitimate businessman. And Brennan won't be too happy with something like this going down on her patch when she's out there lobbying for investment."

Maik watched the firefighters rolling in one of the main hoses, as a prelude to winding down their activities. "Looks like things are just about under control here, if you wanted to get off home. I'll have the report on your desk first thing. In fact, I may as well head on in to the station now. I'm halfway there already."

Jejeune checked his watch. An hour or so later and he might have considered staying up, too. He could have picked up the dawn chorus on the way in to work; that magical hour when the birds were just becoming active and starting to feed. But he was tired, and the prospect of a couple more hours of sleep followed by breakfast with Lindy sounded like an altogether better prospect just now.

He nodded at Maik. "I'll leave you to finish up here. But before you go, please make sure you tell Mr. Christian we are going to be actively investigating Earth Front. That means a police presence around their headquarters for the next few days. And nights. The last thing we need is for him to show up with a van full of his friends with balaclavas and baseball bats, meting out their own particular brand of justice."

"I'll make sure he gets the message," said Maik, his tone leaving Jejeune in no doubt that he would.

Maik moved off to direct a couple of constables sifting through the charred rubble. Jejeune took a final look around the courtyard before walking back to his car. In a case where nobody seemed to have any answers, at least somebody had made up their mind who was to blame for Cameron Brae's death. He just wondered whether Earth Front's conclusions were based on emotion, or on some evidence he had yet to uncover for himself.

23

By the time Jejeune reached the front desk, he could already sense the tension. The desk sergeant, a wizened old dinosaur with wiry grey hair and deeply lined face, had still not fully warmed to Jejeune: likely as much a reaction against the new order that the inspector represented as anything else. Nevertheless, despite his misgivings, the sergeant raised an eyebrow at Jejeune as he passed and nodded his head in the direction of DCS Shepherd's office. "Brennan," he mouthed. After all, when it came right down to it, Jejeune was still one of them. Wasn't he?

Jejeune was just emerging from his office with a manila folder under his arm when DCS Shepherd appeared in the doorway of her own office at the far end of the corridor.

"Ah, Domenic, a minute, please." She held the door open until he arrived. "Inspector Jejeune, I believe you have already met the Right Honourable Beverly Brennan, MP."

Ushering Domenic into the room before her, she closed the door and retired to a chair in the rear corner.

Brennan was already settled behind the DCS's desk when Jejeune walked in, sitting erectly in the high backed chair. She had her gloves off, nestled neatly beside her handbag on the side table. Her hands were loosely clasped before her, resting on the desk, as if ready to grasp any information Jejeune might choose to toss her way. Her blond hair was gathered up behind her neck, neat and manageable.

Brennan took off her glasses, setting them on the desk beside her. This was to be her meeting, regardless of the setting. Jejeune knew Beverly Brennan had made a career of confronting her adversaries on their own turf. Was he an adversary? She greeted him with a smile that did not quite reach her blue-grey eyes.

Jejeune took the seat opposite Brennan, putting his back toward the DCS. If the arrangement struck him as vaguely odd, a glance back toward Shepherd showed that she held no such misgivings. She was apparently quite comfortable to take on an observer's role. But to observe what, exactly?

"Such a terrible business at Mr. Christian's last night," said Brennan without preamble. "As you may know, I paid a visit there myself, to see first-hand what these people are capable of. I am not here in any official capacity, you understand, but I am obviously concerned for the well-being of the local business community. Incidents like last night … well, clearly … Can I ask where your inquiries stand at the moment, Inspector?"

"We have a constable out at Earth Front's offices today, taking statements. We don't hold out much hope of finding the actual culprits there, but if there are some discrepancies in the statements.…"

Jejeune waved an airy hand. If it was a gesture designed to annoy the politician with its seeming indifference, it was a well-chosen one.

The glance at Shepherd was brief, but significant. "I know the DCS would like, indeed we would all like, swift action on this matter. As you know, this is not the first threat toward a member of our community. Now Peter Largemount's situation may or may not be connected, that is for you to determine.

But coupled with this dreadful affair with Cameron Brae, people are beginning to wonder if they are even safe to walk the streets of Saltmarsh anymore."

Jejeune cast another quick look back toward the DCS, but she was looking at her hands and did not make eye contact with her inspector. For her to be willing to sit back and let someone else run this meeting, in her office, seated behind her desk, suggested one of only two possibilities. Either Beverly Brennan had considerably more juice in this community than Jejeune had given her credit for, or the DCS was complicit in this set-up. Jejeune's natural instincts were toward caution when he didn't fully understand a situation, and it seemed better to let Brennan talk until she told him what was really going on, instead of offering any kind of defence that might be used against him later. He smiled indulgently, as if to suggest the politician couldn't really appreciate the intricacies of police procedure.

"The greater concern here, of course, is the overall climate of intimidation and fear. These people cannot be allowed to go around terrorizing members of our business community. It is up to you to restore some sense of calm and reassurance. Instead, you seem intent on following up lines of inquiry that are, quite frankly, puzzling, to say the least."

Jejeune shifted slightly in his chair and crossed his legs. Something about Brennan's tone belied the detached concern for her community she was trying to convey. As was often the case in conversations like this, Jejeune's measured silence encouraged another contribution from the other speaker. Brennan seemed compelled to reinforce her point.

"Inspector, you come here with an impressive reputation, and we all appreciate that your record is one of the highest order. The DCS has great faith that you will get to the bottom of this, but I have to say, from an outsider's perspective, frankly, I'm still waiting to see some results. You can appreciate, I am sure, that your appointment here, with all its attendant publicity, has left us all wondering what all the fuss is about. Now the DCS seems perfectly happy to indulge your, shall we say, unconventional methods. She has been, and may I say, still is, unqualified in her support of you thus far. But when, after this amount of time, the best you have to offer is some theory about a birdwatching list … well, I'm sure you can appreciate our concerns." This time, there was not even a frozen smile to soften the words.

Jejeune felt the DCS shift uncomfortably behind him. He leaned back, but not, as Brennan suspected, to distance himself from the politician's attacks. He had begun to realize how the landscape lay. When a superior has offered someone free reign and unqualified support, it is hard to justify questioning their methods. But if you just happened to be in the room when a powerful and well-connected acquaintance touched upon it under the guise of concern for business interests, well that wasn't quite the same thing, was it? It was, he realized, a sign that his support from his superior might not be as absolute and unqualified as Beverly Brennan was suggesting. Unless he produced some results soon, DCS Shepherd's disillusionment would no doubt take her beyond having to use other people as a shield for her questions.

"How would you characterize your own relationship with Mr. Brae?" Jejeune asked suddenly.

The question may have taken Beverly Brennan aback, but a lifetime of dealing with unpredictable inquiries left her external cues unmoved.

"I suppose you know we had our professional differences. His comments were not always helpful to development in this area. The national park idea, for example. He seemed determined to make the difficult job of attracting new business to the area even harder. My constituents were concerned."

Jejeune consulted his file, although no one in the room believed he really needed to. "'Naive and uninformed,'" he quoted. "'Narrow-minded to the point of negligent. Beverly Brennan appears to lack the intellectual curiosity required of her office.' I would hardly classify Cameron Brae's comments as professional differences. They sound a bit personal for that."

"Do you have a point to make, Mr. Jejeune?"

"You see, that seems to be the problem here, Ms. Brennan. Everyone I speak to in this case seems to be holding back as much information as possible. I am wondering why that might be."

"This is Saltmarsh. People like to keep their affairs to themselves. They don't take kindly to people prying into their private lives when they see no reason for it."

"Unless they're withholding evidence. This is a murder investigation, Ms. Brennan, and the citizens of Saltmarsh can't neglect their duty to co-operate with the police just because of some quaint ideas about minding their own business. However, since it seems that the only way I am going to get any answers is to start asking direct questions, would you mind if I start with you? Can you, for example, give me a complete account of your movements on the night of August 17th?"

The DCS moved forward in her chair, "Oh, I don't think ..." But Brennan raised her hand. Jejeune saw the colour begin to rise in her cheeks and a muscle start to work down along her powdered jawline. A flint of steel entered her eyes. Beverly Brennan's beauty seemed a long way off now, but her poise was still intact.

"Are you implying I'm a suspect in Cameron Brae's murder, Inspector?" She tried to sound amused by the idea, but she missed by some distance.

"You want me to do my job, Ms. Brennan. At this point, anyone who has either motive, means, or opportunity is a suspect," said Jejeune. "You yourself have pointed out that you are among those with a motive, along with most of the business community of Saltmarsh. So now I am moving on to opportunity."

"And if I feel I have good reasons for not answering?"

"Then you would have to convince me why those reasons outweighed the considerations of a murder investigation."

"I see." Brennan drew a breath, composing herself. "On the night Cameron Brae was murdered, I was at home, working on a draft of a speech. I left my office at around five o'clock and went straight home. I made myself something to eat, I don't remember what exactly, probably pasta and a salad, and then went to my study. I was there when my assistant called me with the news at about ten thirty. She will, of course, be able to verify that call, should it become necessary."

Jejeune's expression didn't give any indication of whether it would be necessary or not. "What were you and Peter Largemount discussing at the Hunt Club function? Is he considering draining Lesser Marsh, to expand his wind farm operations?"

There was a flicker of expression, a darted look toward the DCS. Sometimes, if the stimulus was strong enough, all the training in the world couldn't suppress human reactions.

"I consider Peter to be a good, dear friend, but there is no reason on earth why he should share that kind of information with me. And it is certainly no business of yours what we were discussing in a private moment."

"Unless he needed your support to get him over some very vocal objections, from someone like Cameron Brae, for example. Then it does become my business. You're on record as supporting the draining of Lesser Marsh, in theory at least. You do see my problem in this case, Ms. Brennan. So much of the private stuff seems to have much wider implications."

Beverly Brennan leaned forward, as stealthy as a coiled cobra. Her voice was chillingly soft. "I don't know if you follow the goings on in Whitehall, Detective Chief Inspector, but you really should. The political winds are changing. You may well have the ear of the Home Secretary at the moment, but before too long, our party is going to have him by a completely different part of his anatomy. Nothing lasts forever, especially in politics, and that includes a Home Secretary's posting. You would do well to remember that, Inspector Jejeune."

She stood up and gathered up her gloves and handbag. She took time for one further significant glance toward DCS Shepherd before she walked to the door. Jejeune waited until she had her hand on the doorknob.

"Can I ask how you found out about the attack at Archie Christian's?"

"My assistant called me. How she found out, I'm not really sure, but she knows how to do her job. It's what I pay her for."

24

Maik had not expected to be out here again so soon, not that he minded. He had been looking at an afternoon of wading through shadowy alibis and statements until Jejeune's urgent summons. Whatever had set the inspector in motion, it had caused him to move with greater purpose and energy than Maik had seen recently, and when he'd burst into Maik's cubicle, still shrugging on his jacket, the sergeant had been only too eager to abandon his paperwork and join his DCI in a dash to the car park.

They had taken Maik's car, the Mini. The Range Rover had picked up an annoying squeak on the front offside wheel, and Jejeune clearly wasn't in any mood just now to put up with the irritation. He was still flushed from his exchange with Beverly Brennan and he spent most of the drive out to the university staring out the window at the passing countryside. But that suited Maik. With Kim Weston on his CD player begging him to take her in his arms and rock her, rock her a little while, and his boss brooding silently beside him, Maik could afford to lose himself in the odd reverie himself. If Alwyn had been so put out by his previous visit, even though the sergeant had telephoned in advance to set up the appointment, he could scarcely imagine how the professor was going to react to the two of them barging in on him unannounced like this. He smiled at the thought.

Maik would have loved it to have been Alwyn, but he knew the professor was no killer. He had been around men who were, and he could tell the difference. Blimey, listen to him. He was sounding more like Jejeune every day, with his "feelings" and his "intuitions." It was all very well going on instinct, but a bit of hard evidence wouldn't go amiss, once in a while, either. Still, they apparently had something to move on, at last. And to a shoe-leather copper like Maik, that felt very good indeed.

Miles Alwyn was chatting to two graduate students in the doorway of his lab as the detectives approached. The students seemed overawed, not so much by the presence of the small man before them, but by the knowledge that their immediate fate rested very much in his hands. A man like Alwyn would enjoy the knowledge that he controlled others' destinies. But for today, at least, the students were safe. With a slightly pathetic gratitude they accepted the benediction Alwyn bestowed on their work and hurried away to begin the next phase of their research.

From Maik's point of view, Alwyn was disappointingly sanguine about their unannounced visit. He ushered them into the lab with an expansive gesture and closed the door behind them, commenting only briefly on how busy he was.

Jejeune examined the array of equipment on the benches around the lab. He seemed to be paying particular attention, though, as far as Maik could tell, it was all standard lab equipment: flasks, test-tubes, and the like, some of which even he recognized from his meagre science education at the local grammar school. Since Maik had no idea what it was that had brought them out here, it was going to be up to Jejeune to kick things off this time. The DCI had apparently already come to the same conclusion.

"What exactly do you study here, Professor?" he asked, tapping on the side of a glass vessel with his fingertip.

"Yes, if you could avoid standing there, Inspector. We are attempting to simulate exact post-storm growing conditions for those plants. If you block the light source for an extended period, you will render three months' work useless. And please don't tap on the equipment. It will disturb the suspended sediment. Wetland ecology is my remit, and all the marvellous sub-disciplines that come along with it: soil systems, hydrology, vegetation." He waved a hand to indicate the vast boundaries of his realm.

"It's a fascinating area. And an important one."

"Indeed. Wetlands cover less than six percent of the globe, but they may process as much as twenty percent of the world's carbon. And as carbon sequestration becomes an ever more pressing issue in the coming decades, the continuing health of salt marshes, in particular, is going to be vital to us all."

Jejeune listened carefully to the explanation, but not with the air of a man trying to learn something. More like someone listening for the truth. He already knows all this, thought Maik. There was nothing subtle about the way Jejeune was playing on Alwyn's vanity, but, like a lot of sledgehammer tactics, you couldn't fault its effectiveness. The professor had become a good deal less antagonistic since he started talking about how essential his work was. Maik had never met anybody so much in love with his own importance.

"What did you make of Cameron Brae's request for the survey report, considering the nature of your relationship?"

Alwyn seemed unmoved by the inspector's sudden lurching from the general to the specific.

"I daresay his need for high-quality information overrode personal considerations. It would hardly make sense for him to ignore the fact that he has … had … one of the world's leading experts in the field on his doorstep."

"And you've no idea why he wanted that report?"

"None at all. We were no longer in the kind of relationship where he might volunteer that sort of information, I'm afraid."

Maik made a note. He could feel the professor's eyes impatiently following the laboured pen strokes so he slowed down the entry further still. Alwyn shifted, and just for a moment Maik thought he was going to reach out and try to snatch the pen away to complete the entry himself. But Danny Maik didn't have that kind of luck.

"Would Brae not have had his own copy of the report?" asked Jejeune. "After all, he did work on the survey."

"He would have certainly kept a copy of his own data, but as the project leader, the job of assembling the studies into a single coherent report was mine. He was entitled to a copy of the final report, but he would have had to request one through me. I don't recall him ever making such a request."

"Until this time," said Maik.

"Until this time." Alwyn gave Maik his crocodile smile by way of thanks for clearing up the inconsistency.

"Wasn't it strange to have Brae working on a survey that was going to result in the approval of a wind farm in the first place, given his known opposition to projects of this nature?" asked Jejeune.

"I suppose some might have felt there was the potential for a conflict of interest, but with me at the helm, the impartiality of the overall survey was never in question. Besides, I respected Cameron. He was a man of great intelligence and integrity. He lost his way, certainly, but he was basically a good person."

"This respect, it didn't extend to helping his wife though, did it, when she called?" said Maik. "To tell her that she wasn't bright enough to understand her husband's work, that would hardly make things any easier for him at home."

Alwyn had a stab at a disarming smile, but he was long out of practice and his efforts fell well short. "We are a science faculty. We deal in facts here, Sergeant. She was not up to the task, intellectually. I simply told her the truth."

"These survey results," interjected Jejeune, "would you have emailed the report to him?"

"No, I sent him a hard copy."

"What would it have looked like?"

"A standard university report. Spiral-bound. Letter-size paper once white, a bit yellow now. It had a buff cover, I believe."

"And he didn't return it to you?"

"No. If it wasn't at his house, I have no idea what he did with it. Still, I do have other copies, so it really isn't an issue, from my perspective."

Jejeune turned away from the professor and strolled slowly away across the lab. He looked out the window for a moment. *Here we go*, thought Maik, *time for some tinkering with the fixtures*. He was just starting to prepare a question to fill the void when Jejeune surprised him by taking up the mantle again.

"I'll tell you why I think Cameron Brae wanted that report," said Jejeune from across the room. "He was looking for something remarkable. Something rare or unique about Lesser Marsh. Something that might be enough to get it a protection order." He stopped short of telling the professor about Largemount's plans to drain the marsh. "Since he was the macrobiologist, most likely he couldn't find anything obvious among the big orders, the amphibians or the birds, so he was hoping you might have had something on the invertebrates, or the crustaceans. Would he have found it, Professor? Is there something special about Lesser Marsh that might earn it protected status?"

Alwyn shook his head confidently. "Absolutely nothing. All marshes are unique, Inspector, in their species composition, their hydrology, even their drainage patterns. But apart from the fact that it is the only marsh in these parts entirely on private land, Lesser Marsh, I'm sorry to say, is a remarkably unremarkable wetland. If Cameron had asked me, I could have confirmed that for him and saved him the trouble of looking. Really, Inspector, if this is what you came all this way to discuss, the phantom treasures of Lesser Marsh, I must insist on being allowed to get on with my work. I have genuine value to uncover in other wetlands."

Maik matched Jejeune's loping stride along the corridors of the university. Neither man spoke until they reached the sanctity of the car park. They paused beside Maik's car.

"So Brae wanted the survey data to try to put a stop to Largemount's plans to drain the marsh?" Maik needed to be the first to speak, to deflect any questions Jejeune might have wanted to raise about just how the subject of Brae's wife had suddenly cropped up in their interview with Alwyn.

"We'll know if there's anything in the birding records as soon as Senior gets back to us, but Brae was clearly hoping there might be something else, an endangered insect, an invertebrate, perhaps even a worm. Anything that might be enough to put Largemount's plans on hold."

"A worm? Really?"

"Perhaps, if it was important enough. They can be a vital part of a food web, without which an entire ecosystem could crumble. If the survey turned up one important enough, an endemic, for example, found only in this area, it might have been enough to get Largemount's project stopped."

"But Alwyn said there was nothing," said Maik. The two men fell silent. They both knew Brae was not going to go up against an opponent like Largemount empty-handed. "This American Bittern," said Maik carefully, "surely that would have done the trick, wouldn't it?"

Jejeune shook his head slowly. "Not as a single vagrant sighting. And that's the puzzling part."

"Then how about a flock of them?"

"It's a *siege*. A *siege of bitterns*. But they usually occur singly, when they occur at all. The only possible way the ministry would consider a stop order due to American Bitterns was if Lesser Marsh was a potential breeding site, or an identified habitat for an established population. But even Cameron Brae would have been laughed out of the local birding community for making such an outrageous claim."

Still, Maik knew Jejeune didn't like coincidences any more than he did. An earth-shattering event like an American Bittern sighting had to have something to do with Brae's efforts to get the marsh-draining project stopped. But what?

Jejeune was silent for a long moment. "I don't know how Brae was planning to use that sighting," he admitted. "But whatever he eventually came up with, it must have been a pretty compelling argument. I think it was enough to get him killed."

25

If anyone was expecting the new leads about Lesser Marsh to speed the case to a conclusion, reality soon descended in a cloud of scholarly gloom. With Holland stationed at one desk, Maik at another, and Salter at a third, each wading through data on screens or in ancient ring binders, rushed over from various government departments in that morning's mail, a successful resolution to the case could not have seemed farther away.

Each officer was looking for the same thing, as directed by Jejeune when he had handed out the copies of the survey and various other research papers that morning: anything that suggested the marsh harboured a protected species.

Sunlight flooded the room, filling the desks with pools of light.

"Listen to this: 'None of the several species of Odonata of north Norfolk known to have been suffering a precipitous decline in the last three decades were found to be present at this site.' Thirty-one words to tell us something wasn't there! What a load of bullshit." Holland slapped the file down on his desk with a loud report. "Do I look like I want to be a scientist?" he asked the room in general. "I've never liked science, even in school. Nah, mate, drama class, all them potential models and actresses. Now that was a proper subject. Only the uglies took science. Think about it, did you ever see a good-looking scientist? What's he got you doing, anyway?"

"Pond life," announced Salter in a way that made Maik smile to himself. "Aquatic invertebrates, to give them their proper title. I have to agree about one thing, though; these people do seem to take the long way round to say nothing."

Holland shook his head. "Why not ask Alwyn about this lot, for God's sake?" he said. "I mean, the bloke is only the world's leading expert on this stuff."

Maik looked up from his research. "Never you mind why, Constable. You just stick to your task and try to find something that would be worth preserving the marsh for. Remember, *locally rare* is good, *threatened* is better, but *endangered* is the jackpot word here. Besides, you know what they say. Get a good knowledge of marine life, and the world is your lobster."

If Maik was being honest, even he wasn't entirely convinced about this line of inquiry. By now he was beginning to realize that, however unconventional his ideas may be, Jejeune usually had a reason for them, but that didn't make Maik any more comfortable about how they were going about matters. Letting the bird lists go to Senior, for example. Typically, just as he himself was warming to the idea of the four-hundred list having some merit as a motive, Jejeune seemed to be distancing himself from it. But Maik had been watching carefully when Senior and the DCI were talking in the hide. There was something about Senior's "hail fellow well met" routine that did not sit quite right with him. Perhaps a hint of underlying calculation that the joviality never quite managed to hide. Admittedly, Senior could hardly have gotten to the top of the pile in the competitive world of Norfolk birders without some ruthlessness. But was there something more? If there was, Maik couldn't put his finger on it just at the moment. But that wouldn't stop him looking. And while he was at it, there was something else that had been bothering him.

"You know what I don't get," he said suddenly, to no one in particular. "All this talk about Brae's honesty and integrity. The man was having an affair, cheating on his wife. I'm sure of it. And what's more, he'd got form. He'd done it before."

"That's just it though, Sarge. He hadn't, had he?" said Salter. "He was perfectly up front about breaking up his first marriage. Everybody insists that they didn't get together until after he had told his wife he was leaving her. He didn't carry on behind her back. If it had to happen, any woman would rather have it be that way. Unhappiness you can handle. It's the betrayal that cuts to the quick."

This was raw territory for Maik, and he was quiet for a moment with his memories of his mother's perpetual sadness. But where else could Brae have been going at night? To study his beloved marsh? A bit dark for that. His thoughts turned toward Mandy, in the house alone, cradling the receiver in her hand after speaking to Alwyn. Mandy, vulnerable, sad, lonely. She knew, Maik was sure of it. But although infidelity had been responsible for more spousal deaths than he cared to think about, he didn't buy it in this case. *Unhappiness you can handle.* This marsh-draining angle of Jejeune's was flimsy, but even that, he had to admit, had more to it than a scorned wife, at least, this scorned wife. Still, he couldn't shake the idea that Brae's dishonesty and deceit would show up somewhere in the mix when they finally got a result.

Jejeune entered the room carrying a *Birds of Norfolk* tome under his arm. *Did he ever read anything else?* He didn't need to ask if they had found anything. They were under orders to find him as soon as anything, however tenuous, came up. "I'm waiting for a report; coastal flight patterns of shorebirds. Could you see that I get it the moment it comes in?"

"Certainly, sir," said Holland. He exchanged a sly glance with Maik. "This report, sir, is it anything to do with what we're working on?"

"There won't be anything about it in those surveys, Constable. Which is exactly the point. There has been very little study done on how the coastal winds affect the birds' altitude and flight patterns. Even less on how those factors might be disrupted by wind farms. It's the sort of study one might have expected to be commissioned before final approval of a massive wind farm like this went through. But, in this case, it never was."

Holland and Maik exchanged glances again. Everyone knew the approval of Largemount's farm had been fast-tracked, supported by the most emphatic of backings from Beverly Brennan. The numbers that had been bandied about at the time had been impressive — this many jobs, that much revenue. Not much of it had materialized yet, if it was ever going to, but it was easy to see why so much local support had fallen in behind the MP when she started promoting the idea. The thing was, despite the speed with which the proposal was pushed through, no one locally was in any doubt that it had all been done above board. It had been around the time of Beverly Brennan's last election campaign and had been one of her major policy platforms. Brennan's chief rival in the election was an unpleasant little man called Arthurs, not above spreading a rumour or two whether there was any truth to them or not. It was common knowledge he had been all over this process with a fine-tooth comb. If there had been even the slightest hint of impropriety, one regulation not met, one safety check skipped, he would have made it his life's work to bring it to the public's attention. But he had found nothing, and even after the local voters had sent him packing back to his construction business near Peterborough, even then, amid the parting shots and the sour grapes and the generally graceless exit from the public arena, he never once tried to hint that there was anything wrong with the approval process for Largemount's wind farm project.

Of course, Jejeune wasn't around back then. He didn't know all this history. But typically, rather than ask somebody who did, he had gone off on a tangent of his own. Holland would have been happy to let him waste his time just as a matter of course, but even Maik found himself thinking that if Jejeune was going to keep his team in the dark about so many things, then he only had himself to blame if he ended up following leads that turned into blind alleys.

Jejeune gathered up a couple of reports that none of the others had managed to get around to yet. The telephone rang and Maik picked it up. He listened for a moment, his pen poised to take notes until he seemed to think better of it. Finally he asked the speaker to hold and, placing his hand over the receiver, swivelled in his chair to speak to Jejeune.

"Quentin Senior. He seems to think he has found whatever it was that Brae was after."

"In the records? Is he sure?"

"According to him, Brae couldn't have missed it. Something to do with species. What should be there, but isn't. He wanted to give me the particulars, but I thought he might be better telling you directly, it being birds and all."

Jejeune smiled. Maik wasn't a man to shirk his responsibilites, but it had been clear from the look on his face in the hide that he had heard a good deal more about abraded feathers, scapulars, and bill lengths than he ever wanted to know.

"He says he will put together a summary of his findings and fax it over to you, but he could give you the Rabbit Reader version over the phone now if you like."

Jejeune took the phone from Maik. Senior's tone was as irrepressibly hearty as ever, booming his findings down the telephone line with his customary energy.

"Catastrophic decline in some species at the marsh, Inspector. Three in particular, Knot, Sanderling, and Dunlin, over the past few years."

"And are you sure that would have been clear to Brae?"

"Cameron couldn't have missed it. Plain as the nose on your face. Years of consistent numbers, and then, whoosh, off a cliff."

"But there could be any number of explanations why a particular species no longer shows up at a site. Food sources, a population crash, adverse weather conditions along the migration route."

"Indeed, Inspector. But there's only one reason to account for why the birds have stopped going to one particular marsh while they are still appearing in healthy numbers at Cley, Titchwell, and other spots up and down the coast. Or one obvious reason, anyway."

Jejeune replaced the receiver delicately, as if afraid that it might shatter on impact. A few facts and one deduction. It was all Jejeune generally needed to reach a conclusion. He couldn't remember if he had thanked Senior at the end of their conversation. He probably had; politeness was instinctive with him. But even if he hadn't, he was sure Senior would understand why he had been so preoccupied. And if he didn't understand now, then he would in the very near future.

26

Lindy was at the kitchen counter when Jejeune entered. Small piles of chopped vegetables lay on the cutting board awaiting their fate in her crab and avocado medley. But Lindy was peering out the kitchen window at the vast blue horizon with the cottony clouds sitting low over the water's surface. The long summer day was just beginning its descent toward evening and the shadows were lengthening on the grass leading to the cliff edge.

Jejeune took off his jacket and draped it over one of the chairs around the kitchen table. He slumped into the chair and loosened his tie.

"How did the interview go?" Lindy didn't turn from the window as she spoke.

"Fine. Airs in a couple of weeks, I think."

"I hope you weren't condescending to Martin."

Still, the horizon seemed to hold her attention.

"I didn't say a word."

She turned to him. On him. "You don't have to. You just give that look, the one you use at the bank sometimes or with the mobile phone company. Just because people aren't as quick on the uptake as you doesn't mean everybody else is stupid, you know."

Like all police officers, Jejeune had dealt with more than his share of deflected hostility and he had learned not take it personally. But he could not deny Lindy's cold journalist's eye in these matters either, and if she sometimes overstated her case in the throes of an emotional rush of blood, there was usually some substance behind her observations. Perhaps he was a bit off-handed in his dealings with the media occasionally. He made a note to watch his conduct more carefully in future.

He wondered what was really bothering Lindy. Traffic? Work? Another run in with Eric, the Illiterate Halfwit Editor, all capitals, thank you. Jejeune knew how much she liked him, and how much his approval meant to her. If her relationship with Eric was deteriorating beyond their professional squabbles, it would be hard on her. But perhaps it was just something else. It had been a difficult time for her recently. There had been the party, and a couple of tight deadlines at the magazine. Whatever it was, Domenic knew this outburst would have been coming sometime tonight. Better now than later, when they had less time to resolve things before bedtime.

"It's a beautiful evening. Fancy a walk?" Jejeune asked, as if their conversation was still on the leeward side of her attack.

"Heard about a good bird out there, have you?" But Lindy grabbed her jacket anyway, and without a backward glance at the piles of abandoned vegetables, they headed for the door.

With the setting sun came a breeze off the water, but it carried the day's warmth and he held their jackets loosely in his hands as they walked, side by side, in silence. They chose the path along the cliff edge, one of their favourites; a grassy track worn down by their footsteps, and those of others, between the carpet of yellow kidney vetch and those small white flowers they kept intending to identify. Forget-me-alreadys? Further out, seabirds skimmed along the surface of the water. Jejeune noted them but made no comment.

The path drifted toward the edge of the cliff and then disappeared in a collapsed gully of untidy scree and rocks. They stopped on a small patch of open ground, worn smooth by sea watchers and picnickers. In the fading light, the sea had lost its blue. Now it was only a shimmering mirror of movement; light, transience, uncertainty. Its beauty was overwhelming.

"Woman's perspective," said Jejeune when he was sure the wind and views had swept away the last of Lindy's lingering anger. "A man is honest enough to break off a relationship before he starts a new one. Why does a man like that suddenly start a secret affair behind the new partner's back?"

Lindy turned to face Jejeune. Her skin was blushed with the wind coming in off the sea. She passed an elegant hand through her tousled hair to drag it back away from her face. "Who are we talking about, Dom? Someone we know?"

Jejeune thought about keeping it in the hypothetical, as his police training wanted him to. But Lindy, standing on the edge of the cliff, with her arms hugged around her in the not so cold evening air, deserved something more.

"Cameron Brae told his first wife he was leaving her, and who for, long before the fact. As far as I can tell, he kept nothing from her. And that, according to everybody I have spoken to, was perfectly in keeping with his character."

"But then Brae started cheating on Mandy Roquette?" Was Lindy's half smile surprise, or something else? "Miss Party Animal herself? Girl of just about every middle-aged man's dreams? My God, who with?"

"No idea. But does it make any sense to you, at all? That he would do that? That way?"

Lindy looked out at the sea. Relationships; the one mystery even Domenic Jejeune couldn't unravel. She arranged her thoughts, reaching out for Jejeune's hand so he would know her silence wasn't distance. It was the inconsistency, she knew, that he needed to resolve. Behaviour and character. Brae past and Brae present. Brae, sadly, of no future.

"Revenge," she said quietly. "Sometimes, the deception is to punish the other party, for what they have done, what they haven't done, all the promises they broke, the opportunities they caused you to miss. If Cameron Brae was having a secret affair this time, perhaps he wasn't just unhappy. Perhaps he was blaming his wife for something."

The breeze picked up and they slipped on their jackets. The dying rays of the sun began to touch the undersides of the clouds, and they sat down together, Lindy leaning into him, feet dangling into the gully, to watch the show. Whatever it was that was troubling her, it had been subdued for now.

On the rocky beach below, a single set of footprints disappeared off into the distance, the only sign that anyone else had ever trespassed on their private world.

"I've solved the case," he said.

"Really?" She brushed her windswept hair back with her hand again, a casual gesture that set Domenic's pulse racing. "I thought you were nowhere near a result. You really do play your cards close to your chest."

But he could tell that she was pleased for him, genuinely pleased. There would be more fanfare, more media plaudits. Domenic Jejeune, the star attraction again. And Lindy would be leading the cheers. But he couldn't share her pride. In fact, there was no sensation for him at all, just an absence where the unsolved mystery used to be.

"So is this the part where you tell me you don't want to do it anymore?" she said quietly.

It was. But do what, exactly? Be a media celebrity, a boy wonder, the Great White Hope of the police force? Or be a policeman, a detective, at all? What he did want, he didn't really know. He just knew it wasn't this, dwelling in the darkness of other people's psyches, sifting through the layers of deception, uncovering their lies, their duplicity, their crimes.

"So what happens next?" asked Lindy, leaning away from him slightly so she could look into his face. "Back to Ontario? To the birding wonderlands of Point Pelee or Rondeau? Summers at Carden Plain and then off to Presqu'ile for the fall waders? You see, Dom, I have been paying attention. I know them all, those fabulous hotspots, those halcyon days of your youth, you and your brother and those endless seasons of birdwatching."

Despite her tone, Jejeune smiled wistfully. "It's always a mistake to try to revisit your past."

"Even when the present leaves you so unfulfilled, and the future looks so bleak? What a desolate place your interior landscape must be, Mr. Jejeune."

Jejeune said nothing.

"You need your police work, Dom. Really you do. I know you think you hate your job, but you'd be unhappy if you couldn't do it anymore. Think about it. Half the police forces in England were looking for that girl, and you were the one who found her. Alive. Nobody else could have done that. And now you've done it again, solved a case with no clues, no leads, no suspects. You're a detective, Dom, it's what you do. And you're good at it. Would it be so terrible to allow yourself to take a little bit of satisfaction from that?"

Lindy was so beautiful when she abandoned herself to her certainty like this. What it would be like to be so convinced about something, anything, he couldn't imagine. Of course, certainties were always easier when it was someone else's life under the microscope. Ask her about her own future and she would withdraw into a moody introspection. But on the subject of Domenic Jejeune, Lindy was irrepressible. She held such great ambitions for him, he knew. He thought about Senior, huddled down on a bank, watching birds for a living.

What need did he have for ambition? Perhaps ambition was just a luxury unhappy people wallowed in when all their other needs had been met.

"A nice bottle of red, you think?"

Jejeune roused himself from his reverie.

"Well, I'm ready to celebrate your success, even if you're not."

Success? Really? He could name the killer, but the motive still troubled him. But then, finding out who killed Cameron Brae was all they had ever asked of him; the family, the DCS, the media. Motive was nice, but it was a luxury, like ambition. Find the right suspect and they would tell you why they did it. Eventually. They always did.

"There are still a lot of unanswered questions," he admitted.

"Well, perhaps when you bring in your murderer," said Lindy archly, "he'll be kind enough to clear them up for you."

He was impressed, and perhaps even a little bit surprised, that she had been able to follow so closely the self-imposed rules they had hashed out when she had left the national daily to join the magazine. No more inside track. No more ducking under the police tape for an update, formal or otherwise. Until the arrest was announced, he wouldn't say, she wouldn't ask. Still, it must be difficult for her.

They stood up, drinking in the last of the setting sun together. At the far end of the path, the cottage was just visible. The kitchen light had been left on, and burned brightly now in the gathering gloom. Dinner would be a while coming tonight, but that was okay. Jejeune had no real appetite anyway.

27

Domenic Jejeune was hardly ever aware of how he came by his insights, or how he had made connections between them. Certainly, there were the occasional flashes of inspiration, bolts of lucidity right out of the blue, but those moments were rare. Most often, ideas just materialized, like water droplets condensing from the mist of details in his head, so that they were already there, fully formed, when his conscious mind stumbled upon them. He had no way of controlling the process, or marshalling it at will. All he could do was keep accumulating facts until his brain pieced together the various parts of the puzzle. And then the answers came.

The problem was, in this case there had been no blinding flashes of insight, no mystical moments of inspiration, but there had been no gradual distillation of ideas either. Any answers that had come his way seemed to have dropped into place neatly, conveniently almost. It gave him a vague, uneasy feeling that the entire picture might not be as clear and complete as it now appeared.

He looked down at the scrap of paper on which he had scribbled his notes. In murder investigations elsewhere, he knew, this would all have been outlined on a whiteboard in the incident room. But Jejeune was more interested in the end result than its skeleton, and he didn't like to see his thought patterns unfurled on the big canvas until they had reached their final destination. But had they? On one level, it all made sense. The marsh had been contaminated somehow. That was why the birds had disappeared. Jejeune wasn't sure what sort of contaminants might be involved, but it wouldn't take him long to find out. Clean power the turbines may be, once they were erected, but he was sure there were plenty of opportunities for things to go wrong during their transportation and installation. The bottom line was, it didn't really matter. Whatever the pollutant was at Lesser Marsh, Largemount hadn't reported it. Of that much, at least, Jejeune was certain. By now, he was familiar with every piece of official correspondence concerning Peter Largemount's property; certainly enough to know there was no police report, municipal record, or ministry alert of any toxic spill.

There would be hefty fines for a spill large enough to drive away entire populations of wading birds. So Largemount had simply covered it up, kept quiet, and carried on with business as usual. But Brae had pieced together the truth from the bird lists, and he had threatened to inform the authorities. Failure to report a spill was in itself a crime. But even if the authorities allowed the wind farm to continue operating, news of the original contamination would be enough to end Largemount's expansion plans, no matter what sort of high-powered political backing he had managed to assemble. So Brae had found his lever to stop Largemount draining the marsh. And Largemount had killed him to silence him.

But was it really enough to kill for? Murder was like the release of a spring wound too tightly. But this motive didn't seem to carry enough of that tension within it. It was weak, incomplete. Certainly, it could have been at the root of tensions between Largemount and Brae, but Jejeune couldn't help feeling there was something more, something significant that he was overlooking.

He stared down at the paper again. There was one other thing missing, of course. That one piece of solid, irrefutable evidence that DCS Shepherd had been asking for. But that could take days, to get the warrants and then to get the results of the soil and water tests; days when other things could happen, events could spiral out of control. And Jejeune wasn't prepared to let that happen in any of his cases ever again. He would take the risk, gamble that some crucial piece of evidence would turn up, or that the circumstantial evidence would look more compelling when he sat down and actually confronted Peter Largemount with it. But however things unfolded, Domenic Jejeune wasn't going to risk any more casualties by waiting too long. Not this time.

He walked down the corridor to the incident room, where Maik, Salter, and Holland were starting their day as they had finished the previous one, by poring over the survey results from Lesser Marsh.

Holland rolled his eyes. "Sir, these reports, if you could just tell us what it is we are looking for exactly."

"Let's leave those for now. Where are we in other areas?" He turned to Maik. "Have we filled in any gaps? Anyone's movements, witness come forward?" After Shepherd's unexplained familiarity with the four-hundred list, Jejeune wasn't ready to confide this theory to them just yet. But if he could get something else firm on Largemount, there would be no need to sweat the soil and water analyses.

"Not really. Christian's whereabouts are still vague. We do know that Largemount could have managed the run to Norwich in time, just barely."

Jejeune nodded. He had heard about Maik's white-knuckle ride as a passenger in Holland's Audi that had established this.

Salter stirred. "There is this mileage thing. Brae had his car serviced two days before he was killed. We had been assuming he took it straight home afterward and parked it, but there are extra miles on the clock."

"Too much to hope it had a GPS, I suppose?" asked Maik.

"That pile of junk?" said Holland with a sarcastic laugh. "You're lucky it had an odometer."

"But it was definitely a local trip. He couldn't have got as far as Norwich, say, or Yarmouth," continued Salter. "Taking out the mileage from the service station back to Brae's house, there's twelve extra miles — six each way, as I figure it, you know, there and back."

"You'll have plotted the radius from Brae's house already, then, Constable Salter, what with your mathematical wizardry and all," said Maik. "So let's look for destinations around that six-mile mark."

"I'd be willing to do some runs," said Holland. "You know, just to verify the exact distances and such."

"Really?" asked Maik with mock surprise. "You'd do that for us, Constable? Drive that convertible of yours around north Norfolk in the sunshine, and bill the department for expenses afterward? How selfless of you."

"Could he have gone to Lesser Marsh?" asked Jejeune.

Salter shook her head. "Not on its own. It's probably no more than a couple of miles, tops, from Brae's house to Lesser Marsh. If he did go there, he went somewhere else as well."

"Nevertheless, we can't rule out Lesser Marsh as a destination, or at least the property it's on."

Maik tapped the file he was holding against his chin thoughtfully. "So, let's get this right. His last call is to Largemount. He gets no answer, so he gets in his car and drives over to his house. If your call was unanswered, there's only one reason you would do that."

"Because he thought Largemount was home and he wasn't picking up," said Holland, with the certainty of someone who had been on both ends of such situations.

"And why might Largemount not want to pick up? Because he knew what the call was about and he didn't want to talk about it." Maik answered his own question before anybody else could get there.

In the silence that followed, Holland turned to Jejeune. "Oh, by the way, sir, the DCS has been popping in lately looking for updates. Usually when you're not around, funnily enough. Anything I should tell her if she comes by?"

Jejeune considered the question for a moment before answering. "You can tell her that within the next twenty-four hours, we will have somebody in custody for the murder of Cameron Brae."

A stunned silence fell over the room. Perhaps this was just an example of some hitherto unseen Canadian deadpan humour. He couldn't be talking about Largemount, surely. Maik knew that Largemount had been on Jejeune's radar right from the start, but to Maik's mind, their interview with him had been about as colourful as that light grey matte paint until the confrontation over the gull. It was not impossible that something the developer had said, or more likely the way he had said it, had triggered a flicker of suspicion in Jejeune's mind. But to arrest him, on the basis of this evidence? Flimsy didn't even begin to cover it.

A telephone rang. Maik listened for a moment and then hung up. He stood up and reached for his jacket from the back of his chair, as if aware that he was going to need it soon. Jejeune was almost at the door when Maik spoke.

"That arrest, sir. If it was going to be Peter Largemount, I'm afraid you're too late. He's been murdered."

28

Jejeune looked around the site and allowed himself a long sigh. He didn't need anybody to point out that proving guilt was a lot more difficult when your suspect was dead. The motive he had come up with was plausible enough, barely, and Largemount certainly had opportunity to kill Brae. But there still were plenty of holes in his case against the developer, and he knew the DCS would require more answers before she would be able to bring herself to believe, either professionally or personally, in Peter Largemount's guilt. Jejeune hadn't been hoping for a confession right away: Largemount wasn't the type. But once you knew somebody was guilty, you could keep probing until they eventually gave themselves away. He looked over at the inert form lying beneath the blue sheet. Whatever revelations Peter Largemount could have provided, they had died with him.

Jejeune watched Maik march off toward the constable standing nearest the body. He knew it would not take the sergeant long to gather the pertinent information and get back to him. He was good at his job, and his report would be succinct but thorough. Jejeune would soon know everything they had on Peter Largemount's death. The angry red text daubed across the brickwork below the bay window would undoubtedly feature prominently in the report.

Jejeune walked to where the gravel met the meticulously kept lawns at the edge of the forecourt, and looked out over the fields below. The grey forest of wind turbines turned silently. A man's death had had no effect on them. Like nature, they continued their cycles, dispassionate and inexorable. A benign sun shone down from a cloudless china-blue sky. It was the type of day that generally brought Jejeune a feeling of calm, as if the world was in balance. But the world was not in balance today. Just a few feet behind him lay a body from which the life had been taken, not naturally, not as part of any natural pattern or rhythm, but as an act of violence; taken because in some way someone else drew benefit from this death. Money, silence, gratification. Every murderer gained something from their victim's demise. Jejeune took a final look at the peaceful low-lying landscape. He would find no answers there.

Jejeune lifted the police tape and stooped beneath it, making his way to the centre of the forecourt. No lights were on in the house, and the front door was locked. There would be reason enough to enter soon, but for now Jejeune's work, and that of the other investigating officers, lay out here, at the crime scene itself. The body lay off to the right, near the beech trees, awaiting the arrival of the forensic medical examiner. Largemount's Bentley sat where it had been left, slewed in at a careless angle; the driver's door hanging open.

Jejeune leaned in and turned on the car's headlights briefly, and then turned them off again. He stood back and considered the scene. Largemount drives up, gets out of his car, sees someone spray-painting a slogan on the front of his house. He calls out, approaches, and is shot. No. Plenty wrong with that. The slogan was over there, on the far side of the car, the body was over by the trees. So Largemount didn't approach the graffiti artist while he was at work.

He interrupts him, then, takes him by surprise, and chases him over there when he runs, until the murderer turns and shoots. Again, Jejeune gave his head a single shake. Largemount's driveway described a long sweeping arc up toward the forecourt, and the car headlights would have been on as he drove up. There was no chance he could have taken anybody by surprise. Plus the slogan was finished, not neatly, admittedly, but complete to the last word: *silenced*. No, whoever had written this had finished their work and then gone over there, in the shadow of the beech trees, to await Largemount's arrival. Which at least solved one problem: Jejeune had been wondering what kind of person shows up to a crime scene with a gun in one hand and an aerosol can in the other. But this was clearly not about the slogan. This was premeditated murder.

Jejeune walked toward the body. The Rooks in the great beeches at the edge of the clearing cawed and stirred restlessly as Jejeune approached, taking off to perform short circles of flight before swooping down again to nestle in amongst the other dark shapes in the rookery. A photographer was flitting around the body, the flash like bolts of weak lightning. He had folded back the sheet to get his photographs and Jejeune caught sight of what was left of Peter Largemount. He wished he hadn't. When he had finished, the photographer delicately replaced the sheet and moved over toward the car.

Maik approached, the gravel crunching loudly beneath his tread. Jejeune realized how quiet it was up on this ridge. He could hear the murmur of the sea, behind the house and far below, but other sounds seemed muted, as if all of nature was somehow holding its breath. Maik was consulting his notebook and began speaking as soon as he arrived.

"Postman called it in. Found it when he came with the morning delivery, around nine. He got the impression the body had been here all night, though he couldn't really say why. He knew enough not to touch anything, but from what I've seen, this one wouldn't encourage much close examination anyway. The M.E. will be here shortly, but the young PC who was first on the scene says it was definitely a shotgun. Not much of the face left, apparently, but enough to identify him. I've sent the lad off to get some tea for himself and the postie. I think he could use the fresh air."

He cares so much about other people's reactions to death, thought Jejeune. It was a legacy, he supposed, of having seen so much himself.

"What do you make of that?" Jejeune indicated the slogan: *For C.B: The defenders of the planet will not be silenced.*

Maik shrugged. "On the face of it, it looks like somebody else agreed with you about Largemount killing Brae. They need to make their mind up, this lot. Last week it was Christian, now Largemount." Maik shook his head almost imperceptibly. "But I don't know, it's all a bit theatrical for me."

"Better get some people out to Earth Front to take a look around again, anyway. And let's have a look at those threats Largemount received over the Ivory Gull, too."

Jejeune was no more comfortable than Maik with having the culprits dropped in his lap like this. It wasn't impossible that Earth Front had killed Largemount and autographed their work; certainly they were fond enough of the outrageous gesture and the media attention it attracted. But in Jejeune's experience, people cold-blooded enough to lie in wait for a victim and shoot them in the face at point blank range rarely felt the need to leave an explanation painted on a wall. But if the slogan was just a decoy, then perhaps there was another reason someone wanted Peter Largemount dead.

Jejeune approached the body. A large pool of blood had soaked into the gravel around the head, staining the pink stones. From Maik's brief description, and his own snatched look at the body, he suspected that Largemount could have hardly moved at all once he hit the ground. Death might not have been instantaneous, but the wounds would have been too terrible to allow for much movement afterward.

Maik called to him from the far side of the forecourt. "Constable Holland has something he thinks you should see."

He pointed to the stand of beech trees, beneath which Jejeune could see Holland stirring the leaf litter with his foot. The Rooks kept up their harsh, scolding commentary as Jejeune approached, fidgeting nervously above him from branch to branch. Holland was shovelling the body of a bird off to one side with his foot.

"Don't think you can count this one for your list, sir."

The bird's head was twisted back at a grotesque angle, and its black wings were spread out like a cloak. Jejeune could see the distinctive pale base of the upper mandible glinting through the leaf litter. The eyes were already gone, sunken or stolen by scavengers, and there was blood matted over the bird's chest. But there was still enough sheen to its glossy black body to show that it had died only recently.

"There's two more over here, both shot as well. And what looks like part of a nest, too."

Jejeune looked up and could see white patches of sky through ragged holes in two of the stick bundle nests in the rookery. "Have you moved the other birds?"

Holland shook his head. "But I thought there might be ticks or something. You know, contaminate the wounds. That's why I covered the body with that sheet."

"Don't touch any of them. Or the nest material." He went to stand among the massive trunks of the beech trees and looked all around him. Jejeune looked up and manoeuvred himself until he was positioned directly beneath the nests with the ragged holes torn in them. The bodies of the Rooks lay to his right and his left. He stared out from his vantage point into the courtyard, where Largemount's body lay a few feet away. Now Jejeune had his missing pieces, or at least some of them. He didn't know who had killed Largemount, or why, but he was getting a picture of how the event had unfolded.

Maik saw it too, now, having watched Jejeune, having seen him look up into the trees, and then out to where the body lay. Did Jejeune appreciate how easily it came to him, he wondered. Other DCI's Maik had worked with would have thrashed around a scene like this for hours, days even, before they were able to put the scenario together. The slogan, for a start; that would have had them off and running in all directions. But not Jejeune. He had seen it, considered it, and dismissed it, all in the time it took most of the young officers here to decipher the big words. Maik knew he had never seen anybody analyze a scene so thoroughly, so competently, so quickly in all his years of policing. He might not always be right, this new chief inspector, but Maik was pretty sure that he was spot on this time. And if Domenic Jejeune did this often enough, Maik could begin to understand what all the fuss was about.

29

The DCS emerged from her car and hugged her coat around her, although there was only the lightest of breezes up on the rise. Beverly Brennan pulled up next to her and got out. The two women exchanged a hug and a few brief words. Jejeune watched them from a distance, though he was not sure what he was looking for.

The women walked toward him together, carefully picking their way over the gravel in their high heels. Their eyes flickered toward the blue sheet as they approached, but neither woman made a point of looking in that direction. When DCS Shepherd got close enough, Jejeune could see that she had been crying. Fresh makeup had been carefully applied, but he could see the red skin around the base of her nostrils, and the slightly sunken eyes. Beverly Brennan looked as composed and polished as he would have expected. But there was something that connected the women, an atmosphere that hung around them, like the stillness before an electrical storm. There was no animosity between them. Domenic was sure of it. Whatever it was that these women felt, it was a shared emotion.

"I can't begin to express my outrage. This is so terrible," said Brennan. "I just …" She stopped short of saying she couldn't believe it. The body lying beneath the sheet a few feet away was enough to convince even the most resolute skeptic. "I understand Peter was your main suspect in the murder of Cameron Brae. I don't know what to say. I considered him a dear friend as well as a colleague. I would never have suspected that Peter, of all people, could be capable of such an unspeakable act. It must be a mistake, surely."

"It seems to be the most likely explanation, at the moment."

"But you have your doubts?"

"In the absence of a confession, there is always room for doubt," said DCS Shepherd. "What he's saying is that we've absolutely no concrete proof at all that Peter was involved in anything. Right, what do we have here so far?" she asked.

The effort of keeping her composure was obviously taking its toll on the DCS. Her voice wavered dangerously at times, and her attempts to sound efficient and businesslike fell just the wrong side of brusque overcompensation.

"It looks as if the victim's … Mr. Largemount's killer was waiting for him in the shadows beneath those beech trees," said Jejeune.

They strolled over to the damp earth beneath the trees. Above them, the Rooks cawed loudly, descending to lower branches to make their displeasure all the more apparent. Shepherd looked up into the trees. "What the hell's wrong with those bloody birds?"

"They're agitated," said Jejeune. "The rookery took a direct hit from the second shotgun blast. A couple of nests were destroyed and we found the bodies of three adult birds on the ground beneath the trees."

He could see Shepherd's anger building; the frustration and outrage beginning to turn in his direction at his indulgence in trivial details, especially *bird* details. Perhaps, as retribution for the ambush she had set up in her office, he should let her humiliate herself; let her rant about Domenic and his bloody bird obsession, before calmly delivering his findings. It would send the message that he didn't appreciate elaborate charades, where friends probed for answers to questions others were unwilling to ask. But for Domenic, the humiliation of another person was always an empty victory. Besides, at this moment the DCS was vulnerable, wounded by her grief. It would have been a graceless act to seek revenge on someone so fragile.

"It suggests there was a struggle," he said quietly. "The first barrel went off point blank, but the second must have been pointing almost directly up when it was discharged. It suggests Mr. Largemount was grappling for the shotgun at that point."

The DCS nodded. She had already gotten to where Jejeune was going next. For Largemount to have approached this closely, it suggested that he knew his killer. And that he wasn't expecting to have thc shotgun turned on him. Suddenly it all seemed too much for her, the realization of what had happened, the horrible reality of the shrouded body lying on the ground behind them, the constant, manic scolding of the Rooks. She wandered over toward the body, head bowed, silent.

Beverly Brennan watched her go before turning to Jejeune. "But surely you can't be certain that is what happened? There could be other explanations ..."

"There could be," said Jejeune, in a tone that suggested there would not be, in this case.

"If it is true about Peter, even if I still can't quite bring myself to believe it, does this mean this terrible business is finally over? I mean when you have made an arrest in this case, obviously."

"No, I don't think it is. You see, I am not convinced this is about retribution for Cameron Brae's death."

"But the slogan, the graffiti ..."

"I think this could be about the wind farm," continued Jejeune. "It's not the most popular technology. There are the subsidies, and the doubts about its ability to deliver the required power on a consistent basis. Plus the gas-fired plant that is going to be necessary as a backup."

"That's a very short-sighted view, Inspector. You surprise me. There are clear and demonstrable benefits to wind power. This project was central to my election campaign, but I supported it not to win votes, but because I truly believed in it. Peter and I were united in our conviction that it was absolutely vital to the economic future of the area. And I can assure you, the polling numbers suggest it was almost universally supported by the people around here. For that reason, you should know I intend to do everything I can to keep this project going. If nothing else, it will serve as a legacy to a truly remarkable man."

Not for the first time, Jejeune realized his lack of roots in the area hampered his ability to fill in the background. What would the locals, steeped in generations of farming and land preservation, really have made of this wind farm? Perhaps they appreciated the economic arguments and had supported Brennan's position as wholeheartedly as she claimed. But surely there would have been a fair amount of resistance, too? He would have given a lot to have been around during her political campaign, to see how much of this rhetoric she had trotted out, and how well it had been received.

"The merits of wind power are irrelevant at the moment, Ms. Brennan. But the man responsible for bringing the wind farm to Saltmarsh is dead." Jejeune seemed to consider his next sentence very carefully, as if perhaps the wording of it might hold particular significance. "I believe you should consider taking extra safety precautions yourself."

Brennan looked shocked. "Me? Why ever should I be at risk?"

He had not meant to alarm her, merely to alert her to the danger, but he could see she was shaken. Like many politicians, she considered herself removed from the fate of her constituents, sheltered from their consequences.

"You have been very vocal in your support of this wind farm. If this is some form of a reaction against it ..."

She stiffened slightly. "Then I suggest it would be better for everyone if you find these people and bring them to justice as soon as possible."

"I agree," said Shepherd, returning to the group. "This was vicious. It was cold-hearted, and it was premeditated. I want these Earth Front bastards brought in, Domenic."

"At the moment, we have no real evidence that Earth Front were involved."

"Evidence? What do you call that?" She flung a hand toward the slogan on the wall.

Brennan stepped forward. "Inspector, I'm sure we all appreciate your willingness to look beyond the obvious, but there is some merit in taking things at face value. I don't see that you can ignore blatant evidence at a crime scene just because it doesn't fit into your convoluted theories. Sometimes the simple explanation is the best one, surely."

He was uncomfortable discussing the case in front of Brennan, but he was far from certain the DCS, in her current state, would agree to exclude her. In a way that Jejeune couldn't quite understand, Shepherd seemed to be drawing strength from Brennan's presence. But if the absence of compelling evidence wasn't going to carry the argument today, maybe simple logic would.

"As far as I am aware, Earth Front didn't even know Largemount was a suspect in Cameron Brae's murder," said Jejeune simply.

DCS Shepherd stole another backward glance at the

flimsy blue sheet as it rippled in the breeze. "Brae's son did. He's a member, isn't he? And as I understand it, you practically identified Peter for him as a suspect. I want the son brought in, under caution."

"I'm not sure …"

"Immediately, do you understand? Bring him in, Domenic, or I'll find somebody who will."

As she turned to leave, her heel caught in the gravel and she tipped slightly to her left, off balance. Brennan caught her arm and supported her, and once righted, the two women began their ungainly tiptoe through the loose stones back toward their waiting cars.

Maik came over as soon as the women had left, approaching with all the enthusiasm of a man entering a site where a radiation leak has been reported. Despite the breeze up on the ridge, he was sweating.

"Are you okay?" Jejeune eyed him with concern.

"Yeah, just a bit of heartburn. They've started putting more pickles in the sandwiches down at The Boatman's Arms. They think we won't notice they've cut down on the ham. That was me, by the way, who said you'd mentioned Largemount to Malcolm Brae. She had asked if he was in the clear."

Jejeune gestured with his hand to show it didn't matter. He watched Beverly Brennan's Renault make the tight turn in the forecourt and speed away, spewing gravel from beneath the tires. He did not want to be stampeded into a course of action just because the local MP wanted a tidy solution, but at the moment he could see no way around obeying the DCS's directive.

"When I first met Ms. Brennan, she went out of her way to explain her shift toward development from environmental activism. Any particular thoughts on people who volunteer elaborate explanations for their positions, Sergeant?"

"Well, sir, thoughtful as it is of them to help us out like that, I do sometimes wonder if they do it to stop us looking for our own explanations."

"And if we did?"

"There were some whispers about her private life a while back. I didn't pay much attention to them at the time, but I could start digging around if you like. I'm sure Constable Holland isn't short of a few details."

"Let's start with the most obvious motive: money. It takes a lot to run a political campaign. As soon as the wind farm subsidies started to roll in, Largemount would have had more than enough to start bankrolling his favourite candidate. Check Ms. Brennan's bank records, see if any large deposits of cash may have influenced her opinion on the merits of wind farms."

"Can I ask why we're going this route?"

"Because there was something wrong with this wind farm deal from the start. Brae didn't denounce it, he completely ignored it, despite the fact that it was virtually on his doorstep. You heard how vehemently he opposed Archie Christian's GM project, yet even though the potential impact of Largemount's wind farm was much greater, Brae never even gave it a second glance. Largemount wouldn't have been able to make him back off, but maybe Beverly Brennan found a way. Either way, she's just become the leading proponent of wind power in these parts. And I think that might put her in a lot of danger."

30

It just didn't fit. Largemount had been responsible for Cameron Brae's death. Jejeune was sure of that. Whether or not Brae's son had come to the same conclusion, he did not know. But even if he had, was it really Malcolm Brae standing in the forecourt of Peter Largemount's ancestral home that night, waiting to end the developer's life with a shotgun? By the end of this night, Jejeune would almost certainly know one way or the other. But a long shift awaited him between now and then.

Jejeune altered his position in the bushes and turned the observation of the house back over to Maik. In the dark stillness of the waiting, he ran over the crime scene again in his mind. The way the car was parked, the dead birds, the position of the body, the injuries. He had done so many times recently, each time less and less convinced that it incriminated Malcolm Brae. Again, from the top. It's dark when Largemount gets home. He sweeps that big Bentley of his into his driveway. He's probably had one too many at the Hunt Club, but he's not too drunk to get himself home safely. He gets out, fumbling with his keys — dropped by the car — and notices the graffiti. Disorientation, a distraction. He sees somebody. Or somebody calls out to him. They are standing in the shadow of the beech trees. He walks toward the trees and as the security floodlights snap on, he recognizes Malcolm Brae. Malcolm Brae, a little left of normal on a good day, and now holding a shotgun. Malcolm Brae, the son of the man Largemount has recently murdered. Holding a shotgun, and pointing it at Peter Largemount. So what does Largemount do? Run for cover? Dive behind the Bentley, hugging his head in his hands? Fall on his knees and beg for mercy? No. He walks over for a chat!

Jejeune shook his head. It just didn't fit. But with the DCS taking an active role in the investigation now, Jejeune's hands were tied, and he would only start to unravel things once he got Malcolm Brae down to the station. So that's what he was here to do.

From his cover behind the screen of bushes, Jejeune looked at the house again, noting the backlit shadows behind the drawn curtains in the room off to the right. Earth Front had chosen their base well, a roomy, two-storey house on a big piece of land near the edge of the village. The house was big enough to hold meetings and planning sessions, and there was plenty of space for overnighters and out-of-towners to kip down on the floor. And it was far enough from the neighbours that any comings and goings could take place largely unobserved.

Earth Front had a long history of violent resistance to arrests, so a surprise raid had been the obvious choice. Malcolm Brae's presence inside the house had been confirmed by surveillance, but how many other people were in there with him was still unknown. Three had entered the premises after Brae, two of them known to police from earlier encounters. But there could be as many as four or five others, perhaps nine in total, in the house. The DCS wanted a clean arrest with a minimum of collateral damage. Jejeune's experience told him that was a big ask. And the odds hadn't been shortened by DCS Shepherd's decision to bring in an Armed Response Team. True, there was still a shotgun out there somewhere, and Earth Front had form elsewhere in the country with explosives.

"And we are talking about a murder here, Domenic, so it's armed backup all the way, I'm afraid. Full gear and vests for all participants. We take no chances with this lot. And I want no foul-ups. I don't want someone walking away just because we couldn't remember basic police procedure. Do I make myself clear?" She had turned her head here, to include everybody gathered around her, but Jejeune had no doubt who it was she was talking to.

Then to him directly, "I want you there to process the arrest, Domenic, and to secure the scene. And keep an eye on your lot, for God's sake."

His lot was here on merit. Salter and Holland had done the training because racking up the courses was the fastest track to promotion. Maik was here because, quite simply, there was probably no police officer on the east coast better suited for this type of operation.

A crackle in Jejeune's earpiece was followed by the hushed voice of the ART commander. "They're in position," Jejeune told the team huddled behind him.

They were all quiet. Holland's jaw was working a wad of gum as he stared, unblinking, at the house. Salter looked a million miles away. Thinking about her son? Jejeune had seen her, looking at his picture on her desk just before they had left to come out here. Maik was just still. Preternaturally still, like a stalking animal about to pounce. Centred, focused, composed. This was Maik's territory, night operations, the action. Jejeune could see the sweat glistening on his brow and at his temples. *All composed on the outside, Sergeant? How about on the inside?*

Jejeune was always surprised by how calm he found himself on operations like this. He was not much for the action side of things. If push came to shove, he could probably manage either, he supposed. But his thoughts rarely strayed in the direction of physical confrontations. For some reason, though, he never felt worried. Tense, certainly, but when events were so far outside your control like this, worrying about how things might turn out seemed like a waste of energy.

The order came down from the ART commander, and Jejeune mounted the stone stairs. He knocked loudly on the door, announcing the police presence and demanding entry.

Afterward, the inquiry put the sound down to wood; either a plank falling hard, slapping loudly against the floor, or even a hammer blow; there was plenty of placard-making equipment found in the house. Certainly, the search of the house turned up nothing in the way of firearms. A couple of hunting knives, a length of cord, and various chemicals that could have become explosives with time and skill, but that was it. No guns, no ammunition, no weapons of mass destruction. But on the night, with the air still and silent and the officers' knuckles white on their weapons, the loud, sharp report coming from inside the house, perfectly timed to be a response to Jejeune's knock, was enough to spring the tightly wound task force into action.

Jejeune heard the shattering of glass and the splintering of the back door, the shouts, the commands, even before Holland had muscled past him and smashed the front door lock with his boot.

Most of the inquiry's later findings were based on Jejeune's own observations, backed up in the significant details by the ART commander's contributions. But he had been in the thick of the action, rounding people up and forcing them to the ground, while Jejeune, positioned as he was in the front doorway, had the perfect vantage point to watch it all unfold.

It was really two operations. The four officers of the ART had piled in through the back door, but their surprise entry had been met by aggressive resistance from at least six Earth Front members gathered in the kitchen. The kitchen was in direct sightline from the front door, down the long, narrow hallway, and there was already blood by the time Jejeune got his first view of the scene, so at least one of the Earth Front group had been hit by the shattering glass from the back door. Jejeune saw a young couple scurry down the stairs to the cellar with an ART officer in pursuit. He also noted the four people in the front parlour to his right. They had been sitting on sofas around a low table when the ART made their move, but they were up on their feet by the time Jejeune's squad got to them, making active confrontation easier. He saw the thin, pale-faced man race past him up the stairs to his left, toward the bedrooms, and Maik follow him, taking the stairs two at a time. He heard the window break upstairs in the bedroom, and now, down here in the parlour again, he saw the girl with the blond ponytail launch herself at Salter, sending her hurtling backward, where the corner of a large old oak desk caught her under the armpit, just beyond the protection of the flak vest. He saw Holland fling himself toward the girl, taking a blow above the ear from the machete swing of a wooden stake, and he saw the constable fall heavily onto the blonde. Later, at the pub, Holland would tell his friends what a great body she had, but in truth all he saw was the dirty yellow ponytail as his black vest hit her full in the face and pressed it into the wooden floor.

Jejeune saw it all, so why didn't he see the ART officer follow Maik up the same stairs, so that it came as so much of a shock when he heard, as clearly as if there had been silence in the house instead of mayhem, the strident command, shouted into the officer's shoulder-mounted radio. *"Officer down, officer down. Request ambulance support now. Repeat ..."*

The others must have heard it, too, even over the din and the crashing of furniture and the bellowed commands from the kitchen and the shouted defiance, because they stopped. They all stopped. Eyes turned toward the stairway, toward Jejeune, who was up the stairs now, two-at-a-timing them like Maik, and now looking at the soles of Danny Maik's shoes, and then at a long grey figure stretched out on the carpet in the bedroom hallway, face down.

By the time Jejeune came back downstairs, the chaos had leaked from the house like the air escaping from a balloon and the Earth Front members were being shepherded meekly out through the front door. The police van was already crowded, so two of the suspects were eased into the back of one of the police cars that had responded to the radio call. Two ambulance units had responded, as well. Holland sat on the rear step of one of them, holding a blood-soaked towel to his head. Six stitches, expertly put in by one of the medical crew on the spot. *Fine to drive himself? You're having a laugh, Sir.*

Beside Jejeune, two members of the ART were discussing with the commander whether the Earth Front group had been expecting the raid. The element of surprise hadn't given them nearly as much of an edge as they had hoped. But then again, who goes unarmed up against a fully-equipped ART squad? If the Earth Front members had been tipped off, they would have either been tooled up, or gone altogether. It was an important discussion, with ramifications that could have reached right into the heart of the division, but Jejeune couldn't concentrate on it at the moment. It was just another impression, another sensation crowding into the kaleidoscope of images swirling around him. The inquiry would decide later that the group had received no advance warning of the raid. They were simply a group of people used to violence, and quicker to react to it than the average law-abiding citizen. All clear.

Salter stood beside Jejeune, favouring her left side. She was looking at the house, bathed in the flickering blue lights, at Holland, at the police van, only half-listening to the earnest young medical attendant who was speaking to her: "Likely no broken ribs, bruising only, but if I let you go home, you've got to get yourself properly checked out in the morning. Promise?"

Promise.

"I'll just have to hug Max with the other arm," she told anyone who wanted to listen.

She seemed on the verge of tears. Perhaps it was the pain, thought Jejeune. But then again, she had been fine a few moments ago. Until the inert body of Danny Maik had been stretchered past them to the ambulance that was waiting, doors open, ready to take him to hospital.

31

Jejeune entered the interview room and slapped a file down loudly on the desk. He sat and closed his eyes for a moment. The last of the adrenalin from the raid had stopped jiggering through his body. In his mind a blue light was twirling slowly; Maik, fitted with an oxygen mask, a flimsy grey blanket draped over him, was lying in an ambulance. No wounds, no injuries. Something internal, most likely, they'd said. But Domenic Jejeune still had plenty of emotion to fuel his interview with Malcolm Brae without putting on any act. His own misgivings could be put aside for now.

Malcolm Brae sat slumped in a chair, sideways on to the scarred wooden desk. His sweater was torn at the neck and there was an angry scoring along the knuckles of his right hand, but otherwise he seemed to have suffered no physical damage during the arrest. He kept his eyes averted as Jejeune settled himself in and opened the file. Right to counsel waived. No need. Not guilty. Of anything. For now, Jejeune would hold off on any charges, despite the DCS's wishes. He would see where the interview led him first.

"I imagine you had high hopes when you first joined Earth Front, a genuine belief that you might be able to make a difference. It must make you angry, the way things have gone. I mean, really, what do these people care about environmental issues? Might just as well be the G20 they are protesting against, for all the interest they have in your cause. How disappointing for a true believer like you, to be stuck with a bunch of people who have little in common beyond a love of violent protest."

Malcolm Brae stirred. He shifted in his chair to face Jejeune and laid his forearms on the desk. "You're right, of course. In fact, I feel so darned disillusioned right now, I might as well just confess to everything. Got your pencil ready?" he asked in a flat, dead tone. He looked up and Jejeune saw his eyes for the first time: dark, sullen, defiant. Brae's tone hardened. "Earth Front's manifesto is quite clear. We are a legitimate environmental activist organization. Now either you know this and are pretending not to, or you are as incompetent as everybody seems to think you are. Not me, by the way. I think you're the real deal. I do hope you're not going to disappoint me." He looked around the room and spread his hands. "My liberty does rather depend on it."

"When I spoke to you at your father's house, on the night of his death, you said you disapproved of your father's work."

"My *stepmother*'s house, Inspector. And that was true. He didn't go far enough. Always a little too afraid of upsetting the establishment. Argued a good game, but when it came down to really taking action," he leaned forward conspiratorially and lowered his voice, "lacked the stones for it, actually. Don't look so shocked, Inspector. Father-son disappointment can go both ways, you know. Any chance of a cup of tea? A biscuit would be nice, too. I missed my dinner tonight," he said archly.

"We have evidence linking Earth Front to Peter Largemount's death. We found writing equipment in the house that matched one of the threats he received for refusing access to the Ivory Gull. We also recovered cans of spray paint, an exact match to that used on the wall at the murder site."

"Evidence? Really, Inspector, you're embarrassing yourself. But you don't really believe it was us at all, do you? People would like it to be us, of course. Our passion and commitment makes them uneasy. Society is not comfortable with such uncompromising approaches. They're used to the politics of accommodation. *Can't we all just get along, find some common ground, agree to disagree?* Well, no, we can't, because the earth is being raped by ruthless people with no morality and no shame, and unless somebody stands up and fights these people on their own terms, nothing is ever going to change. Earth Front does what we need to do, what others would like to do, if only they dared."

"Uncompromising points of view *should* make people uneasy. Start denying the inconvenient details and it is easier to believe the ends justify the means. But I suppose once you have a casualty or two under your belt as an organization, it's hard to go back to how things were before. Everybody gets bound up by the guilty secrets, and the only way forward is to become even more extreme. We have completed an inventory of the weapons at your house, by the way. You keep very good records."

"It makes the insurance company less nervous."

"One gun is missing. A Churchill, 1982."

"Really, imagine my surprise. Still, I've no doubt it will show up at some point, covered with my fingerprints. Probably just prior to the trial, I should imagine."

Jejeune ignored the remark. "Do you know where it is?"

"No idea, but it's worth over two thousand pounds, so I suppose robbery could be a motive. You've been to my workshop. Not the most secure of environments." He leaned forward confidentially. "We tend to go by trust a lot in this part of the world. Bit of a mistake, it seems."

"Perhaps criminally so."

"Not really. I'd be willing to bet the gun's firing mechanism is still locked up in my safe. Ammunition too, stored separately, as per the applicable laws. Still, it would be easy enough to install another firing mechanism, if you knew what you were doing. For the record, I do."

"Was it functional? With a mechanism fitted?"

"Enough to kill Peter Largemount at point blank range, you mean? Oh, I should think so. Of course, even if you recover the gun, the rifling won't help you. Still, I'm sure you have other ways of determining if it's the murder weapon. Has it been fired recently, for example. And you'll want to be testing suspects for residue. Unless the killer wore gloves, of course. Or had a wash in paraffin in the last couple of days."

Both men stared down at the rough, workman's hands splayed on the desk, scarred with tool slippages and impacts with hard surfaces. Hands that had not seen soap and water recently.

"Earth Front is aware of the consequences of its actions. But we're not mad. Whatever we do, it's carefully thought through, maximum impact, consequences, ramifications. If we had decided to take it upon ourselves to kill Peter Largemount, do you really think we wouldn't want to claim responsibility afterward? I am telling you, Inspector, Earth Front isn't responsible for Peter Largemount's death. And neither am I."

Brae paused for a moment and pushed himself back from the table. "If you fancy taking our chat any further, I'm afraid we'll have to do it without that." Brae's thumb indicated the digital sound recorder on the desk beside them.

Jejeune thought for a long time, as the silence of the interview room closed in around them. He leaned toward the microphone. "Interview suspended at 11:43." He switched off the machine.

"You were aware that your father suspected Lesser Marsh was contaminated? I think he was threatening to go public with the news, unless Largemount abandoned his plans to expand the wind farm. And that's why Largemount killed him."

"And you think I killed Largemount to avenge my father's death?"

Jejeune was aware that if he got the confession now, with the tape off, he would have a lot more work to do. But Brae shook his head, as Jejeune suspected he might. "No, I would have. Perhaps I should have, but I didn't."

"The absent waders, they alerted your father to the contamination?"

Brae flickered a glance at the constable by the door. Eyes front, back straight, hands folded behind him. "A sandwich would do, anything really. I'm famished."

Jejeune signalled to the constable. The cafeteria would be closed at this time of night. He would have to hunt around for something. It might take a while. That was okay.

As soon as the door closed behind the constable, Brae sat more upright. "My father knew about the contamination because Largemount told him," he said. "When they did the survey of his land, Alwyn found it and he went to my father. They confronted Largemount and he admitted it. A big spill or something. Sometime in the past. But he said it was contained, swore it."

Malcolm Brae sighed, as if poisonous gas had finally escaped from within him. But now that he had started, he wanted to get it all out. He began talking faster, more urgently, looking at Jejeune's face directly, to make sure he was getting it, taking it all in. There wouldn't be a second time for this.

"Largemount needed that wind farm approval or he faced ruin. The estate was drowning in debt. Usual story. Upkeep of an ancient pile. No income from the serfs anymore. Largemount was in dire financial straits. He risked losing everything if Alwyn and my father refused to sign off on the survey. But he still had some influence. They always do, don't they, the blue bloods? He told them he could get them what they wanted. Funding for Alwyn's research? Well, he was on the university's finance committee, wasn't he? And for my father? Someone he knew in television was looking for somebody to host a little documentary he had an idea for, about the value of wetlands. In the end my father decided the television program offered him the chance to reach more people, have a bigger impact. The greater good. How many times has that been used to justify a sin? Or a crime?"

Jejeune was silent for a long moment. "You found out about your father's arrangement with Largemount. That's what your argument was about." It was a statement.

Brae shrugged. "I suppose it was, though neither of us mentioned Largemount specifically. I know he was angry, with himself, mostly, for being such a fool."

"That must have upset you. First to find out he had compromised his integrity like that, and then for him to show no remorse."

"Oh, he was extremely remorseful. But only in the wider sense. He actually talked about betraying his public, if you can believe it. Not a word about his family, of course. He just could never bring himself to consider the small details. And, unfortunately, in my father's world, his family, his proper family, well, we were the smallest details of all."

"You didn't expose this deal yourself, even after your father was killed. Why was that, I wonder? Were you trying to protect your father's reputation? Or was there some other reason?"

"Blackmail?" Malcolm Brae laughed, a genuine laugh this time. "Please, Inspector. I had no proof, only my father's word, and with him dead, Largemount would have simply denied there ever was an arrangement. And Alwyn would have backed him up, obviously. No. I wouldn't normally approach a man like Peter Largemount without a large dose of hand sanitizer nearby anyway. I certainly wouldn't want any of his money. I told you. I never saw Largemount after my father's death. I didn't kill him."

Malcolm Brae's eyes went to the door. He leaned forward, needing the closing of the space between the men to add emphasis to his words. His eyes were bloodshot and his breathing was getting faster. He was on the fast track to somewhere, and both men realized he was running out of time. Jejeune hoped he got to his destination before he came off the rails completely.

"I don't want this getting out, Inspector. If it does, I'll deny any knowledge of a deal. My father made a mistake. Was he weak? Certainly. Stupid? Possibly. But he believed in his work, and he gave his life to it. And who's to say he made the wrong decision. Do you know how many marsh monitoring programs have been initiated in schools up and down the country because of *The Marsh Man*. Not to mention all the other people who have been brought to conservation work through his activism. He doesn't deserve to have his legacy spoiled by one moment of madness."

So now Jejeune had it. The missing piece. That was the hold Brae had over Largemount, one that would have been enough to force him to abandon his expansion plans. The agreement between the three men to keep the contamination quiet. Revealing the pollution spill itself wouldn't have been enough to kill for. It would have destroyed Largemount's business, but not the man himself. But bribery, falsifying government reports, that would have been enough to send Largemount to prison, to ruin him personally. And for a man like Peter Largemount, that *was* enough to kill for. So now Jejeune could close the file on the Cameron Brae murder. But there was no sense of triumph, no satisfaction, merely a vacuum where the questions had been, a vacuum soon to be filled, Jejeune knew, by other uncertainties.

Malcolm Brae had gone silent, and when Jejeune looked up, he saw tears running unchecked down the younger man's cheeks, tracing their way through the dirt and smudges. Whether they were for his father's memory, or regret at how their relationship had ended, Jejeune couldn't say. He only knew they were not for Malcolm Brae's own predicament. Because at that moment, he realized, Cameron Brae's son could not have cared less about his own fate.

32

Jejeune wasn't a big fan of intuition, but what else could it have been, really? He stood in the entrance hall of the university and listened, straining to hear beyond the buzz of the sulphur emergency lights, and the empty, eerie silence of the night outside. A footfall? He took another step inside and paused. All quiet. Gently, he eased the big door closed behind him and began walking along the darkened corridors toward Miles Alwyn's laboratory.

Large swathes of shadow fell across his path. Only a greyish, ghostly light filtering in from the clerestory windows high above offered any illumination. Jejeune's steps echoed off the walls. He felt a momentary movement of air, as if some phantom was tracking him, moving with a stealth to match his own. Jejeune stopped abruptly and peered back along the corridor into the darkness. The shadows could have given shelter to a thousand forms, earthly or otherwise. He listened, but only the hiss of the silence came back to him.

Alwyn did not look as surprised as he might have at Jejeune's unannounced nocturnal visit. "Inspector, I hear congratulations are in order. It must be a terrible time for poor Katherine, of course. To have lost Cameron, and now

Malcolm's arrest.... Still, to have resolved both murders so quickly, well, your reputation clearly does you justice."

Though a general sense of relief was normal when a murder suspect was arrested, there seemed to be more than a few people in these parts keen to rush things to a conclusion Jejeune felt might still be some way off. He wondered, too, where Alwyn was getting his information. Malcolm Brae's arrest had not been shrouded in any particular secrecy, but it was hardly a matter of public record yet, either. Quentin Senior's earlier warnings about the Saltmarsh rumour mill seemed well-founded.

"I am trying to fill in a few gaps, Professor. I was wondering if you could shed any more light on Cameron Brae's request for that survey."

Alwyn had turned back to his experiments, and seemed to find nothing in Jejeune's question worthy of drawing his attention away from them. "I thought you had already answered that, Inspector. Something about some rarity he was hoping to find. How is your sergeant, by the way? His health, I'd heard?"

"Doing better, I believe." Jejeune wandered over to a window and drew back a blind a short way with a fingertip. The university car park was dark and quiet, the few cars scattered throughout it empty. He turned away and took a seat at Alwyn's desk.

"He's not a university man, the sergeant." Alwyn wasn't posing a question. "It's a pity, he has a good mind. We could have made something of it, if we had gotten him early enough."

"I'm afraid the army beat you to it."

"Ah, military. I should have guessed. Must have been a difficult transition, I would imagine, from the black-and-white world of army life into police work, with all its shades of uncertainty."

Alwyn waited a beat for Jejeune to comment. Seeing he would be disappointed, he continued. "It's funny; I would have thought a man like Sergeant Maik would find the clarity of science comforting. And yet he seems to hold me responsible for Cameron's marital problems, simply because I told his wife the truth. Problems in relationships are inevitable, in any species, but they are hardly the fault of the scientists who observe them. It is like blaming the disruptions in cetacean mating behaviour on the scientists who discovered that the oceans are becoming louder."

Jejeune couldn't help himself. "Louder?"

"Oceans are becoming more acidic with climate changes, and higher acidity allows sound to travel much farther. The impacts on the mating calls of animals such as whales and dolphins are potentially enormous."

"I think for the sergeant it's more a question of whether it was necessary to be so forthright," said Jejeune.

"Or whether I should have withheld the facts, you mean, out of some sort of loyalty to my former colleague?" Alwyn smiled smugly. "Surely my greater loyalty must be to the truth." The professor's tone softened slightly. "Regardless of what you might think, I did like Cameron, despite his obvious flaws. He was a little brittle, perhaps, in some respects, for such an accomplished person, but then ambitious people so often are, aren't they?"

Jejeune apparently did not consider he had spent enough time among such types to form an opinion. He rose silently from his chair and walked to the door. He peered out into the darkened corridor. "Are any of the other labs in this wing occupied just now?"

"Shouldn't think so. Can I ask what you're looking for? Visitors rarely call at this time of night. It's one of the reasons I like working late. It's nice and quiet here."

It would be necessary to see Alwyn's reaction to Jejeune's next question. He walked around the lab bench and stood silently behind the rack of test tubes, waiting, saying nothing, until Alwyn eventually straightened to meet his gaze.

"What did Cameron Brae actually want that report for, Professor? Was it to confirm the findings at Lesser Marsh? The ones that showed it was contaminated?"

Alwyn's smile was indulgent, but probably not as reassuring as he had hoped. "It is not unusual for a survey to find contaminants, Inspector. One litre of oil has the capacity to contaminate a million litres of fresh water. It would be barely detectable at such levels, but it would still be present."

"But concentration levels high enough to drive away bird species permanently? That would have been sufficient for the ministry to have denied Largemount his permit for the wind farm. And yet somehow one was still granted, wasn't it?"

Alwyn's soft brown eyes were wide and owl-like behind the spectacles, but Jejeune detected for the first time a flint of steel. So many academics he had known seemed unsuited for a role in the real world; naive, innocent, even, as if they thought their pursuit of higher knowledge isolated them somehow from the realities of everyday life. But Alwyn had a nervy edge, a survivor's instinct about him. Jejeune supposed that in academia, like any other field, to get to the very top, you had to know how to take care of yourself.

Slowly, and with great clarity, Jejeune laid out the details of the deal Malcolm Brae had revealed to him. Alwyn listened patiently, the same wide-eyed look of indulgent curiosity on his face. When Jejeune had finished, the professor clasped his hands in front of him, as if he was afraid that the truth might somehow escape from them.

"Well, Inspector, Malcolm Brae's story certainly has the appeal of neatness and simplicity, two things that are undoubtedly of great importance to the general public. Unfortunately, neither real life nor science tends to offer us such tidy solutions.

As far as I am aware, Peter Largemount's influence on the funding committee was no greater than that of any other member." Alwyn spread his hands to indicate his little empire. "Certainly, nobody could deny the investment has been amply repaid. Over the past five years this department has gained an international reputation. I am myself now considered one of the world's foremost authorities on salt marsh ecology. I am also, by some considerable measure, the most widely and frequently published member of the faculty, which, frankly, appears to be the raison d'être for all of us academics these days. But to return to your point, while it may well be true that Cameron entered into an arrangement with Peter Largemount, since neither one of them is any longer able to either confirm or deny it, I'm afraid all you are left with is one more unsubstantiated rumour."

Jejeune seemed to be listening to something beyond their conversation. He walked back to the door and eased it open slightly.

"The thing is," said Jejeune, peering into the pockets of darkness, "despite the contamination showing up in the original survey, Largemount was still granted his development permit." He turned to face Alwyn. "I am told that some contaminants are remarkably stable. It would be a relatively straightforward process to re-examine the soil samples you submitted and extrapolate the contaminant levels back five years. You were aware that the ministry keeps the samples submitted with land survey reports?"

Jejeune had half-expected Alwyn to take refuge in his experiments again, to become suddenly busy or preoccupied. But Alwyn needed no time to compose himself.

"May I ask who it was you consulted about this? There are very few in this field who would be comfortable challenging the findings of a survey conducted by a peer of my standing. Robertson, perhaps? Envy in academia has a particularly unpalatable flavour, I find. Still, it is perhaps to be expected from someone whose own career has so spectacularly failed to flourish."

Jejeune's silence confirmed that his sources were confidential.

"Perhaps it was Stiles. She's a good scientist. At least she knows what she's talking about, most of the time. But, yes, your source, whoever he or she is, is perfectly correct. If they were to do it properly, the results would accurately reflect the contaminant levels on Peter Largemount's property at the time of my original survey."

Alwyn's confidence was beginning to unnerve Jejeune. He had seen brazen denials before, but there was something about Alwyn's assured manner that didn't seem right. He was an intelligent man, and he knew all the bravado in the world wasn't going to alter the outcome of an independent examination of his survey results.

"But if the results you submitted were accurate, then why would the ministry approve the permit, unless ..."

"It is the bane of your profession, I suspect, to consider only wrongdoing. If it is not in one area, then it must be in another. There is no corruption in the ministry, Inspector, at least none that I am aware of. The approval of the permit was perfectly lawful, based on an accurate set of readings from Peter Largemount's land."

"Then I don't understand."

"That is because you are unwilling to consider the one obvious truth: the contamination levels did not exceed the thresholds at which the ministry would deny a development permit. And that is because there has never been any contamination spill on Peter Largemount's land."

"But, surely ..." But Jejeune's protest petered out as he realized he was unsure of what to say.

Alwyn took off his glasses and turned to stare directly at Jejeune. He tipped his body slightly forward across the desk, ready to deliver his wisdom, as he did to his PhD candidates on their first day.

"There are a number of contamination types, but we are talking here about the difference between static and transitory. A static contamination would be the result of a spill or a release, where the contaminants remain largely in the immediate area. This creates an immediate stochastic event, an ecological catastrophe, large or small, at the site. It results in high readings in the immediate vicinity, for protracted periods. In such circumstances, the ministry would require a controlled and monitored cleanup and subsequent retesting before they would consider issuing a development permit. But transitory contamination moves through the site, windblown sometimes, or via surface water. It delivers a constant supply of contaminant, enough to eradicate or drive away species, perhaps, but never accumulating in sufficiently high qualities to exceed threshold levels. This is what is happening at Lesser Marsh."

Having spent so much time in his life fielding lies, Jejeune recognized the truth when he heard it. He was stunned into silence. He felt the acidic bile rising in the back of his throat. How could he have been so wrong? Belatedly, he realized that in considering his own failings, he had missed the bigger picture. If Brae had no hold over Largemount about any contaminant spill, then the developer had no motive to kill him. Jejeune's investigation into Cameron Brae's murder was back at square one. Worse. Without Largemount, he had no suspects at all.

"And there could be no mistake? You're absolutely certain?" Jejeune heard a hint of panic in his voice. Had Alwyn detected it?

"I can assure you that these contaminants did not originate on Peter Largemount's property, Inspector. The concentration values throughout the site are far too low."

Jejeune was silent for a moment. This close to the coast, there would be many different water sources flowing into Lesser Marsh. Any one of them could be delivering the contaminants. The actual source of the spill could be miles away, in any direction.

Alwyn's head snapped round at the same time as Jejeune's. This time there could be no mistake, a footfall, a shuffling, something in the corridor. Alwyn, nearer the door, was first into the corridor, but Jejeune passed him easily and sprinted along the dark hallway back toward the entrance doors. Both men changed direction as they heard something, skittering shoes, off to one side, and ran toward where the sound had come from. At the end of the long corridor Alwyn doubled over, winded, and waved Jejeune on.

Jejeune ran blindly along the corridors, following sounds and echoes, twisting and turning until he was completely disoriented. He found himself at the end of a long hallway opening out onto a central atrium, a wide open space with exits in many directions. Jejeune paused and listened. He could hear his own breath, and feel his chest heaving. He surveyed the scene before him: a rabbit warren of corridors, hallways, staircases, doors; half-lit from above and deeply pocked with shadows. Whoever he was chasing knew that the darkness was their ally. Stillness and silence would be all that was needed to avoid detection, while he ran around in circles, chasing phantom footfalls and following imagined sounds. He moved out into the centre of the open space, pausing cautiously every few steps. Nothing. He paused again to look all around and listen. Somewhere back in the direction of the lab he heard hurried footsteps. Alwyn. *Where was he?* Jejeune sprinted back in the direction of the sound, hurtling around corners, jacket flailing, feet skidding on the polished floors. He saw the professor huddled against the wall.

"Did you see them?" asked Jejeune breathlessly.

Alwyn shook his head. The two men walked quickly back toward the lab.

Jejeune stopped suddenly as he reached for the door handle. "Have you been back here?"

"No."

Jejeune knew that some people would have found it difficult to remember whether they had left a door open or not. He wasn't one of them. The door had been open when they'd left. It was closed now. He placed a protective arm in front of Alwyn and opened the door slowly, using a handkerchief. The lab was empty. Except for the smell; a rich, sweet aroma he had smelled only once before — on the stock of Malcolm Brae's vintage Churchill shotgun.

Jejeune turned to Alwyn. "Any idea why someone would want to target you, Professor?"

"None at all. Surely this is all just some harmless student prank." Except he didn't believe that; Jejeune could see it in his eyes. Alwyn knew why he was being hunted, and it scared him. Enough that he was prepared to lie about it.

"Whoever it was, they're gone now. I don't imagine they're still on the university grounds," said Jejeune. "But I am going to call the university security service and ask them to escort you to your car. I'll wait here until forensics arrives. It's a warm night. Perhaps whoever it was forgot to wear their gloves."

33

Something had gone from the atmosphere of the incident room, and a stilted uneasiness had seeped in to fill the void. Beyond the basics, nothing had been said about the events at the Earth Front offices, and the lack of discussion had hardened by now into a willful avoidance, encouraged by the DCI's own willingness to treat the subject as toxic. They knew that if Danny Maik was here, there would have been a few assurances about their own conduct at least; an avuncular squeeze of Salter's shoulder as he went past, a quiet back-handed compliment to Holland: "*Well done, Constable. I'll know who to send next time there's a punch-up at the infants' school.*" Something to let them know they had done okay, got the job done, despite the general shambles that the arrest had become. But from Jejeune, there had been no acknowledgement, no mention, nothing. It was as if he would have liked to wipe the whole episode from his memory. As a result, everyone was left nursing their wounds, and their suspicions, in silence.

Jejeune's similar unwillingness to discuss Danny Maik's condition in any way was unnerving in its resolve. Any attempt to bring the subject up was summarily shut down with an abrupt change of topic, so unsubtle and transparent that the message was unmistakable. So they didn't even try anymore,

Holland's attempt that morning representing the last foray into the subject.

"Good news, about Danny, er, Sergeant Maik, sir. He's back at home. Nothing too serious, he tells me. I was thinking ..."

"Yes. That is good news, but for the moment let's press on with our briefing.... So, where are we on Beverly Brennan's financial statements? You were going to see if the sergeant's inquiries had turned up anything."

Holland pulled a face, but shifted gears as required. "Her finances are as clean as a whistle, but I tell you what, she certainly came about her convictions overnight. For years she was all about the environment, save the whales, anything you like, so long as it was green. And then all that changed, and it was all economic development and wise use of resources. But if she did sell her soul, there's no evidence of it in her bank account."

Jejeune pulled his bottom lip between his thumb and index finger. Of course, illicit funds could be hidden in any number of creative ways these days. But perhaps it was something else that had persuaded her to give up a lifetime commitment to environmental causes.

"Ideas?" he invited.

"Surveillance on her during a possible security threat some time back turned up something odd, secretive, like, about her comings and goings," offered Salter reluctantly. "But there are some questions us local coppers find it better not to ask, so it never went any further."

We, Constable, *we* local coppers, thought Jejeune. Life with Lindy had developed in him a pedant's intolerance for grammatical errors. He considered the substance of Salter's report instead, and thought about the two of them, Largemount and Brennan, at the Hunt Club dinner. If it was an affair with Largemount, the timing certainly fit. But where did that leave the DCS? Was it over between them before Shepherd began seeing him? Did she know about their affair, or care? Or was he completely on the wrong track with this? Was it just, as everybody claimed, a friendship between the DCS and Largemount? It was just one more ambiguity in a case that was nothing but. And again, Peter Largemount was at the centre of it all.

Jejeune felt an anxiety he had never known before. His case was falling to pieces, crumbling to dust in his hands. Nothing connecting Largemount to Brae's death had been found in the developer's house, and now even his motive had disappeared in a puff of smoke. Absent Malcolm Brae, who he believed innocent, Jejeune had no suspects, no motives, and no evidence for either murder. He remained convinced that Largemount at least knew something about Brae's murder, but was what he knew tied to his own death? Inquiries in that direction had failed to gain any traction whatsoever. For the first time since the investigation began, he was staring at the very real possibility that these murders would be taken away from the division before he was able to solve them.

Jejeune had shared nothing of his thoughts with the others since his interview with Alwyn. He spent his time on his own, sequestered in his office with the door closed, going through the evidence on a more or less continuous loop — *once more, from the beginning* — leaving his officers to puzzle over the ever more bizarre assignments he handed out. Today had been more of the same.

"Every water source, large or small, that connects with Lesser Marsh, Constable Holland. Don't rely on published data. Get the maps out and verify everything yourself. And Constable Salter, let's shift your research on marsh invertebrates to concentrate on what sorts of pollutants might cause their decline."

"While he looks after all the leads involving people," said Holland as soon as the door closed behind Jejeune. "Remember them, the real live human beings in this case?"

Salter picked up a file and riffled through it listlessly. "I don't like this," she said. "I can see not using Alwyn, if he thinks he might be involved. But there are plenty of other experts out there. Why does he want us to do all this stuff ourselves? And why, now, all of a sudden, is anything we find supposed to go to him directly, and nowhere else? What's he up to?"

"Wants to solve it all himself," said Holland simply. "Banjoed it all up first time around, so now he has to prove he's still their Golden Boy."

Possibly, thought Salter. But understanding it didn't make her like it any more. And it didn't alter the fact that it wasn't good police procedure, either.

"It would help if he could tell me what I'm supposed to be looking for in this lot," she said irritably.

"It would help if he knew," said Holland. "I don't think he has a clue anymore. He's just groping about in the dark. Not that there's anything wrong with that," he said with a smirk, "but it's no way to run a murder inquiry. This far in to the investigation, and he can't even tell us for certain that these two murders are related. How's that for progress? For all we know, they could be completely unrelated incidents. This could just be the settling of two separate accounts."

Lauren realized with a jolt that Holland was right. She had never even considered the possibility. "They have to be connected, though, don't they? We don't have people killing each other left and right out here. This is Saltmarsh, not Dodge City, for God's sake. Two unconnected murders?" She shook her head firmly. "Sorry, I'm not buying that. I'm just not."

Holland came over to sit on Lauren's desk, in that dangerously close way he had. He took the file off her and flipped back to the title page: *External Inhibitors in Copepod Reproduction Cycles.*

"Tell me he's joking. How are drainage patterns and shagging sea lice going to get us any closer to a result? If Jejeune wants to trace where the local waters flow, why doesn't he just get some of those rubber ducks they use up at the tidal bore races in Blakeney?"

He looked thoughtfully out the window behind Salter's desk before standing up abruptly and walking out. Salter watched him leave. It was a nice day for a drop-top drive in his A5. And she was sure he would pointedly avoid passing on his DCI's best wishes to Danny Maik when he saw him.

34

A thin Norfolk drizzle spattered the windshield, slanting in on that near horizontal approach that was, as far as Jejeune knew, unique to this part of the world. Since the storms of the previous week, the elements had been jousting for control of the north Norfolk skies. Today the rain was almost fine enough to be considered mist, but it was still capable of soaking a person through to the skin in a matter of moments. Lindy was probably already regretting her decision to accompany him today, thought Jejeune, even if she had said nothing and was gazing contentedly out the window. Still, he had his own problems. They drove through the lanes in silence, each locked in their own thoughts, willing to let the slow rhythmic slap of the windshield wipers fill the void between them.

On the horizon, Jejeune could see the turbines of Peter Largemount's farm. The wind had always been a part of life here. From the low scrub of the coastal areas to the flat plains of the inland farms, this entire landscape was shaped by wind. Wind and water. And it was to the water they were heading now.

By the time they arrived at Great Marsh, the rain had stopped, though the overcast skies threatened a return at any time. They made their way along a rough grassy track toward a tiny wooden hut, all but hidden from view by the surrounding hummocks. Quentin Senior emerged from the hut just as they arrived.

"Ah, Inspector, and lady friend. Can't stop, I'm afraid. Just about to go out and check the nets. You're welcome to come along if you like, or you could wait here. I won't be long."

Jejeune already knew what Lindy's decision would be. She wasn't going to miss a chance to observe something like bird netting for the first time. They caught up with Senior, who was tromping through the shoulder-high vegetation, showering fine sprays of raindrops from the tops of the grasses.

By the time they emerged into the small clearing, Senior had already drawn the mist net toward him and had begun the delicate task of extricating a small brown bird from the netting. The net stretched across the entire clearing, a distance of about ten feet, supported by narrow white posts at each end. Although it was easy enough to see now it was gathered, when stretched out, the fine netting would be almost invisible, especially to a bird emerging on the wing at speed from the surrounding vegetation.

"Doesn't it hurt them?" asked Lindy, watching the skilful way that Senior gathered bird and netting together in one hand and delicately slipped the mesh from the bird's feet.

"Injuries are surprisingly rare," said Senior over his shoulder, without pausing in his task. "No doubt the initial impact shocks them, but the nets are very fine, so they offer a soft landing, so to speak. Of course, predators will move in quickly if they see them all strung up and defenceless like this. Sad to say, they are as opportunistic as the rest of us when they see vulnerability exposed. I've had herons take all sorts of things out of nets before I could get to 'em." He nodded affirmatively at Lindy's horrified expression. "*Nature raw in tooth and claw.* And beak, too, apparently. But the main threat if you leave them hanging around too long is the cold. They're surprisingly susceptible, especially on a damp, drizzly sort of day like this. A bird's feathers provide a wonderful insulation, but if one is tipped up stern afore aft, like this feller here, the feathers can become displaced, allowing the cold air to get to their bodies. That's why we get them out and upright again as soon as we can."

Senior had been working swiftly as he spoke, disentangling birds and putting each in a small linen bag, which he gently tied at the neck before tucking it into a larger leather satchel on his hip. With the net cleared of captives, he began making his way back to the hut, with Jejeune and Lindy again falling into step behind him.

Inside the hut, Senior set about his tasks with the same brisk precision he had used in removing the birds from the netting. He fished each bag from his satchel in turn and gently laid it in a box lined with grass. Methodically, he took the first bag and weighed it, before carefully removing the bird inside. Holding it so that its head protruded between his first two fingers, he turned the bird over and examined it, spreading it wings and tail gently to examine its feathers. Lindy watched intently as he held the bird in one hand and meticulously recorded his findings on a small chart with the other. When he had finished, he fished a small metal ring from a compartmentalized box on the counter and recorded the number on his sheet. Then he slipped it over the bird's leg and squeezed it with a pair of crimping pliers until it was firmly fastened on the bird's leg. The whole process had taken seconds.

He turned to Lindy. "Would you like to do the honours?"

"Oh, I don't think …"

"Just cup your hands. There, like that. Gently, now."

Senior delicately set the bird on its back into her hands and closed her fingers loosely over it. She could feel no weight at all, only the warm soft movement of feathers, and the fluttering of a heartbeat as the bird's chest rested against her curled fingertips. She moved to the door, cradling her treasure, and stood for a moment in the open doorway before opening her hands. The bird flew away immediately, not with the graceful fluttering of doves she had seen in those symbolic releases at peace ceremonies, but with a frantic whirring of wings and feathers that took her by surprise. She realized she had been holding her breath and she released it now. Jejeune smiled at her.

"That was fantastic," she said, "even if it was just a transparent attempt to win me over to birding."

"Not a bit of it, my dear," scoffed Senior. "You are just helping out an old man with his research, that's all, eh Inspector?" He took up the second bag, and began the process again. A few faint raindrops pattered down, dappling the dusty grey glass of the hut's windows.

Jejeune wondered aloud about the effects of another heavy rainfall, so soon after the last deluge. "If it causes the seawater to flood into the marsh again, it will decrease the salinity even further."

Senior nodded his agreement. "It is a worry. I doubt the marsh has even had chance to recover its equilibrium from the last floods. If it remains out of balance for a long time, it could have an impact on which species remain here."

"Increased, darling," said Lindy to Jejeune. "When you add seawater, the salt content increases. Science not your strong subject?"

"Much as I hate to take a gentleman's part against a lady, I'm afraid your beau is quite correct, my dear," said Senior with a kindly smile. "It's so counter-intuitive; it's only natural to assume the speaker has made a mistake. But salt marshes are actually more salty than the sea. When seawater enters a salt marsh it dilutes the salinity. If it persists over any length of time, lower-saline tolerant species can survive, so you can get a shift in the species mix. Quite fascinating, really, the flux that these salt marshes go through."

Senior crossed to the door and opened it. He watched the bird flutter away from his huge palm with a soft smile on his face.

"So what are you doing this for, exactly, ringing the birds?" Lindy asked, when he returned to the bench for the third canvas bag.

"A number of migratory bird species are suffering serious declines. Not any of these chaps, I might add. This Reed Warbler and those Reed Buntings you and I just released are quite common enough around here, thank goodness. But we are collecting data to see if we can work out what the reasons for those declines might be."

"Surely, there can only be a couple of things that would affect bird numbers," said Lindy. "The availability of food and habitat, climate, that kind of thing."

Jejeune had seen this before in Lindy, this attempt to reduce the unexplained to a logical premise, even nature and natural processes. She was comfortable with things this way, when she could break them down and analyze them. It was when things got more toward the emotional end of the spectrum that she became a bit less sure of her ground. But who knew, perhaps she was right. Perhaps the simple, straightforward solutions did hold the answers. It was just that Jejeune had seen nature defy reason often enough to make it always worth looking beyond the merely rational for explanations.

"There was something I wanted to ask you," said Jejeune suddenly. "Brae had a complete set of lists on his desk when he died on the Thursday. You said you hadn't seen him for at least a week, yet one of the birders, Ivan, told me he didn't drop his records off with you until the Sunday night. I am wondering how they could have ended up on Brae's desk if you hadn't seen him."

Senior fixed his sapphire-blue eyes on the detective directly. "D'you know, you're quite right, Inspector," he said evenly. "I popped Ivan's list in Cameron's mailbox on my way out on the Monday morning. Didn't bother knocking. It was early and I didn't want to wake anyone. It must have slipped my mind."

If Senior was expecting something from Jejeune, a nod of understanding, a smile of reassurance, he did not receive it. An uncomfortable silence descended over the interior of the hut.

"This ringing effort," said Lindy, valiantly trying to rescue the mood, "is it anything to do with the missing species you told Dom about? From those lists?"

"Partly. Sanderlings and Dunlin are abundant everywhere else along the coast. No reason other than pollution for them to avoid this place. Not as far as I can see."

"This place?" said Jejeune with a start. "I thought you meant they had disappeared from Lesser Marsh."

"Good God, no. There is nothing much at Lesser Marsh anymore. Apologies, Inspector, I sometimes forget that you are not from around these parts. Lesser Marsh has been known to local birders as a dead zone for years. No, I was talking about Great Marsh, this magnificent wilderness out here before us. This is where we're seeing those catastrophic declines in waders."

The realization that he had misinterpreted Senior's report struck Jejeune almost like a physical blow. He could see Senior's apologetic smile, hear his words, but he couldn't take in anything that he was saying. The ramifications of his error came flooding in to him now, almost too quickly for him to process in real time. He realized he needed to get back to the station immediately, right away, to start looking at the evidence again, in light of this critical new information. He bade Senior a swift farewell and reached for the door almost before Lindy had time to realize what was happening.

By the time they got back to the car, they were both soaked through. Lindy jumped in the Range Rover and shrugged back her hood, spraying the tawny upholstery with raindrops. She shivered slightly as Jejeune started the engine.

"Brrr. Still fancy birding as a full-time job, Dom?"

She realized her mistake immediately. What was it the lawyers said? Only ask a question if you already know the answer, and only then if it's going to help your case. But when she looked across, it wasn't rapture she saw on Domenic Jejeune's face this time. It was alarm.

35

When the early citizens of north Norfolk carved tracks out of the surrounding countryside, they had not considered motorized vehicles, much less behemoths like the Range Rover. Still, at least Jejeune was high enough up that he could usually see others before they saw him, and find a wide spot, like now, to pull into to let oncoming vehicles squeeze by. If he had known yesterday that he would need to be out this way, he would have squeezed the trip in before going to see Senior. It would have saved on the petrol. He was aware of the criticism about driving a gas-guzzler like this, but it seemed to him that one's carbon footprint was a pretty mutable idea these days. He didn't take many plane trips, so he felt he was entitled to drive a less environmentally responsible vehicle. If he had been a frequent flyer, he would have found another justification. The Beast, as Lindy called it, was a part of his lifestyle, and despite Lindy's periodic sniping, it was here to stay.

He drummed his fingertips on the steering wheel as he waited for the stream of oncoming cars to pass, some barely squeezing between the Range Rover and the overgrown hedges on other side. The courtesy on roads and the patience in shop lines out here was something that he was still coming to terms with. The city-dweller within still wondered how people could approach life at such a leisurely pace — didn't these people have jobs to go to, deadlines to meet?

His mind wandered once again over the encounter he had witnessed in the incident room just before he left. Holland, idling as ever in a corner, had begun casually strolling toward him with a file. "I was thinking, sir, perhaps I should have a go at interviewing the wife. You know, new perspective, new set of eyes."

Salter had laughed out loud. "I don't think the Party Animal is quite ready for your particular brand of consolation just yet, Tony. Besides, what would Danny say?"

"Danny? And Mandy Roquette?" Holland had considered the idea briefly. "Nah, no chance. He's old enough to be her father."

Salter had said nothing, just offered a smile that seemed to ask "When has love ever respected age?" But she seemed like a woman who wouldn't often be wrong about these kinds of things, and Jejeune was willing to give her credit for having picked up on something that he had missed. It was playing on his mind now as he was jerked back to the present by a friendly toot from the last of the cars going past. Perhaps it wasn't significant, but how many more details like that were there in this investigation, details he had failed to pick up on? As he pulled away, the piercing squeak from his wheel bounced back at him off the hedgerows, overloud, through his open window. He would need to get that seen to, soon.

Jejeune followed Nancy, the PA, along the wide hallway into a drawing room off to the left. He hadn't been in the room before, but it was a matching bookend to the one on the opposite side, where Malcolm Brae had sat brooding into the fireplace the night of his father's death. Mandy Brae sat in a wing-backed wicker chair set sideways and facing toward a large bay window. The glint of water from the surface of the marsh was visible through the tangle of brambles and hedgerows at the foot of the garden.

Mandy Brae turned her head as Jejeune entered the room and offered a weak smile of greeting. She indicated a chair opposite her, and Jejeune sat.

"How's Danny doing?" she asked.

"Fine, I believe. He's back at home."

"But not ready for active duty yet. So they sent you instead? You're the one who gets all that great publicity, aren't you? You ought to get yourself an agent. A lot of celebrities would kill for column inches like that. So tell me, Mr. Jejeune, Domenic, how are you enjoying your fifteen minutes of fame?"

Jejeune inclined his head. "Fifteen minutes can be a very long time."

She nodded knowingly. "Still, it must be different when they are writing about your brains rather than your dress sense. With us the audience seemed to be split between schoolgirls who wanted us to join them for a pajama party, and creepy blokes looking for a memory to keep them warm in the old age home. Women loved us, of course — all that empowerment and girl power. In fact, about the only group we didn't connect with was boys our own age. It probably explains why Ally and Tammi are out there shagging everything in sight these days."

Jejeune remembered the stories about the acrimonious breakup of The Roquettes, and the subsequent tabloid exploits of Mandy's former partners. But why did she feel the need to bring it up now? To make a comparison with her own stable relationship? If so, for whom?

"Do you know much about you stepson's dealings with Earth Front? Perhaps you saw some literature, or some of his friends came by."

She shook her head. "No. He would have kept anything involving Earth Front's activities at his place. And he would certainly never discuss something like that with me." She smiled. "It's funny. I actually would have had some sympathy with them, the less radical side, obviously. You see a lot of the dark side of humanity in the music business, the waste and the excess. You sometimes wonder if it would be such a bad idea to let Mother Nature take over the running of the planet again. She could hardly do a worse job than we have, could she?"

She was being flippant, but Jejeune recognized there were seams here that Earth Front could mine in another, less worldly individual.

"Your stepson believes you married his father ..."

"I know what he believes. That I'm just some airhead who needed Cameron to give my IQ rating a boost. A sort of Marilyn Monroe to his Arthur Miller, I suppose. Thanks for bringing it up, Domenic. It's just a teeny bit bloody insulting, as a matter of fact. I did go to a grammar school, you know. Mastered joined-up writing and everything."

"I'm sorry. I didn't mean ..." But he stopped. After all, it was exactly what he did mean.

She looked at the inspector carefully. Jejeune suspected that, consciously or otherwise, she had spent most of her adult life trading on her sexuality. She was used to men being attracted to her, comfortable with it, even. His detachment was making her uneasy. He considered reassuring her that it was no reflection on her, that she was really very attractive, but that would have taken the interview in a different direction entirely.

"I did believe in Cameron's work, Domenic. I *do* believe in it."

Her childhood accent slipped its leash momentarily. She had had many years of practice in keeping her working-class background out of the limelight, but when she spoke with conviction, sometimes the roots still showed.

"Were there any other threats or problems in your husband's life?"

Jejeune's question shocked her out of her contemplations. "I thought you had solved the case."

So did he, once. But not now. And yet, he wondered if he was acknowledging this for his own benefit at least as much as for hers. This was dangerous ground. Alwyn's information had shaken him more than he wanted to admit, and added to the misunderstanding over Senior's findings, it had left him reeling and uncertain.

"You're talking about his affair, aren't you?" She shrugged. "What can I say? I don't know anything."

"Your stepson, he knew about your husband's infidelity." It wasn't a question.

"He couldn't wait to point it out — 'Called Dad at the uni yesterday. They hadn't seen him. Any idea where he was?'"

A weaker woman might have succumbed to the tears that had started to her eyes, but she drew a fluttery breath and was soon back on the topside of her self-control.

"Could he just have been encouraging doubts where there was no reason for them?"

She shook her head, perhaps just for a second not trusting her voice. "He enjoyed it, obviously, but he was right. Cameron was seeing someone. Danny believes it, too. I think he may have found some evidence, only he was too kind to tell me."

It was Jejeune's turn to shake his head. "There is no evidence."

"Danny even thinks I might have had something to do with Cameron's murder because of it. You know, revenge or something. He doesn't want to believe it, but he can't help himself. I could see it in his eyes, the last time he was here."

"He likes to consider all the possibilities. It's what makes him a good policeman."

"I didn't kill my husband, Inspector. Whatever Cameron was up to when he wasn't with me, I loved him. I could never have hurt him."

"I believe you. Can you tell me, how did your husband seem, the last time you saw him?" he asked.

"The last time I saw him, he was fine. A bit distracted, maybe, but nothing out of the ordinary. By the last time I spoke to him, though, something had changed. He was moody, telling me he loved me one minute and then so angry the next he could barely speak."

"Angry about what?"

"He wouldn't say, but I don't think it was me. Malcolm perhaps? They had had a fight a couple of nights before. That always used to upset him, though it was rarely him who started them."

The fight Jcjeune already knew about. And the reasons for it. It had to be something else. "Can you think of anything else that could have made him that angry?"

She inclined her head slightly. "Sorry. All I can say is it wasn't like him to get so bent out of shape like that. He normally handled stuff pretty well. It was one of the things I loved most about him."

Nancy tapped discreetly on the door. "It's almost time for your conference call."

Jejeune stood up abruptly. "I should be going anyway. Thank you for your time."

"Say hi to Danny for me, would you? I have some of his records here. Should I give them to you?"

"I'm sure he would prefer to come over and collect them himself. I'll remind him you have them."

36

"So this is the message?" Lindy stood before the untidy red lettering splashed across the front of Largemount's house, just below the bay window. Large and bold at first, then tailing off as it drooped to the right, as if either the anger or the strength of the writer had waned the longer the work went on. "At least they got their capitalization right. Perhaps I should let Eric know. He might want their resumés."

"Yes, and when was the last time you saw a graffiti artist worry about punctuation?" Jejeune was standing behind Lindy, halfway between the house and the stand of beeches, where the Rooks swirled and looked down on them from on high.

"No confession from the son, then. Do you think he did it?"

Jejeune didn't need to think long about his answer. "He has the entire package, the motive, the means, the opportunity. He even says he would have liked to have killed Largemount. But he didn't do it. I'm sure of it. The trouble is, his story about a deal between Largemount and his father only makes sense if you're prepared to take a lot of other things on faith."

"You've got to trust your instincts, Dom. You did before, when everybody else was telling you you were wrong. And that didn't work out too badly, did it?"

She smiled, and he knew she was reliving the drama and the glory of it all once more. It was a high point for both of them, he piecing together the evidence, she reporting his progress, formally at first, and then, even after they began seeing each other, still with as much professional detachment as she could manage. Until the day he made the arrest, and saved the girl, and she reported it, and the world exploded into fireworks around them. It must be hard for her now, thought Jejeune, seeing him involved in another high-profile case, more media scrums, more scrutiny and public interest, and having to keep her distance.

A Sparrowhawk flew low and fast across the forecourt, causing an outburst of cawing amongst the Rooks. Jejeune watched it go, a silent, lethal arrow without a target. Yet.

"Remember that ex-soldier you interviewed last year, the one who had come back from the Gulf and started a pacifist movement?"

Even from a master of non sequiturs like Jejeune, this one took Lindy slightly by surprise. "He was not on his own, either," she said. "He said he could name half a dozen others, even from his own regiment, who felt the same way. I suppose it's natural, to see what they have seen, and want nothing more to do with war."

"I don't know about natural. But it is understandable. And that's the thing. Whether you agree with his position or not, there's a rationale to it, a logic. But what about the other way? A life-long pacifist suddenly develops a taste for warfare. Not too often you see that, is it?"

"Why do I get the feeling we are not talking about my soldier anymore?" asked Lindy in that guarded tone she used when she realized Domenic was about to launch into one of his musings.

"I believe the development of the human conscience has a certain pattern to it," continued Jejeune. "Whether it's an attitude to war or anything else. The destroyer who gradually turns to creating. That's an understandable progression. It's redemption. Not everybody follows it. I'm not even saying it's always right. But it makes some kind of sense. But going the other way, from being an advocate for nature to becoming an exploiter of it with little or no regard for the environmental consequences?" He shook his head.

"Like Beverly Brennan, you mean? I take your point, but if you're thinking she may have had some help with her decision, well, underhanded dealings involving an MP? Say it isn't so! Besides, you have to admit, there is a certain appeal to the imagery. One day, flowers in her hair, the next a hard hat. Talking of hard hats, how is Sergeant Maik?" she asked, changing the subject. "You should go and see him. We could go up there for a drive tomorrow."

"He doesn't want any visitors. Besides, I need to focus on these cases. Now more than ever. I need to find some evidence that lets us move on from Malcolm Brae, one way or the other."

Lindy squeezed Domenic's hand. She realized this business had shaken his faith in himself. His carefully constructed theories about Peter Largemount and disappearing waders and contaminated marshes had turned to dust and blown away, and taken a good portion of his self-confidence with them. "You'll get there in the end, Dom. You've just got to keep believing in yourself."

But the hard sell never really worked with Dom. and now that Lindy had planted the seed it was time to switch to lighter fare. "By the way, what's this I hear about you fawning over aging starlets? That nice Constable Holland called yesterday and said you would be late because you were visiting Mandy Brae. He said you had been there all afternoon. At least somebody cares that I was sitting at home all alone, abandoned."

"I would hardly call thirty-three aging. Mature, maybe. Knowing. Experienced. Besides, what can I say? She gave me an impromptu concert."

Lindy looked into his face, unsure whether to believe him or not.

He nodded. "She did 'Party Animal' for me."

"Really? Omigod, I used to love that song." Lindy was suddenly a young girl again. *"I'm a Party Animal. Let me be your cannibal ..."*

Jejeune, who had been intending to listen to the song as soon as possible, decided against rushing into anything. By now, he was beginning to wonder if he was the only person in the U.K. who had never heard it. He had certainly heard of The Roquettes when he was back in Canada. Their success was worldwide. So why couldn't he remember any of their songs? Perhaps, like so many things in this wired-up global village, it was only the fame that had travelled, and not the substance it was based upon.

"So why did you go to see her, really? Is she a suspect? An affair would have been hard for Little Miss Party Animal to deal with. A woman like that would need to feel like she was the only one. Convince her of that and she would be yours for life. But if she slipped to second-best, chances are you'd never get her back. So I'd say that's definitely motive, and for a woman with her money, means would be no problem. Does she have an alibi?"

"Are you asking as a member of the public who is not privy to such information, or merely as a journalist who has not been assigned to the case?"

Lindy stuck out her tongue. "Looks like it's no cannibalism for somebody tonight." She danced over toward the trees, humming "Party Animal" and doing something very interesting with her shoulder.

Jejeune scanned the treetops with his binoculars. He found the Sparrowhawk perched on a snag high up in a dead elm tree on the far side of the forecourt. He watched it for a long time, a small, grey, innocuous presence sitting motionless on the bare branch. They like their high ground, our predators, thought Jejeune. Their penthouse apartments, their mountain retreats, their clifftop mansions. They can see their prey better, sit there unobserved and wait for us to drop our guard. Had Largemount been a predator, perched up here in his hilltop aerie? If so, who had been his prey? Brae? Brennan? DCS Shepherd? Jejeune walked toward the edge of the rise and looked out over the vast grey forest of wind turbines. What if Malcolm Brae was telling the truth? What if Largemount had claimed responsibility for the contamination on his land? It was such a preposterous story, even more so now that Alwyn had taken away any reason for Largemount to do so. But just suppose for a moment that it was true. Would Largemount go as far as murder to preserve his deception? Would he kill to protect his lie?

Lindy joined him at the edge of the rise and laid her head against his shoulder, trying to see whatever it was that Domenic was seeing among the turbines. She was so afraid of losing him. But she knew if she started to, that there was nothing she could do to prevent it. Dom's philosophy was that if something was outside your control, it was pointless worrying about it. But that was okay if you were Domenic Jejeune and you had pretty much the whole world on a string. But what if you were Lindy Hey, sometime famous journalist, now anonymous magazine columnist? Belinda Ann Hey, who barely had control of her temper sometimes, let alone her life. What good was a *laissez faire* approach then, when other people could make decisions that could affect your work or your relationship and there was not a damn thing you could do about it?

Then it was a little harder to trust in the fates. Then, worry was about all you had left.

A sudden frenzy of scolding shattered the stillness, and they turned to see the Rooks rising in a black mass as the Sparrowhawk made a half-hearted pass over the colony. In a moment, it was all over and the birds settled quietly again into the beech trees on the far side of the forecourt.

"Perhaps Largemount was involved," said Lindy softly, "just not in the way you think. Perhaps he and Brae had other issues, besides the contamination of the marsh. Not everything in life is about birds, you know." She stroked his arm. "It's okay to be wrong every once in a while, Dom. You can allow yourself that little luxury."

But he couldn't, could he? Not where police work was concerned. If he was ensnared in this job, this career, then it was because he had a gift for it, a talent. But he had been wrong this time, wrong about everything, from the start. And if that was true, then he had lost the only excuse he was prepared to give himself for doing a job he found so desperately unfulfilling. That he was good at it. And he got results.

Lindy withdrew her hand. "I've got to be getting back. I have a deadline, though for the life of me, I can't see why people clamour for details about the misappropriation of government funds. Eric reckons they are probably mostly looking for tips on how they can get in on it." She didn't smile.

She took a last, lingering look at the slogan scrawled across the wall, with its message dipping toward oblivion. A couple more words and it would have disappeared completely. Above her, the Rooks offered more half-hearted caws as the two of them walked to the car, but with the sun beginning to set, the birds had started to settle into their roosts for the night, and energetic protests were apparently altogether too much work.

"Are these those birds Senior was talking about, the ones that play just for the fun of it?"

Jejeune didn't answer. Preoccupied, he turned to her: "Largemount never allowed birders onto his property. So how did Senior know there was a rookery here, let alone that it was near the house?"

Lindy shrugged. "Perhaps he came here in a non-birding capacity at some time. You know, as a regular human being."

But the humour was lost on Jejeune, who got back into the car with the same preoccupied expression as before. When they reached the end of Largemount's driveway, he pulled the Range Rover over and got out. He walked out into the middle of the driveway and looked back toward the property. From here, neither the stand of beech trees nor the rookery was visible. With his binoculars, Jejeune could just make out faint black specks circling in the distance. You would have to be a very good birder indeed to identify those black dots as Rooks. But then, Quentin Senior was a very good birder, wasn't he?

37

Alwyn was scared; genuinely, palpably afraid. This wasn't the panic that Jejeune had seen at the lab. This fear had had time to embed itself, and it was unsettling Alwyn on a far more visceral level. But one thing was for sure, it wasn't this break-in that had frightened him. Whatever it was, it carried far more menace than the destruction of some old sticks of furniture and the smashing of a few lamps.

Jejeune stepped over the wreckage in the doorway and entered Alwyn's cottage. He knew the professor's fear would make him vulnerable. But enough to tell the truth, finally?

"I have left everything exactly as it was when I came home, Inspector. Thank you for coming. I wasn't sure housebreaking was within your remit."

"Sometimes. Depending on the circumstances." Jejeune surveyed the interior of the small cottage. Debris was everywhere; spilled papers, scattered clothing, drawers upturned. He stepped carefully among the items on the floor and made his way to the window, bending slightly to peer at the view. It was majestic, a fringe of chalk cliffs, and beyond them an unbroken horizon of sea.

"Your neighbour told you she thought she had seen someone lurking up here earlier in the day, I understand."

"Her word, Inspector. I simply put it down to her mistrust of outsiders. We don't get many visitors up here. But I was obviously wrong to dismiss her suspicions so casually."

Jejeune joined Alwyn in looking around at the mess. He bent down and picked up a pile of papers. It was an academic report of some kind, pages still in order, one to twenty-one. Jejeune set it on a desk.

"And nothing has been taken, as far as you can tell? Any idea what the intruder might have been looking for?"

"None at all. I don't have personal possessions of any great value, and I rarely bring home important documents. As you know, I prefer to work at the university."

Jejeune looked around the room. Alwyn was right. There was little here to mark this as a home. No photographs, no mementos; not even any plaques attesting to the professor's brilliance or standing in the academic community. For Alwyn, this delightful little cottage perched on the edge of a cliff was a place to live, nothing more. Jejeune bent to look out the window again. There was not a single body of land between here and the North Pole. In winter, the storms off the North Sea would be punishing, but in the spring, Sand Martins would patrol these cliffs with dazzling feats of aerial acrobatics. The runnels at the cliff's edge would blaze with the magnificent deep red marsh orchids. It would be a beautiful, spectacular place to spend your days. And Alwyn would notice none of it. His studies and his academic standing were what brought him reward, not the sky ballets of cliff-dwelling birds. Jejeune sighed inwardly. Professional success seemed a high price to pay if it robbed you of the appreciation of nature's gifts.

"Four hours," he said, "between your neighbour's report and your calling the police."

"Yes, I went out directly after Mrs. Paddon came over. It

was only when I came back that I discovered this." He spread his hands to indicate the room.

"So the burglar must have been hanging around. Unusual that. Especially in such an exposed spot as this."

"I can't tell you how distressing it was to come back and find my home … despoiled like this."

"Yes, I imagine it would be. Cameron Brae believed Great Marsh was polluted, didn't he? And he thought Peter Largemount's land was the source."

He stopped to look at Alwyn. The professor looked puzzled, stunned. He was in his home, his violated home, his possessions strewn all about him, and Jejeune wanted to talk about the case. He took refuge in his expertise.

"With respect, Inspector," he said cautiously, "I can accept that Cameron had some idea that birds were disappearing from Great Marsh, but we can't possibly know that he put it down to pollution, much less that he suspected Peter Largemount."

"I believe we can," said Jejeune, taking a folded paper out of an inside pocket. "How many water sources feed into Great Marsh, Professor?" he asked politely.

"Four major ones, innumerable smaller ones." Alwyn looked around the room again, as if trying to remind Jejeune of the reason for his visit; his, Alwyn's, distress, his problems, not those of a dead colleague. But Jejeune was resolute.

"You would have a monitoring station at all the main inlets?"

"That would be common practice in monitoring marsh hydrology, yes," said Alwyn. "Do you think you will want to dust for fingerprints in here, Inspector? I understand that is standard procedure at domestic break-ins."

"I don't believe we will find anything to help us, Professor Alwyn. Do you?" Jejeune opened the map he had taken from Brae's study on the night of the murder. "Of the four monitoring stations at Great Marsh, Cameron Brae was only interested in one. This one."

Alwyn leaned forward and peered at the red *X* Jejeune was tapping with his index finger. He said nothing.

"The data he asked you for wasn't the old survey report on Lesser Marsh, was it? He wanted the readings from this monitoring station."

Alwyn tented his arms on his knees, tapping his hands gently against his lips. He let his eyes wander around the desolation of his living room before finally settling them on Jejeune's face, which was waiting there for him, patient and unwavering.

"He wanted the most recent readings, and the set before. He thought he could prove that the pollution at Great Marsh was coming directly from Largemount's land. But the data from that monitoring station showed no contaminants. I tried to tell Cameron that, as the lowest-lying area for many miles around, Great Marsh is an extremely dynamic wetland. It would be impossible to definitely pinpoint one source for a pollutant. But he insisted, so I gave him the data, and the next thing I knew he was dead. I had no idea what the connection was between the two events, or whether Peter Largemount was involved in any way, but obviously …" He shook his head. "It was a stupid thing to do, lying to you. I apologize."

Jejeune stood in front of Alwyn, towering over the tiny, shrunken figure on the sofa. First an admission of error, now an apology. It was turning into a red-letter day for Professor Miles Alwyn.

"Here's what I think, Professor. I think there was a deal between yourself, Brae, and Largemount to cover up the pollution on his land. But then, for some reason, probably to do with the pollution in Great Marsh, Brae decided he couldn't keep silent about the deal any longer. He was going to go public with the details."

Jejeune left room for Alwyn to comment. He seemed to be considering something. But the professor's instincts for self-preservation were strong, and even now he couldn't bring himself to reveal the truth. Not in real terms. He took refuge in a hypothetical situation, a "little scenario" he asked Jejeune to imagine with him.

"Let us say two analysts perform a government survey, and they find contaminants in the soil and in the surface water. It is their duty to bring this to the attention of the landowner; to ensure that the source is identified and cleaned up. Now, this can be a costly and time-consuming proposition for the landowner, who has suddenly become accountable, and based on their previous experiences, these analysts might expect denial and bluster, personal abuse even. But let us suppose this particular landowner reacts differently. Let us suppose he acknowledges that his land is the source of these pollutants, confesses he knows all about it, in fact, and assures them that he is willing to assume all responsibility and costs for cleaning up the spill. A most satisfactory outcome, one might think. Except that one of the analysts, the leader, shall we say, has doubts. More than doubts, actually. He knows for a fact that this pollution cannot possibly have originated on this land. But before he can even voice his concerns, the landowner is already admitting that he desperately needs a clear survey, and furthermore, he is willing to use his influence to help the careers of the analysts, in return for their assistance. Well, the pollution is to be cleaned up. Future negative impacts to human health would be negligible. So where would be the harm?"

Alwyn stopped for a moment, looking into the middle distance. But despite the free-floating narrative, or perhaps even because of it, Jejeune couldn't escape the feeling that Alwyn was still deciding on what, and how much, to share. Domenic Jejeune had seen too many confessions, too many times when the dam broke and all that pent-up conflict came bursting forth in a flood of spilled secrets and suppressed emotions, to mistake this for the real thing.

"So you said you would *falsify* the report for Largemount, to ensure he received his development permit?" Jejeune chose the word carefully, just to remind Alwyn that they were talking about a criminal offence here, after all. But Alwyn merely smiled.

"Falsify? Not at all. All our analyst would have promised, absolutely all, was that the survey results would in no way impede the landowner's application for a development permit. And that would have been perfectly true, you see, since our hypothetical lead analyst already knew the pollution levels were within the acceptable thresholds." Alwyn smiled demurely. "I did already tell you, Inspector, the survey results submitted to the ministry were entirely genuine. Of course, I may have been a little more forthcoming, at least the lead analyst in our little tale might have, if it hadn't been for the arrogance of the man, believing he could simply buy the findings he required like that. It's our culture, of course, this notion that everything has its price. But surely some things must be above such considerations. And the truth must be one of them. Don't get me wrong, Inspector. I am not naive enough to think that scientific data is never altered for profit, but it was the sheer callousness of Largemount's approach, as if it was no more than another one of his business transactions. So if this boorish lout wanted to offer a reward for their reporting the truth, then our analysts would be perfectly prepared to accept it. Don't look so shocked, Inspector. You may see things in moral terms, but I can assure you, science does not. Peter Largemount volunteered to take responsibility for the pollution, insisted upon it. I have no idea why, but do you really think it would have made any difference to him what the actual concentration levels were?"

"So when pollution showed up at Great Marsh, Brae thought Largemount had reneged on his part of the deal by letting the pollution continue on his land. And he wanted the monitoring data to prove it. Only it proved the opposite."

Alwyn sighed, and finally, for a brief, flickering moment, Jejeune seemed to get a glimpse behind the veil, a faint telltale sign that the truth was ready to step out into the light of day. It had been a long time hidden.

"Cameron was convinced the pollution was coming down from Lesser Marsh. He said he was going to expose Largemount, tell everybody about the pollution on his land and the deal we had made. I tried to tell him that Largemount's land could not have been the source of the pollution at Great Marsh. The monitoring data proved it. I offered to go over the results with him, explain them, but he wouldn't listen."

"So when Brae left you, he was still going to see Largemount? Even though you could prove that the pollution wasn't coming from Lesser Marsh? Why would he do that?"

"I have no idea, but when he left he was beside himself with fury, unwilling to listen to reason. If he did go to Peter Largemount's house in that state of mind, I'm afraid anything could have happened."

Jejeune looked down at Alwyn, head bowed again, small white hands clasped before him. He made for a pathetic figure, a frail old man sitting on a worn-out sofa amid a sea of scattered possessions.

"The thing is, Professor, with the other two now gone, you are the only one left who can testify about the deal with Largemount. Does that bring us any closer to a reason why someone might be targeting you, I wonder? Who else knew about this deal?"

"I know of no one."

But he did. Jejeune could tell. And despite his fear, Alwyn still wouldn't say who it was.

"I hope you are not going to make the mistake of thinking you can negotiate with them. Two people who may have believed that are already dead."

As Jejeune reached the door, Alwyn called to him. When he turned around he saw the professor's hands splayed to indicate the room.

"Inspector. About all this?"

"Oh, I think it will be okay for you to start cleaning it up," said Jejeune.

38

Holland and Salter watched with something approaching disbelief as Jejeune departed from the incident room. "And just how, exactly, does one go about setting up a protection detail without letting the subject know it's there? And more importantly, what's the point? I thought protection was at least partly to reassure the subject."

Holland smiled. "He wants to see what Alwyn will do if he thinks he's still under threat."

"But there is no bloody threat. Not if the DCI really believes Alwyn staged the break-in himself." Lauren's tone was charged with frustration.

"Well I agree with him on that, at least," conceded Holland. "Alwyn wouldn't have the *nous* to make a break-in look convincing. For all his faults, and his requests for maps of drainage patterns between Great and Lesser Marsh ..." Holland flapped the written request Jejeune had just handed him. "I think we can trust the DCI to spot a set-up when he sees one."

They both knew the signs: a clumsy, impossible-to-miss entry point; nothing of value damaged or destroyed; the soft stuff, clothes and pillows, tossed around for over-the-top disorder. Just like in the television shows. And like it hardly ever was in real life. Burglars didn't stand around in the middle of the room throwing things around like they were at a chimpanzees' tea party; they got in, took what they wanted, and got out again.

"No, this fake break-in was Alwyn's way of getting protection from the person who came after him at the uni. But until he is ready to tell us who that is, our intrepid leader is going to let him swing in the breeze a bit."

"Maybe he really doesn't know."

Holland shrugged. "Maybe. One thing's for sure though, whatever Alwyn's got himself involved in, it won't be Brae's murder. I've told you before, this is about Archie Christian, not some pencil-necked wonk who likes splashing about in mud puddles."

She knew Holland was already laying the groundwork for when the higher ups did eventually lose faith in Jejeune's bird theories. And Jejeune himself. She had seen Tony in the DCS's office the day before, when she was having her lunchtime salad with Sheila from Traffic. Sheila was a bright, personable young police officer who had at one time become another trophy in Tony Holland's ongoing quest to plate every woman at the station. Salter herself excepted, of course. And the DCS, presumably.

"I can hear him now," Sheila had said, nodding toward the window in DCS Shepherd's office, where Holland was standing to attention.

"It's not about the new leadership method, ma'am. I'm sure if the DCI prefers to assign things and just let us go off and do them, instead of a more lead from the front approach, well, no doubt that's just his style. It's the same with his approach to basic police procedure. I mean, everybody at the station is all for this thinking outside the box business. It's just that, well, just at the moment, ma'am, it doesn't seem to be producing very much in the way of actual results. And that's what has got some of the

officers wondering, you know, this hands off approach, the lack of hard leads ..."

Salter had nodded. The mocking pitch had been spot on. She had been watching Tony Holland operate for a long time, and she would bet Sheila's version wasn't more than a couple of *ma'ams* off.

"Plenty of *we's* and *us's* in there, too," added Salter, "just as added cover in case anything comes back off the fan later on. And no alternatives, either."

"Too right," Sheila had concurred. "Tony's far too canny to nail his own colours to the flagpole outside Archie Christian's house, or anyone else's."

But they both knew that Holland's report would be getting a more sympathetic hearing than usual. Shepherd normally had her bootlicker detector set on high, and she was quick to snuff out anything that would threaten the morale of her squad, developed so carefully through all those teambuilding exercises. But it was common knowledge around the station that, if the DCS didn't exactly blame Jejeune directly for Peter Largemount's death, she certainly held him responsible for putting the developer in Earth Front's crosshairs in the first place.

Salter looked down at the file on her desk: *External Inhibitors in Copepod Reproduction Cycles*. This had to stop. She walked out of the room, following the path Jejeune had taken back to his office a few moments before. It wasn't the best time, she knew. But it wasn't her style to back away from a confrontation, and this needed to be done. She took a little steadying breath and opened the door to his office.

Jejeune was sitting behind his desk, papers spread all around him. He flipped the file before him shut and looked up. Was there something familiar about the file? Perhaps not. They all looked the same; dingy buff covers, dog-eared corners. Salter had seen enough of them lately.

"Yes, Constable?" Jejeune waited.

She drew another breath. "The waders stopped going to Lesser Marsh because these copepods died off. Isn't that what you told me?"

Jejeune looked at her warily. "According to the birders' old records, three particular species of waders were the first to disappear from Lesser Marsh. I think it was because their food source disappeared."

"And if I can find out what kills them, these copepods, we will know what was spilled at Lesser Marsh." Salter delivered it in a way that suggested there was more coming.

"I'm sure there's more than one substance that will kill copepods," said Jejeune carefully, "but if we could even narrow down the list it would be a good start, yes."

"So this is all about Lesser Marsh?"

Jejeune didn't answer.

"Then perhaps you'd like to explain why you've asked Tony for the drainage maps between Lesser Marsh and Great Marsh?"

And perhaps he wouldn't. But it wasn't Jejeune's style to take cover behind some bluster about insubordination. And they were going to have to know about the link soon enough.

"The same three species — Sanderling, Knots, and Dunlin — are disappearing from Great Marsh, too," said Jejeune. "Cameron Brae would have recognized the pattern from when he did his original survey of Largemount's property. I think he became convinced that Great Marsh was being affected by the same contaminant as Lesser Marsh."

Salter's eyes widened. "My God, he would have been livid if he suspected that Largemount had polluted his precious Great Marsh as well."

"Enough to confront him, threaten him, get into a life-and-death struggle with him?" Jejeune raised an eyebrow. "Yes. But Alwyn's data from the Great Marsh monitoring station doesn't support that. In fact, it shows no pollution flowing in from Largemount's land at all." He looked at her evenly. "Let me know when you've identified those substances, will you, Constable. We'll see if that sheds any more light." His picked up a paper and began reading again.

"You know," said Salter flatly, causing Jejeune to look up again. "I expect to have to look for motives for criminal activities, but not for why my DCI is assigning me my duties. You've got me doing one thing, Tony doing another, and you're in here doing God knows what, and it's pretty obvious you don't want anybody else to get the big picture. You trust us enough to do the work, but not enough to tell us why we're doing it? Frankly, sir, it's insulting. You're not the only one who wants a result here, you know. We're from this area, and these were local people who died, people we knew. My dad used to see Cameron Brae down at the post office, when he was buying his newspaper and dad was getting his tobacco. Peter Largemount used to give generously to the local fair; my son won a bike he had donated one year. Don't you think we've got a right to be involved? This is not just about getting a case closed, so we can all get our picture in the *Police Gazette* and then go on about our business. This is about our community. You can't shut us out of this just because you want to solve it all by yourself, because you think you bollixed it up first time around. You've got officers here who are interested, really, truly interested in the outcome. I know we don't all have them fancy college accents or that ever-so-clever way with words you might be used to down in The Smoke, but we're not as thick out here as you seem to think we are, either. It wouldn't hurt to rely on us now and again to do our jobs. It's not right to make us sit at our desks looking at mouldy old reports without knowing why, all because you're too bloody stubborn to ask for help. It's selfish and it's self-indulgent and it's … it's wrong."

She was angry at herself for having gotten flustered, but she knew the overall message had gotten through. She hadn't had enough experience with this new boss to be able to read his reaction. Was this cold, quiet, almost eerie stillness how he normally took personal criticism? Normal or not, it was very unnerving. Should she have kept her counsel? Not over this. Lauren Salter, Detective Constable first-class, wasn't about to let anybody tell her she couldn't be trusted. Not at any price.

"I'll keep it in mind, Constable. Was there anything else?"

Jejeune drew some papers toward him, but not the file he had been reading when she had entered. He had closed that and pushed it away when she had begun speaking, Lauren remembered. A witness statement. The handwriting, she thought. She had recognized it. As she should have; she had seen it often enough. What was Jejeune doing reviewing *that* statement, of all of the ones he had on his desk? *My God, it's not us you don't trust at all, is it?* Her hand was halfway toward her mouth before she managed to stop it. She didn't think Jejeune had noticed.

She stood outside Jejeune's office for a long moment, leaning against the closed door, breathing normally to calm herself. She could imagine Jejeune inside, just the other side of the door, with the file open again, his head bent over the contents, studying them carefully, trying to decide if the flimsy handwritten statement before him actually constituted a viable alibi for DCS Colleen Shepherd or not.

39

"Barbeque? The DCI?" Jejeune heard a familiar voice saying as he entered the station "Hardly. He thinks a griller is something you find in a zoo."

"Eh up, Gaffer's here. Well, mine anyway." The desk sergeant slipped a wink to someone half hidden behind the door, out of Jejeune's sight.

"Need your keys, Dom," said Lindy. "You wanted me to drop The Beast in today, remember?"

Apparently not. She was going to take it in to the local garage to have them fix the squeak on the Range Rover's wheel. In the city, Jejeune might not have even noticed it, but out here, where he always drove with his windows down whenever he could, the sound had become too much of a nuisance to be ignored. But Jejeune had forgotten this morning when he left home, and he realized now that he still needed the Range Rover today, after all, so her trip had been in vain. His apology was fulsome and genuine.

"Not a problem, darling." She held up a battered enamel mug. "The sergeant here makes a mean cuppa, and we've been having a great old natter, haven't we, Sarge? We've been comparing bosses. I have to say, compared to you, Eric seems like an absolute dream to work for."

The sergeant looked suitably abashed, but Jejeune offered a smile to show Lindy's comments hadn't struck any vital organs. He thought about Lindy and her relationship with her boss. Did it make any difference to her who was sharing a bed with Eric, the illiterate halfwit editor, capitalize as necessary? Did she know, or care, or even give it a thought? Why then should he have to entwine himself in the private life of DCS Shepherd? Why did he have to worry about who she might have been sleeping with? Why did the intimate details of her life have to become part of his?

The sergeant gathered up Lindy's mug and set it on the counter next to its twin. Lindy gave Jejeune a playful peck on the cheek and swept out of the station with a jaunty swing of her hips, jangling her key ring as she went. The sergeant watched her go with a broad smile.

"Lovely girl," said the sergeant, whose name Jejeune remembered as being Coulter. "Reminds me of my daughter. Same devil-may-care outlook. She's up at Norwich, doing Social Studies, though what she's going to do with a degree like that, I don't know."

Jejeune smiled to himself. Lindy Hey, Goodwill Ambassador to the masses. A trip to Afghanistan and by the third cup of tea the Pashtun warriors would be falling all over themselves to lay down their weapons before her.

"Gave me a start, mind, when she came in. I saw that blond hair and I thought it was that politician, Brennan, again. Not a way you'd want to start the day, eh? Not after the last time." Emboldened by Jejeune's smile, Coulter thought he would try his luck. "Any news on when we might be seeing Sergeant Maik again, sir? Very popular around here is Danny. A lot of people are asking after him."

"Nothing, I'm afraid. I'm sure it won't be too long."

Jejeune's features had closed, ready to shut off the topic

if the sergeant was foolish enough to try to raise it again. But instead, a strange expression of understanding spread over Coulter's face.

"Ah well, no news is good news, I suppose."

Jejeune went on to his office. He closed the door and sat down. He needed to think.

He had spent the morning at a beach. He had no idea which one, just some open stretch of coastline reaching out into the sea. An unbroken mantle of soft grey clouds was sitting low over the water. Only on the horizon was there a glimmer of light, a faint blue band of promise. The beach was deserted, not another soul on the vast, wide expanse of sand that stretched out in front of him. Having come from the city, it never ceased to amaze Jejeune that you could be that alone in the world. He walked along the beach, feeling the satisfying softness as the sand gave way beneath his slow, deliberate strides. He ventured as close to the tide line as he dared, the white noise of the waves breaking on the shingles. A set of paw prints ran along the sand, with an unbroken line in between. A small dog, dragging a stick in its mouth. Always the detective, even if, these days, he wasn't a very good one.

Jejeune's path became blocked by a narrow tidal creek carrying its silty cargo out to the sea. On each side of it were shallow lagoons and rock pools. When the tide washed in they would teem with new life, but at that moment they looked barren and empty. Jejeune looked inland, back to where the dark smudge of Corsican pines marked the edge of the coast road. He traced the creek's sinuous course back to where it emerged from a tidal salt flat, and watched the water for a long time as it eddied and churned, meeting the incoming tide in an erotic swirl of water, the fresh intermingling with the salty in a turbulent, roiling dance, until it was no longer possible to tell one from the other.

He looked out at sea, at the motion, the colour, the light. A Black-headed Gull swooped in and settled on a piece of driftwood a few feet away. Picture complete, thought Jejeune. For him, a landscape by itself, no matter how beautiful, seemed an empty thing. It needed a flicker of life, a tiny quiver of existence, to validate it, to confirm that other living things found a home here, too.

Side by side, they looked out over the sea, the man and the bird, two beating hearts in this otherwise empty landscape, with no connection beyond their desire to be here, at this time. Was it the birds that attracted him to places like this, he wondered, or the solitude, the absence of demands, of expectations? But if Jejeune was unsure of his own motives, he knew this bird would have a purpose in being here. Nature always had her reasons.

He chanced a sidelong glance at the bird, now settled to his presence. It had already completed its summer moult, crisp clean feathers having replaced the ones abraded by the harsh demands of eking out a living on this wild, windswept coastline. The gull stayed for a long moment, allowing Jejeune to rest his eyes softly, unthreateningly, upon it. And then, as if deciding it had allowed him enough time to appreciate its beauty, the bird spread its wings and effortlessly lifted off, wheeling on the invisible air currents, drifting away over the sea toward the horizon.

Dark under the wings. Not a Black-headed Gull, then, a Little Gull. It wasn't a mistake he would have normally made. He put it down to distraction. Still, it was a novice's error. A Little Gull. But not a little gull, right, Lindy? Jejeune turned and looked at the roiling water, the salt and the fresh coming together. He stood up and began swiftly retracing his steps back along the beach toward his car. Perhaps he wasn't such a bad detective, after all.

And that was why, now, back in the quiet of his office, he had to think.

40

Danny Maik wheeled his Mini into the car park and got out. He looked up at the steep incline before him. Once he would have taken it without a second thought, his progress constant and his posture upright as he mounted the slope without even breaking a sweat. Now he had to consider things more carefully, pace himself, possibly even stop for a break halfway up. It was not a thought that filled him with joy.

He was panting heavily when he crested the rise, and doubled over for a moment to catch his breath. But the view when he straightened up was spectacular. You didn't have to climb very high in north Norfolk to get a commanding view of the surrounding landscape, and on this rise he could see for miles.

"Greetings, Sergeant," said Quentin Senior, looking over his shoulder. He was standing at a scope set up to survey the coastline to the east. He would have been able to watch Maik arrive and track his progress up the rise, if he had chosen to. Maik had no idea if he had or not.

"Come out to do a spot of birding? Or are you back at work. Pursuing inquiries, as they say?"

"Not yet. I just thought I'd come out for a breath of fresh air."

"You could hardly have chosen a better place, could you?" Senior indicated the vista in front of them. A vale fell away to his left, and in the early afternoon sunlight it presented a scene of picture-book tranquility. Checkerboard fields rolled off toward the horizon, dappled shades of green and gold as far as the eye could see.

"Beautiful, isn't it? Hard to believe it didn't always look like this. After the war, the government needed to move to large-scale agriculture, you see: wheat, barley, potatoes, celery. Feed the masses in the post-war peace. So they decided to make the fields bigger, three times the size of what they once were. They tore out eight thousand miles of hedgerows in East Anglia. Understandable, I suppose, but a damned shame, just the same. Imagine it, eight thousand miles of pristine hedgerow habitat lost, just like that. It's a wonder the Dunnocks survived at all. Hedge Sparrows, they used to call them. Lovely little things; feisty, lots of personality." He paused to duck down and look through the scope again. "I hear you've been spending a fair amount of time chatting to our members since you've been off. Learn anything interesting?"

Maik shrugged. "Mostly that birders are just like the rest of us. Some good, some bad."

"And most of us somewhere in between, eh, Sergeant?"

"Something like that. From what I hear through the grapevine though, it does look like you can reassure the local birders that their records pose no threat to anybody else."

Senior straightened up again and turned to face Maik. "I'm sure they'll be most relieved to hear it." He took a slow sweeping look out over the fields again. "I wonder what it'll all look like in another generation. You know they're expecting half a million new people in East Anglia in the next decade. Where are they going to put them all?" He shook his head ruefully. "So what of the cases, Sergeant? What does your grapevine say about them?"

"I believe the inspector has some solid leads on Peter Largemount's murder."

"Really? And on Cameron's?"

"That one is still wide open, as I understand it," said Maik, looking straight into Quentin Senior's face. "Although Peter Largemount's own motive appears too weak now. Not even as good as a four-hundred list." Maik gave a flat smile, but there was no real mirth in it.

"The four-hundred list, it's also out of the running?"

"That's the general feeling, yes."

Maik drank in the scene before him. It was a landscape in constant motion. The sea, the trees, the gently rocking grasses. It was such a pretty place to have to conduct such prosaic business.

"That day you dropped off that list to Brae," said Maik, "the Monday before he was murdered. You said he was still asleep."

"Once a policeman, eh Sergeant? Yes. At least I assumed so. There were no lights on."

"Cameron Brae was a notoriously early riser, always had been. You must have been there very early."

"Indeed I was."

"Where were you going at that time in the morning?"

Maik's questions were becoming more abrupt now, lacking his usual preamble or polite couching. It was as if he sensed he was nearing the end of something, and he just wanted to get there. Either that or he was just beginning to tire of the whole process.

As if to counterbalance Maik's haste, Senior took a slow look over the surrounding land once more. He was silent for a long moment. "My father worked on those hedgerows. Ripping them up, casting them aside, burning them. Perhaps some of your relatives did, too. I do sometimes wonder if that's not why I followed the course I did. Righting past wrongs, a bit of penance, as it were. I was going out to Feltham Bog, Sergeant. I had heard a report of a Cetti's Warbler. A remarkable absentee from my year list, to that point."

"Rarity, is it?"

"Yes and no. They are fairly reliable at Strumpshaw Fen, but they are few and far between otherwise. I would say it's a sought-after bird, yes. This one would have saved me the trouble of going all the way out to Strumpshaw, so I thought I would try to see it while it was still around."

"Can I ask how you heard about it, this Cetti's Warbler? Was it on one of those rare bird alerts?"

"D'you know, I can't remember. Probably a bit of tittle-tattle in one of the hides, I should think."

"Plenty of other birders out there looking for it, were there?"

"I didn't see anybody," said Senior, after not very much reflection at all.

"Nobody? A bit strange that. You'd have thought there'd have at least been a couple of other birders out there after it, if it's as rare as you say. I imagine my boss would have been there, for example, if he'd have heard about it."

"There may have been some people on the far side, of course. It's a big area. Have you ever been to Feltham, Sergeant?"

Maik hadn't, but he knew it well enough. It was a place where somebody could lose himself quite easily. You could spend all day there, and nobody would ever know. Or vice versa.

"So did you ever see it, this bird?"

Senior gave his great white head a shake. "No. They can be elusive little devils when they're not singing. Still, I've seen one since, so no harm done. That's the way it is with birding sometimes. You might miss something at the spot you expect to find it, only to catch it later somewhere completely unexpected."

"You know, it's a funny thing, that's just the way it is with policing, sometimes," said Maik.

Senior raised himself and gathered his belongings. He took a final look out toward the sea. "That's Cley over there," he said, pointing. "Cley next the Sea. You can tell by the shingle banks. Locals put 'em up in an effort to stop the sea's inexorable march inland. But the banks themselves are being driven inland by about a metre a year. Next the Sea, indeed." Senior shook his great head sadly. "Trying to tame nature. Will they never learn? I wish you the best of luck with your investigations, Sergeant. When you return to your duties, of course."

Maik said nothing, simply nodding in reply to Senior's raised hand. He watched the rambling figure of Quentin Senior disappear down the slope, still robust, but now favouring a hip or a back that was starting to protest against a lifetime negotiating the uneven landscapes.

Maik sat for a long moment on the top of the rise, feeling the blustery wind wash over him, alone with his thoughts. He had had time to think during his enforced break. Think, and read. Who was he kidding; he had been in a position to do little else. Life listers, county listers, fly in/fly out to get a checkmark listers, he had studied them all. He knew more about bird listing than he ever imagined he would want to, probably even more than Jejeune by this point. But he couldn't find murder in it. He had read about the world's top listers, the eight-thousand-species merchants. These were the hardcore birders, where all the joy of the pastime had long since evaporated, and only the quest of adding ever more species to the list remained. He had become familiar with the stakes, with the current trend of defining subspecies, so that the bird you saw in Anglesey, and then again in Orkney a few years later might now be two different entries on your list after all, driving that lifetime tally even higher. He knew about the serious rivalries, the petty jealousies. He knew about the mischief and the rancor, and the resentments, and the outright anger of some birders toward their competitors. But try as he might, Danny Maik could find nothing to support his boss's premise that it might all lead to murder.

Maik knew a lot of the local birders personally, and as obsessive and obsessed as they could seem to an outsider, he couldn't find a murderer among them. He knew he had done his duty. He had taken his superior's idea seriously, done his research. He had explored the idea, and examined it, and given it far more time than it deserved, really. He was disappointed for Jejeune, who had invested so much in this. Maik would have liked it to have been about these bird lists, but he knew now that Cameron Brae's murder had nothing to do with his quest to see four hundred birds in Norfolk. He wondered if, in his heart of hearts, Jejeune had ever really believed it himself.

Maik stood and looked out over the landscape once more. He hadn't brought binoculars, but even with his naked eye he could still pick out the landmarks. The university, with its solid stone towers puncturing the skyline to the north; Archie Christian's hilltop house, looking down on all around it; a little farther to the east, Largemount's wind farm; and just beyond, the telltale glint, even from here, of the waters of Great Marsh. There it was, in one great, sweeping vista, the canvas on which the tragedies of the recent past had been painted. The answers were down there, too, somewhere. But where? He turned away from the view, and began the slow descent to his car.

41

Taking their lead from the chief inspector, there were only the most muted of greetings for Danny Maik on his return to the station. Salter squeezed his hand gently as she walked by, and Holland delivered a steaming mug of tea to his desk. They all knew that, given the slightest encouragement, Salter would have been all over an occasion like this — cakes, cards, a little present in a shiny gold gift bag. But they also knew Danny Maik would not be comfortable with that kind of attention, from her or anybody else.

The DCI's presence in the incident room today seemed mainly to oversee Maik's return to duty; in other words, to see that they didn't dwell on it. Jejeune himself made only the slightest of acknowledgements that Maik had ever been away, and judging by the sergeant's response, that was just fine with him. The briefing itself had been little more than a series of updates, with nothing new on offer, and no new leads or directions. This case was bogged down, going nowhere, and petering out into an *unsolved* quickly, and it appeared there was nothing anybody could do about it. Maik had already suggested he start going through everything again from the start, a suggestion to which Jejeune readily agreed. But they all knew that there would be nothing new to find. Danny Maik wasn't the kind to miss anything important the first time around. And much as they begrudged admitting it, Jejeune wasn't, either.

"The data set from that monitoring station at Great Marsh, the readings Alwyn sent over to Brae, any joy there, Sergeant Maik? Any little rays of sunshine to brighten our morning?"

But it didn't suit Jejeune, this forced lightheartedness. It was all Salter could do to keep from looking away. Holland simply rolled his eyes.

"I've spent all morning going over them, and, from what I can see there are no changes between the previous records and this last set. All the concentration levels are the same. I'm no expert of course, but there's nothing to suggest that there was any contamination entering the marsh from Largemount's property."

"Maybe the contaminant was dumped into Great Marsh directly," said Salter. "Let's say Brae found out who it was, caught them in the act even. He storms off to report them …"

"And they follow him back to his house and finish him off. A hanging, making it look like a ritual killing, to throw us off the track." Holland finished her premise, though not with any particular conviction. "Sorry, remind me again why we even think that Great Marsh is polluted."

He already knew the answer. All they had was Jejeune's missing birds. The species lists, the *Scolopacidae* of Great Marsh. That's what they were basing this entire line of inquiry on. Even Maik, still struggling to play catch-up, was aware of that much.

To end the deafening silence that followed, Jejeune tried a couple of half-hearted efforts to cajole Maik back into the fold, but after a few uncomfortable exchanges the DCI retired to the sanctuary of his office, to his own review of the case files, for the umpteenth time. The tension eased noticeably when Jejeune left the room.

Tony Holland got in early with his explanations to Maik.

"So as soon as I mention I might have a few minutes to come and see you again, what does he do? Drops more files in my lap. So now, instead of another visit to my favourite sergeant, I'm chasing all over north Norfolk trying to trace where the waterways run." He turned to Lauren. "What about you? Did you ever find out why those sand lice stopped having it off? Headaches, was it? Perhaps they need advice from somebody who's been getting some action lately."

Tony Holland was getting frisky again. It was about that time for Salter to rein him in, but she wouldn't do it today, not on Danny's first day back. "I've moved on to the fascinating world of organotins, now."

"Organo …what?" asked Holland, throwing in a look of incredulity toward Maik as if to say *see what you've been missing while you have been away?*

"Antifoulants, to you lesser mortals. They kill copepods, along with a fair bit of other marine life, from what I can gather, which isn't much," admitted Salter. "My dad tells me he used to use this kind of thing on the hull of his boat, to clean off the barnacles and limpets."

"Must be strong stuff," said Maik. "I did a bit of that work myself as a kid, down on the quay. We only used scrapers, though, back in those days. Useless, really. You couldn't have shifted those things with dynamite, some of them."

Holland came over and scooped one of the ring-bound folders off Lauren's desk. "*Organotins: Environmental Annihilators*. Oooh. Scary. I shan't be able to sleep when I get home tonight."

"Yeah, it's all very well for you, all young and fit and full of yourself. But I've got a six-year-old boy whose idea of heaven is going down to play in the tide pools. If these reports are anything to go by, I shouldn't let him anywhere near the seashore ever again."

"You don't want to believe all this rubbish. They're always trying to scare you with something. It'll be toxins in fish and chips next, or somebody will discover that sea salt causes impotence. Who writes this dreck anyway? Greenies, no doubt."

"Only the leading experts in the field," said Lauren testily, snatching back the file. "Not everybody's in it for their own purposes, you know. Some people do this because they actually care. There's tons of this stuff all along the coastlines of Britain, and the highest concentrations, wouldn't you know it, are from the Wash to the Thames Estuary."

"Here, wait a minute." Holland took back the file for a moment and flipped through until he reached the page he was looking for. "This tributyltin, what they call TBT? This is one of these antifoulants? If you want to know about this stuff you should have a word with Traffic. They picked up a bloke from Hull a couple of months ago, travelling with some big drums of it in the back of his truck. Did him for transporting hazardous without a permit. Funny how that works, isn't it? You go through your whole life without ever hearing about something, like this TBT, and then it crops up twice in a few weeks."

"What was he doing driving around with it?" asked Maik, approaching from the far side of the room.

"They suspected he was looking for somewhere to get rid of it. Apparently with the regulations and red tape involved these days, it's a very expensive proposition to have this stuff properly disposed of. But he wouldn't say where he was going with it, and they didn't have enough to hold him, so they had to let him go after they had ticketed him. They did impound the stuff though." He turned to Lauren. "If you fancied having a first-hand look, it's probably still out in the storage unit. Unless they've already had it picked up by the Hazardous Squad."

"What you need to do, young Holland," said Maik closing the gap between them ever so deliberately, "is to get on to your source in Traffic and find out all you can about whoever it was who was transporting this stuff."

Holland scratched his head slowly, making his blond locks bounce. "Yeah, might be a bit of a big ask that, Sarge. We're not really talking anymore, Sheila and me. Didn't exactly part on the best of terms, if you know what I mean."

Salter did.

Holland shook his head slowly, as if he was actually considering the idea for a moment. "Nah, can't see it happening, to be honest."

"Oh, it's going to happen, Constable," said Maik, close enough now to Holland for him to see the results of that morning's fresh shave with a new razor. "It's going to happen, even if you have to take her a nice box of chocolates and a bunch of flowers and ask her if she can ever forgive you for being such a prat. Because we need that background, Constable, that info that never finds its way onto the official arrest docket: how he acted, what he didn't say. And you are going to get it for us. Am I right? Of course I am."

Holland watched Maik grab his jacket and head out the door. "Chocolates and flowers?" he said to Salter after the sergeant had left. "Blimey, I can see why he doesn't get much these days."

Lauren, however, simply watched Danny's retreating form with a sad, sympathetic smile.

Jejeune entered the room moments later, carrying a sheet of paper.

"Anything I can do for you, sir?" asked Holland. At this point, he was even willing to consider washing the DCI's Range Rover, if it meant getting him out of having to read any more reports on drainage patterns.

"No, I don't think so." Jejeune crossed to Salter, her desk awash with scientific papers and charts. "Anything?"

"Well, there's obviously a strong connection between the antifoulant levels in the water and the decline in the copepods in the mud, but honestly, there's so many big words, most of them look like Max's set of wooden alphabet letters after he's dropped the box. I think I'm getting the overall idea, but there's still a lot of things that I'm not clear about."

"Then why don't you call the people who wrote the reports?"

"I can't do that. You're talking about some of the world's leading experts. I can't go calling them like I know what I'm talking about."

"You'd just be asking the questions, Constable. They would be the ones giving the answers."

"But that's just it, what if I don't understand their answers?"

"Then clearly, I'll have to start looking around for somebody with a fancy college accent."

After Jejeune left, Holland looked over with a disgusted expression on his face. "What was all that about? Beneath him, is it, to pick up a phone himself? Typical, leave us to do all the grunt work, while he swans off to look for the Lesser-spotted Whatever."

But Lauren Salter, Detective Constable first-class, was still smiling as she reached for the telephone and began to dial.

42

"You've ruled out Senior?" asked Salter.

She and Maik were alone in the incident room, sifting through the details one more time, the Motown song from Maik's laptop their only company. Maik nodded. "His only motive is that list. And if he was going to kill Brae, he would have had the ideal opportunity on that Monday. Quiet morning, no one else in the house, no one knew he was going to be there. Why just drop off the list and then go back a couple of days later to kill him? That said, there is something a bit off about him."

"That's what my dad says, too. Senior came down the workingmen's club last year, trying to get up a petition for a statue to Sydney Long, the doctor who founded Cley Marshes. He gave a bit of a presentation, went on about the economic value of birding to the area, and the historical significance of Cley. He said he was going to put a suggestion to Beverly Brennan for a statue near the new visitor centre. Claimed he could get as many names as he liked from birders from all over the world, but he was looking to get as many local names on the petition as possible, birders or not. He thought they would carry more weight. Dad said he felt a bit sorry for him. He was obviously so passionate, so committed to this idea, but everybody in the club could tell that it was a complete non-starter. Mind you, that said, he must have made quite an impression. I remember Dad coming back and saying we should take Max out to Cley to see the place, let him learn a bit about his local heritage. So we all piled in the car one Sunday and went out there."

"And?"

"And it was a nice enough place for a walk, I suppose, but there are plenty of other places I would rather take Max if we were going out for the day."

Maik went back to his work, the music from his computer in the background, just barely loud enough to hear. The Four Tops.' "I Can't Help Myself." Salter stood up and approached his desk, taking the chair opposite him. Maik finished the sentence he had been laboriously scrawling on the paper, laid down his pen, and looked up at her.

"Sarge, I've been thinking …"

"Have you, Constable? A lucky day for us."

"If the DCI is still trying to put Peter Largemount in the frame for Brae's murder, shouldn't we be looking at his movements a bit closer? You know, maybe checking his known associates, seeing if anyone could put him with Brae in the period just before the murder."

"We've checked all of his knowns, and nobody can put him anywhere near the victim or the murder site."

"All except one. Nobody has really looked into one of his known associates too closely, have they?"

"No, Constable, they haven't."

"Somebody needs to ask, though, don't they?"

"Yes, they do."

They both looked up as Tony Holland entered. There was something approaching reserve in the way he slouched over toward his desk and slumped heavily into his chair. He picked up a couple of papers and shuffled them around listlessly. Maik and Salter waited patiently.

After a couple of moments, with only Levi Stubbs and the boys taking the edge off the silence, Holland turned around to look at them, his face still slightly flushed. "Some people, honestly. You go there all friendly, ready to let bygones, and all that, and all they want to do is bring up ancient history."

Maik raised his eyebrow.

"Sheila. I got your info. But I think it's safe to say, I won't be getting any more from her. Info that is. Or anything else," he added with a grin. He was back already.

"*Our* info, Constable," said Maik. "Not mine. The division's, society's, the wider world's."

Lauren crossed over and took the sheet of paper from Holland's outstretched hand. She passed it to Maik and went to sit back at her own desk. But not before she had slipped him a significant glance. Not about this paper, he knew, but about their earlier, interrupted conversation.

If they did question DCS Shepherd, thought Maik, and she did have something to tell them this late in the case, she would never get out from under it. Even if it was something benign, with no impact on the case at all, the fact that they had had to ask, instead of her volunteering the information in the first place, or at the very least when Largemount became an active person of interest, would be enough to warrant a further look at her conduct. It would be a situation for the Special Investigation Unit. They would question her officially, and if she was anywhere within touching distance of this thing and had kept it secret, it would be as good as over for her. She might survive the investigation, likely would; the DCS was tough, and clever, and a good police officer, but her career would never recover from it.

But if a slow-as-molasses sergeant like him, just back from an enforced layoff and still half-hopped up on medications could figure all this out, how long ago did Domenic Jejeune get there? And at what point would his desire to solve the case overcome his reluctance to entangle the DCS in it, and go beyond these recent lukewarm, ever-so-casual inquiries about DCS Shepherd's private life. It had better be soon, thought Maik, because as far as he could see, putting it off like this wasn't going to make it go away. And now Salter had gotten here, too, and if she didn't see any results from this little off-the-record chat with him, it wouldn't be long before she went to somebody higher up the ladder, somebody outside the division, perhaps, and sat in a chair across the desk from them to tell them she had been thinking …

Maik laid Holland's paper beside his computer and machine-gunned a few strokes onto the keypad. He stared at the results on his screen intently. He scribbled a note on the pad beside him and then opened up a new window. After more rapid-fire keystrokes, he grabbed Salter's report on organotins and began leafing through it, looking for a particular passage. When he had finished, he checked one more thing on his computer before disconnecting his radio station feed and lowering the screen of his laptop. Slowly, but with great purpose, he eased himself out of his chair and reached for his jacket.

"Let's take a drive, you and me," he said to Holland.

"Where to?"

"Hull. We're going to find out where Steven Baker, of 44 Larkin Street, was going with all that TBT in his truck."

"I already told you, Traffic questioned him. He wouldn't say."

"That's because they didn't know the right way to ask," said Maik, holding the door open for Holland and following him out the door. He looked back at Salter, immersed in her paper swamp once again. "You know what to tell the DCI if he asks."

She nodded. "I know. On inquiries. Asking questions the right way."

43

Under the bank of heavy grey clouds, the dark water seemed to trap the light, drawing it in to its murky depths. The fringe of dry reeds around the edge of the marsh stirred restlessly in the wind. From the top of the rise, it was the only movement the men could see. Maik sighed with irritation. His drive back from Hull had been a trying one, as most long journeys with Holland for company tended to be. But there were nuggets of information from the interview that led him to believe he was on the right track. He hadn't had time to discuss them with Jejeune yet. The call to join the DCI out here had come as soon as he had returned.

By the time Maik arrived, Jejeune had already dismissed Alwyn's arm's-length protection, a young constable who looked like he might have trouble protecting someone from a strong breeze. Surely even someone as self-absorbed as Alwyn must have sensed a shadow by now. But according to the constable, the professor had been as cautious as ever when he left his home that morning. All indications were that he was still unaware of his protection, and still feeling vulnerable. Maik could live with that.

The detectives saw Alwyn as soon as they descended to the water's edge. He was standing a little way from the shore in knee-high water, wearing a heavy green fisherman's jacket and thigh waders. He was facing away from them, bending over to examine a tall, tube-like contraption suspended in the water. The light reflected off its metallic surface with a dull glint. If the man sensed the presence of the two detectives, he gave no hint, but when he had finished entering his data, he tucked his small hand-held device into the overlarge pocket of his jacket and straightened to look directly at them.

"We need to ask you some questions, Professor," called Jejeune across the water surface. Alwyn waded toward the shore but stopped, still in the water, a few feet from the men standing on the bank.

"Couldn't this have waited until I got back to the lab? You seem to have no qualms about dropping in there unannounced, Inspector, but I really must protest about you tracking me down in the field. Data of this type is extremely time-sensitive. I must insist on being allowed to continue my work here."

Maik had his hands in his pockets and his collar turned up. Jejeune could tell he didn't want to be here. But just at that moment, Jejeune couldn't think of any place in the world he would rather be.

"We'd like you to tell us what happened when Cameron Brae realized you had falsified the data from that monitoring station there." Jejeune nodded toward the gunmetal tube in the water.

Alwyn half raised a hand before letting it fall to his side again. "I'm afraid I don't know what you're talking about."

Jejeune continued as if the other man had not spoken. "Scientific data is, as you like to point out, irrefutable. The data should have convinced a trained scientist like Brae that there was no contamination coming from Largemount's property. Yet instead of simply accepting that, he still tried to telephone Largemount, to confront him. Why would he have done that, unless he knew the data you had given him was false?"

Maik felt the anger begin to rise within him. So that's why they were here, he thought, standing on this forlorn wind-swept stretch of mud; to arrest the one man he had written off from the start, about the only one he had felt was incapable of killing Brae. This condescending little mongrel? And his DCI couldn't find it within himself to confide in him before now, so Maik might, just for once, not feel like he was the last man in a two-man race, never seeing anything but the back of his DCI's heels disappearing over the hill in front of him.

Alwyn tried something resembling a contemptuous laugh, but it didn't quite come off. "And you came to this ridiculous conclusion how, exactly, if I may ask?"

"Because my sergeant told me."

Despite his anger, Maik looked surprised.

"He compared the two sets of monitoring results from this station, the ones you sent to Brae." He turned to Maik. "You said the results were the same. And as I said before, you always say what you mean, Sergeant. Not *similar*, or *close*, but *the same*." He turned back to Alwyn, who was now backing away slightly. "But they couldn't have been the same, could they? Not in one particular category, anyway."

Alwyn waved a hand ineffectually. Jejeune's casual familiarity with his area of expertise seemed to be having the desired effect. "I'm afraid marsh hydrology is a good deal more complex than simply comparing columns of numbers. To trust it to a … well, no offence, Sergeant, but there are a great many nuances that lie well beyond the reach of the layman."

Jejeune sensed Maik tensing next to him. His temper, never far from the surface, had been even less predictable than usual since his return to duty. Lashing out at inferior intellects may well have been Alwyn's form of defence when put under pressure like this, but it was not a course of action Jejeune would have advised where Danny Maik was concerned. Not today.

"You never told Brae that Largemount wasn't responsible for the contamination at Lesser Marsh, did you?" said Maik slowly. "If he had known that, he would have realized Largemount couldn't possibly have stopped the pollution, even if he had wanted to. So you let Brae think Largemount had it all under control. It was the only way you could have gotten him to agree to the deal. He would have never signed on if he thought the contamination was going to continue."

"Was that really my duty, Sergeant? Peter Largemount claimed he was responsible. If I had not been so well versed with the subject matter, I might well have believed him myself. If I am guilty of anything, it is merely of keeping my suspicions to myself."

Jejeune wasn't sure if it was Alwyn's admission or his attitude of amused detachment that Maik found so antagonistic. But his face had darkened. The DCI hadn't intended for things to go this way, but he decided to wait, now, to see what further results Maik's anger might produce.

"You know, I've seen a thousand like you," said Maik, moving forward until the water was lapping around his shoes. "Nasty little chancers, ready to do anything to get ahead. So where was all your concern for the facts then? Having a day off, were you, from your pursuit of truth in its pure, untarnished form? You didn't seem to have any trouble finding the truth when it came to telling Mandy Brae she wasn't bright enough to understand her husband's work."

Maik stepped closer, and Alwyn took an unsteady step back into the water.

"It was Brae's success you couldn't stand, wasn't it? His fame, his marriage. It was eating you up."

"Jealous? Of his silly little TV show and that pretentious fool of a wife? A woman with barely enough sense to learn a few dance moves? How dare she think that with a few quick conversations she could take her place at the grown-ups' table. Please don't imagine the rest of us are so easily beguiled by her, even if it is obvious how you feel about her yourself."

Jejeune watched as Maik continued to advance on Alwyn, circling the professor, stalking him, making him retreat, stumble backward, splashing the water around both of them as he did so. Alwyn looked across to him, a fellow intellect to connect with in the face of the sergeant's aggression. Maik had closed the gap between himself and the professor now. The water was lapping around his shins, soaking his trousers. Alwyn retreated further in the face of his relentless approach. He was shaking his head, backing away, until the water reached the tops of his waders. That stare. Danny Maik, eyes as cold as a November rain. Alwyn tore his eyes away and looked to Jejeune again. Surely he, as the senior man, should bring a stop to this, introduce a sense of control, of sanity.

"Couldn't you see how much she cared for him?" asked Maik. "Couldn't you see how much she wanted to be a part of her husband's world, how important it was to her to understand? She came to you for help. That poor lost girl. She came to you for help and you crushed her. You dismissed her, like you dismiss everybody who is that little bit slower than you, that little bit less well-educated. And then, even afterward, even after you had killed her husband, it wasn't enough. You sent her the watch, to cause her more pain, more sorrow. Didn't you? Didn't you?"

Maik's anger filled the marsh. His face was dark, the sinews in his thick bull neck twisted like lariats, his eyes cold with fury as he leaned into Alwyn's face.

And then, there it was. Finally. In Alwyn's eyes, at the mention of the watch. The guilt Maik had been looking for. Jejeune saw it too, the merest flicker of acknowledgement. But it was enough. Now it was time to end this. He moved forward to the edge of the marsh, ready to call Maik back in, to calm things down. But he was already too late.

Afterward, Jejeune wasn't sure. Perhaps Alwyn had already lost his footing. Perhaps Maik's lunge was just a reaction to that. At the time it was just a flurry of action; Maik's sudden grab, Alwyn's half-raised arm and his stumble, the water splashing up around the pair of them as they came together, Alwyn fighting to retain his balance. And then Maik, standing over the professor as he lay on his back, flailing around in the water with his arms outstretched, half submerged, with his heavy, saturated clothing dragging him under. Maik, with his hands on Alwyn's jacket and then off, empty, held above his head like a sinning footballer. Never touched him. Honest.

Alwyn's face disappeared beneath the water, a foamy trail of air bubbles running like a white scar across the dark surface. Jejeune saw Maik reach under the water and grab the front of Alwyn's jacket once again, wondering, uncertain, just for that split second, about his intent. And then Maik hauled the professor up, fighting the weight of the wet clothing, the panic of the man, the pull of the water. Alwyn's breath exploded from him with a gasp, but his body remained limp. Maik held him just above the surface, fighting his own balance. The professor's rag doll body was splayed backward from Maik's grasp, fingertips still in the water. He was spluttering and coughing, choking for breath.

Maik staggered once more, trying to retain his balance and keep hold of Alwyn's jacket. Even from here, Jejeune could hear the mud sucking at Maik's shoes as he dragged the limp, half-submerged body of Alwyn to the water's edge. He dumped him on the ground and staggered over to a dry area farther up. He sank down to the ground heavily and sat with his arms resting on his knees, his head bowed between them, his upper body heaving with strain.

Alwyn choked and then rolled heavily onto his side, coughing out a stream of dirty water. He lay still for a long moment. Jejeune waited patiently until he had recovered sufficiently to pull himself up to sit on a rock at the water's edge. He was leaning forward, hands on knees, his wet clothing clinging to him like guilt. He was whimpering slightly; shock probably, thought Jejeune. Water dripped from his lank hair and face as he sat, head bowed, staring down into the water, the dark, non-reflecting water. He seemed to find nothing of comfort there.

Jejeune approached him.

"It was the bittern, wasn't it?"

"That bird?" Maik looked up, still breathing heavily.

"No, Sergeant, not the bird. The water. The mix of salt and fresh, it's called bittern. Cameron Brae had no way of verifying the results the professor had sent him, but he knew that, after the storms we had recently, all that sea water flooding into the marsh would have diluted the salt content. Especially in the morning. Those results, the bittern, the *am. bittern*, one from before the storm surge, one from after, those readings at least should have been significantly different. But as you said, they were the same."

The reeds rattled as a renegade breeze passed through them like the hand of a ghost. In a moment, there was silence on the marsh again. Alwyn was shivering slightly, his teeth chattering and the skin around his lips turning faintly blue. He spoke to the ground again, his voice barely audible.

"A stupid oversight," he said sullenly. "I told you, Cameron was extremely bright. I would have never deliberately underestimated him. I knew I couldn't send him the real results so I simply reran the previous report and tinkered with a few readings. But as you say, I neglected to alter the salinity levels." He shook his head. "Stupid. Unforgivable, really."

Alwyn's voice was dull and lifeless. The resistance had left him now, completely, stripped away layer by layer until only the truth was left. He had been prepared to deny things as long as he was the one who held all the facts, but it was clear now that Jejeune had them, too. There no longer seemed any point in denying anything. A violent coughing fit overcame him, seeming to rack his frail body to the core.

"Brae realized that you must have known right from the start that the pollution was continuing. Every monitoring record you took from here must have confirmed it."

Alwyn nodded weakly and wiped tears from his eyes with the back of his hand. Jejeune knew they were the result of the coughing fit. The professor wasn't the weeping kind.

"He came to see me after he got the results. He was incandescent with rage, screaming about how I had betrayed him, stood by while we allowed an ecological catastrophe to unfold. He said he was going to confront Largemount, to demand that he pay for the bioremediation, to clean up the contamination and restore the marsh to health."

"But bioremediation processes on this scale would cost hundreds of thousands of pounds," said Jejeune.

"And that's why you killed him." Maik's voice was as cold and flat as the overcast sky. He was standing beside Alwyn now, heedless of his mud-caked shoes and waterlogged trousers, hovering over the small shivering form, as dangerous and as threatening as ever. "Because Largemount would have to take that money from somewhere, and your funding would have been the obvious place to start."

Alwyn shook his head, looking up at Maik. "Still, Sergeant? Even now you fail to understand? Cameron said if Largemount refused, he would go public with the details of our original deal, expose him, expose all of us. But it was already too late to help the marsh, you see, even if Largemount had agreed to pay. Cameron seemed to think if we just stopped the pollution, turned off the tap as it were, and employed some biological remedies, the marsh could revert to the way it was in a few seasons. But for salt marshes, bioremediation can never be fully effective. The systems are far too interconnected. What corrects one issue inevitably exacerbates another. The only way is self-attenuation, the slow, gradual process by which the marsh heals itself. It has to go through the cycle, you see, of self-cleaning. For a wetland system as complex as this one, it will take decades. To all intents and purposes, Great Marsh is a dead zone in waiting. The worst, much worse, is still to come."

"You told Brae that?" asked Jejeune, watching Alwyn's face closely.

Alwyn nodded abstractedly. His teeth had begun to chatter again and his skin was beginning to show pale blotches. They would need to get him away from here soon, out of his wet clothes and into some warm blankets. Soon, but not yet.

"Cameron refused to accept it, of course. For all his so-called expertise on marshes, it turns out he had a surprisingly simplistic view of their ecosystems, after all. We argued for a few moments more, but then he left, abruptly. But I swear to you, Inspector, Cameron Brae was alive when he left my house."

"Perhaps so," he said thoughtfully, "but not the last time you saw him. Correct?"

Nothing moved in the marsh; not the light of the grey sky, not the dark surface of the water. For one brief, elastic moment, everything ceased. There was no wind, no sound, no birdsong. The men, the marsh, all of nature waited. Jejeune was anxious to get this over with now, to have it ended and to move on, away from this marsh, this desolate place with its dark, still water and its fading reeds and its end-of-life feel. Jejeune waited to see if Alwyn would begin on his own. He would not.

"Let's take it from the moment you arrived at his house, shall we, Professor?" said Jejeune patiently. "On the night Cameron Brae died."

44

"Suicide, Domenic. Really? We're sure?" DCS Shepherd put her elbows on the desk and buried her head in her hands. "God Almighty, what a mess. How the hell did you not see it before?"

Jejeune ignored the question. "Brae was dead when he got there. Alwyn went to the house first, to the study. Then he went out into the garden and found the body. After that, it was just a matter of putting on the chains and the sack and removing the ladder."

"Did he say why he did it?"

"He claims he wanted to spare the wife the knowledge that her husband had committed suicide. Not this wife, the first one, Kathleen. A murder would seem more heroic, somehow, he said, less like an admission of guilt. A more likely explanation is that he wanted to deter people from looking into the possible reasons Cameron Brae might commit suicide in the first place. Being responsible for polluting Great Marsh would have been high on most people's list. Alwyn couldn't afford the closer scrutiny of everything — the runoff from Largemount's land, the original survey — that would have resulted if Brae's suicide was investigated too closely."

"Please don't tell me we missed Alwyn's prints in the study."

"No, but he doesn't deny being there. He says he went to recover the monitoring results he sent to Brae. There would have been a suicide note, probably written in red ink. It almost certainly laid out the details of their original deal with Largemount. Alwyn claims he saw no note, meaning he has destroyed it, most probably. He would have panicked when he saw it, and gotten rid of it, even before he really realized what he was doing."

Despite herself, the DCS couldn't help pausing to snatch an incredulous glance at Jejeune.

"Red ink? How the hell…? Oh, of course, the pen…. And the watch?"

"Brae removed it, as suicides do. Watches and glasses. He left the watch in the study. The glasses would have been easy enough to slip back on Brae's face. They would have been in the top pocket of Brae's shirt most likely, but the watch was a different matter. Alwyn couldn't leave it in the study, but the wrists would have been too bloated by the time he found the body to put it back on. That's why the chaining of the arms was done so loosely, around the shirt cuffs rather than the wrists. Alwyn ended up taking the watch, but he wanted to be sure it got back to Mandy Brae. He had no idea it would cause so much distress. About that, at least, I believe him."

It was the small details, she thought, the red pen, the glasses in the shirt pocket, that gave Jejeune's report such a sense of certainty about how events had really unfolded; a certainty that she knew wasn't really there. But he had the big picture right. Of that, she was sure.

"Alwyn." She shook her head. "I never cared for him. Still, I imagine this has taken the sheen off some of his arrogance. I presume his academic career is over."

"He doesn't seem to think so. With the other principals both dead, he knows we would struggle to prove the existence of a deal. As long as he continues to deny malice or intent, he's in the clear — on the major charges, anyway. To be honest, I think he's even looking forward to his notoriety."

Jejeune's mind went back to Alwyn's comments during his confession, back in the safe, warm interrogation room — with Danny Maik nowhere in sight: "Scandal is hardly the impediment to an academic career that it once was, Inspector. Quite the reverse, in fact, a hint of the dark side does wonders for one's reputation these days."

"The pity of it is, he's right. He'll probably end up with a TV show of his own." Shepherd sighed. "Once this gets out there will be a lot of questions. The resources, the manpower, the time we've poured into this. And all to come up with a suicide we might have gotten to on the first day, at the scene even!"

Nobody could have called a suicide at the scene. Jejeune knew it and DCS Shepherd undoubtedly knew it, too. But Jejeune knew, too, that suicide wasn't a satisfactory result, whatever that meant. The public wanted justice. Well, unfortunately, it didn't always work like that. Instead, they got a death; they got a solution. A man died, under tragic circumstances. It wasn't Jejeune's job to ensure an ongoing saga for the networks, or to apologize if the outcome wasn't entertaining enough for a gawping public.

"So this whole business of the four-hundred list was nothing to do with the case? This bird he saw, this … bittern thing, it wasn't really a factor at all, even if we still don't know why he chose not to report it?"

"Cameron Brae never saw an American Bittern. That *should* have been obvious, really. He didn't capitalize it. Every bird in Cameron Brae's list, going back as far as his earliest records, was capitalized. It's a matter of personal style, rather than grammar. But the entry in his diary that morning was *am. bittern*, lower case *b*. I missed it," said Jejeune simply.

"And you're quite sure now that it was Alwyn, and not Peter, who Brae went to see the night he died."

It wasn't a question. She had known all along it wasn't Largemount who Brae had gone to see that night. Peter Largemount had been at his house, ignoring an incoming telephone call so he could continue denying to his guest any involvement with Beverly Brennan, insisting on it over and over again, his need to convince her so great that he was almost late for his presentation, having to race through the lanes of north Norfolk to deliver his speech at the hotel in Norwich. Shepherd watched Jejeune's face carefully. How much of this did he already know, or had he guessed at? Did he know even now what thoughts she was reliving about her last private evening alone with Peter Largemount?

"I believe Brae's original plan was to go to Largemount's house after he had confronted Alwyn. To tell him he was going to expose everything. But when Alwyn pronounced his death sentence on Great Marsh, Brae simply went back home. Alone in the house, he must have agonized over the marsh, and his part in its destruction. Eventually, his guilt became too much for him."

"Of course, the irony is that you … that *this* has done Cameron Brae's reputation irreparable harm. As a murder victim, he was a martyr to his cause. As Alwyn rightly suggests, suicide implies guilt or, at the very least, complicity. I doubt his followers will be able to forgive him for his betrayal."

"He did a lot of good work. A moment of weakness? People might understand. In time."

Shepherd suddenly straightened her back and switched into damage control mode with her characteristic brusqueness. "This still leaves us with Peter's death. Are we any closer to charging Malcolm Brae? We're going to have to move ahead soon, or risk losing him altogether. What does the CPS say about the evidence?"

Jejeune searched her face. For all his sins, Largemount had not been responsible for Brae's death. Had he really been killed in the mistaken belief that he was? Or would charging Malcolm Brae just allow a killer with another motive to slide into the shadows?

"They've found a couple of people who heard him wishing Largemount harm, and worse, and since the missing Churchill hasn't surfaced, there is no way of ruling it out as the murder weapon. Plus, of course, the various bits of incriminating physical evidence recovered from the Earth Front house. But ..."

"And let's not forget that nobody knew Brae had killed himself. We've only just found out about it ourselves, for God's sake. As far as Malcolm Brae is concerned, he still believed Peter killed his father. So there is motive, declared intent, and opportunity. No one can verify Malcolm Brae's whereabouts?"

"I don't think ..."

"We're going ahead. Have Malcolm Brae formally charged with the murder of Peter Largemount. And I want a press conference to announce it. This is your area, Domenic. This is what you were brought in for: to handle the big stuff. Now, I want you to get out there and do your job. I want a major announcement, loud and proud, with all the bells and whistles. Fireworks, too, if you like. I want the nationals in here, TV and print. This is our only chance to redeem ourselves after spending all this time chasing a suicide. I want the public to know that we have wrapped this up, and I want there to be no question that we've got it right. We're all singing off the same hymn sheet today, Domenic. Do I make myself clear? Let's see if we can't drown out some of the background noise over Cameron Brae's suicide."

Was this his job? He was a police detective, not an impresario at a pier-end pantomime. This wasn't entertainment. It was life. And death.

"I'm not sure Malcolm Brae is guilty."

"That is for a jury to decide. CPS believes we have enough evidence to proceed, you're telling me. I want the case brought. Unless you have a more viable suspect in mind …"

Jejeune met her steady gaze and held it. He wasn't quite ready to offer his alternative just yet. He needed one more piece of evidence. He just hoped that this time it wouldn't come too late.

45

Jejeune looked out at the night sky, mesmerized. If he had to give up everything about this part of the world, it would be the skies he would hold onto until the last; the endless, blue, forever skies of the days, and these nights, vast and clear and soft with stars spangled across them as far as the eye could see. The day's thin tracery of white clouds had been peeled away by the evening's breezes, and above him now was a spectacular velvety black tapestry shot through with glittering points of light.

Down here, the darkness was complete. There was no moon, and the fields around them were no more than dark voids, as empty and impenetrable as the spaces between the stars. Maik and Jejeune were hunched in the back of a police car, nestled into a layby along the main road. Their own vehicles, the Range Rover and Maik's Mini, were parked in a field on the far side of the road, hidden from view by the cover of high hedgerows. It was a warm night, and they had the windows wound down, so the sounds of the night seeped in; insect calls, the occasional hiss of tires from a passing vehicle; even, in the silence, the distant crush of waves breaking on the beaches far to the east.

"Are we sure they will have cause to stop it, Sergeant? I don't want this one going away on a technicality."

Maik smiled to himself in the darkness. In deference to the rising optimism he was beginning to feel, he allowed himself the indulgence of confirming what the DCI already knew, as much for the satisfaction of hearing it himself as anything else.

"We have an earlier report of a vehicle being driven in an erratic manner as it left the car park of The Boatman's Arms. Anonymous tip, I believe. Traffic will have every right to pull over any vehicle matching the description, which this one does, coincidentally enough. They will stop it as soon as the tires hit the public road."

"And we're sure it will be tonight."

"As sure as we can be. Everything points to it."

After the recent events, the temptation was constantly there to check on Maik, ask if he was okay. But Jejeune knew he had to resist the urge. As if in answer to Jejeune's concerns, Danny Maik got out to stretch his legs. He was no doubt feeling the tension, too. It was, after all, his lead they were pursuing. He had more than a passing interest in how things worked out.

Tony Holland was discussing Norwich City's latest loss with one of the uniformed constables when a staccato burst from a radio rattled the air.

"On the move, sir."

Maik's voice was as clear and crisp as the night air. "Ready, everybody. And remember, there's still a shotgun out there somewhere, so I don't want anybody playing silly buggers tonight. Let's all take it seriously. Understand?"

Straining to peer into the darkness, Jejeune could just make out the faint metallic shimmer of a van moving across the field in the distance. It was moving slowly, lifting slightly every now and then as it negotiated the rutted ground. Jejeune tried to keep calm, but he could feel the tension beginning to build within him. Everything depended on this. If it didn't go right, it would be over, the lead, the case. *His career?* He was aware that, at this moment, it mattered to him. It mattered very much.

"Here we go."

But just as Maik spoke, the glint from the distant vehicle's bodywork slowed, then very gradually began to change direction. It had been heading directly for them, for the gateway between the hedgerows that opened out onto the main road. Now it had begun a slow arc back toward the darkness on the far edge of the field. The driver was taking it easy, whether to avoid alerting anybody watching or to avoid getting bogged down in the rich peaty soil it was hard to say. What had tipped the driver off? It could have been a glint off one of the police cars' reflectors, perhaps even the glow of a cigarette. Those who live by their wits take their cues from any sources they can get. Whatever it was, it was obvious the vehicle was no longer coming this way.

"No." Jejeune had not realized he had spoken aloud until Maik replied.

"The van's still on private property, sir. We can't touch it."

"Stay here." said Jejeune, sprinting across the road toward the Range Rover. "And be ready."

He was glad Maik hadn't asked for specifics, because he didn't have any just then. But by the time the big engine coughed to life, Jejeune's plan had started to form. The Beast bounced roughly out of the field and lurched out onto the road, accelerating away between the hedgerows with the headlights off. The narrow laneway he had seen on the maps earlier was about a quarter of a mile ahead of him, but in the darkness it came up too suddenly. Jejeune slammed on the brakes and wrenched the steering wheel right, the big vehicle rocking dangerously as it fought the physics of the turn. He accelerated again as soon as the wheels hit the road and sped down the lane along the side of the field, still hidden from view by high hedgerows. He saw the opening at the last moment, a gateway leading into the field, and wrenched the wheel around once more. Without braking, he accelerated toward the gate. It smashed backward violently, dangling forlornly from a single hinge as the Range Rover bounced through the gap and into the field. Now Jejeune flicked on the headlights. He picked up the van immediately. It was on the far side of the field, trundling across the ground toward an area where the land sloped away from view. Jejeune accelerated again and headed straight for the van.

The twin beams of his headlights locked onto their prey like lasers. Despite the darkness surrounding them, it was obvious that Jejeune was on a direct course to intercept the van, and coming on at a recklessly high speed. The van lurched forward, headlights still off. If the driver could just get beyond the arc of Jejeune's headlights, the surrounding blackness was waiting to swallow the van up. A flick of the steering wheel locked The Beast's headlights back on to the van, but in a second it was gone again, slithering off down the slope, out of sight. Jejeune turned off his own headlights and rolled to a stop. He lowered his window, listening for sounds, rattles, engine noises, anything. Silence. Jejeune feathered the accelerator and let the Range Rover's quietly purring engine ease him forward. He heard at once the metallic squeak of the front wheel. The surrounding silence amplified the sound, echoing it around the empty field, announcing his position. He knew he had no choice. He turned off the engine and eased his door open quietly. He got out, feeling the soft earth give beneath his tread.

Jejeune stood still and silent in the middle of the darkened field, senses taut with strain. The peaty smell of the earth filled the air. Nothing moved in the blackness, but in the distance there was a sound, the quiet tick of a gently idling engine, somewhere just beyond his sightline. Jejeune advanced slowly toward the edge of the slope, guided by his finely tuned birder's ear. And all the time, Maik's words played on a loop in his brain. *Remember, there's still a shotgun out there somewhere.*

Jejeune stopped. The sound was clearer now, reaching him more evenly across the silence of the night. The van was near. It had not moved during his approach. The driver was waiting, watching, scanning the fields for any sign of the Range Rover's approach, listening for that tell-tale squeak to reveal it was slowly creeping over the uneven terrain toward him. Just those few seconds' advantage might let him disappear into the darkness for good.

Jejeune did not see the van until he crested the rise, but by then it was too late. The driver flicked on the headlights, the beams fixing Jejeune against the horizon. He heard the change in engine pitch and reacted, turning and sprinting away. The van accelerated up the slope toward him with a high-pitched whine. Jejeune stumbled in the mud, scrambling to his feet and fighting for his balance as he ran over the uneven ground. The van's headlights bore down on him now, pinning him in their path, closing fast. Jejeune could see the Range Rover, lit up in the beams, and changed course to head for it. He heard the whine of the van's engine, heard the creaks as it rattled over the furrows in pursuit. He felt the heat on his back and flung himself to one side, reeling as the side mirror clipped his head with a sharp crack.

Jejeune lay low on the earth, dazed. The brake lights. The brake lights were on. The van was coming back to finish the job. Jejeune saw the van begin to crank into a turn. The headlights went off again, leaving only darkness. Jejeune scrambled up and sprinted to the Range Rover, feeling a sticky wetness running down his neck.

He flicked on the Range Rover's headlights just in time to see the van heading straight for him. Jejeune turned the key and stamped the accelerator in one motion, lurching out of the path of the oncoming vehicle half a second before it reached him. By the time he had regained control the van had turned around and was coming in for another pass. If the driver had a shotgun resting across his arm, he would have a clear line of sight through the side window as he passed. Jejeune gunned the engine again, slewing the big Range Rover around as the van plunged past into the night. It rattled on into the darkness, heading for the far side of the field. Jejeune cranked the steering wheel round hard, feeling the big tires bite into the soft earth, the extra traction of his four-wheel drive giving him the edge he needed. Now he was directly behind the retreating van and making up the ground between them.

He could see the van swaying dangerously as it hurtled across the uneven surface, spraying mud in its wake. Jejeune turned on his wipers, smearing the mud across his screen. He kept the Range Rover's big headlights locked into the van driver's rear-view mirror, to let him know he was right behind him. And closing fast. The van swung hard right, making for the broken gate where Jejeune had entered. Jejeune raced after him, piling on the speed. The van smashed through the remains of the broken gate and careened into a hard left-hand turn onto the lane, slewing the rear end as its mud-caked tires slid on the unpaved surface. It hurtled along the lane, retracing the route Jejeune had taken a few minutes earlier. The Range Rover bounced out of the field into the lane in pursuit.

They earn their money, those guys in Traffic, thought Jejeune. The patrol cars screeched to a halt across the top of the lane seconds before the van arrived. The van driver slammed on the brakes and skidded to the left, losing the front tire in a ditch. Right behind, Jejeune barely made the stop himself, veering to the right to give himself the extra yard he needed.

Jejeune was first to the van, but he stood back and allowed Maik to approach. He had generated the lead that had led to this operation; he deserved the satisfaction of ending it. The sergeant approached the van from behind, keeping his body well away from the line of a swiftly opened door, just like the manual said. Jejeune touched his head wound again and examined the fresh blood on his fingers. He put his hands in his pockets; no need to show everybody how much they were shaking.

Maik tapped a gnarled knuckle against the driver's window and waited patiently for it to be lowered.

"Any chance of a lift, Archie? I'm going down the station." Maik's glance swept past Archie Christian's hunched form, toward the containers in the back of the van. "And if those drums contain what I think they contain, so are you."

Maik straightened up from the window, as the arresting officers from Traffic moved in to begin their work. He caught one last glimpse of the defiant figure of Archie Christian as he was taken, resisting, from the van and bundled into the back of the waiting patrol car.

Maik approached Jejeune, unable to keep the note of triumph from his voice.

"Definitely chemicals, eight drums that I could see. Don't know if it's TBT yet, but whatever it is, it's a safe bet it's not something you should be transporting unsecured and without the proper documentation. Certainly enough for a warrant to search his premises, and do soil tests on his land. By the way, sir, just so you know, the boys have asked me to pass on their apologies. What with it being dark and all, and us having a bit of a chat about football, none of us could really make out what went on out in that field. Completely passed us by. I suppose we should have been paying more attention, but there you are. Oh, and you might want to get that bang on the noggin looked at, too. It looks nasty."

Jejeune nodded. The gate, the pursuit, it would all have happened exactly as he chose to put it down in his report. Nobody was sure exactly where the legal chips had fallen tonight, but Archie Christian wouldn't have any friends left in places of influence, not now he had finally fallen from grace.

Jejeune got into the Range Rover and pulled in behind the convoy of police cars, pursuit vehicles, and van, successfully reversed out of the ditch and now driven by Tony Holland, all heading toward the station.

Maik watched them go. He leaned on a narrow stile and looked out over the darkened fields. He felt the warm evening breeze on his face. He had no idea where things might lead from here, but whatever Archie Christian was eventually convicted of, Maik was fairly sure that, when added to the drug thefts from the vet's offices, it was a safe bet that the outside world had seen the last of him for quite a while. He eased himself up from the stile and began the walk back along the quiet, dark lanes toward his car. On the whole, he decided, it was nice to be back.

46

Katherine Brae made herself very busy after ushering Jejeune into her front parlour. First it was tea, then, while the kettle was boiling, it was the cushions that needed attention. Finally, a few of the ceramic statuettes on the mantelpiece above the fireplace needed rearranging, though if they were returned to a different position, the change was not immediately clear to Jejeune. By the time she returned from her second visit to the kitchen with a tray of tea things, they had been in the house together for at least ten minutes with only the barest of pleasantries exchanged. Clearly Jejeune was not the only one for whom this was going to be a difficult meeting.

"You should get stitches for that head wound, Inspector," said Katherine Brae, handing Jejeune a cup of tea. "Men are so silly about these things sometimes. It wouldn't make you look weak, you know."

"Professor Alwyn claims he only acted to protect Dr. Brae's reputation," said Jejeune, anxious to change the subject.

"Did Cameron's reputation deserve protection, I wonder?" She dismissed her thought with a wave of her mottled hand. "Miles Alwyn never acted in any way other than to serve his own interests, Inspector. If it was to protect anyone's reputation, it was his own. What will happen to him?"

"Obstruction of justice, evidence tampering. There may be other charges. Likely no custodial time."

"Cameron must have realized there was something wrong with the marsh some time ago. He never actually said as much, you understand, but you could tell, if you knew him. There was something in his face whenever he returned from there, a sadness I had never seen before."

"He noticed that some of the waders were disappearing, though they are still showing up in healthy numbers at Titchwell, Cley, and other spots along the coast. He reasoned that Great Marsh was being contaminated by something. An antifoulant called TBT, as it happens."

"But the other birds at the marsh," said Katherine Brae, "they won't all be affected, surely?"

"I'm afraid so. The Godwits, the Oystercatchers, the longer-billed birds are still there because they probe deeper for their food, beyond the present contamination levels. But problems will show up in their food sources in a few more seasons, as the contamination accumulates and works its way through the ecosystem. Eventually, they will all be gone."

"How terribly sad. Poor Cameron. What it must be to watch something you love so much dying by degrees like that." A thought seemed to strike her. "It won't be enough for Colleen, I expect. A suicide, I mean. It should be, shouldn't it? Surely society benefits if it is proven that there is one less murderer among us than we thought? But she will have been looking for something more … well, dramatic. Poor Colleen, life never seems to satisfy her expectations."

She looked up at Jejeune's silence, but did not intrude upon it. For some moments she made herself busy with her tea cup. "Do we know who was actually responsible for contaminating the marsh, Inspector?"

"We have made an arrest in connection with that."

"Mr. Christian?" She looked at Jejeune. "Of course, you can't say until charges are formally brought."

"We believe we have the right person."

She poured more tea for both of them, although her own cup was still half full. "I understand Malcolm is to be formally charged with Peter Largemount's murder." She let the act of pouring claim all her attention.

Jejeune looked around the room, at the comfortable furniture, the ornaments along the mantelpiece. Was this any kind of a setting to be talking to a mother about her son's arrest for murder? But then, what was?

"There will be a press conference at 5:00 p.m. today at which I will be announcing an arrest and charges. I wanted to let you know beforehand, in case there were any arrangements you had to make."

Katherine Brae was silent for a long time. From the next room, the unremitting ticking of a clock sounded. *They could be so quiet, these country houses*, thought Jejeune. Outside, a Pied Flycatcher alighted on a bush for a moment. Migration was underway already, another sign that summer was coming to an end.

"I see. Well, I suppose I should thank you for your courtesy in coming here, at least. You should know I have engaged the best firm of solicitors in the area. The senior partner was a personal friend of Cameron's." She paused for a moment. "You seem to be far too good a policeman to bring a case on such flimsy evidence, Inspector. Is there anything I should know? Has Malcolm confessed? He didn't do it, as I suspect you know."

"No one has confessed. I'm sorry. I can't say anything more about it at the moment."

But she had already moved on, to a place that only she could see, somewhere in the space between her chair and the empty fireplace.

"That deal with Peter Largemount was Cameron all over. Ambition and pragmatism in equal measure. He never could see the risks his aspirations posed to the things he loved. He became so frantic toward the end. It was most unlike him. I suppose he was closing off many of his peripheral projects so he could channel all his energies into saving the marsh."

"You appear to be very well informed about your ex-husband's recent activities."

She paused for a moment, as if considering the counsel of invisible voices. When she spoke again, a new tone of kindness had come into her voice.

"And you seem to understand things to a degree quite remarkable in one so young, Inspector." She smiled and set down her cradled tea cup in its saucer. "You're quite right, of course. Cameron wanted to share things with her, truly he did. But despite her best efforts, she just wasn't quite up to the mark, intellectually, I'm afraid. Cameron felt he simply didn't have anywhere else to go where he could discuss matters, so he came here." She gave her head a small shake. "It was so typical of him, to want the best of all worlds. Still, he is not entirely to blame. The users of the world need enablers, don't they?"

Jejeune began to stand up. Katherine Brae smiled at him from her seat, but made no move to get up.

"Thank you for coming, Inspector. I shall not be at your press conference, but I suspect my solicitors will have a representative there." A softer smile touched her lips as she turned her gaze away from him. "You know, Cameron could be quite irresistible when he set his mind on something. The trouble was, he never seemed entirely sure what it was that he wanted." She shook her head sadly again. "Poor dear. I shall miss him."

47

There was music coming from the sunroom. Maik went around to the side of the house. The door was open.

Mandy Brae was sitting at the piano, playing to the empty room. Her slender white arms were poised delicately above the keyboard, her head bowed slightly toward the keys. She was singing softly to herself. Maik recognized the tune. Classical? Not with words. A show tune, perhaps? He couldn't place it.

Her pitch was perfect, her timing flawless, holding each note and then releasing it expertly, so that it floated out into the empty room. She played simply, the music an accompaniment to the voice only. It was a spellbinding performance, played out to an audience of none.

Maik stayed in the doorway for an eternity of small moments. Perhaps the light shifted, sending a shadow across her sightlines. Perhaps she just sensed him there. She stopped playing and twisted sideways on her piano stool. The way the light fell on her face turned her skin to alabaster. A strand of hair had escaped her untidy ponytail and tricked down her neck like the path of a teardrop. She was almost unbearably beautiful. It was all he could do to stop himself from sighing aloud.

"Danny."

"Don't stop on my account."

She smiled, "I know it's not Marvin Gaye, but there is some other good music out there, you know. Come in. Have a seat. How are you feeling?"

She swivelled around.

"I just thought I would come by to see if you had any questions," he said. "It's just that sometimes, with suicides, well, the family members, you know, they wonder …"

"Cameron felt he had caused the death of Great Marsh. Nothing I could have said or done would have changed that. He worshipped that place. I knew that when I married him."

"I wanted you to know … we found no evidence that your husband was having an affair."

She held a fist to her heart. "Other than in here, you mean? Thanks, Danny. That's very kind. I'm not sure it really matters, though, now. I lost my husband a long time ago. To what, doesn't really seem important anymore. It hurt then and it hurts now, but that's the way it was." She offered Maik a brave smile that almost broke his heart.

"Any idea what you will do now? Will you stay on here?"

Was there hope in his question? She looked up, as if she had heard something behind the words.

"My agent is in talks over a documentary about the session musicians during the glory days of Motown. I could really get behind a project like that. All those behind-the-scenes stories. Perhaps I might even get to find out why Smokey would never credit his wife Claudette for her contributions on those beautiful a cappella tracks the Miracles laid down."

She seemed to be considering the proposal to herself, letting the fingers of her right hand play a little ripple of the keys as she thought.

"I would have to go over there, of course. Most of the big Motown stars have long since moved to the west coast, I suppose, but the sessioners, the ones with the real stories, I don't imagine many of them will have strayed very far from home. Ever been to Detroit, Danny? We played there quite a lot. For some reason they seemed to have a thing for a bunch of silly white girls jumping around singing 'Party Animal.' I could never really understand it myself, especially considering the musical pedigree of *that* city, of all places, but they were always very nice to us."

Visiting these people, chatting about some of the sessions they had worked on, listening to all those stories about the Funk Brothers, Babbitt, Jamerson, all the greats? Maik couldn't imagine a world where these sorts of things were possibilities. He felt, more sharply than he ever had, the distance between her world and his. It was a divide that could never be crossed, no matter how much she referred to him as Danny and asked about his health.

"I may get back into music, too," she said, tinkering with the piano keys again. "I really did like it at one time, in the early days. Before the madness. It might be nice to do some writing. Soundtracks perhaps."

Not performing, she didn't say. She didn't have to. It was harder each time Maik met her to imagine this delicate, private person performing for thousands, bustled and bundled around by the animal called fame.

"It's important to be happy in what you do," he said.

"You should tell that to your boss. He hates his job, doesn't he? He wants to be somewhere else, not asking widows if they know why their husbands are dead."

"It's a hard job to like sometimes."

And it never seemed to give you a satisfactory ending. Maik looked out the window at the garden, and the marsh beyond, still and quiet with the sunlight upon it. Motown songs were better. Three minutes, problem to solution, and everybody goes away, if not happy, at least knowing the answers.

"Still," said Maik, "he's good at what he does. Apparently, even the media get things right sometimes."

"You should know better than to trust the hype, Danny. Heroes will disappoint you every time. Even Marvin didn't turn out to be quite who we thought he was, did he?"

She offered a sad smile and Maik repaid her in kind.

"That reminds me, I've got your records."

She got up and went over to a desk and came back with a pile of singles and albums, each stacked neatly and arranged by release date, just as her father's collection was.

"I've pinched all the ones I wanted, uploaded them onto my iPod. It seems only fair, given the amount my accountant tells me I've lost through illegal downloads."

She didn't really seem to care. Perhaps for some people there really was such a thing as enough money.

"I'd better be going." Maik nodded toward the piano. "Leave you to your music. It was nice to have met you," he said awkwardly.

"You make it sound as if we'll never see each other again. You meet a lot of people twice in life, Danny. Once when you're not ready, and then again when you are. Thank you for your kindness. You've been a big help through a very difficult time. I won't forget it. Or you."

She turned back to the piano, but she was not singing as Maik left, just playing. Was it a different tune, he wondered. Or did it just sound different without the words?

48

DCS Shepherd parked her car some distance from the mayhem and walked through the stand of beech trees to a spot on the far side of the forecourt, where Maik was standing with his hands in his pockets, watching the TV camera crews set up for their broadcasts.

"They had better get somebody to rope off those cables, or there's going to be a lawsuit," he said by way of a greeting.

"Just what the hell is he playing at, Sergeant? Why has he chosen this location for the press conference?"

"Developments, ma'am. He said he tried to get a hold of you, but he couldn't reach you. He said if you wanted the announcement in time for the evening news, this was where it had to take place."

"Developments? What developments? He is still going to announce the arrest, I take it. Where is he, anyway?"

"Just over there, by the podium." Maik saw Jejeune watching them as they spoke. In fact, Jejeune's eyes hadn't left the DCS since she had arrived on the scene. "As I understand it, ma'am, he's going to announce the arrest of Archie Christian just now. Christian is over there, with a couple of uniforms keeping an eye on him."

"He's having Christian attend the public announcement

of his own arrest? Where does he think he is, for God's sake? Hollywood? The CPS will have a bloody fit, parading him out here in front of the media like this. We'll be lucky if Christian doesn't sue us all."

She saw Jejeune, making his way now through the media throng toward the front of Peter Largemount's house. He paused for a moment and looked up into the beech trees. She could hardly believe her eyes. At a time like this, he was watching bloody birds.

"I understand Inspector Jejeune asked Christian if he wanted to be present and he agreed. He has signed a release, ma'am."

"How on earth did he get him to do that? What is going on here, Sergeant? Is he going to announce the arrest of Malcolm Brae or not?"

But before Maik could give an answer, or avoid one, Jejeune mounted the front steps of Peter Largemount's ancestral home and turned to face the media.

The DCS stirred uneasily by Maik's side. On the back of the suicide announcement, the arrest of Archie Christian would be a sideline at best. The people gathered here were expecting an announcement in the murder case — Peter's murder. Had Jejeune really orchestrated this big production simply to disguise the weakness of their case against Malcolm Brae?

But Maik was calm. He wasn't sure of all the details yet, but he could see that Jejeune was. The DCI looked utterly composed behind the bank of microphones, with a look that took on all comers, frank and calm and confident. Whatever he was about to tell them, it was his show now. And it would stay that way until he decided otherwise.

"Yesterday evening, police arrested a fifty-two-year-old male on suspicion of the illegal transportation of hazardous materials. Today, Archibald Reginald Christian has been formally charged with a number of offences relating to the unlawful storage, transport, and disposal of organotin tributyltin, otherwise known as TBT. Inquiries are ongoing, and further charges are anticipated in this case."

The stir among the media was not one of approval. Surely, Jejeune hadn't brought them all the way out here just to announce something most of them had already picked up from tittle-tattle in the station canteen. There were a few cursory looks across toward Christian, subdued between two officers, but he barely acknowledged his name, or the attention being focused on him. He was scanning the crowd desperately, looking for someone in the sea of faces.

"Inquiries made subsequent to this arrest suggested a link between this crime and the murder of Peter Largemount on August 29. A few moments ago, the police made an arrest in connection with this crime. A charge of murder has now been brought against Ms. Beverly Joanne Brennan of Saltmarsh, MP for Norfolk North East."

The chaos that followed the announcement took on a life of its own. Several journalists shouted out questions simultaneously, repeatedly calling Jejeune's name in order to get his eyes to fall on them. Others reached for their mobiles, texting, calling, spinning around frantically to locate a stronger signal. Reporters jostled one another for position, thrusting microphones in the direction of the chief inspector, Christian, constables, anybody who might have a contribution to make, a headline to offer. Jejeune ignored them all. He had said all he had to say.

A scuffle broke out to the side of the podium, where Christian was trying to break free of the officers holding his arms.

"No," he shouted. "No, it's not true. I was with her that night. I swear it."

Finally Christian found her in the crowd, off to one side, arms pinned between two female officers. Brennan looked frail, small, not at all the finished, polished article the public was used to. Beneath the makeup her complexion was pale, almost a deathly white. A strand of hair had fallen across her face.

"I was with her," repeated Christian. "I'll swear to it. We were together, at my place. Tell 'em Beverly. Tell 'em they've got it wrong."

"No, Archie," said Jejeune flatly. "You were nowhere in sight. Beverly Brennan was here alone when she emptied that shotgun into Peter Largemount's face."

It was a comment Jejeune regretted immediately, and more so over the following days as it was played again and again on a seemingly never-ending loop in the media.

Beverly Brennan looked at Christian. Tears had made wavy tracks through the makeup on her cheeks, but she wasn't crying now. She bit her lips and her voice wavered as she spoke. "I'm sorry, Archie, I'm so sorry. I couldn't let him …"

"Don't you say another word, Beverly. Please. Not till you get lawyered up. Not another word, my lovely. We'll get this sorted. I promise."

The police constables moved each of the detainees off and eased them toward separate waiting cars with special care, as if aware that the media might be scrutinizing their every move. The scrum continued, following them to the cars in a jostling, jousting procession that threatened to erupt into disorder at any moment.

Maik watched Jejeune closely as he stood on the steps, his eyes moving everywhere as usual, taking it all in, surveying the chaos he had set in motion. He looked unmoved, unaffected by the commotion going on all around him. Nothing, thought Maik. No elation, no relief, no sense of satisfaction. It means nothing to him. Job done, that's all. Shame, really, with all the work he put in, that he wasn't able to take anything away from a stunning success like this. Did it really mean so little to him, or was it just a way of protecting himself? Maik didn't know, but it wasn't really his business, anyway. Jejeune had gotten them their killer; he had closed their cases for them. In the end, that was all they had ever asked of him, and all he had ever promised to do.

DCS Shepherd stood in stunned silence on the edge of the forecourt, watching the remnants of the media horde as they wrapped up their cables and packed away their lights. It was just another headline to them, with plenty of backstory for them to pursue. It would run for days. For her, it would run forever. She moved off swiftly, hunched against the calls of the reporters, avoiding eye contact, until she reached the sanctity of her car. She drove away without a backward glance.

Tony Holland sidled over to Maik. "Well, he certainly knows how to put on a show, I'll give him that. The DCS must be over the moon. I told you, though, Archie Christian, front and centre, and not a bird list in sight. How did Jejeune get on to Brennan, anyway?"

Maik looked up at the Rooks milling around in the beeches above all the frenzied action in the area of the forecourt below them. "Those trees you were standing under, with Christian. Did Inspector Jejeune ask you to stand there?"

Holland nodded. "Very specific, he was. Stand here and listen. 'To what?' I says. But he just says *listen*. But there was nothing to listen to, not until Archie had his strop."

Maik nodded. "Apparently some birds, Crows, Rooks, like that, they can recognize faces. And they have long memories for anybody who poses a threat. They're not afraid of showing it either. Jejeune must have remembered the ruckus they caused when Brennan met him here, the day after Largemount was murdered. The birds obviously recognized her as the one who fired the gun and destroyed the nests."

Holland looked skeptical. "All this rumbled by a few birds. You're having a laugh."

"You remember he was out here again with his girl a few days later. Same blond hair, same build. If there had been no reaction from the Rooks …" Maik gave a slight tilt of his head. "It wouldn't have been enough on its own, of course, but it would have set him off in the right direction. And once he started looking, well, between Brennan and Christian there could only be one connection that made any sense, really. True love, Constable, about the only place we didn't think to look."

"Brennan up for a bit of rough? Didn't see that one coming, I have to admit. Still, stranger things, I suppose. Like Largemount helping himself to a bit of Shepherd's pie now and again, for example."

Maik held up a gentle hand. "That's enough. Too many people have been hurt by this business already. Let's leave it at that, shall we?"

Holland shrugged. "See you down The Boatman's tonight? Should be drinks all round, I'd imagine. DCS's shout, though, probably. I doubt Jejeune will be putting his hand in his pocket."

Maik watched Holland's retreating form until he had gotten into his car, which was parked beneath the beeches. Only the slightest stirring of the Rooks accompanied the sounds of the car door closing and the ignition coughing to life. A couple of birds lifted off and described languid arcs in the air before settling again into the leafy branches. To the untrained eye, their landing spot was chosen at random, but according to the articles Maik had been reading, their places would have been carefully predetermined by their position in the hierarchy of the roost.

"Complex social structure?" he asked the birds aloud. "I wonder what that must be like."

49

DCS Shepherd was standing by the window when Jejeune entered her office.

"The chief constable has been on the phone. I understand there have been congratulations from the highest level."

Jejeune said nothing. It had not hurt that Brennan's arrest had opened up a parliamentary seat formerly held by a member of the opposition, but perhaps there were other reasons the case had caught the attention of the Home Office.

"The CC himself didn't sound overly impressed with the way we've handled things, but professional standards and our own legal team seem to agree that we did nothing wrong. So you never had any intention of charging Malcolm Brae? It wouldn't have hurt to let someone in on your suspicions about Beverly. I could have been trusted, you know, despite our friendship. Or what I took to be our friendship, anyway."

"I wasn't sure," said Jejeune. "Not until …"

"Not until that little pantomime with Archie Christian? Tell me, was it necessary to haul him over to Peter's to make the announcement? His arrest was properly processed, by the way, so we're in the clear there." She turned from the window and looked at Jejeune. "In case you were wondering."

He wasn't. There was no anger in her voice, not about any

of it, the secrecy, the breaches of protocol. But it was clear that whatever congratulations had come down from on high, DCS Shepherd wasn't feeling moved to add her own to them.

"I didn't know if Christian was with Brennan on the night of the shooting. If he was, we would have had no way of proving which one of them shot Largemount. I told him I was going to charge her. I gave him the chance to provide her with an alibi, if he agreed to attend the press conference."

"As long as he signed the waiver." Shepherd nodded slowly. "And of course, when you brought Christian there, you had him wait near the beech trees, right next to the rookery."

"There was no reaction from the birds at all. Christian wasn't there that night."

She said nothing. She was remembering the way Jejeune had stared at her when she had gotten out of her car and made that same walk under the beech trees. Had he been watching her, or was he watching those birds?

"I first met Beverly at uni, you know. I've known her for a very long time. I wonder, does that really mean anything, to say you *know* someone? Obviously, I knew nothing about her affair with Christian. Or what she might be capable of." She stood up and walked to the window again, resuming her study of the parking lot. She spoke with her back to Jejeune. Some things were easier to ask without eye contact. "And Peter's role in all this?"

"As soon as Brae and Alwyn went to him about the contamination, he must have realized Christian was the real source. One of the major water sources from Christian's land runs right into Largemount's property. Perhaps he even knew beforehand. He also knew about Christian's relationship with Brennan, somehow. He offered to keep quiet about it, and even take the blame for the contamination, in exchange for Brennan's support for his wind farm project." Jejeune seemed to hesitate. "Whether or not Christian forced her into it, in some way, we're not sure."

Was there ever, even in a matter like this, degrees of guilt? The DCS shook her head emphatically. "Beverly was stronger than that. No, she did this, all of it, because she wanted to. She was a willing participant."

Jejeune continued. "Once Brae had uncovered the contamination, Largemount realized that whoever was the actual source would have had a strong motive for his murder. And he was already on record with Miles Alwyn as having claimed responsibility for the spill. He must have confronted Christian and told him he was going to tell Alwyn the truth about the contamination, that he wasn't responsible. He would simply have been looking to remove himself from suspicion in Brae's death. But Brennan knew it wouldn't take a man of Alwyn's abilities long to trace the real contamination back to Christian, once he knew it wasn't coming from Largemount's property. A third conviction, even one on a hazardous materials count, and Archie Christian was facing a long prison sentence. Brennan simply couldn't allow that."

DCS Shepherd looked outside again. Below her, in the parking lot, life was going on with its ever-present comings and goings.

"Peter would have trusted her," said Shepherd to her reflection in the window. "Even with all of this. It would have been no more than a straightforward business transaction for him, a simple *quid pro quo*. My silence for your support. Seeing Beverly, even holding a gun, it would never have occurred to him. He would have gone right over to her. Walked right into …"

She turned around suddenly, arms hugging herself tightly about the waist, eyes searching the room for something to focus on.

"Two men dead," she said shaking her head. "And almost a third."

"Brennan needed to be sure Largemount hadn't already talked to Alwyn, so she went to see him. With Brae and Largemount both dead, there was no need for Alwyn to hide his suspicions any longer, so he told her that, despite Largemount's claims, he was convinced that any pollution at Lesser Marsh was coming from another source. It was all she needed to hear. Ironically, it was probably our protection detail on Alwyn that prevented her from getting close enough to kill him, after she failed at the university that night."

"Really? So we actually managed to get something right in all this, even if it was by accident? I suppose that's one positive to take to the chief constable. Are there any others, Domenic? If there are, perhaps you could point them out for me. Because from where I'm standing it's just a little bit bloody difficult to see them at the moment. A celebrity suicide and an MP on a murder charge. Not exactly the public relations coup we were hoping for, is it? This case has carved a swathe right through the heart of Saltmarsh society, Domenic. I realize not all of this is your fault, but it's not going to make your job any easier going forward."

Jejeune hadn't really been looking for a public relations coup. Or anything else, for that matter. And as for not *all* of it being his fault, on another day he might have inquired just exactly which parts *were* his fault. But today he let it go.

Jejeune looked at the DCS, at the still-fresh redness around her eyes. In his expansive post-interview mood, Alwyn had been damning in his assessment of Peter Largemount: "Not guilty in Cameron's death, Inspector? Then hardly innocent either. There are those in these parts who will see Largemount's death as a settling of accounts for his many past environmental sins." Jejeune looked at the DCS again, at the desolation in her red-rimmed eyes, and thought about the professor's final comment before he had been led away: *"Really, Inspector, I expect few tears will be shed for Peter Largemount."*

Shepherd resumed her seat behind the desk, drawing a set of papers toward her, ready to start studying them when she had dismissed Jejeune. She drew a breath to compose herself. "Well, I suppose you'd better write it up for me. Don't leave anything out."

He was almost to the door when she spoke again. "By the way, how is Sergeant Maik? I've been hearing rumours…."

Jejeune's expression was impenetrable.

"You haven't forgotten the conversation we had, when I first assigned him to you. Any signs, anything at all suggesting he is no longer fit for the job?" She waved a flimsy sheet in his direction. Jejeune supposed it was his incident report from the night of the raid on Earth Front's headquarters. "Wishy-washy comments about incapacities sustained during the course of an arrest barely warrant a mention in his file. It's practically indistinguishable from the reports about the injuries the other team members received."

"Nothing has come to my attention that suggests Sergeant Maik is unfit for duty."

"Have you even tried to find out? You can hardly keep abreast of the situation if you wait for the information to fall on your desk, can you?"

"No, I don't suppose I can."

"And what was this business at the marsh? Maik rescued Alwyn, I understand, but there seems to be some discrepancy as to exactly what went on beforehand."

"Alwyn was in obvious distress."

"But what was Maik doing in the water in the first place? That seems to be the question. According to Alwyn he was already there, next to him, when he went under."

"The sergeant obviously anticipated the problem beforehand."

Jejeune's stare was frank and unflinching. It's the only solution, his gaze seemed to say, unless you care to come up with another reason why a police sergeant might want to go wading through knee-high water in his suit and loafers. A flicker of something flashed across Shepherd's features, but it was gone too quickly for anyone, perhaps even Shepherd herself, to register what it might have signified.

"Yes, well," she said uncertainly, "keep an eye on him. One loose cannon on my team is more than enough, thank you very much."

She brought her attention back to the matter at hand, the mass of paperwork on her desk.

"One more thing, before you go. Would you mind having a look at this?" She held out a sheet of paper, and Jejeune returned to her desk to retrieve it. "A statement for the nationals." She looked at Jejeune. "The CC feels this one might be better without any theatrics, so I'll be handling it myself."

Jejeune skipped through the facts to the final paragraph, the DCS's exit lines. This would be the impact statement. This was what she wanted to leave them with:

> This terrible tragedy has shocked our entire community. Our deepest sympathies go out to the families of all victims in this tragic case, and indeed to all those who have been harmed by the actions of some of our most respected citizens. It will take Saltmarsh a long time to recover from this series of tragedies, but we are a strong community, a resilient community, and we will heal from these tragedies in time. The process of healing begins today.

Too many tragedies, thought Jejeune. But he simply nodded and set the paper down on Shepherd's desk. She hadn't picked it up by the time he left.

50

The process of healing begins today.

Jejeune leaned on the railing of the walkway, looking out over the marsh. A glassy blue sky offered the water a brittle light to reflect. A brace of Mallards dabbled in the weeds near shore, while farther out, on a raised mud bank, a pair of Curlews probed for food.

"It's still beautiful, Dom," said Lindy, joining him at the railing. "For all that crap that Archie Christian has been dumping into the water, the marsh doesn't look any different." She put her forearms on the railing and leaned forward, looking down into the dark water.

"Not yet."

A generation. Alwyn's projections were that it would take an entire human generation for the wetland to recover, before the contamination could leach out completely and the marsh could restore itself to health. Leave it for the next generation. *Not quite what you had in mind, was it, Marsh Man?*

Jejeune felt the boardwalk move with the pressure of another set of footfalls. Quentin Senior joined them at the railing, watching the Mallards dabbling among the weeds.

"Ah, Inspector and reluctant companion. Still fighting the call, I take it." He smiled indulgently at Lindy. "Only a matter of time, my dear. You have that intellectual curiosity, you see, that need to define. The challenges of bird identification are but a step away."

"When you see a herd of pigs soaring above this marsh, Mr. Senior, that's the day I'll become a birder."

Senior barked a short laugh of delight. "A drift, Ms. Hey. A collection of pigs is a drift. At least, on the hoof, that is. Not so sure it would apply on the wing. Still, deny it if you like. You mark my words; I have an eye for a latent birder. We'll have you decked out in olive green yet."

Lindy looked at the Mallards. "They're so pretty. I love the way the sun makes their necks shimmer."

"Indeed. Look at this one, down here below us, working away, completely oblivious to us, not a care in the world. This was how it all started for us, wasn't it, Inspector? Watching a few birds, wanting to know a bit more about them. Before we all got caught up in lists and numbers and races to four hundred and all that nonsense."

"But surely you'll carry on trying to reach four hundred?" said Lindy. "After everything you've put into getting this far."

"I suppose I will. Though I must admit there is something missing now that Cameron is no longer in the race." He shook his head softly at some private memory. "You know, I sometimes think as we get older we lament the passing of our rivals every bit as much as that of our friends. And ours was quite a rivalry, I can tell you. Even if it was not quite worth killing over."

Senior smiled to show there were no hard feelings. But Jejeune knew Danny Maik had been following reasonable suspicions. Even if Senior had eventually been proven innocent, neither Maik, nor anyone else in the department, had anything to reproach themselves for. Nevertheless, Jejeune was glad Maik's suspicions had proven groundless, all the same.

"I suppose with Cameron Brae gone, it's the end of an era," said Lindy suddenly.

Senior nodded. "In one way, perhaps, but one of the joys of our pastime is that new blood is always coming through, younger, keener, and certainly with a damned sight better hearing and eyesight. Look at young Duncan, for example. Breathing down my neck already, and he has nearly two decades on me. I may well be the first to four hundred, but I doubt my record will last for long. Not that I'd mind handing the mantle over to Duncan one day. He's an excellent birder. In the truest sense. Understands them, loves them for what they are, not as a tick on his list. Always talks about *seeing* a bird, or at worst *hearing* one. Never hear him going on about 'having' birds, you know, 'had a Yellowhammer yesterday.'"

Lindy nodded to herself. She and Domenic had had a similar discussion a few days before, about two friends of theirs who were looking for a new holiday destination, having "done" North America last year.

Jejeune saw her tacit agreement and he smiled to himself. Despite their differences, he suspected the more time Lindy and Senior spent with each other, the more common ground they would find. Both had such a certainty about life, a conviction of how things should be, a conviction he could only dream of possessing.

"So there never were any American Bitterns here?" Lindy was peering into the reeds, though whether it was in hope or just curiosity wasn't really clear.

Senior shook his shaggy white mane. "Not this time. But there will be, one day. You mark my words. Everything comes to Cley, they say. And points around." Senior lifted his binoculars for a lazy scan across the marsh. "Bitterns and bitterns, eh, Inspector? We've had quite a siege of them lately."

"And that's about the biggest mystery of all, as far as I am concerned," said Lindy. "Why a siege, for God's sake?"

Senior smiled. "Ah well, you would have to ask Juliana de Berniers. She's the one who first catalogued these wonderful collective nouns. Some do say it's a corruption of *sedge*, but there are enough strange entries in Ms. de Berniers' *Book of St Albans* to suggest that it was probably *siege* right from the beginning."

"But why have a collective noun for bitterns at all," asked Lindy, "if it's so unusual to see more than one at a time? I mean, nobody's ever felt the need to come up with a collective noun for intelligent men, have they?"

Senior barked his delighted laugh again. "Ah well, I suspect it's back to the dinner table for that one. As in, *I understand you are entertaining tonight, my Lord, I'll have cook prepare a siege of bitterns for your supper*. But it's an interesting question. And that's exactly why we need bright new minds like yours in our ranks. Old hands like myself and the inspector here, we tend to simply accept the incongruous wisdom of our pastime without questioning it."

It's her energy, thought Jejeune, this connection she has with older men: Senior; Coulter, the desk sergeant; Eric, the Illiterate Halfwit Editor. Few men in their later years could help being attracted to such a stunningly beautiful young woman, but it was more than that. It's her vibrancy, her positivity. It restores their faith in life. It reminds them that there are still some things worth believing in, however much their own romances or careers or lives have failed to deliver on their dreams.

"My interest is purely etymological, I can assure you," said Lindy. "It has nothing to do with birding at all."

"*My heart in hiding, Stirred for a bird,* eh, Inspector?" said Senior with a wink. His smile held a flicker of regret, despite his jocular tone, and there was a hint of sadness behind the bright blue eyes. "You'll have read the ministry's decision."

Jejeune nodded. In an effort to aid the natural regeneration process, the government was proposing to designate the lands surrounding Lesser Marsh and Great Marsh as an Area of Special Protection. It was likely the entire area was going to be off limits to the general public from now on. Not exactly the expropriation Largemount had feared, but largely the same result anyway. It was the final irony in a case riddled with them.

Senior sighed. "An AoSP. Still, a few signs, a few fences. People will still enter if they want to. Certainly they would to see an Ivory Gull. How often do they occur here, once every thirty years or so? Perhaps the marshes will be fully restored to health by the time the next one shows up, and they'll be letting people back in."

"Perhaps."

Lindy looked up. "Have you ever seen one, Mr. Senior?"

He nodded. "Once. A long time ago. Up in the Hebrides. Beautiful bird. Unmistakable, eh, Inspector?" He smiled at Jejeune, taking in his sad expression. "Don't worry about this place. Thirty years is a mere spit in the ocean for Great Marsh. And when it has recovered, the birds will come back, too. Let's not forget, when Dr. Long bought the marshes at Cley, Avocet, Marsh Harrier, and Bearded Tit had already been lost as breeding birds. And the Bittern."

"But, surely, they're all here now, aren't they?" She turned to Jejeune. "I've heard you talk about them," said Lindy.

"Recolonized by birds from the Netherlands," said Senior with quiet satisfaction. "Great Marsh will recover. Don't you worry. I might not be here to see it, but you will. And your young 'uns, should you be so blessed." Senior straightened up from the railing. "It's this area, you see, the birds and the people, we're all intertwined, caught up in one another's history. We could never let it perish, a place like this."

The family of Mallards had lost interest in the weeds and moved off toward the reed beds on the far shore, motivated by invisible forces, beyond the senses or understanding of humans. Jejeune took another long look at the marsh, at the freshwater reeds, and the brackish scrape beyond, at the tidal salt marsh with its sinuous creeks snaking out between the dunes to the beach, and, finally, to the sea. Links and divisions, interconnections and separations, all borne of a dependence on each other and a necessity to maintain the balance, to continue the process, to preserve the cycles that had been going on here for millennia.

Well, I'd best be off," announced Senior, suddenly having found the resolve to detach himself from Lindy's presence. "There's a report of a Thrush Nightingale down at Stiffkey. Probably nothing, but I thought I'd better go along to check it out. Don't suppose you would be interested in accompanying me. Either of you?"

To Lindy's surprise, Jejeune declined. "Perhaps later," he said. "For now, I think I'd like to stay on here a while. As you say, around here, you never know what might turn up."

The Bittern

The Eurasian (or Great) Bittern, *Botaurus stellaris*, was once widespread in the lowlands of the U.K., but hunting and habitat loss led to the species' extirpation by the late 1880s. In the early twentieth century, the species returned to Britain, and by mid-century numbers had increased encouragingly. However, numbers began to decline again, and by 1997 just eleven males, at seven sites, were known to exist. Only a concerted effort to restore and create reed beds saved the species from a second U.K. extinction. Since 1997, numbers in the U.K. have continued to rise. Because the birds are secretive by nature and difficult to observe, counts are extrapolated from the distinctive "booming" vocalizations of individual males. In 2012, 106 males were recorded from 53 sites, suggesting an overall resident U.K. population in excess of 200 birds.

However, the birds' future in the U.K. is far from secure. Bitterns require freshwater habitat, but many of the U.K.'s largest reed beds are in coastal East Anglia, and are highly vulnerable to tidal inundation. Bittern habitat is also under pressure from a number of other sectors, including the thriving thatching industry. Clearly, there is still much work to be done if we are to save this iconic wetland species.

Fortunately, there are now a number of habitat conservation and creation schemes in operation around the country. New reed beds are being created farther inland and existing reed beds are being expanded. This work offers much hope for the future of the U.K. population, but it is time-consuming and demanding work. In addition to monitoring the birds' numbers and breeding patterns, regular audits must also be conducted of water quantity and quality, reed extent and structure, and fish and amphibian populations. Much of this work is done by volunteers.

The U.K. Bittern Monitoring Programme is funded by RSPB and Natural England as part of its Action for Birds in England (AfBiE) project. For further details, or to support the important work of conservation initiatives, please visit the Natural England website at *www.naturalengland.org.uk* or the RSPB website at *www.rspb.org.uk*.

Turn the page to read the opening of...

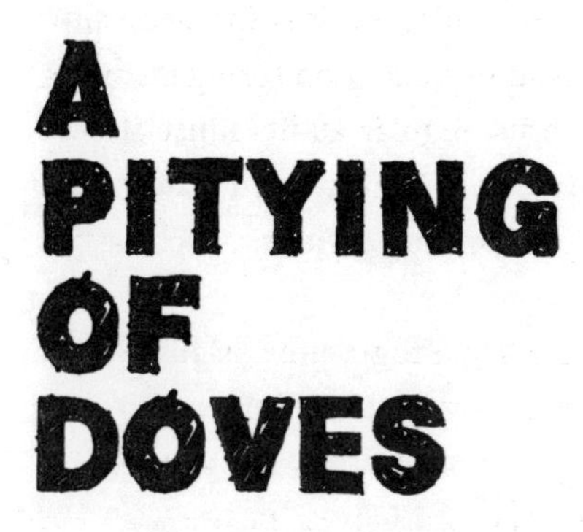

The gripping second installment in the

BIRDER MURDER SERIES

Why would a killer ignore expensive jewellery and take a pair of turtledoves as the only bounty?

PUBLISHED JUNE 2016

PROLOGUE

AUTUMN 2006

It was like driving into death; a grey maelstrom of ferocious rain and roiling storm clouds that cloaked the landscape with their dark menace. The storm of the century, they were calling it, worse even than '53.

It had been building for days, hunkering offshore, marshalling its power as it waited for that one perfect confluence of weather systems. In the previous hours there had been a couple of tentative incursions over the land — high winds and swift, angry rain squalls — but at 9:32 that morning, as the tide rose to its highest point in fifteen years, the storm began to unleash its full fury on the north Norfolk coastline. By now it had built to its peak, bringing evening to the afternoon in a sinister twilight of bruised skies and vast, swirling sheets of rain. The low-lying coastal lands were being inundated by the deluge from above and the storm-driven tidal surges from the sea. And now the floodwaters were headed this way.

The man urged the tiny car onward, a shiny sliver of light creeping over the oily blackness of the road. He wondered how long it would be before he saw the first evidence of flooding in the fields on either side. The river had already burst its banks, according to the latest report that had come over the car radio. Soon the waters would begin creeping insidiously across the flat black earth of the farms, swallowing up every feature, every hollow of the land. It was no wonder the radio announcers had started rolling out the Noah's ark references, even if they didn't know what they were talking about. *Two by two?* He had turned the radio off in a fit of exasperation at that point. How could you trust their storm updates when they couldn't even get basic scripture right? Seven: that was the number of clean beasts God had commanded Noah to take on the ark. Seven and seven, of each species, the male and the female. Not two.

At least somebody knew his Bible.

A momentary wave of lightheadedness passed over him. This snail's pace driving and those earlier diversions had taken him long past his scheduled time to eat. Still, a glass of orange juice and a couple of digestives when he got home …

The man blinked hard to clear his blurred vision and concentrated on the narrow country lane in front of him. The incessant hammering of the rain on the roof seemed to fill the car. In the feeble headlights, he could see the manic devil-dance of raindrops falling so hard they were bouncing back up from the surface of the road. All around him, the storm was attacking the land with such terrifying ferocity that it seemed almost to have one single purpose: to obliterate Saltmarsh from the map. When the storm finally passed, thought the man, the destruction left in its wake would be devastating. It would take the local communities a long time to recover from the day this veil of misery descended upon them. Perhaps some never would.

Violent gusts of wind tore at the tops of the overgrown hedgerows along both sides of the narrow lane, scattering leaves like tiny wet messages of the storm's destruction. A burst of wind-driven rain came out of the darkness like an ambush, rattling against the driver's window and startling the man into a momentary oversteer. *Careful. Get stuck in a ditch tonight, with the north Norfolk countryside disappearing beneath this storm of biblical proportions, and who knows when they'll be out to rescue you.* According to the radio reports, the emergency services were already stretched to the limit, clearing people from the path of the relentless brown tide that was bearing down on them.

And besides, there was his precious cargo. He didn't want to have to explain that to any potential rescuers. He patted the lid of the large cardboard box on the seat next to him and wiped the back of a clammy hand across his forehead, blinking his eyes once more to clear his vision.

There were those in his church, he knew, who would argue that this storm was a punishment from above; divine retribution for Saltmarsh's sins, past and present. He wondered if his actions counted among them. He had committed a crime, yes. He was prepared to admit that much. A perfect crime, as a matter of fact; but not a sin, surely. After all, he had acted with the best of intentions — compassion and mercy and pity. There could be no sin in that. The sky lit up as tendrils of lightning clawed their way across the towering bank of cloud on the horizon. The thunder that followed threatened to tear the swollen sky apart with its force. Somewhere over the noise of the storm, he heard the splintering crack of wood and saw the severed arm of an ancient oak crash onto the road ahead of him in an explosion of leaves and debris. Motive: that was what made it a sin. The man understood that now. His act of kindness had only ever had one real motive: his own gain. He knew it. And God knew it, too.

He steered cautiously around the fallen limb, gripping the steering wheel tightly as he feathered the accelerator. Silver sprays cascaded up against the bodywork as the wheels found a deeper patch of water near the edge of the road. He felt tired;

the constant focus, the concentration, was taking its toll. And all the time, the metronomic beat of the wipers slapping back and forth against the wet windshield filled his senses, as measured and constant as a heartbeat, lulling him toward the rest he so badly needed.

In the dark, he almost missed the driveway. The little yellow carriage lamp had been torn off the gatepost by the wind and lay shattered across the road. What a shame. Maggie loved that lamp. An irrational sadness moved him almost to the point of weeping. He pulled into the driveway and parked. His body was bathed in sweat and he was shaking.

He sat in the car, watching the rain stream down the windows. The house beyond was dark. His mind fogged with confusion. *Where was Maggie?* Of course. Working. He would call her from the house; make sure she had arrived safely at the hospital. But first he needed to rest, to close his eyes. Just for a few minutes. Not in his bed. Too far away. Here in the car, next to his prize, the spoils of his perfect crime. He fumbled in his jacket for a pen and scrawled a spidery note on the top of the box: *For my Turtle D…* The pen slipped from his grasp and fell to the floor. Too far away. The drumming of the rain on the roof of the car was almost deafening now. He felt the weariness, the overwhelming weariness, pressing down upon him. He needed food, but it was in the kitchen. Too far away in this storm. Too far away. Just rest, then.

Maggie knew before she reached the car. Not when she alighted from the bus, stopped so thoughtfully by the driver a few feet past the actual bus stop, so she could avoid the massive puddle: not as she was walking along the lane, with its vegetation still dripping and heaving from the effects of last night's storm. But by the time she turned into the driveway, she knew.

The threat of death had been a constant in their lives ever since his diagnosis all those years before. Though it sometimes drifted to the back of their consciousness, it never really left them. So she approached the car with a strange mix of reluctance and haste, pressing in to look through the passenger window, through the clearing morning mist on the glass, where she saw her husband slumped against the steering wheel. She opened the door and put a finger to his neck. Even to her, it seemed a cold, professional gesture. Perhaps it was best that she was still in her nursing mind-set. Sometimes it took her hours to switch off after a shift, especially after a night like last night, with all the stress and trauma of the storm-related injuries. She withdrew her hand, noticing for the first time the box lying on the passenger seat, and the words, his last words, scrawled on the top. She gently lifted the lid, peered in, and then replaced the lid and carried the box into the house.

Inside, she set the box on the floor and sat for a moment at the kitchen table in the cold, empty house. Then she crossed to the computer, typed out a short note, and printed it off. Folding and refolding the paper a couple of times, she opened a drawer of a battered old filing cabinet and stuffed the note into the middle of an untidy sheaf of papers, closing the drawer again with exaggerated care.

By the time she had swept the seat and floor of the passenger side of the car with a dustpan and brush, and emptied the dustpan onto a flowerbed, the shock was starting to set in. Back in the house, now barely aware of her actions, she put away the dustpan and brush and picked up the telephone. And then, having called the police to report the death of her husband of thirty-five years, Margaret Wylde sat down on her living-room couch and cried.

1

SPRING 2014

The thing about death is, it never taunts you with false hope. There is never any chance that things will reverse course, or get better, or even change. So in that respect, death never disappointed Danny Maik. Only life could do that. Still, even a detective sergeant as familiar with death as Danny was entitled to wonder, just for a second, whether encountering this scene the second time around would make it any easier. But when he re-entered the room, he was greeted by the same frozen tableau of horror; the silent, empty absence of life that was witness to the violence that had gone before it. And so Danny's own reaction was the same, too; an overwhelming sense of sadness. It came upon him whenever he encountered death, but perhaps this time the feeling was even a little stronger than usual, now that he could properly take in the pathetic innocence of the girl in the cage, and the peaceful repose of the man lying at her feet.

It was hard to believe that anyone's first reaction to the news of these murders could have been optimism. But if Lindy Hey could have witnessed this room for herself, experienced the blood, the stench of soiled feathers, the grotesque posture of the girl's body, Danny suspected that her response would not have been quite so upbeat.

"I don't suppose he's there," Maik had asked when Lindy answered the phone.

"Weather like this? Peak migration season? Nothing wrong with your detective skills, is there, Sergeant?"

"I thought perhaps if you knew where he was, we could send a car. It might be faster."

"Sorry, he could be anywhere along the coast at this time of year. Texting is your best bet. His phone will be off, but he's pretty good at checking his messages. Is it a bad one?"

Danny could imagine Lindy cringing at the seeming insensitivity of her question. She knew that, for him, there were no levels to murder. For Danny Maik, it was only ever the extinction of life, terrible in its finality, no matter who the victim was, or what the circumstances. But he knew Lindy wasn't being callous. Murder had once again intruded into her partner's life. She was simply trying to gauge how it would affect him, them, their relationship.

"If he calls, can you tell him to come to the Free to Fly Sanctuary on Beach Road?"

"Really, that bird rescue place?"

It wasn't just his imagination, that note of hope in her voice. He was sure of it now, considering it for a second time. Lindy was thinking that the presence of birds could possibly turn this into the one case that finally engaged Domenic Jejeune. And she might be right. A murder in a bird sanctuary might just capture the inspector's interest in a way that previous cases had so obviously failed to do. Whether it would be enough to ultimately convince Jejeune to commit himself to the career everybody seemed to believe was his destiny, well, that was another question altogether. As the title of one of Maik's beloved Motown titles might have put it: "Yes, No, Maybe So."

Danny returned to the present and swept his eyes over the scene once again. Two rows of floor-to-ceiling cages lined the breeze block walls of the sparse room, separated by a narrow walkway. In every cage but one, birds huddled silently in the farthest corner, away from the light. The survival instinct, he recognized. Sit still and avoid drawing attention to yourself. In another life, Danny had employed the same tactics himself, when his own survival had depended on it.

Detective Constable Tony Holland approached and nodded toward the bodies on the other side of the wire. "Murders in a bird cage," he said. "He's going to love this one, isn't he? Where is he, anyway? Off communing with his feathered friends somewhere, I suppose."

Maik ignored the question. "Uniforms made sure they left the scene exactly as it was? Keys hung in exactly the same place?"

Holland's look told Maik that even the uniforms had enough experience in dealing with a Domenic Jejeune crime scene to know what was expected of them. They would have disturbed nothing during their initial inspection, relocking the cage and replacing the keys carefully. The DCI would see everything just as it was when they first arrived on the scene. If any messages had been left, intentional or otherwise, Jejeune would be able to interpret them *in situ* before SOCO started sifting through things.

Maik asked for the background on the victims and Holland did his best to provide what they knew so far. It wasn't much.

"The kneeler is Phoebe Hunter. She runs the shelter. Ran. Him, we have no idea. No ID or phone, either on the body or in the car. Nice *shine*, though." Holland indicated an expensive watch and ring on the man's left hand.

"There's a car?" Maik couldn't remember seeing anything other than familiar police vehicles when he arrived.

"Round the back, tucked away in the corner. It's a local rental from Saxon's Garage. I've called Old Man Saxon. He'll pull the file and get us an ID as soon as he gets in." Maik's silence unnerved Holland and the constable checked the time on a flashy new iPhone. "I could go and get him if you like...."

Maik dismissed the idea with a wave of his hand. He peered into the cage once more, forcing himself to look beyond the carnage to take in the details. The body of a young woman knelt in a pool of her own blood. She had slumped far enough in death that her knees were resting on the concrete floor of the cage. But her upper torso remained suspended upright, impaled on a broken branch that protruded like a spear point from a dead tree limb that had been stretched across the cage as a makeshift perch. Her head rested against her chest in an attitude Maik remembered from the crucifixes of his church-going youth. Beneath her, almost at her feet, lay the body of a man. He wore an expensive-looking turtleneck sweater, finely tailored trousers, and high-quality leather shoes, all in black. The man looked almost peaceful, curled on one side as though sleep had suddenly overtaken him. Maik wondered if it was the serenity of the man's pose that made the girl's own situation seem so grotesque by comparison. But no, Phoebe Hunter's death really needed no point of contrast to appall anyone.

Maik looked at the dark blood pooled on the floor around the girl. He had seen blood spilled on many surfaces, but only on cement did it seem to settle like this, flowing outwards and then drawing back slightly from the edges, as if shrinking back in revulsion at its own progress. In that strange way of things, the blood had flowed to within inches of the man's body, but had not touched it. There was not a trace of blood anywhere on the man's black clothing.

Maik considered the girl's clothes carefully: well-worn shoes, a short skirt, and a skimpy baby-blue top with tiny embroidered flowers around the neck. The top was bunched and one of the spaghetti straps had been torn as her killer grabbed her and thrust her onto the branch. Maik wondered what she had been thinking about when she got dressed the previous morning. These birds? The tasks that awaited her? Excitement about what the new day might bring? All for it to end like this, kneeling on the floor of a locked cage, amid bird droppings and spilled seed, in a pool of her own blood. *Yes, Lindy, it was a bad one.*

To Maik's right, Detective Constable Lauren Salter was pressing her face against the cage, gripping the wire with her fingers. She seemed unable to pull her eyes away from the scene inside, terrible as it was.

"Everything all right, Constable?"

"He's not from around here," said Salter, "I'm sure of it." She seemed distant, distracted. Sometimes, the nervous system put mechanisms in place to shield a person from shock. But Salter had seen her share of traumatic deaths. Maik wondered if it might be something else. She nodded toward the well-dressed man with his dark complexion and jet-black hair. Even in death, he was startlingly handsome. "Trust me, quality like that would have stuck out a mile from the local gene pool."

Tony Holland readied himself for a response, but he seemed to think better of it. Sergeant Maik liked a bit of decorum around his murder scenes, and he could get very testy if he thought people weren't taking things seriously enough.

"An out-of-towner and a local, then," mused Maik. "So what were they doing here together, I wonder."

Holland smirked. "You're kidding, right? He's away from home, meets plain Jane here; game over."

Holland held up his hand to fend off the looks he was getting from both Maik and Salter. "What? I'm just saying, a no-frills number like her, with her *maybe* outfit on, just to let you know it was a possibility. If he had the chat to go with his looks, it would be a foregone conclusion. I'm just saying," he repeated.

Maik was silent, which was probably the safest response Holland could have hoped for from him. But Salter wasn't in the mood to indulge Tony Holland's singular view of the world. "And they chose this place why, exactly, Tony? The ambiance? Believe it or not, there are other reasons a man and a woman could be together. That is, unless the man is a complete brain-dead moron with a one-track mind. Oh, wait ..." said Salter with heavy irony.

Salter's outburst was so out of keeping with her normal demeanour around Danny Maik that both he and Holland shot her a surprised look. But while Maik had always put her previous self-control down to simple professionalism, Holland had long ago identified a different cause. When you had been striving as long as Salter had to get Maik to even notice your attentions, let alone respond to them, you didn't want something as unattractive as a temper tantrum spoiling your chances.

"What's up with you, then?" asked Holland. "Touch of the hot flashes?"

"Oh, for God's sake, grow up."

Both fell silent under the sergeant's stony stare. In his present mood, if Danny Maik decided to start banging heads together, the lab team would have more than one mess to clean up when they got here.

"I'll go see if I can light a fire under that lazy bugger, Saxon," announced Salter, striding off angrily toward the doorway. Maik stared after her retreating form, but neither she nor the silent Tony Holland met his gaze.

Maik considered the bodies carefully once again; the man's smart black attire, the girl's clothing. What had Holland called it, her *maybe* outfit? A little low up top; a little high down below. At this stage anything was possible, but a romantic pairing looked off to him. Death was the ultimate leveller, but appearances suggested that in life these two would have inhabited very different worlds. Still, Danny

Maik was hardly an expert on what attracted people to each other. More the opposite, truth be told. And he had known stranger relationships in his time. If somebody came up with a sighting of the two of them huddled together over G and Ts in the local bar, he wouldn't dismiss it out of hand.

But, regardless of why these two people had come here together, or what they intended to do, one thing was clear. They hadn't been alone. Someone had killed them both, then deliberately manipulated the evidence before fleeing the scene. As to whom that someone might have been, the only person Maik knew who might be capable of working that out was currently occupied with other matters — specifically, the spring migration of birds along the north Norfolk coast.